MW01505533

S. K. STAPAR

MIDNIGHT GATE

S. K. STAPAR

MIDNIGHT GATE

AN EPIC FANTASY ROMANCE

Copyright © 2025 by S. K. Stapar

All rights reserved.

No part of this publication may be reproduced, distributed, or transmitted in
any form or by any means, including information storage and retrieval systems,
photocopying, recording, or other electronic or mechanical methods, without the
prior written permission of the author.

The story, all names, characters, and events portrayed in this publication, other
than those clearly in the public domain, are fictitious. No identification with actual
persons (living or deceased), places, buildings, and products is intended or should
be inferred.

No generative artificial intelligence was used in the writing of this work. Without
in any way limiting the author's exclusive rights under copyright, any use of this
publication to "train" generative artificial intelligence technologies to generate text
is expressly prohibited. The author reserves all rights to license uses of this work
for generative artificial intelligence training and development of machine learning
language models.

Paperback ISBN: 978-1-7637871-1-7
eBook ISBN: 978-1-7637871-0-0

Visit **www.skstapar.com** to find out more about S. K. Stapar's books. You will also
find information on news and events, and you can sign up to the e-newsletter to be
the first to know all the latest updates.

For those who bear the load of responsibility,
and who seek the balance in control.

Author's note

Midnight Gate is an exciting fantasy romance set in a land where cursed monsters roam and stakes are high. The story describes some scenes of battle-related violence, blood, death, grief, graphic language and sexual activities, shown on the page. Readers, please note before you step into a land of cursed magic, gripping secrets and agonising romance. Welcome to Midnight Gate.

CHAPTER ONE

ROUGH WIND SHOVED STRANDS of thin, ebony hair into my eyes as I gripped the crumbling ledge of the Amber Gate tower. Cold gravel waited below, silent and invisible under darkness, promising a painful drop should I slip.

Not something I could afford if I wanted to compete in the Ranking at dawn.

I spat long hair out of my mouth and tested the protruding stone carving of a gargoyle, thanking the old fae who had built this wretched tower for their commitment to intimidatory art. The monster's long head groaned in complaint as it held the weight of one trembling leg, and then a second. My bedroom window was somewhere high above, much too far to climb back to safety.

That was fine. I never wanted my old life back.

Up until now, my life had involved relative comfort. I had been afforded a warm bedroom to myself. Three cooked meals per day. Safety from the bloodthirsty Cursed—all luxuries for common folk, I was assured. But these luxuries were provided within the solitude of the Amber Gate tower, and there was no one to keep me company—except if you counted dead bodies at the tower's base. After more than a decade of solitary confinement, I was sure some certainly might.

As I shifted to a crouch, repressed fantasies crept along my mind like the protruding vine carvings I reached for. Surely no one would recognise me. Someone might even clap my shoulder as I returned from the perilous Smed Forest clutching a full bottle of miran nectar, the only healing substance left in Veligrad. The thought of warm touch against my skin was enough to invite a shiver down my spine.

But first, I needed to escape the tower that had held me for thirteen years in its stiff walls.

At least this time, there was definitely no one around to watch my slow descent. No guards held sentry in the Amber Gate manor's back courtyard below, nor along the tiers of the manor's formal gardens. The Ranking Eve bonfire drew all Amber Gate townspeople to the ceremonial feast that preceded the competition for the chance to become a Protector for one of Veligrad's seven cities.

Only a couple more powdery footholds down some tongue-blearing heads and fertile stone vines, and I could compete in it, too.

I took a shaky breath. The only other time I had tried—and failed—to escape my tower, someone had died. This time, I needed to make it, or they would lock me away with no window at all.

A trembling foot found another rough protrusion. I could do this. After running the length of the tower's stairs all my life, my legs were strong enough to keep—

A scrape against gravel disturbed the wind-brushed silence from somewhere below, and panic gripped me as hard as I clutched the disintegrating stone wall. Little light reached my tower from the distant street lanterns beyond the manor's estate, but my eyes were already well-accustomed to the dark.

The figure of a male crept through the courtyard beneath me. The angle of his dark head told me his gaze was travelling over my ill-kept tower, focusing on the window far above me.

And not noticing a woman partway through an escape.

Perhaps my shape looked like a gargoyle in the dark. I thanked the long-dead gargoyle sculptor again.

I held my breath as the stranger continued his survey around the curvature of my tower. It was a long hold. Not ideal when my fingers and toes were starting to prickle from the awkward angle at which I gripped the wall.

Why was he here? Nearly everyone else was at the Ranking Eve bonfire now, feasting on burek and the sweet, honey-roasted nuts I could smell under the current of the wind. Or covertly betting on which competitors would succeed this season for a Protector position and which would die.

Just as I released my breath, his careful footsteps over crunching gravel sounded closer again, walking the length of the pristine courtyard, dividing his attention between the two buildings.

While he strolled, the sensation in my fingers and toes turned from prickling to sharp stabs, and my mind caught up to the fact that I did not have the gravitational defiance of a spider, but that I was a mortal woman holding a brittle, vertical wall.

The stranger needed to leave.

Usually, I could scare people away with my title alone. Most knew me as the Cursed Mortician, but a favourite version I had heard was Firer of the Death Kiln. It made me sound powerful—which almost caused me to chuckle. Those who chose to be more dramatic would tell stories of a hidden woman with no soul, trapped in the Amber Gate tower, forced to burn the dead, as she was a vukodlak herself.

That one was half true.

While I did not carry the witches' Curse that thirteen years ago had turned all fae into vukodlak—rabid, wolf-like creatures that thirsted for blood—I felt cursed just the same. I had no memory prior to the day I was found wandering in the Smed after the Fall of the Fae, and so I had been locked in the mortuary tower, isolated in case the Curse was latent. Forced to cremate corpses mangled by the once ruling fae. Even after thirteen years of clearly growing no fangs or tail, superstitions held strong in Amber Gate. The worse the rumour, the more folk liked to believe it.

And now I wondered how I could use the only power handed to me—others' fear of my profession—against the man wandering below, wasting precious time that could remould the shape of my life.

Perhaps if I managed to show myself, he would run. Afraid of my supposed Curse, just like everyone else in this town. He might alert the guards, but it would still give me enough time to run towards the Smed Forest, the place where no one who wanted their blood kept in their own veins would venture. I could then follow the tree line near the Ranking start point and wait until its commencement at dawn.

But if this stranger ran after me instead, I would not win.

From the angle I peered down upon him, he seemed around my age. That was where any commonalities stopped.

Shadows highlighted a sword-sharp jaw coated in full stubble. His frame was huge, and strong shoulders topped the straight spine of someone who used their body as a weapon. Was it in defence or to strike? There was something else about the way he carried himself, something in the slight forwards lean of his neck, that told me he was no simple guard. This man was too careful, cautious.

Numbness overtook my fingers, and pain spread to my biceps and thighs, trembling from the exertion of tensing my body as tightly as it could to grip the tower. I begged the moon for him to be gone soon.

At least he could not see me.

"I can see you," spoke a smooth male voice, its quiet timbre reaching my height on the tower.

Shit.

"Are you trying to get in or out?"

Even in my panic-addled state, my thoughts were clear enough to realise that was a peculiar question to ask someone you had just met clinging to a wall. And it meant he did not know who I was.

"Out!" I snapped.

I hated that I was engaging with him. Once I had a decision made, I wanted to execute it exactly the way I intended.

"Why?" the man asked steadily, curiously.

Because it's the only way to secure my freedom without Caster Leden threatening to recapture me, or worse. Because if I can enter the Ranking and retrieve the miran flower's nectar, I can prove for certain that I'm not Cursed.

A strangled cry was all I could manage, as my strength was close to giving out. Even that was a mistake. The force of air through my chest further destabilised my weakening position, and I desperately tested my foot for another hold before any other momentum pushed me off the wall.

Except, everywhere I reached, the stone all crumbled away.

I'm going to fall.

The next gargoyle below was too far. Shallow breaths quickened in my chest—the panic of losing control. Something I never allowed. I could only try and slide down the wall and hope that I would land squarely on the gargoyle's head, and that the impact would not break its neck, or mine.

I squeezed my eyes and clenched my muscles tighter, ready to release, when a whistling sound coasted past my ear.

Thwack.

"Take it." The end of a rope was looped over and around the closest gargoyle, and its bristly length bumped against my shoulder. "The rope's enchanted," the man quietly called from below. "It's safe to hold."

It went against everything in me to admit my own failure, and I was too close to falling to wonder why the stranger was helping me. It was only the fact that I was nearer to ending as a crumpled pile of bones than I was to reaching the Ranking that allowed me to shakily seize the rope.

My stranger was right.

I tugged, and somehow the rope held taut, as if knotted thrice to welded iron rather than failing stone. Wasting no more time, I descended down the curved wall face.

It took all of the remaining strength I had, and then borrowing some more from panic. Cuts and burns from the rope's sharp fibres almost made me want to let go and take on the quick, brutal pain of the fall instead. But no, this was a pain I could endure if I wanted to make it to the Ranking in mere hours.

Still, I winced as I finally landed and adjusted to the fact that, for the first time since I was eleven years old, I was outside of the Amber Gate tower.

Exhilaration and panic rushed through me at the same time. The sensations felt basically the same. There were also other, new sensations. The bumpiness of gravel beneath my thin boots. The looming presence of the tower before me, as if leaning over to scold me.

And the weight of the stranger's gaze, watching me.

Wavy, ink-black hair hung over thick, curious brows—a curiosity without the morbid fascination that anyone who sought a glance of me through my window wore. He was not close enough to reach, but I bet the touch of his bronze skin was warm. That broad body could easily enclose me, hold me, and I could not help wondering what he would smell of up close.

Stop it.

These thoughts were redundant. I would hopefully never see this man again, because I needed to run now and—

"Why?" he repeated, the word stopping me just as I tensed to bolt.

Dark hair fluttered into my eyelashes, and I pushed it back towards the failing bun at the nape of my neck, falling apart from the weight of my waist-length hair battered against the wind.

He was clearly trying to analyse my escape, though I wondered for what purpose. His garments told me he was definitely not a guard—no dark-orange vest peeked from beneath his heavy canvas cloak—but he could pass for a mercenary. My garments told him I was not a criminal—thick woollen leggings and a knitted pullover were not standard issue in the cells. Nor was the hammer strapped to my waist with a buckled belt.

The stranger's dark brows narrowed, and he stepped towards me. Not near enough to touch, but it was close. "You're being kept against your will." Silver glinted from something on his lower teeth as he spoke, adding sharpness to the smooth glide of his words.

The contrast pulled at my attention, but something else distracted me more.

Genuine concern.

It had been so absent in my life that its sudden appearance was jarring. I had seen pity from the guards who knew I didn't carry the Curse, but who would not jeopardise their positions by advocating for my innocence. The way this stranger gazed down at me was different.

His dark eyes darted, registering my dull, ashen skin, the limpness of my hair, and then flicked between the rapid rise and fall of my chest, to where I rubbed my palms against the rope's burn.

I should have started moving—towards my target, away from this stranger. But indulging in his gaze felt like taking a very hot bath after not washing for weeks.

"In a way," I finally breathed.

"And the Caster of Amber Gate," he spoke through clenched teeth. "Does he know about this?"

The bared words offered me full view of the lower teeth of his strong jaw—they were entirely coated in cold metal. I had not been in contact with many people throughout my life, but even I knew something about it was unusual, disconcerting. Yet it suited him just the same. Insinuating ill of the leader of Amber Gate was dangerous, especially to a stranger.

Caster Leden did not only know about my captivity but was solely responsible for it. Although Leden was the only one of

Veligrad's seven Casters not to possess a Heightened Power, he bandied mortal powers just as compelling as magic—fear, zealotry, respect. Dangerous powers against anyone who tried to oppose his rule. The man before me did not appear to be under the same influence, and a sweep of admiration loosened some tightness in my chest. But trust was not a gift to be given lightly.

"He . . . condones it," I said carefully. "If that is what you're asking."

My stranger's expression shifted into something as cold and hard as the silver on his teeth. He must have caught a flash of my thoughts, for the cords in his thick neck loosened. "Do you have somewhere to go?"

My gaze drew to lips that spoke with a deep, even smoothness that stroked the length of my spine. *Yes*, I did have somewhere to go, and I should leave now. It would take me at least half an hour to reach the border of the Smed Forest.

"Hmm." A rough sound reverberated from his chest as he followed my unintentional glance west. "You want to compete in the Ranking."

Oh, Vuk. He was too observant. Intelligent. And now he sounded even more curious. "Are you going to tell the guards?"

He dropped his voice to the low howl of wind that tunnelled between the manor and my tower. "*A river dammed is still water flowing. Battering rain makes a tranquil lake.*" I caught my jaw before it could drop, as I recognised the century-old poem about inner strength and indomitable will. My mouth went dry as he bent his head a fraction towards me. "I have no intention of hindering your path. But will you tell me why Leden has done this? Why the Ranking, of all things, is your escape?"

Even covered in wool, the frigid night crept under the fibres, yet I grew hot under his direct attention. This stranger was definitely not from here if he did not know about my tower. My lips were ready to form the shape of a perfect response, another poem from the same worn book I had sorrowfully left behind in my room.

Rivulets may disappear while
Rivers spill into seas high.
One defines existence while
Another defines itself.

Would that I had time to exchange poetry with this strange man, who spoke the words that had been my only company on my loneliest nights, but I did not.

I cleared my dry throat. "I need to go, now."

He swiftly drew back, allowing me space, expression somehow soft and hard at the same time.

Legs, move.

They did not listen. A gust of harsh wind blew the dark-haired stranger's long cloak apart, revealing leather suspenders attached to his trousers like two vertical baldrics. Four pairs of tiny daggers, each the size of a finger, tucked into slits along the leather running down his chest.

Noticing my hesitation, he pulled a dagger from the sheathe over his heart and held it out to me.

"Take good care . . ." He paused, waiting for my name.

Palms tingling, I hastily took the pointed sliver of metal from him, pleading with myself to run, and realised this was the first time in my life I was introducing myself to someone.

"Nevena," I said, my chest feeling light. A foolish feeling, really.

As I uttered my name, his face shifted to an expression I was more acquainted with.

"Nevena . . . *Nightfall*?" The question was soft. No longer a *curious* kind of soft, but an *uncomfortable, wary* kind of soft.

Instinctively, I backed a step away in response, the movement a confirmation of my surname.

He huffed a soft breath. "Well, am I pleased to meet you," he continued in a gentle tone that sounded not pleased at all. While he remained where he was, he seemed somehow bigger now, his chest broader. "Do I look familiar, Nevena Nightfall?"

All warmth leached away, leaving a familiar cold as empty as my lonely tower. Shaking my head, my saliva was thick when I swallowed, dreading the reason this stranger recognised my name.

"Come on, Nightfall," his voice was almost a whisper. "I'm Edric. Edric *Silvan*."

A soundless gasp left me as he emphasised his surname. A name that I had tried to forget. Had spent sleepless nights unable to clear from my thoughts.

"That means . . ."

"It means"—Edric spread his shoulders to their full width—"that I'm finally meeting my brother's murderer."

Memories flooded my vision, ones I had tried to repress for two years. Veins bulging underneath a young man's desperate eyes. The lack of fight in him as I swung a hammer at his head.

I dragged my mind away from the depth of those visions and back to the brother of the man I had killed. He looked at me

the same way he had when he'd spoken about Caster Leden.
Furious. Unforgiving. *Dangerous.*

"Run." The command was little more than a sigh of wind.

I listened to that deadly softness. And ran.

CHAPTER TWO

M Y HEART WAS STILL pounding against the inside of my chest like a trapped fist trying to break through. Even after I knew I was not being followed, even when I made it to my destination alone.

Edric Silvan.

A shudder coursed through my limbs while sweat coated my skin.

The guards had told me a hooded family member had collected Ander Silvan's remains after that night two years ago. The young, blond man had arrived in Amber Gate earlier that day and introduced himself to merchants as a traveller. Distorted spawns of rumours spread through the town following *that* night, the only accurate part being my name. Edric must have heard the rumours that failed to tell him the truth of why Nevena Nightfall, the Mortician of Amber Gate's Cursed, had killed his brother.

After the deadliness in Edric's voice, I was not going back to correct him.

In a long-abandoned farm at the Smed Forest's edge, I finally doubled over, clutching my thigh muscles with stinging, rope-burnt hands. Outside of my tower, I was more fragile than I had expected. Running hurt my feet and left my face numb. Years of climbing that long, winding staircase were almost for nothing against the unexpected cold burn of shards grating my insides. Or perhaps that was the memory of my previous escape attempt, ripped open from the seams I had tried to hastily stitch over and never touch again.

But I was out.

Gloriously and terrifyingly—out.

Mere footsteps away, the Smed stood in imposing, expectant silence. At any moment, a vukodlak howl could tear away the false calm—as well as tear out my throat and drain my body of blood. That was how corpses ended up in my mortuary at the base of Amber Gate tower, all victims of the vukodlak's Cursed bite, and it was why I could not simply disappear to another city in Veligrad. Emerald Gate was the next closest city, reachable only by a journey south through the Smed Forest and mountainous Serpent Ranges, both infested with vukodlak and impossible to survive alone.

I wiped beads of sweat from my upper lip, creeping quietly along the tree line between the forest and an abandoned field of wild grass. All manner of creatures had once lived in the Smed before the witches Cursed the fae for their cruel reign, their unyielding dominance over witches and mortals. Now, no warm-blooded creatures remained in Veligrad's cold, northern wilderness, not even the grey wolves mortals once worshipped. Only things that could burrow or fly.

I could do neither, so vying for a Protector position at the Ranking was my only option at freedom. If I could find the elusive miran flower and collect its healing nectar, then return fast enough to Rank, that would finally prove I wasn't Cursed.

Well, that was if I could avoid running into any vukodlak.

My ears strained for any sound within the Smed. Further down the tree line, a monotonous chorus of gathered voices travelled from the Ranking Eve feast at the base of the giant Amber Gate arch, where the competition would commence at dawn. Ranking Eve was one of the few occasions townspeople ventured outside after dark, protected by the guards, the four Amber Gate Protectors, and Casters—the leaders of each of Veligrad's seven cities—who attended the competition. For the next few hours, I needed to remain covered in the Smed's shadows where no one would see me—mortal or Cursed.

I patted the hammer at my hip, its cold curves and points offering a sliver of comfort but doing nothing to ease the memories of its past use. It had proven all too reliable before.

My trembling legs shuffled to crouch between the tall buttress roots of a beech tree just inside the forest line. Perfect for hiding from bloodthirsty fangs. I hoped.

As I settled into a ball, damp forehead on my stinging palms, I couldn't help but release a long, silent groan. It was time to allow my common sense to berate me.

Deservedly.

I should never have accepted a stranger's help, and definitely should not have stayed to chat. Even if he quoted favourite lines from poems that I had rewritten on pages and pages of my notebook in the desperate moments I had felt most alone. Loneliness was a foolish beast, unfairly powerful. Yet another thing I needed to wrangle within my control.

A loud moan of wind through branches pulled me out of my thoughts. There was so much to become accustomed to. There was the unbothered intimacy of the breeze that touched my wrists, my neck, so unlike the indifferent wind of my high bedroom window. There was the endless space around me that even in the darkness was stocked with movement. Not dead stone or neat, dry wood. Not bodies awaiting their cremation. Not the hunger of kiln fire. But all things alive.

Too alive.

I pressed my palms into my eyeballs. Was I truly ready for this?

"Nev," a familiar voice quietly called from the darkness, and my head shot up.

Oh, no.

"Nev!"

It found my ears again. The high, urgent tone of the last voice I wanted to hear, even after Edric Silvan's. The one person I wanted to keep safe.

"*Shh,*" I reluctantly hissed. "I'm here."

Malina Summerfield hurried over as I unfolded from the ground, her unbound, flaxen hair frizzing outwards from her temples, glinting silver in the weak light reaching us from the Ranking Eve bonfire. This was the sole person who had noticed my isolation and risked her livelihood to convince guards to sneak her into my room when she was meant to be leaving new ceramic urns in the mortuary. Well—there was one other who had snuck into my room, but he counted as something else.

My only friend stopped within arms' reach. For the first time in our lives, I stood before her surrounded by living greenery rather than my grey stone walls.

"You did it," she breathed.

Not yet. The reality of what I needed to do next sobered away any sense of accomplishment. "Why in Veligrad's Seven Gates are you here?" I hissed. "I told you my plan so you wouldn't worry, not so you could follow me." I wanted to turn those narrow shoulders around and push her beyond abandoned, tall grass, towards the safety of impenetrable bricks and bolted doors.

"You're always fussing about me." Malina rummaged for something in her apron still flecked with clay, left beneath her thick woollen coat. "These came in today. You can't go without taking them with you."

She pulled out a bundle of envelopes and held them towards me.

"Absolutely not."

"They need you."

I knew that.

The letters looked like pale hands reaching out for help. Help that I had provided for the last thirteen years in *The Northern Serpent* newspaper. Malina had set up the anonymous advice column, "Do Tell," as a joke when we were eighteen. It should have been hilarious, providing advice from someone whose only life wisdom was learnt through gossip from Malina, or from bored tower guards who vented their woes through the tower door to someone who did not matter.

Turned out, I was good at it. Turned out, a lot of people kept secrets like knots, capable of unravelling their relationships or livelihoods, and *The Northern Serpent* found themselves in demand of the columnist that knew how best to untie them.

Unbeknownst to anyone except Malina, that was me.

It also turned out that "Do Tell" was partly what kept me from making any escape attempts—bar the one I wished I could forget. The people of Amber Gate needed me, so when I was not cremating bodies or cleaning the mortuary, I would dedicate my mind to their lives, and I would write.

"If I don't make it, then their letters will be lost, and they'll think they weren't important enough to receive a reply." I never missed a single letter. "They need someone to respond to them, Mal. You need to keep it going."

Where I was stubborn and closed, Malina was earnest and open. Now, however, the muted light that reached us illuminated a forehead as furrowed as mine.

"You know, you've spent a lot of your life telling me what to do. What I *should* do. If you're really going to do this, you need to listen to me." From the depths of her apron, Malina pulled out something else. A tiny glass vial the size of my pinkie finger, half filled with the most precious commodity in all of Veligrad—nectar of the miran flower.

Attaining the only healing magic left in Veligrad would have cost her months and months of her ceramicist apprenticeship wage. An amount she had not been able to accrue in time while her father was on his deathbed and whose passing left her with grief's vicious burden for a long while. I could almost hear my heart crack, threatening to splinter with the kind of pain so beautiful it could destroy me if I did not stifle it now.

"You're going to take this nectar—"

"Mal, I—"

"—and take the letters—"

"They'll be lost if I—"

"—and you're going to keep this miran nectar on you so that you *will* survive."

"I can't," I choked out. Any reminder of Malina during the Ranking would surely break me. A reminder that I was actively trying to part with the one person who made my confinement feel like somewhat of a home. "You need to keep it for yourself. Please."

Her furrowed brow remained in place. "You can't expect to face things alone all the time. Letting someone else help you is not weak, you know. Especially, letting *me* help you. Why don't you just listen to me, and we can find a place for you to hide for a while? Or I'll run away with you. I *told* you, I'll be happy enough. We'll chop off all our hair"—I restrained a shudder—"find different jobs. It wouldn't matter what, but at least you'd be properly free. We would make it, Nev. If you just ask me to run away with you, I'll do it." She dropped her arms by her sides and lifted her chin. "I'll do it now."

My chest was torn paper, and each word from Malina made that tear grow larger, bit by bit, word by word.

I did not deserve her kindness, and this visit risked her apprenticeship. Malina had tried hard to take over her father's pottery workshop after his death three years ago, but with her skills unable to match his, the regular customers soon closed their accounts. Under duress of poverty, she had sold her beloved workshop home and struggled to find a ceramics master with an apprenticeship to spare. She finally had one—the strict Master Patrizia who valued obedience above all else—and I would not risk that for her when jobs were never plentiful in Amber Gate town.

"That's not freedom, Mal," I said as gently as I could. "Even if I cut my hair"—something I would never do—"there would always be the risk of running into a guard or someone who knows my face. It would just be another kind of confinement. I don't want to live a hidden life any more. Collecting the miran nectar is the only way I can prove I'm not at risk of spreading the Curse. Leden would never let me out otherwise. It's convenient to keep me in the tower when everyone else is too afraid of the bitten dead rising. But imagine if I get a

Protector position. I would get some allowance, then I can buy us a home, so you don't have to worry about relying on an apprenticeship to sleep safely at night. And imagine if I could Rank at one of the seaside Gates?"

Living by the ocean was a dream we shared, but the reminder did nothing to clear the worry from Malina's face.

"I need to live without fear of being captured and kept in a cage again."

The letters crumpled slightly in Malina's fist.

"I know, Nev, but . . . what if you have no old magic in your veins? The miran flower won't open for you, and you won't get a Rank at all. And then what will they do to you?"

Malina was right. The flower that bloomed twice a year, in between sun-ray and shadow-light season, would only open for those with pure intentions—and magic in their blood. But I had already deliberated over every detail of my strategy.

"There's no rule on how I collect the nectar. I've planned for this. I promise no one else competing has as much to lose as I do."

It would not be long before Master Patrizia realised Malina was gone. The quicker this visit was over, the better it was for my friend. The more she thought she could help me, the more she would risk her livelihood.

It was tidier if I left my own mess to myself.

"I'll be fine. I promise." While I willed my sharp cheeks to lift into a rare smile, I suppressed a shudder of dread at what would happen to me if I failed the Ranking after forcibly escaping the tower. I would not allow it. "You know I can't take the nectar. Just in case . . ."

In case you get sick like your father. Like the countless others who don't survive the illnesses of shadow-light season.

Malina did not need me to say it.

I reached a shaky hand out and closed it over the one holding the vial, the only healing substance left in all of Veligrad after the witches' magic faded at the same time the fae became Cursed.

Her hands were cold.

"Your hands are warm," Malina said with a touch of surprise.

"Please keep it," I begged, as I held that small contact. It threatened to burn down my world, yet made my determination grow hotter. If I wanted this to be my norm—simple touch, human interaction, a life outside my rooms—I needed to carry on.

I broke contact first, releasing her hand still holding the vial. I could hug her if I wanted to. If she wanted to. We had laid alongside each other in my bed before, as we chatted and plotted dramatic escapes from each of our lives. But maybe now, after all my time in the mortuary tower, she did not want that.

Distant firelight reflected off her water-glazed eyes. "This isn't how I pictured your freedom." She took a half-step forwards, then stopped. Knowing there was nothing to do to convince me otherwise, Malina wiped her eyes. "At least eat this now, then."

I dodged a bread roll she tried to push at me from another pocket of her apron.

"Can't. I'll vomit."

"Then take the letters."

I shook my head.

In a stubborn move she probably picked up from me, Malina dropped the letters at my feet regardless and backed away.

"I'll see you once you finish the Ranking, Protector Nightfall."

Tears pushed against my lids, threatening to loosen some of that tight control I had instilled in myself since I was eleven years old. If I wanted to survive outside of the crumbly, gargoyle-guarded tower of my life, I could not lose a single fleck of control.

"You'll see me then."

CHAPTER THREE

AMBER GATE'S GIANT STONE arch stood oppressively in a clearing facing the Smed. Like my tower, the monument was made of slate-grey stone carved with vines and the faces of frightening creatures lolling their tongues, all the way up to its tall, pointed peak.

Dry grass grew at the feet of its two flat-sided columns. At the arch's peak, a round indentation marked the space which had once held the Gate's *dragul*—a crystal imbued with fae magic that mortals had chipped away from the arch, then split amongst Casters and Protectors of each of Veligrad's seven Gates. The dragul was the only source of power to defend against vukodlak, activated by the distant strands of magic in a mortal's veins. Most mortals had some fae or witch blood amongst their ancestors. My problems today would be halved if that magic resided in my veins, too, but luck rarely granted me her favour.

It's fine. I have a plan.

I peeked carefully around a beech tree from my position just inside the forest. Excited conversation and the clinking of glass carried across the weed-ridden clearing, where spectators gathered near the low-burning bonfire on the gently rising slope town-side of the Gate, as far from the forest as they could manage while maintaining a view.

Woodsmoke curled into the forest as I brushed the seat of my woollen leggings. I had spent the final hours of the night balled tightly between tree roots, fearing every whisper of wind or creak of branches. The vukodlak must have been roaming elsewhere, as nothing had visited me apart from scraggly mice.

"Competitors, over here." A man clapped his hands. I recognised him as Caster Leden's assistant. A young man who tried to cover his youth with a large, dark moustache, and who always seemed to leave Amber Gate manor wringing his hands.

Over a hundred stern-faced competitors approached the Gate, all dressed in padded linen or leather and armed with sharp weapons against the Smed's dangers. Inferiority swooped at me like a mocking crow. I tried to bat it away.

"The Ranking will commence shortly. Stand in one line before the Smed." He indicated exactly where I was standing, now visible in between the trees amongst growing grey daylight. "Who are you? A competitor?"

A hundred pairs of eyes looked my way, and my cheeks stung. Only a mite of relief wriggled within me that Leden's assistant never cared enough to peer up at my window when I had watched the comings and goings of the grand, pillared manor.

I nodded, and the young man tutted in impatience at what he saw—some farm girl poor on coin, hoping to get lucky but more likely never to return from the Smed.

"Get in line with the others then."

I dropped my gaze, trying to ignore the crawling feeling over my skin where eyes judged me, in sympathy or repugnance, as I joined one end of the forming line.

Maybe I should have asked Malina for different clothes. In my wool, I stood out like a sheep in a wolf pack.

Orange-vested guards moved along the line of competitors, handing each person two empty, longnecked glass bottles stoppered with corks.

It was already too bad that my grey, woolly set made me noticeable amongst the dark fighting attire other competitors wore, but I hoped my lowered head would keep any guards from suspecting the Cursed Mortician stood in the ranks of competitors before them. While Protectors had the best chance of killing the Cursed with magic, there were only four at each Gate. That was why two hundred guards at Amber Gate had been trained at maiming with silver-tipped arrows, swords and axes. For those who didn't possess magic like Protectors or Casters, silver through a vukodlak's heart would do.

Hammers also work. I shook away the thought as my stomach churned at the remembered crunch of iron on skull.

A pair of boots entered my view, and two glass bottles were pushed into my hands.

"I hope you know what you're doing." It was a murmur, only loud enough for me to hear. It belonged to the only other living person I had ever touched. Toma Ceran left before I could even meet his gaze. If he still held any fondness for me, he did not show it now. It was fair enough, I told myself. We were both only a convenience for each other—he, who had been raised in Tide Gate and shunned by other guards for the resented safety of his upbringing, for the fact that he had lost no loved ones in recent years, while many of them had. And me, for being—me. Judged as Cursed, and never to be released.

One way or another, this might be the last time we would see each other.

I watched his sword-strapped back as he strode down the line, checking everyone had received their bottles. And that was when my attention caught a pair of thick, dark brows further down the line. Directly facing me, sharp jaw sitting at least a head above anyone else.

Edric Silvan.

The blades running down Edric's leather suspenders were as bright as the full moon, matching his lower teeth. Matching the glare in his dark-blue eyes. He looked like steel if it could take human form. Whatever poetic depths he had revealed to me last night had vanished, along with any softness.

A gap in his suspenders remained in the space over his heart. I was sure he regretted gifting me the missing dagger which now lay flat against the back of my wrist, secured with a linen hair ribbon.

Great. I had an enemy amongst the competitors already.

I sunk back into the line, hoping to escape Edric's view, and pulled out the only other useful item I had brought. A hessian sack with a single, looped strap. As I drew it from my waistband, Malina's letters slipped out and fell onto damp grass. A rude snicker sounded from the person next to me—an attractive woman with mousy hair, pulled back into a tie at the nape of her neck—as I shoved the letters down the front of my top. The sneer on her face told me it must be a habit of hers to laugh at others' misfortunes.

All conversation ceased as the Council of Veligrad's Head, Caster Leden, approached to stand between the giant columns of Amber Gate. He faced the crowd on the Gate's bonfire side, offering the back of his grey head to competitors. Three of Amber Gate's Protectors stood near his side, amber dragul crystals sparkling on chains at their necks.

That was why we were all here.

"Today," Caster Leden's flat voice boomed, "there are seven Protector vacancies across the Seven Gates of Veligrad."

Internally, I recoiled at the voice of the man responsible for sentencing me to a life of confinement. Sure, it may have been reasonable at the time when the Curse first occurred—finding a girl wandering the Smed, covered in scratches, claiming to have no memory. Guards naturally suspected it might be a symptom of the Curse. But after weeks, months, and then years of clearly remaining mortal, it went beyond any caution to keep me isolated against my will. It was true that those bitten could turn into vukodlak—but only if they survived the blood loss when the Curse corrupted their veins. Rumours still brewed across Amber Gate that the bitten dead could turn, too, and so someone needed to burn the corpses that guards deposited in the tower mortuary, before the bodies supposedly rose.

I wondered if the Casters from other Gates that now stood watching Leden's speech knew of my injustice, or if they even cared. Did the other Casters rule their cities with the same brutality Leden did? In Amber Gate, the theft of an apple could land someone with a noose around their neck. I silently begged the old wolf-god, Vuk, that it was not so elsewhere.

"The positions are as follows. One position at Moon Gate."

Backs straightened at the mention of the third-most southern city in Veligrad, including mine. The three southern Gates lay along the continent's south-western coast and boasted no vukodlak attacks in over a decade. The coastal cities were safely situated far from the Smed Forest and Serpent Ranges that snaked from Veligrad's north-west edge before cutting across to the east.

"One position is vacant each at Amber Gate and Glass Gate," Leden continued.

Set amongst flat lakes in the centre of Veligrad, Glass Gate saw few attacks. It would be an improvement to the numerous bodies I saw mauled every couple of weeks. Life in my tower was lonely, but I couldn't say it wasn't busy.

"And four positions at Midnight Gate."

Murmurs broke out across the gathered crowd like the buzzing of flies on an old corpse. *Four positions*. That was the most positions ever announced for one Gate. In fact, that was *all* of the Protector positions available at a Gate, not including the Caster.

I bet some would refuse the title rather than accept a position at Midnight Gate, the most dangerous town in Veligrad, isolated by a vast swathe of forest to the north of Amber Gate.

"To be a Protector is to undertake a burden. The burden of carrying the only remaining magic in Veligrad. Yet it is great a privilege to channel the magic that once ruled mortals." The clearing fell silent, faces furrowed in thought. "Magic that *we* now rule. It has been thirteen years since the fae were Cursed by deceitful witches. Since the Curse's strength corrupted the witches' own magic. Thirteen years since mortals were last forced to suffer substandard lives in slums on the outskirts of cities, oppressed for centuries under the rules and whims of those with magic." Leden's words were met with the complete silence of a crowd enraptured, enraged by past harms, and enamoured with righteousness. This was why Leden ruled.

My hatred of the man filtered away any zealousness.

"While we found ourselves free of their domination, the small magics we relied on were lost, and we became targets for attacks of the Cursed." Not many liked to speak the name *vukodlak*—in the old language: ones who wore the coat of a wolf. "Witches once sold protection and healing to us, in exchange for whatever payment or price they deemed fit. With the witches' magic vanished, the only magic available to us remained in the old fae Gates of Veligrad."

The sparkling, amber dragul at his neck was larger than those of the Protectors beside him. I hastily lowered my head towards my dew-sodden boots as Leden turned around to address the competitors.

"I warn you. Be sure of your purpose in entering the Ranking today. The miran flower opens only for those with pure intentions, who carry threads of magic from ancestors that once lived in a time when mortals and the magical coexisted. If you believe you are worthy, you will enter the forest and retrieve the miran nectar while the miran flower blooms today. You will prove your worth against the dangers within the Smed and return with the nectar that can soothe all pains and heal all ills."

Only if you can pay for it, I thought, my mind drifting to the small vial in Malina's hand. Another tear ripped along my chest. She offered me her kindness in a way no one else ever had. I hoped I could repay her. To do that, my heart needed to be stone, not paper any longer.

I took a steady breath, preparing for the end of Leden's speech, bracing for the Ranking.

"You will be Ranked first by the weight of nectar you return with, and second by the speed of your return." Leden's pale, grey-moustached face always bore the same rigid severity. A look that many took for decisiveness, for knowledgeability, and one that I took for cruelty. "You all know what resides inside the Smed. My own son was lost to—" Leden's stern voice broke. I had heard this was the reason for Leden's unyielding rule against all magic. His son had been bitten, left alive, then risen as a vukodlak, before almost killing his own father. Leden's children were the only parts of him that evoked any emotion, and the townspeople soaked his misery with their own shared griefs. "Consider the Cursed again, and be sure you want to enter."

A couple of competitors near me, including the woman next to me, pushed out their chest with certainty. These, no doubt, were the ones who already knew they carried old fae or witch blood from their recent ancestors, the faint strands of magic that were the key to opening the miran flowers. Fae had always considered mortals too lowly to mingle with, making it rare to find anyone carrying more than a great-grandparent's portion of fae blood. As for witches, Leden had seen them all hunted after their magic disappeared, should their loss of magic mean they, too, would become Cursed. While his ruthlessness was deemed necessary to save mortals, it was not a perspective I could share.

"A final rule. No blood is to be spilled. Not your own, nor your competitors', should you want to attract the Cursed. Those of you here from the southern Gates will not have seen a Cursed attack. Here in the north"—he paused—"we know it too well."

As stress wound a tight net around my lungs, two guards carried over a tall pendulum clock, placing it beside the arch. Above the giant monument, my tower loomed in the grey distance as if admonishing my absence. Scolding, yet safe.

Fists beat within my chest like a drum.

Was I truly certain I wanted to leave?

"You have until noon to return and cross the Gate's threshold." Leden surveyed the line before him, and my limbs tensed, though his eyes barely registered my presence.

"Begin."

CHAPTER FOUR

ALF OF THE COMPETITORS sprinted into the Smed's spindly branches, while others approached the tree line warily. I was one of the latter.

So was Edric.

He prowled closer to the first row of crooked trees, keeping in line with my movements. He was tall. And wide. The bulge of his shoulders screamed he was clearly a strong fighter. How was it possible that he looked more weapon than man? I could either wait for him to go first, or I could run, maybe climb up a tree if I was desperate. Surely he had his own Rank to worry about. He looked too big to move nimbly across a forest floor, but then again, he had looked too brutish to recite poetry. The calculating expression in his narrowed eyes told me there were likely other hidden surprises to this curious male.

Carefully, I drew closer to the forest's entry when another body broke into my peripherals—a tall woman with a thick, dark braid running to her waist, a few years younger than me. She drew in a sharp breath through her nose as she took in my pilling, dew-soaked wool and paltry array of weapons. While her interruption from Edric's cold gaze was welcome, her stare full of warm pity was not.

Pity only ever led to things half-hearted.

Before the woman could offer me any sympathy, encouragement, or help—whatever those brown eyes were threatening to do—I sprinted into the Smed.

A rush of cold, dense air misted my face beneath the forest's dark boughs. Bent and knotted limbs blocked out the rising day, leaving the forest in a deep gloom as if the sun was reversing its climb.

This was the second time in a matter of hours that I had needed to run from Edric Silvan. My feet slipped across green moss and squelched into water-logged soil, unused to the changing surfaces compared to the hard floors of my tower. Hopefully Edric was slower than me, and I wouldn't have to face whatever his murderous glare had threatened.

While my focus was honed on staying atop my feet, of creating a distance between Edric, of not smashing the glass bottles jostling in my canvas satchel—I lost sight of the other competitors who had been ahead of me. The confident-looking ones. Those were the individuals I needed to follow.

My lungs blazed with a now familiar icy burn, but my legs held strong. Thirteen years locked in a tower could have meant that I had wasted away. Sometimes I thought that was nearly the intention against a young girl of what origin no one knew. But I had run the tower's stairs each day, from my bedroom at the top, all the way to the sweltering ground floor where the cremation kiln burned. I had also kept a close eye on the guards when they trained in the courtyard below my window. The captains never knew that while they instructed their subordinates to become defenders and killers, they were unintentionally teaching me, too.

Even so, those competing today had likely trained harder than me, had likely had access to more knowledge about the

Smed. All I had gleaned through half-heard conversations and vague book references was that the miran flowers grew sporadically deep within the Smed, and only those with magic could sense their pull in its vicinity. And, of course, the deeper one travelled within the Smed, the more likely one was to encounter the forest's Cursed creatures.

When I was certain Edric had not followed me, I slowed. Towards the flowers, I felt nothing. No magical awareness or clues where they might be. So I attuned my ears to listen for the shuffles and crunches of those somewhere before me.

In my rooms, time always passed quickly when I was cremating or when one of my visitors bribed certain guards to sneak them in. All other times it was slower than the passing of clouds. Here, I could not tell how long I had spent wandering.

The forest grew darker the deeper I entered. Thick, wet air dampened any sounds. Trees became wider, the ridges in their rough bark deeper, as if engorged with ancient stories long forgotten. It felt like trespassing. Like the trees' gnarled faces were silently judging me, even now calling to the Smed's monsters to come and remove the intruder.

I wondered whether Edric felt the same, or whether he could wield that enchanted rope, using his strength and simmering rage to—

Stop thinking about Edric.

I shook the unhelpful thoughts from my mind. Before I could delve back into analysing any further about Edric's anger or his strength, a cry broke through the silence of the forest.

It was close, some way to my left. Fear flooded my chest. What could it be but a vukodlak, latching its fangs into a competitor's neck? The trees seemed to leer at me in satisfaction as I changed direction away from the sound's origin.

Then I stopped. What if someone had found nectar already? The nearby monster was likely distracted. As harsh as it was, someone's hard luck presented me with the opportunity I had planned for. If I couldn't take nectar from the miran flower itself, I could take it from a competitor. The hammer at my side was almost painfully cold as I gripped its head.

I turned back towards the sound of the cry.

My footfalls were careful and quiet over slimy, mossy roots as I weaved through wide trees, seeing little ahead of me. Grasping the wooden handle of my hammer tight, I finally arrived at the source of the cry.

A different kind of monster stood before me.

In between branches, I spied a male contestant with a thick neck clutching a drooping, dislocated shoulder. The corners of his lips pulled so far down that they twisted his already cruel face. A short sword with a mother-of-pearl inlaid hilt was strapped to his hip, as was a quarter-filled bottle of thick, gold liquid. The miran nectar.

Opposite him was the same woman who had stared at me before entering the Smed. Sweat beaded on her sienna forehead as she panted heavily, clutching a glass bottle with a little less miran nectar than the male's. The sword at her hip was similar to his with a curving design of mother-of-pearl at the hilt, too.

Moon Gate.

The man broke his stare and whipped his neck in my direction. I faltered a half step back, as both pairs of eyes noticed me. But he suddenly lunged towards the woman—who blocked his approaching arm with a slim wooden club, then thrust it square into his chest, sending him flying onto his backside.

"Stop this, Kavi," growled the bear of a man, painfully raising himself back up. Trickles of sweat ran between the bristles of his shorn hair and into his eyes. "You'll only draw consequences to your parents."

"I thought you might be here to change. To escape your mother's influence. Why don't you use this opportunity, Ryker? You could free us both."

If the pair were already returning from retrieving nectar, miran flowers were surely nearby. Perhaps they were still dripping after being opened recently. I started creeping away from the scene before me, allowing the fates of Kavi and Ryker to unfold themselves. Neither of these two would return from the Ranking to a half-life in a stone cage. I needed to focus on myself.

What if Kavi is escaping something important, too?

That voice sounded more like Malina's than mine. My friend's earnest face flew into my mind. The way she had been a child holding her father's clay-caked hand and had possessed the courage to ask the guards outside my door why a girl had to be by herself, and didn't she need someone to play with? Malina had no idea why I was confined, just that I might be sad and lonely. It was she who had convinced her father to bribe guards to let her be in my company. Malina had changed the trajectory of my life by using her courage, her care.

What if Kavi needs a Malina right now, too?

I filled my cheeks with air and blew hard. Then turned back around.

Kavi was still trying to block and dodge Ryker's lunges at her bottle while she staggered with fatigue.

"What the—" Ryker realised too late that I was already close behind him.

"She might not be able to do this right now, but I certainly can." I yanked his dislocated shoulder down hard, and the man gave a guttural scream. A kick to his stomach sent him sprawling. One part of me rejoiced that my training was working, while another part—one I tried to ignore—recoiled in disgust at intentionally causing someone else such pain.

Ryker lay on the ground panting, but his gaze was hard and unyielding.

"Get away from her," I said.

Ryker tried to raise himself to retaliate, but I swiftly yanked on his dislocated arm again. This time his scream was more restrained, but I knew I was causing damage.

"Get. Away. From. Her."

The large man remained, his eyes darting between Kavi and me.

"Alright," I said, "here it comes—"

"Not again," he barked.

"No? Then leave, *Ryker*. You're injured and you're slow, and if you keep trying to take her nectar, I'm going to keep doing this over and over again. Think you'll make it back in time to Rank for a position?"

Ryker snarled, saliva spitting from the corners of his mouth. "I won't forget this." He heaved himself away from me, before stomping unevenly, painfully, into the trees.

That made two enemies within only hours of my escape from the tower. Maybe I was safer confined.

At least Malina would have been proud of me.

"Thank you," Kavi breathed when Ryker was out of sight.

"It's fine," I said, and made to move away.

"If you go that way"—Kavi pointed in the opposite direction I had started towards—"there's a patch of flowers a little further along. They only dribbled a bit of nectar, but better than nothing."

I only nodded before promptly leaving for the direction Kavi pointed out. Maybe I had judged her too harshly earlier. It only took minutes for the deep, bitter floral and honey scent to fill the air. And then, in a tight circle of trees, I saw the miran flowers.

Vibrant crimson streaked with violet along the outside of their closed petals, with buds as large as closed fists. They grew to my hip from stalks whose roots wound around protruding tree roots, as if receiving their nutrition there rather than from the earth.

Shrivelled flower heads littered the ground, their stems cut clean. I suspected someone else had come here before and attempted to force the nectar out. Had the shrivelling occurred once they had been cut or after they had been used? I wiped sweat from my stinging hands on my pullover, then reached to a flower, ready to pry its petals open.

At the first hint of my touch, the petals burst wide apart, and nectar shot out in a stream all over my front.

I quickly pulled back, panting. Staring at the stickiness. Were these the same flowers Kavi spoke of?

The petals constricted once more, but plump drops of nectar continued dripping in rhythmic beats, as if leaking with pent-up pressure. I angled a bottle carefully, and gently brushed my fingers against the petals again. They reopened, and nectar flowed from a long pollen tube and into the bottle like a tap. After a few moments I pulled away, blinking slowly.

Glowing in my hand was a full bottle of sunshine. Miran nectar.

It could not be. I had never felt magic run through me. Had never had any special power. In fact, there was nothing special about me at all. That was how Caster Leden could justify keeping a lost, forgotten girl locked away, so that only I would suffer should a bitten body rise to attack. If I had as much magic as the volume of nectar indicated, I certainly would not have been stuck in a tower for thirteen years.

Who am I?

It was a question I had buried long ago in the cemetery of my mind that broke through hard soil as a green shoot. It had never mattered who I was and would not have changed my confinement.

But perhaps it mattered now.

The second jar filled next, just as easily. That was when another thought entered my mind, making me bite my lip. If I had the most nectar, maybe I would not only escape Amber Gate, but I could end up at Moon Gate, the safest city out of the positions available. Shock transmuted into adrenaline, and I shoved the corked bottles into my satchel.

I could do it.

Too bad I heard the quiet tread of boots a second too late.

A tiny, familiar dagger glinted beneath my throat while its owner's breath warmed my temple.

"Hello again, murderer," Edric Silvan snarled.

The fucking hypocrite.

With a flick of my wrist against my leg, the twin to Edric's dagger was in my palm, and angled at what I presumed was a valued piece of anatomy.

"What position are you competing for then?" I hissed. He kept a distance between his front and my back, as if he didn't dare touch me any more than he needed to. But I could feel the space between us as if it was tangible. "A position where Protecting *doesn't* involve killing those who are Cursed?"

Edric's breath paused, and I felt a gleam of satisfaction. Whatever he thought of me, what I did to Ander had been out of defence, not out of enjoyment.

We both remained still, trapped between our daggers. Both knowing if blood was drawn, then so were the vukodlak, and we would fail the Ranking. Edric's next move all depended on how badly he wanted to avenge his brother.

"Ander was not Cursed."

Those soft words hit my lungs like a barrage of rocks. It was the one thing that I could not let go of when I thought of Ander Silvan the night he had appeared outside the tower door. The veins beneath his eyes, the intensity with which he rushed after me into the mortuary—

Stop thinking about that and move.

I couldn't. Edric's dagger beneath my throat was too close. With his spare hand, Edric reached for my wrist, but my blade pressed against the fabric of his inner thigh, halting his attempt at retrieving the dagger.

"The silver in your hand is mine," Edric growled against my ear. "It doesn't belong to butchers."

"I thought it was a gift."

"Then why don't you repay me with a gift of your own? Hand me those bottles, and then show me again how well you can run."

I scoffed, the sound as rare as my laughter. "I preferred you reciting old Rieka poetry. Or was that the only line you knew?" My cheek inclined towards his chin. "I don't know if metaphors about empowerment within hardships suit you.

Try the one about being two-faced: '*Seven wishes over seven moons, / None of them left me with what you returned.*'"

Edric's breathing stilled again, and I gathered myself, similarly surprised. I guess slinging poetry in argument was not something I expected to do on my first day outside my tower.

"I take back what I said earlier," Edric said. "Rieka's water poetry doesn't suit you. You don't have the power of a river or the grace of a lake."

"No," I breathed, ignoring the unexpected flinch at his words. "I'm a rivulet. I define myself."

I lunged an elbow at Edric's ribs—that he swiftly avoided. He gripped my satchel, but not before I hugged it into my chest, pulling Edric's arm along and ending up with him wrapped around me in another lock, my back flush to his front. A wave of scent rushed into my lungs, something between citrus and salt.

Ignore that. Unhelpful, new sensations.

In the scuffle, my dagger moved to a kidney. If he did not release me, I would have no choice but to stab. He was probably thinking the same thing.

Whoever went first, then.

"You know what?" His closed fist pressed onto my sternum, dagger tilting my chin upwards towards his face. Daylight had worn away all softness from the previous night. He looked meaner, the angles of his face harder. The soothing voice from last night could not possibly have issued from that firm, angry jaw.

"What?" I straightened my back against his front, channelling the guard captains I had watched over and over again. Never losing control of their body, their emotions. "That you're a hypocritical, uncultured prick? Or that I'm going to make sure you don't finish the Ranking?"

Edric leaned forwards in our locked position, his firm arms holding me securely, and whispered into the shell of my ear, "*Fight me. It'll* be more fun for me to know you struggled so hard and failed when you're back in that tower, rotting alone for what you've done."

His breath against my skin triggered an involuntary shiver. I forced my voice to respond in a flat tone. "I would hardly call fighting an amateur poet *fun.*"

Edric glanced down to where my arm still hugged my satchel, but my hand clutched Edric's hard forearm.

"You sure?"

My breath hitched.

Edric took my moment of distraction to rip the satchel off my shoulder, his dagger leaving my throat. I whirled and caught the strap, but he tugged it hard towards him.

The weak fabric split in two.

Glass smashed open against the forest floor, spilling the most important commodity in Veligrad.

"No! *Not the nectar.*"

I understood he hated me. I understood he wanted me to fail. But I did not understand why he would do something so careless as to deprive the ill and feeble of the only medicine in Veligrad that could heal them.

"*Fuck.* I didn't—"

With a shriek, I shoved a shoulder into Edric and dove for the intact half of one remaining bottle, scooping its body into the crook of my elbow before any more could chug out.

Once again, I found myself running.

Nectar slopped out of its open, jagged top as I navigated the forest back towards Amber Gate, while heavy steps followed close behind me. If I faltered even for a half step, I would be within Edric's grasp.

But my lungs felt clear now, and my limbs moved quickly, freely. I dodged protruding roots with ease, and the ground that had been slippery now gripped my feet, helping them along. Perhaps it was the effect of the "Do Tell" letters tucked into my chest, urging me on. The people I had helped somehow helping me. Whatever it was, a clearing suddenly opened up between the trees, revealing Amber Gate, ominous and intimidating ahead. Lumpy earth changed to flat stone. A crowd watched with collective curiosity as I ran across the clearing and through the threshold of the giant arch.

I gasped for air, not from fatigue, but from a settling realisation of something I had almost been too afraid to truly believe was possible.

I did it. I made it.

"Congratulations!" Kavi beamed as she approached. Some distance away stood Ryker, and a handful of others who had returned with nectar.

The sound of footfalls behind me was absent. Panting, I turned to find no one there.

A moment later, Edric broke through the forest line in a slow saunter. He paused before he reached the arch, scanning those that had arrived before him, ignoring me as if we had never shared a glance, let alone daggers pointed at important arteries.

Then out of the trees, the woman that had sneered at me emerged and joined my pursuer. Together they strode through the arch.

CHAPTER FIVE

"**N**AME, CITY, AND OCCUPATION?" Leden's assistant asked each competitor in turn as the weighing of nectar commenced. Only eleven of the hundred had returned with meagre volumes of nectar. Two had not returned at all.

"Kavitha Khalili. Moon Gate. Student."

I had slipped from Kavi's side, hoping if I was last that the weighing would create enough distraction for the guards to pay no attention to my name and face.

"Edric Silvan. High Gate. Traveller."

While my gaze remained firmly on the weed-fractured pavement, my ears couldn't help but strain towards Edric's response. Traveller. *Sure.* It was a good cover, I had to admit, for whatever Edric's real job was. High Gate was the largest and wealthiest city in Veligrad. By virtue of being the southern-most point of the continent, furthest away from the Smed, it was the safest. Folk could afford to *travel* at their leisure.

I tasted bitterness at the back of my tongue. Living by the ocean at High Gate was a dream. Had life been too cushy and boring without the threat of danger lingering at the city's borders? Did that curiosity account for his excursion to my tower last night?

Something told me it was more than that.

"Jelena Altan. High Gate. Jeweller."

It was Edric's companion. Another privileged competitor. That explained the way she had sneered at me with superiority. *Spoilt, ignorant brats.*

Didn't they have safer careers to pursue? I certainly would if this wasn't my only choice. While Protectors were held in high esteem, this career was dangerous, unless you Ranked at the southern Gates. At the end of each six-month season, Protectors from the northern towns would often try to Rank again to secure a position in the south.

The remaining nectar swilled thickly around the base of my broken bottle as a notebook was shoved into my vision.

"Name, city, and occupation?"

My tongue felt too thick to speak. This was the moment that could undo everything. If I lied, it would only make things worse when the tower was discovered empty, and I was eventually recognised. Leden would be present when the dragul crystals were bestowed to the new Protectors, and he was not a man to be undermined in front of his subjects.

But I was not Cursed, and with the nectar between my clammy hands, I could finally prove it. Uttering my cursed name could finally ensure my freedom.

Leden's assistant tutted with impatience. "Well?" He plucked the broken bottle from my grip, passing it to a guard to be weighed.

"Nevena Nightfall," I murmured quietly. "Amber Gate . . . Mortician." It was hardly a whisper.

"*Pardon?*"

I cleared my throat. "Nevena Nightfall. Amber Gate. Mortician."

The moustached man stumbled backwards and cried loud enough for nearby guards to hear, "*You're* the Cursed Mortician?"

The chatter of the watching crowd stopped in waves, like quietening wind gusts. A handful of guards stepped closer, swords glinting with menace beneath burnt-orange vests.

"Did you say the Cursed Mortician is here?" said one guard, his pinched face travelling up my attire and to my ashen face. Another shouted, "The Cursed Mortician? Who the fuck let her out of that tower?"

My muscles tensed tight into my spine, trying to make myself smaller, to disappear.

"Nobody let me out," I tried to speak over the raising voices, "I—"

"How is she a Mortician? She doesn't look like she could even lift a spade."

"No, she's the Mortician for the ones found in the forest. The ones killed by the Cursed. They don't get a burial. They get burned."

"Then she must be Cursed!"

"I am *not* Cursed." The clamour silenced as my voice finally cut through. "Is over a decade cremating the bitten not proof enough? Look at me. In all that time, I have not become Cursed. I'm *mortal.*"

The rise and fall of my breath was the only sound as wide, suspicious eyes took on my invitation and *looked*. Vuk. It was too much attention on me, too many pairs of eyes making their own judgements. My chest constricted. Less room to breathe. My lungs pumped faster, trying to swallow air—

Then a voice like strong, black coffee broke through the jittery silence.

"Her eyes are clear."

"What?" the assistant snapped.

Guards parted as a handsome man built like a blacksmith strode forward. His thick hair gleamed bronze under the frigid, noon sun, reminding me of the old fae statues that stood poised around the manor beneath my window. A dark blue-black dragul sat between the prominent swell of his pecs, visible between the undone top buttons of his shirt.

The Caster of Midnight Gate, Tavion Hartley.

Hartley calmly continued, his dimpled chin lifted. "There are no swollen veins around her eyes, and her irises are unclouded. Fingernails are still intact, no claws. She doesn't look like someone just bitten, to me. How long's she been in that tower?"

Wind whipped against the arch's unyielding stone. No one wanted to respond with a truth that would reveal the fallacy of my confinement.

"Too long." Toma's hollow voice carried from where he stood some distance from the ring of guards closing in on me, finally putting words to what the other guards failed to admit. That they were complicit in the wrongness of my confinement.

"Well, it only takes a couple days to transition to the permanent wolf form. I think we can all see that Nevena Nightfall is *not* a vukodlak."

Guards and townspeople visibly flinched at the true name of the Cursed.

"But—"

"This might only be my second season as Caster, Prosek"—a corner of Hartley's mouth hitched into a half smile—"but as a former guard myself, I would hope you trust my judgement on what the Cursed look like." Though he spoke at Leden's assistant, Hartley's words travelled in Leden's direction as the Head Caster slowly approached.

Something tingled with heat at Hartley's defence of me, like a first sip of steaming tea, thawing some of the chill of Leden's presence. Caster Hartley was clever. Should Leden denounce the Midnight Gate Caster's judgement, he would be admitting his own Council was unfit, that a weakness lay amongst Veligrad's strongest. However, admitting Hartley was right meant he had wrongly confined an innocent person for the majority of their life.

"Well," spluttered Prosek, his pink lips bursting through his moustache, "she can't be a Protector. She's only ever been kept in the tower. She won't last a minute."

"She lasted in the Ranking. As far as I can count, she's one of only eleven who managed to retrieve nectar and return before noon. The miran flower deemed her intentions pure to offer her nectar. That's the criteria fulfilled. Isn't that right, Leden?"

Competitors slunk away as Caster Leden's piercing, grey gaze struck an unflinching Hartley. Watching townspeople held their limbs in stiff angles of indecision, ready to run at my supposed affliction, but too enraptured with the scene before them.

"Nevena Nightfall," Leden's resounding voice commenced, his stern face not betraying a hint of his thoughts, "has tested an important theory for the good of her townspeople."

Fear deflated within me, making space for rage. I wanted to sweep Leden's glossed leather boots from beneath him. I had been no test, merely a convenience to do the dirty work no one else wanted.

"She was found in the forest as a girl, claiming no memories of what occurred to her. Instead of eliminating her in the manner of the risk she presented, she was treated with mercy. We placed her safely away from endangering others, should she be Cursed. At the same time, Amber Gate was presented with another problem. We wanted to bury our kin who were devastatingly slain by the Cursed, but what if those bitten awakened again, as Cursed themselves?"

Large gems sparkled from beds of thick, gold rings on Leden's fingers, while his hands remained stiffly by his sides. The extravagant array of colours contrasted strangely with his sterile manner.

He continued with solemn heaviness. "The Fall of the Fae was a time of unknown. Too many mortals had been lost already. Thus, this young lady was given a role of high regard: to safely cremate those bitten. All these years she has worked to protect our town while we protected her."

The power of righteousness was infectious. Just like that, my forced confinement was made benevolent. The grey days of my childhood when I had scraped my nails bloody against the mortuary door, begging for sunlight and freedom, were shrugged away with condescending ease. Caster Leden could make torture sound reasonable if he chose to. Chatter rose from the crowd like strengthening rain.

"I see. Well"—Hartley clapped his hands and rubbed them together loudly, breaking the grip of Leden's speech—"seems all clear now. What do you say, Leden? Is Nightfall a free woman?" Hartley's tone was easy, light. But the challenge was unmistakeable.

He's standing up to the Head Caster. . . for me.

Except, was this a challenge for my freedom, or a challenge to Leden's authority? My instincts said I was a pawn in the Caster's game of politics. There was nothing good in that for me.

Bodies drew closer like roots towards the Lutava River, awaiting Caster Leden's response. Over his straight nose, Hartley held Leden's gaze with gleaming eyes.

"Of course."

Leden's grey moustache bristled very slightly as his gaze flicked to me. His expression was arranged exactly as it always had been. Stiff and stern. Yet that single movement conveyed his thoughts.

I was the source of his embarrassment. If I failed to Rank, and when all these Casters were gone, any mercy he had claimed to bestow would disappear.

Under my wool, I began to sweat.

"Jakov." Leden gestured to his assistant. "The final Ranks, if you will."

The flustered assistant reddened at the use of his first name. Retrieving the weighing notes from a guard, he cleared his throat.

My heart beat harder against the brittle twigs of my rib cage as silence fell once again. This was the announcement that would determine my future.

"The seven vacancies shall now be awarded. Those who place first, our strongest and fastest individuals, are posted at Veligrad's largest cities. Protectors in need of more experience are posted to Veligrad's least populated regions, to hone their skills without risks to the populations."

"Bullshit," muttered a nearby competitor, his white-blond hair bright in my peripherals. "We all know it's a punishment."

"The new Moon Gate Protector is Jaya Chand."

While many competitors' shoulders drooped in response to missing out on the safest Gate, Kavi's nemesis Ryker fell to his knees and savagely beat his uninjured fist on the ground, like he was pounding a face. Those nearest to him shuffled away. The nectar I had seen him with must definitely have been stolen. There was no way the miran flower would consider his intentions *pure*.

Glass Gate was called next, awarded to a snobby-looking male that could rival Edric's friend for sneers. The raging Ryker was positioned at Amber Gate, and then the final four positions were announced. My pulse throbbed in my veins.

"The new Protectors of Midnight Gate are Kavitha Khalili, Aksel Ivkov, Edric Silvan and Jelena Altan."

No.

It felt as though every bone around my heart exploded into splinters.

I tried to draw in air, but my lungs felt punctured, unable to ever hold breath again. The pale afternoon sun was too intense. My exposed skin suddenly too vulnerable. Too many eyeballs turned my way.

I failed.

It was all because of Edric Silvan.

My clenched fists trembled with the rage I wanted to inflict on the sullen, prejudiced male that stood brooding next to his friend.

You won, Edric. Celebrate. You did this.

No victory lifted his thick brows as he rubbed his knuckles slowly up and down his sternum.

What would happen to me now?

"The celebratory feast will begin shortly in the manor," Prosek continued, as if his previous declaration hadn't just upended my world. "Protectors will then be Stepped to their new positions prior to sundown. All others will be required to leave by the method which they arrived, so please—"

"Excuse me, Jakov," Leden interrupted the assistant, Hartley looking poised by Leden's side. "In light of the unique challenges of Protecting Midnight Gate, Caster Hartley and I have made a decision to benefit our land's northern-most town."

Jakov Prosek's cheeks reddened again as he conceded to Leden's interruption.

"An additional Protector will join Midnight Gate," declared Leden. "Congratulations to Midnight Gate's fifth Protector, Protector Nevena Nightfall."

Chapter Six

I wasn't sure whether my legs floated or dragged as I pulled myself before the quiet Amber Gate tower. It was unguarded.

By the Seven Gates of Veligrad, is this real?

Exhilaration pressed against the inside of my skin, yearning to be released. Too bad it was compressed within a tightly knit layer of dread.

Nothing felt real.

There was little to collect from my room, but I dared not go inside, should the tower shut me up and never let me go again. The gargoyles I had trodden across on my way down leered at me as if resentful of my escape. I could almost sense the heat of the cremation kiln waiting hungrily on the other side of the arched wooden door, trying to lure me back inside with its warmth.

I had hardly waited three breaths when Malina came rushing around the corner of the manor, scattering gravel as she crossed the courtyard to reach me. News and gossip spread faster than spilled mead in Amber Gate.

"Clothes," she said and pushed a stuffed canvas pack into my arms. She did not need to ask why I hadn't stepped inside my tower to change.

"Mal—"

"You still got the letters?"

"Yes, and Mal—"

"I'll keep sending them. You better respond so I know you're still alive and breathing and—"

"*Mal.* I promise it'll be okay." My friend's lip trembled. So did my legs. "I've done it, Mal. I'm free."

Free enough. For now.

Malina's expression did not lighten. Her voice shook. "You know why Midnight Gate lost all four of its Protectors this season."

Thanks to gossiping guards, I knew.

Vukodlak had attacked and drained two Protectors. The other two were forced to stay until the end of the season, with Casters not allowing them to Step back through the Gates to return to their home cities. After which, they retired.

Midnight Gate was blocked from the rest of Veligrad's cities by the vastness of the Smed Forest entirely surrounding it. It took two dragul crystals to cast enough power to Step between the ancient Fae Gates, and one of them needed to be a Caster's dragul, since they carried the strongest portion of magic. Without a Caster's dragul, anyone at Midnight Gate was essentially trapped.

"I should have tried to talk you out of it." Malina placed the heels of her palms over her eyes. "Now, it's too late."

"It's alright," I whispered. "This is the best way." I gently pulled her hands away from her face, squeezing them. They were still cold.

She sniffed.

Then she lifted her chin. "You better be back here next season, Nevena Nightfall." There was that tone again, the one which mimicked my own stubbornness. "You better be here, competing for another position to get out of Midnight Gate. Do you hear me?"

"I hear you. I'll be back in six months." I squeezed her hands harder.

"Do you promise me?"

I sighed. Anger was so much easier to handle than the kind of sadness Malina covered me with now, as warm and prickly as tears. But I could not deny the only person that had made my life feel like a home. It was because of Malina that my bed was covered in warm blankets and that I had books stacked in piles against the walls. It was why all my clothes were warm wool, like the ones I wore now. She was the only person who had advocated for me when I had been powerless.

Until today. Until Hartley.

"I promise that at the end of shadow-light season, I will be back at the next Ranking."

"Good."

She threw her arms around me.

My shoulders relaxed in her hold. It was a hug full of the comfort of warm bread and the stable mellowness of unfired clay. That was what safety felt like to me.

The "Do Tell" letters crumpled inside my woollen pullover. I would remain connected to Malina in this way. She'd send me letters, and I would send the replies she would publish.

One season, and then I could return and sweep us both out of our insecure positions in life and into real safety and freedom.

Remaining in my soiled, woolly clothes was a mistake.

The other competitors had changed, and their families were dressed respectfully in formal shadow-light season attire. Trousers with jackets, long gowns with coats. Garment colours mostly representing the Gate from which they had arrived. I was dressed like one of the corpses found in the woods that would end up on my worktable. Disarrayed and trodden.

At least it reflected how I felt.

Amber Gate manor's windowless ballroom glowed from the countless candle sconces that dramatically highlighted intricate floral mouldings, flourishing across the walls and ceiling. The appearance of warmth did nothing for the cold glares coming my way from the guests crammed around long tables laid with food.

My stomach sunk. Although I had expected wariness, a small part of me had hoped for acceptance. I was now proven "not Cursed," but deep rumours were never easily doused with reasoning. I itched for the formalities to begin soon so I could escape the watchfulness of those who had been happy to let me rot in the tower.

Let this time pass quickly. Let me be back here, whole, in six months to compete again.

I was not sure who I prayed to. Mortals used to pray to the moon and to Vuk, the wolf-god. Fae used to pray to the stars. Witches used to pray to the Earth Mother, before they were hunted by mortals when their magic disappeared. Whatever magic was left swirling in Veligrad could take my words in exchange for my gratitude.

An empty corner far from the raised stage seemed like the best place to wait for this ceremony to be over with. The crowd parted like a spoon through lentils, while I kept my gaze on the ground.

"Nevvy, over here."

Toma's voice called from nearby, and I whipped my head towards it. That meant I wasn't looking when I slammed directly into someone's large, solid back, and landed flat on my ass. Something clattered to the floor at my feet.

"Nevvy, are you alright? You dropped this." Toma pushed a small, leather book into my hand as he helped me up. I recognised the title of my favourite poetry book and cringed. "Come on, let's go near the front. They're about to present the dragul."

"This isn't mine. It's—"

"Nevvy?" Edric towered over me. He raised a brow as he snatched the poetry book from my grip and slipped it into his pocket. "That is, without a doubt, the worst nickname I've ever heard."

Being honest, I wasn't a fan of Toma's nickname for me either, but it was a small price to pay for what he had done for me. It was because of Toma that I had nearly been successful in escaping two years ago, but—*stop*. I would not think of that night if I could help it, especially with Edric in my face.

Toma thrust his chest forwards like a male bird in mating season. The tip of his short hair barely grazed Edric's chin. "Look, man—"

"Don't hide the book now, Silvan," I stepped in front of Toma, so close to Edric our fronts were nearly touching. "You must be one of those men who opens a book in public places, pretending to read, just to be seen trying to look mysterious." I had seen men do that in the courtyard below my window, in deliberate view of others who took their daily walk around the manor's formal gardens. "If you actually read a line of *Water Music*, you'd know the poems encourage choosing self-restraint over force. Maybe you should consider that next time you open your mouth."

The silver on his lower teeth glinted hard and dark in the dim ballroom as Edric peered down at me with disdain. He hooked his thumbs under those dagger-lined suspenders, parting his lips to retort, just as Jelena Altan appeared at his side, angling to lead him away. She mumbled something to him I couldn't hear, but the sneer beneath her nose told me she thought I wasn't worth a glance, let alone a conversation.

"That's one interpretation, *Nightfall*," Edric ignored his companion. "Another is not to underestimate one's own power. '*Strong currents carry gentle ripples. / Formed of salt, heed them both.*'"

Vuk. He wasn't wrong.

The collected poems of *Water Music* had endless interpretations. I swallowed my irritation, ignoring the fact that I was growing hotter and hotter the longer we stood together.

The closely listening crowd was something I could not ignore, however. In the hours I'd been free from my tower, silence seemed to follow me whenever I spoke. Those in our vicinity were no longer ravenous for food but for the entertainment before them. As much as I wanted to hurl better interpretations back at Edric's irritatingly intelligent face, it would only fuel the crowd's amusement.

Toma pulled at my forearm. Though he was right in wanting to lead me away, there was something about the gesture that had me slipping out of his grasp.

"Alright, *salty*." I cringed internally the moment the insult left my tongue. Maybe I should have gone with Toma. "Why don't you run along with your friend? Surely there's more nectar around you're willing to waste."

A flicker of emotion scrunched his brow, so fast that I was not sure if I had truly seen it.

"Hmm." He dropped his head, as if sharing a secret. Toma mumbled a warning that Edric ignored. "Well, that's easy to answer. You see, I can't simply *run along* when the woman in front of me is a violent murderer who has just been promoted to one of the most powerful positions in Veligrad. Do you see my problem there?" Edric's warm breath tickled my face. His voice lowered to a quiet rumble I felt in my chest. "You enjoyed your time as Mortician, didn't you? Carving up the dead. Watching their bodies burn. How else could you have stayed there so long without losing your mind?"

Heat quickly cooled, solidifying into a chunk of ice in the pit of my stomach.

"Like I had a choice. You on the other hand? Whether you deliberately destroyed that nectar or not, you freely chose to be careless. You freely chose your own anger over the lives that nectar could have saved. I have never been free."

Got him.

Toma gripped my shoulder, trying to steer me away, at the same time Jelena pulled on the crook of Edric's elbow. Apparently, they had decided our duel was over.

Before Edric could respond, a blaze of light issued from the front of the ballroom.

A dragul sphere.

My mouth dropped at seeing one for the first time. The orb was larger than my head and shone with brilliant white flames that leapt and wound around and around each other.

This was the magic that Protectors and Casters could wield with a dragul crystal. When projected at a vukodlak, the circle of burning light consumed the Cursed creature that had once been fae, killing them instantly.

Standing behind the dragul sphere with palms upturned was a Caster. A tall woman with dark, voluminous curls that did nothing to soften the harshness of her thin, pale skin stretched tight over sharp cheekbones. The dragul at her chest was a large pearl the size of an eyeball, threatening to see all.

The Moon Gate Caster, Renata Rada.

The Caster whose Heightened Power was the ability to read thoughts.

Jakov Prosek stood some distance apart from her, as did the other Casters, all dressed in the colour of the dragul that represented their Gate, except for Leden. He appeared stern and sterile in a grey jacket and trousers, instead of the deep orange of his Protectors, while Rada looked like a warrior in her cream, snakeskin-like leathers.

The brilliant, weaving sphere of magic vanished, and Jakov warily stepped forwards as he cleared his throat, his too-large moustache matching the disproportionate importance he placed on himself.

"To all the competitors who entered the Smed today and retrieved nectar, Veligrad gives our thanks. It is only twice a year that the miran flower yields Veligrad's only healing substance. Today's collection will supply Veligrad with approximately one thousand and six hundred vials."

Disappointment plunged inside my stomach. *One thousand and six hundred* for a population of over half a million. It was not enough. Rage flared hungry flames towards Edric—the man that had cost Veligrad's people what was close to eight hundred vials' worth of healing medicine from my two full bottles. And he had the audacity to call me violent.

Another thought temporarily cooled my anger: How had the miran flower offered me so much nectar? The more nectar it produced, the more power in someone's blood. I would have to be a close descendant of a witch or a fae for the miran flower to produce so much nectar for me—but not close enough to fall to the Curse. Was that why I had no memories? Had my parents wiped them to save me from being hunted by zealous mortals? Saved from Leden's order to slay any remaining witch or fae?

It didn't matter. I had wasted countless lonely hours creating stories in my head about who I might be, who my parents were.

What *did* matter was that I needed to keep my head down. Make it through Midnight Gate, and finally allow Malina and I to live a free life made of our own decisions.

"We will now move on to the presentation of the dragul necklaces, to those who have shown their worth in protecting Veligrad today. The dragul will activate once Protectors arrive at their respective Gates. Protectors will now recite their vow before us all."

My limbs trembled as the first Protectors were called to receive their dragul necklaces, the Protector's vow a drone against the loud whooshing in my ears. Kavi gave me a reassuring smile as she joined my side. One I could not return.

This is real. Too real.

This was the only way I could freely exist in Veligrad without needing to run away and hide. Escaping now was no better. Even with a dragul, I would be as good as dead in the Smed on my own.

A shimmery, pearl pendant was presented to the new Moon Gate Protector, a smaller version of Rada's. A smooth, brown

jasper for Glass Gate, detailed in layers of light and dark brown.
Ryker accept his multi-faceted amber crystal dragul, handed
to him by Caster Rada. As she smiled, I noted that his high,
burnt sienna cheekbones closely matched the structure of her
pale face.

His mother.

"Congratulations, son. I trust you feel proud."

Ryker's entitlement made sense now. A pampered Caster's
son. However, the smile Rada gave her own child was serpen-
tine. *Strange.*

He accepted the dragul and her words with a stony blank-
ness that was not difficult to glean as uncharacteristic for this
raging beast compressed into human skin.

"And finally, Midnight Gate."

The unmistakeable clinks of coin passed through hands
nearby. Bets on who would resign, or who would die.

My name was called last.

My stomach curled into a deeper unease as I neared Caster
Rada. Her serene smile was at odds with her narrow eyes.

Unease turned to dread, slamming into me all at once as
I stopped before her. What a revolting power, to violate the
private space of another's thoughts.

"It is, isn't it?" said Rada, and my dread doubled. "The Vow,
dear."

Better to get this over with, though repulsion still crawled
over me like beetles. "Alone, I offer my full self to my duty. As
one, the Gate is a channel, as am I. May the many be protected
by my Vow."

"Interesting," Rada whispered, her smile widening. Despite
the muck that had congregated on my wool throughout the

previous night and day, only now did I feel dirty. What had she seen? I would need many baths.

Leden watched with an unreadable expression as Jakov passed the dragul necklace to Rada.

It was not the indigo iolite crystal like the others of Midnight Gate.

"You're lucky the Council was able to collect the leftover shards from when the Midnight Gate dragul was divided all those years ago," said Jakov. "They cast it in resin at very short notice, you know."

The only reaction I allowed to show was a hard blink at the opaque pendant containing floating indigo slivers of the Midnight Gate crystal. I was being given leftovers. Not even a small portion of intact dragul, but crumbs.

The larger the dragul, the more power it contained. It was why Casters wore the biggest chunk of the gem pried off each Gate, allowing them to Step between Gates. And *shards*? I would have nowhere near as much power as any other Protector.

So Leden really wanted me to die.

Resentment simmered in my blood as Rada hung the pendant around my neck. Despite its shattered form, the dragul was beautiful, like the night sky in inverse, brilliant indigo sparkles within a pale-yellow sky of solidified resin, hanging off a fine silver chain.

All for nothing.

Panic dug its sharp talons into my sternum. I was going somewhere far from Malina, far from the safety of my tower, towards a dangerous town where Protectors faced their deaths, armed with a paltry magic at best. I had convinced myself that copying the guards' training was almost the same as learning to fight, but really, what skills did I have apart from running away? Midnight Gate was isolated. Once I arrived, there would be nowhere to run.

I sunk into line with the Protectors on stage, trying to hide my clawing panic, when shuffles and shouts sounded from outside the manor.

A guard flung open the arched, oak entrance doors. "Two guards found drained in the manor gardens. Wounds are fresh. Two more are missing. It's a vukodlak attack!"

Guests screamed and tables scraped as those closest to the door scrambled away.

"Remain and protect the manor," Leden commanded the Amber Gate Protectors. "New Protectors, follow your Casters. This will be your first demonstration on how to kill a vukodlak."

Chapter Seven

"Midnight Gate, this way." The soothing scent of peppermint leaves fanned from Hartley as he swept past my side. "The guards are split into units to find the missing two and kill any Cursed near the perimeter. We're our own unit. Stay behind me and you'll be fine."

No blood marred the gravel beneath the hedges at the manor garden's lowest tier, every drop sucked away before it could fall. The bodies had already been removed, but I knew what they would look like. Dark veins pronounced under shrivelled skin devoid of fluid. They were the ones who, until now, I had been charged to cremate.

Hartley's broad back strode confidently ahead of our group as we left the manor estate, following orange-vested guards into Amber Gate's cobbled streets. I needed to thank Hartley for his part in prying me from Leden's clutches, but now was not the time. Guards shouted orders, some splitting off to search narrow lanes, while others made for the forest.

Everything felt starkly real.

I was outside the tower. My position as a Protector was guaranteed. And now I had to face the reason for all the deaths I had seen.

"This is ridiculous," grumbled Aksel Ivkov, the blond Protector who had called *bullshit* on the Ranking posts. "Our dragul won't work until we get to Midnight Gate. And I thought the Cursed only came out at night?"

The back of my pendant pressed strangely against the top of my sternum, as if nestling into my skin. A small magic, I guessed. A lump of heaviness in my stomach told me to expect little more than that when we reached Midnight Gate.

"You know anything about Heightened Powers?" Hartley asked without looking back.

"Yes, obviously," Aksel narrowed his eyes.

"Go on."

A huff. "Most Heightened Powers come through after a couple of seasons, except for Caster Leden's, who never got one. But yours came through after only one season."

"Well, you're not wrong. But I was more leading towards what my powers actually are." One moment Hartley was offering a half grin over his shoulder—the next, he became a dark blur as he circled our stunned group with a speed that made my eyes sting. He stopped right before Aksel. "Heightened speed and strength. You'll be safe with me, Ivkov."

Aksel refrained from rolling his eyes before falling in line with Kavi and I as we entered the abandoned grassland bordering the Smed—a weed-ridden buffer separating the clustered town from the thick forest.

So far, Kavi had not said a word to me since we'd left the manor, merely maintaining a warm presence by my side. I liked that. If I glanced at her, I knew her grounded, brown eyes would meet my gaze with ready understanding. An invitation to share, but no expectation to divulge. We had helped each other in the Smed at a time we most needed it. Was this all it took to make friends? I knew from my experience writing "Do Tell" that it wasn't always the case. But after what had happened in the Smed, I felt like we were two different links of a chain that had somehow snapped together.

"Vials," someone ahead called as the first unit of guards neared the Smed. The guards each pulled a small, glass vial from their belts and knocked them back like rakija shots.

"Here." Toma appeared at my elbow, drawing me aside while guards continued streaming around us into the Smed. Something smooth and cold slipped into my hand. "Take mine."

"I'm not injured." I slanted away, trying to push the vial of nectar back to him, but he refused. Kavi stopped a few paces ahead, a slight crease on her brow.

"It doesn't just heal illness, it gives you more energy. We use it only for active assignments like this."

My jaw went slack. Even against the trepidation at searching for vukodlak, Toma's statement was enough to jolt away fear in exchange for shock. When Malina and her father could not afford the nectar, Djordje had simply died. And all this time, the guards who knew of her father's illness—guards like Toma—could have saved his life.

"I don't want it."

Hartley called from further ahead, ready for our unit to enter the Smed together, but before I could protest further, Toma gripped my jaw and poured the vial's contents down my throat.

"You deserve more life than what you have experienced. I should have tried better to help you leave the tower. This is the least I can do to keep you safe now."

I choked against the nectar's sudden invasion into my mouth. Kavi yelled at Toma, something I couldn't distinguish while I coughed. The liquid was stronger than plum rakija, the flavour of bitter, unripe fruit and sickly sweet honey, tied with something too harsh to ever be palatable. It was the second time today I felt violated.

I wiped my mouth of the thick liquid, reluctantly licking it from my lips. "I told you I didn't want it. Don't ever do something like that again. And I don't need you to keep me safe. I can do that myself."

"But, Nevvy—"

Toma was suddenly shouldered away—hard—by a tall, strong frame.

Edric's tall, strong frame.

Edric didn't even glance my way as he continued on as if nothing had happened, though I heard him mutter under his breath, "If I have to hear that name one more time . . ."

I snapped my teeth together. My stomach flipped, the heavy weight gone. For a supposed fan of inspiring poetry, Edric seemed unopposed to collecting more enemies than uplifting others.

Whatever. So he hates everyone.

Toma rubbed his shoulder, unfailingly noticing Edric's posture, his size, his weapons—all marks of a fighter. Without an apology, Toma glanced between Edric and I before pivoting away to join his unit of guards.

"Alright," said Hartley as Kavi and I hurried to rejoin him at the Smed's edge. Hartley's gaze followed the back of Toma's short hair, before snapping to us. "We're splitting from the guards now and going north. Move as quietly as you can. Listen out for panting that sounds like quick, raspy breaths. That'll be the vukodlak."

The dim grey of the clouded afternoon disappeared under the Smed's thick canopy. Though the forest looked almost identical to what it had a few short hours ago, a threatening presence hung closer, almost tangible. As soon as we moved away from the direction of the guards, all noise grew muffled. The crunches of our own steps and the swishing of fabric were the only sounds inside the thick, stiff air. Vukodlak could easily be lurking nearby, stalking us as we tried to stalk them.

"The Casters and Amber Gate Protectors should be in the forest with us, not the guards," Aksel grumbled to Kavi. "It's quite specifically *their* purpose, to cast dragul spheres at vukodlak so others don't have to get close to their fucking fangs."

I agreed with him. While guards could slash and stab, vukodlak possessed the irrepressible craving of a vicious thirst.

Snap.

I swivelled towards the sound from where we had just walked. "I heard something over—"

A root caught my retreating heel, and my body flipped backwards. Firm hands caught me under my armpits before my head could hit a jutting rock.

I was quickly pushed back on my feet, as Edric murmured low enough so only I could hear, "Careful, wouldn't want you to slip and hit your head. Caved-in skulls don't look pretty. Or did you like it when you killed Ander? Is that what your little hammer is for?"

I hauled myself away from Edric's lips. "Don't worry about me or my *little hammer*, you—you *giant dick*."

Oh, Vuk.

Could one's insides implode from cringing too hard? I would rather shove my pullover over my crimson face and happily walk into a vukodlak den than look at Edric Silvan's annoyingly half-amused, half-tormented face ever again. That would also help in avoiding the second-hand embarrassment emanating from Kavi, Hartley, and Aksel. Jelena merely snickered.

"Oh, um, don't think there's anything there, Nevena. All clear," Kavi said, her voice slightly too high. She was more precious than the indigo iolite around her neck, trying to dispel the awkwardness.

Pity it didn't work.

Edric raised a brow that matched his quirked, full lips. Behind the dark stubble across his face, long dimples appeared on either side of his mouth.

Why could I not think of anything better? With a pen in my hand, curated words flew onto paper like a formation of synchronised birds. But the words that fell off my tongue? Life shut in the tower was almost better than the burn of embarrassment that cooked me inside out.

We continued walking, the *snap* behind me forgotten.

"I didn't expect anything less of you, Nightfall," Edric murmured, leaving Jelena's side to fall into step with me. He tightened a familiar rope above his thigh. "I guess you've had a lot of time to think about all sorts of things while you were locked up. But I'd rather you keep my *giant dick* out of your thoughts."

Spluttering in indignation, I had nothing with which to respond. My face burned. I had no idea my skin's temperature could rival that of my bedroom hearth.

Kavi and Aksel exchanged curious glances.

"Do you two know each other?" asked Aksel.

"Yes," said Edric at the same time I said, "No."

The Moon Gate and Tide Gate citizens shared another glance, rendering my face even hotter under the attention of my new peers. Hartley was pretending not to listen, while Jelena watched with the attentiveness of a predator ready to rip into its prey's neck.

It was time to change the subject, and quick.

"They like valleys, the vukodlak do," I said, my mind going over *The Northern Serpent* articles I had read. I slowed my pace to put distance between Edric. "Or slopes. That's where their dens—"

Crack.

Everyone heard it this time. Collectively, breaths held. In the silence that followed, another sound grew, almost like buffeting wind—if wind could sound like short, raspy breaths.

"Vukodlak!" shouted Hartley.

The ground thundered as three huge vukodlak charged directly at us from behind, hairless, grey maws snapping with saliva, above which completely white eyes streamed with pus. My dragul pendant seared hot against my skin, as if yearning to—

A bright, indigo orb shot from Hartley towards the nearest vukodlak, followed quickly by two others. As soon as the dragul sphere hit their targets, the vukodlak were consumed by a violent, deep-blue fire. They dropped and writhed. Their long, high-pitched howls of agony pierced my ears like a thousand pins.

And then there was silence.

Three burnt figures lay steaming on the ground—half-formed creatures, somewhere between wolf and fae. Long spines curled over wiry limbs that looked like they could run on four legs or two. Sparse fur spurted from the back of their heads and down to their short tails, while their grey, slimy fronts were bare. Their ears held elongated points with more cartilage than a dog's.

"I might be able to move fast, but casting dragul spheres takes more concentration and energy. Especially outside of Midnight Gate," said Hartley, gripping his indigo iolite pendant.

The smell of charred hair reminded me of my tower's cremation chamber. A scent I wished I could leave behind.

"That's why when we get to Midnight Gate, we'll patrol in teams so—"

My dragul burned again, and I twisted to see five more vukodlak pounding through the trees. Too many for Hartley's magic to dispatch quick enough.

"Run!" Hartley shouted as he cast blazing orbs, one at a time.

But there was nowhere safe to run. Swords were pulled from scabbards as more milky eyes appeared between the thickets. Kavi and Aksel struck first with a practiced grace, metal meeting grey flesh and claws in a wail of ghastly screams.

Heart pounding, I reached for my hammer. My pendant pulsed against my throat. Was that usual? A buzzing, vibrant energy pooled in my stomach, rising to my chest. At the same time unfamiliar, yet somehow known to me. Then it trickled through my veins, like sugar. Energy. *Magic.*

An explosion of light erupted before my palms, forming a sphere of indigo flames shot through with gold. Disbelief rocked me. The flaming orb shouldn't be possible, yet here it was, pulsing as if waiting on my intention.

Over there.

My magic shot towards a vukodlak, striking it squarely in the back just as it was about to latch its teeth onto Hartley's shoulder.

Bewildered glances flicked my way only for a moment, as they slashed and stabbed the dwindling onslaught of Cursed.

An intoxicating hit of energy rushed in my blood as I turned to the nearest wolf-creature, ready to use my new power again. But as quickly as the magic had appeared, it deflated.

Oh, Vuk.

My veins were empty of anything but ordinary blood. It was just me against the onrushing vukodlak.

Swallowing the sour taste of death, I whipped out my hammer. The Cursed fae dodged my swipe, putrid saliva splattering my face. I swung again. Too hard. The momentum rendered me off balance, and the vukodlak lunged. I tried to swing upwards as my vision filled with a wide, rotted jaw, but something yanked hard around my middle, knocking the breath from my lungs.

I landed at the base of a tree—with Edric's enchanted rope cinched around my waist.

Reflexes faster than I anticipated, Edric stabbed the creature's heart with a shallow dagger. The vukodlak crumpled to the earth as Edric sent me a glare as sharp as his weapon. My stomach tightened. Then he was off, hurtling his small daggers into the eyes of the vukodlak nearing Jelena.

Fingers trembling with shock, I managed to loosen the thick rope from my waist.

Did Edric really just—I couldn't finish the thought.

Shrieks of pain rung from all angles as the number of vukodlak dwindled. Kavi and Aksel exercised their swords like a dance against the Cursed around them. Three vukodlak battled Hartley, but unlike Aksel and Kavi's smooth ducks and blows, Hartley's power was slowing. The others were too distracted by their final battles to notice Hartley close to defeat. Only I noticed one vukodlak baring its sharp fangs above the Caster's neck.

Stumbling towards Hartley, I hurled my hammer. It struck, denting the creature's head.

My stomach roiled at the familiar sight, even as my actions allowed Hartley enough space to put down the remaining two. They were the last to fall.

Burnt and slaughtered bodies lay strewn in twisted angles on the forest floor, black blood and pus putrefying clean earth.

The six of us drew into a tense circle, back-to-back, surveying the silent trees. I managed to hold down the rising vomit at the sight of slimy skin and horrific faces of the dead vukodlak.

Several minutes passed as we waited. And then several more. It was only when the sweat on my back had turned cold, that Hartley decided it was safe enough to leave.

Aksel turned to me first. "Where'd that power come from? You don't even have a proper dragul." His expression shifted to suspicion. "What did they put in that?"

"Pine resin." Hartley responded in a monotone as he studied my face. "You saved me, Nightfall."

Edric stiffened in the corner of my vision. The rope was back in its resting place against his thigh. I swept away a mote of confusion. Edric couldn't taunt and insult me, and then expect my gratitude for . . . *saving my life?* Anyway, an apology needed to come first.

I swallowed, focusing on Hartley's puzzled brows. "You saved *me*." I ignored the sound of a scoff beside me. "From the tower. From Leden. From a life of misery. Thank you. You didn't have to do any of it."

That easy grin crept back onto Hartley's blood-specked face, his stubble the dark-gold of precious jewellery. "Any reason to poke a little at Leden." But I knew that wasn't the full truth of it. "Let's get back to Amber Gate. We may have just killed the pack that attacked the guards. Good first day, Midnight Gate Protectors."

Maybe, despite Edric's presence, Midnight Gate was not going to be so bad.

Chapter Eight

WHENEVER I LOOKED AWAY, I could feel Edric's hard gaze studying me.

So what? My dragul shards worked. Was he disappointed? Jealous? I tried to smooth the wrinkles of annoyance from my brow, but they kept returning.

"One hand on the shoulder of the person beside you. One hand on your dragul."

Hartley's voice echoed strangely as we stood in a line under the Amber Gate arch, wobbling slightly as if reflecting off water. His palm hovered above a small engraving of a wide-branched tree, Midnight Gate's symbol, carved onto the inside of a flat column. I stood at the end of the line, gripping the supple leather of Kavi's jacket with a clammy hand.

This is it. Sweat beaded above my lip, under my arms. *I'm about to leave Amber Gate.*

The missing guards had not been found. Amber Gate was dangerous, but Midnight Gate was renowned for being worse. At least my dragul worked, and one of Leden's plans to sabotage me had failed. The leftover dragul shards were more powerful than Leden had estimated. I stroked the smooth resin in which indigo fragments floated as inconspicuously as stars.

"Stepping between Gates usually only takes a Caster's dragul plus one other dragul. Since there's six of us, this should be quick. As soon as I touch the Midnight Gate symbol, the Gate will Step us through. Ready?"

I don't know.

The empty space around me felt too large without my walls, leaving me choking. But the paths I had trodden today were all spaces I had dreamed of standing in for over a decade, that I had traced across the thin paper of maps and illustrations. Real life was now before me in all sorts of unexpected dimensions and shades.

I was ready.

"Let's go!" Hartley pushed his palm to the tree symbol, just as I looked up to find his gaze—and met Edric's instead.

Energy rushed through me like ten spoonfuls of sugar. A climax of brilliant light burst through each indigo dragul, imprinting an image into the back of my eyes before I squeezed them shut. The glint of Edric's silver teeth. The wave of his side-parted black hair, helplessly fallen over his forehead. Rough, dark-blue eyes, pinning me with twin storms about to break.

Why was Edric the first person to look at me like this? Even with Toma there had not been this intensity during the times he had managed to sneak into my room.

A second later, my knees hit hard, dusty earth.

Kavi gasped from beside me as we slowly rose together, my heart pummelling against the inside of my chest.

"Welcome to Midnight Gate," said Hartley.

Standing on the barren top of a flat hill, the blue-grey Midnight Gate arch was surrounded by an endless, rolling forest. The Smed absorbed the growing dark into its depths, as the sky overhead glowed violet with the day's final rays. To the west, the jagged mountain line of the Serpent Ranges was a blue-tinged shadow on dusk's horizon. Barely a brush of wind sounded against the frigid, wild landscape, as if it paused to watch our arrival.

"Where's the town?" Aksel's flat, suspicious tone jarred unpleasantly against the dark peace. Edric and Jelena stared out into the expanse, unsurprised.

Hartley chuckled with all the dark spice and rich possibilities of too many goblets of mead. The sound echoed against hard earth, and he secured his hooded jacket tighter against the hilltop's frigid chill.

"Midnight Gate was positioned here to best view the stars without interference from any light." Above us, white pins already twinkled. "The town's an hour's walk away, next to the Lutava River. You'll get used to navigating amongst the trees around here."

"You mean to tell us we have to pass through the Smed again—*at night*?" Aksel's pale face was as stony as the immovable arch above us. "No wonder Protectors keep fucking dying."

"There are safe paths the vukodlak don't cross." The curve of Hartley's mouth did not dip. I had the sense Hartley enjoyed remaining in control while others grew frustrated. A calm demeanour was a virtue for a leader, but Hartley's expression made me wonder whether his was born of amusement . . . or was it superiority? No, it had to be amusement. "One of the safe paths starts here. It travels due east until you reach the town."

"Right. I'm sure it's a safe path if your Heightened Power is speed," Aksel muttered.

"*And* strength. You can always hop on my back if you like?" Hartley grinned, and Aksel glared back. "No? Well, let's hope your Heightened Power becomes the ability to fly. Don't think we've seen that one yet." Hartley glanced to the violet sky quickly transitioning to indigo, the shade of the Midnight Gate's dragul. "I'll tell you all about the safe paths later. Let's get on with this before night really falls. Everyone, touch the arch. Anywhere except for the symbols of the other Gates. You're going to establish a connection with your dragul and the arch. This will release your magic, as the dragul only works strongest near its own Gate."

I placed a hand beside Kavi's onto the arch, touching stippled stone carvings dedicated to the emerging constellations above us, so worn they were almost undistinguishable. For the first time since I could remember, my lungs filled with fresh air that was empty of the smoke of charred remains. One part of my plan to escape Amber Gate had been achieved. Now I just needed to survive Midnight Gate. Kavi's warm, knowing eyes met mine, and my cheeks crinkled in return. Almost a smile. Maybe once I was used to being outside my tower, it might happen more.

"The arch you can see is only a portion of the stone buried deep within the earth," Hartley began when all of us touched the cool surface.

At the arch's peak, a round depression marked where the indigo iolite crystal used to sit before it had been removed and adapted into dragul pendants. An odd sense of heaviness settled on my shoulders at the defacement. I tried to shake it off.

"Let your mind dive into those roots. This is where the remnants of old fae magic live." Hartley's voice seemed to warp.

Something urged me to press my hand harder into the column. My pendant thrummed. My fingers tingled, and the stone turned hot, stinging like a needle cushion, daring me to pull away.

"Feel the magic drawing up from the arch, connecting to your blood, to your dragul."

The same sensation returned as when I had used the dragul earlier. Energy wrangling within me. But now it was different, transmuting into something that melded into my very skin and poured into my blood.

"Now press your lips to the Gate. Hold your dragul and speak your name."

I did, kissing the rough stone before softly stating my name. In a thousand whispered voices, I heard it speak back.

Nightfall.

Gasping, I opened my eyes wide. A buzz of energy travelled through my veins as fast as a diving eagle, before abruptly fizzling away, leaving me with a new awareness.

Magic. Settled under every cell of my skin. Under my control.

"Everyone feel that?" asked Hartley, as others' sharp inhales sounded nearby.

Tears tracked thin rivulets down Kavi's sienna cheeks. Aksel wiped his eyes on the back of his hands, and Edric and Jelena faced away to the east where the sky already matched the colour of our draguls. It wasn't until I blinked that I realised my eyelids were ready to spill salty drops, too. I reined them back in.

"Congratulations, you're officially Protectors of Midnight Gate. You now have the power to wield dragul spheres and defend Midnight Gate's people against the vukodlak. Well"—Hartley flicked me a smile of straight, white teeth—"those who didn't already have the power before." My stomach dipped under his attention. "Now, this is the only training you'll need. A dragul sphere is a ball of flames, stronger than any earthly fire. It will destroy anything you aim it towards, but your own flames will never hurt you. They're a part of you."

A part of me. While I carried this dragul, I could never be caged again.

"Place your palms out and feel the heat of your dragul," Hartley continued. "Imagine that heat in your hands. Take a breath. Then make that heat real."

It was easy. Much easier than earlier. All it took was the same energy as bending my knees and jumping into the air, and the orb of magic fire flared to life.

Kavi cried out in delight as indigo light burst above her hovering palms. Four other deep-blue spheres illuminated the darkening hilltop. Mine was the only one marbled with gold, deeper than the yellow resin of my pendant.

"Aim them at the sky."

Streaks of light shot towards the waking stars, then exploded in fireworks. A soft, male exhale sounded near me, and I couldn't help but catch the light reflecting off Edric's lower teeth, while his mouth opened in gentle awe. Why did it remind me of a poem he had recited to me?

Strong currents carry gentle ripples.
Formed of salt, heed them both.

"Not bad, Protectors." Hartley grinned. "I guess it's time for you to meet your new home."

Hartley led us down a barren crack of path, unkept and riddled with twisted roots. He kept a dragul sphere to illuminate the way, baring light upon churlish trees that resented the intrusion. I followed directly behind, drawn towards Hartley like cold hands towards a warm hearth.

"You'll get to know all the safe paths," Hartley said. Something about the forest seemed older than the Smed at Amber Gate, the trees taller and stiffer. I brushed off the looming feeling that reminded me of my tower. "The only thing you need to remember is this: Don't disturb the teeth."

I stumbled over a root, and Kavi caught my elbow with wiry strength before I could fall. I thanked her with a close-lipped nod, though Hartley's warning made me shiver.

"'Don't disturb the teeth'? You've got to be fucking kidding me. As if this place isn't creepy enough," muttered Aksel from Kavi's other side. While Aksel's manner could be described as *direct* at best, I could not help but agree with his sentiments.

This was unnerving.

"Yep. The people of Midnight Gate are . . . traditional in their ways. When the vukodlak killed most animals in the forest, the townspeople collected the teeth of wolves that had been slain. They marked paths with their teeth, and for whatever reason, vukodlak don't cross them. Memorise the paths, look out for any wolf teeth on either side, and if you see them, don't disturb them."

"So they still worship Vuk here?" asked Kavi. "Maybe that's why the wolves' teeth work."

"I hope that's the reason," Hartley replied.

Night fell true as we pressed onwards, dry branches reaching low, skimming my hair like fingers. My ears strained behind me, hoping to catch any words from Edric speaking to Jelena, unable to help the nibble of curiosity as to their relationship. They remained silent. Had Edric's supposed travels already led him to Midnight Gate before? I wouldn't be surprised.

Just stop thinking about him.

Simple wisdom. Not difficult to accept. Was it?

"Caster—" Kavi ventured, before Hartley interrupted.

"Hartley's fine. Or even Tavion."

"Right, *Hartley*. Why are there so many deaths at Midnight Gate if there are safe paths that vukodlak don't cross?"

Hartley took a breath before responding, his powerful shoulders lifting. "Most deaths in recent years have been Protectors, not townspeople."

Protectors? We were meant to be the ones with the power, the ones who were most safe, and meant to keep others safe.

"Right. I suppose that's our role. To take on the brunt of the Cursed and Protect the townspeople." The acceptance in Kavi's voice sounded like selflessness, like bravery. I moved closer beside her. "Is that how they met their deaths, Hartley?" she asked.

Hartley's head dipped forwards. He shook it slightly. "The teeth get disturbed."

Get disturbed. It took me a moment to understand the tense of Hartley's sentence. That meant—

"Someone doesn't want us here," said Kavi, finishing my thought.

Snap.

Hartley swung his dragul sphere to the left, hovering it in the direction of the sound, followed quickly by Aksel and Kavi stepping forwards with their own flames of indigo light ignited. Instinct had me pulling out my hammer, while Jelena's and Edric's stiff presences beside me suggested they reached for their weapons, too, and stood tensed like coiled springs.

Under the scanning light, nothing moved, only shadows melding and shifting. After three heavy beats of my heart, a small movement finally revealed itself at the foot of a nearby tree.

A tawny bird lay tangled in the dried twigs of a dead bush. Its eyes were wide as two yellow suns as it struggled weakly against its cage. One wing flapped while the other stuck stiffly away from its side.

"It's a bittern," said Kavi, slim brows raised in concern. "They're bad luck."

Hartley moved to continue down the path, but Edric lit his own dragul sphere. Frowning, he knelt before the bird.

"Silvan." A hint of annoyance entered Hartley's tone. "What are you doing? Let's not linger in the dark when—"

"There," growled Edric as he stood, the long-beaked bird cupped against his chest. Its injured wing stuck out at a painful angle.

"Didn't you hear what Kavi said?" Aksel let his dragul sphere vanish. "Everyone knows they're practically Cursed."

"Maybe everyone's wrong."

He brushed past them and took the lead ahead of Hartley, who quickly increased his pace to walk beside him.

I swallowed, trying to ignore the scent of something bright and tangy that washed down my throat.

Kavi flicked me a glance that looked far too knowing.

We carried on towards the town, now with a feathered addition to our party.

When the hour's walk was near its end, a different light began to filter between trunks and bushes.

Trees pressed closer together the nearer we drew. Twisted branches snagged my pullover as I squeezed between tightening limbs, gnarled hands trying to drag me back the way I had come. Then as quickly as the woods had contracted together, they suddenly separated once more, offering a full view of the town ahead.

I held back a gasp.

Midnight Gate was nearly unchanged from its fae influence. It was no town, in the mortal sense. Rather, it was a woodland realm of enormous trees—trees that were inhabited by people.

Zhivir trees.

Their wide trunks were set with oval doors. Giant branches acted as walkways between the trees, or wrapped around trunks in a spiral, connecting the rooms of each home. Soft glows emanated from small hollows, while outside, thousands of lanterns were strung like vines, throwing a silvery light to illuminate the moss below that made up the streets of Midnight Gate.

Tranquil and enchanting, Midnight Gate looked directly plucked from the illustrations I had seen in books brought to me by Malina, depicting old fae cities before they were replaced by the mortal's favoured stones and mortar. Wood could be wily, a flare of magic sparking it to move or change. Zhivir trees liked to move branches of their own accord, even on days without a hint of wind. But stone always set and remained as it should.

I preferred wood.

"What sort of fae-loving place is this?" sneered Aksel.

"You'll need to be more careful, Ivkov," said Hartley. "People here carry some more traditional sentiments towards the fae. If we want to hang around longer than last season's crew, we'll need the townspeople on our side."

Right. So that they wouldn't sabotage our safe paths. My gaze travelled over the throng of people, trying to spy anyone appearing suspicious. But the looks I received mirrored suspicion back. For the most part, we were ignored. While half the town worked—some wielding crafts, some selling wares—the other half wandered leisurely or sat on artfully carved wood logs, eating with friends. Fresh garlic cooking in oil weaved its way towards me from zhivir trees that hosted diners outside their trees' bases. Low branches draped flowering vines above patrons' heads, while well-tended fires offered warmth against the chilly northern air.

Most townspeople dressed in long cloaks the colour of stars, or earth, or sky. Between the parts of their cloaks, shirts and gowns were embroidered with intricate, whirling patterns of silvery thread. I itched to change from looking less like a lost sheep and more like someone who could Protect them.

We approached the tall, buttress roots of a zhivir tree wider than most others. Branches melded into walkways that spiralled around its trunk, leading to dozens of doors set high into the tree.

"While each of Veligrad's cities has a tower, Midnight Gate has this. The Night Tree," Hartley explained.

The zhivir tree was similar in size to my Amber Gate tower, only grown from wood rather than placed by stone. Healthy vines looped between branches and crawled up the trunk, the Amber Gate tower's carvings now seeming like a flimsy attempt at mimicry of something more vibrant and strong than stone could ever hope to be. This tree held its own presence, one of might and secrecy, things hidden and things that thrilled.

Like midnight.

The Lutava River, as black as strong tea, ran silently behind the zhivir tree, a stark contrast to the town's busy nightlife.

"Zhivir trees are all safe from the Cursed. Nothing malevolent can enter," Hartley said as he led us closer to the mouth of the walkway.

Was that supposed to make us feel better? Didn't seem like safe zhivir trees had done much for our dead predecessors.

"Hartley, the placing of the Night Tree . . ." Kavi began. "At Moon Gate, the Protectors take patrol from the Moon Gate Tower. It offers a view across the whole city. Here, it seems it might be . . . *tricky* for us to patrol with the level of visibility blocked by trees." Kavi worded her question carefully, unlike Aksel who was murmuring in agreement but with phrases like *got to be fucking kidding.*

"Long ago, when the city was established," replied Hartley, "the biggest threats came from the river, not the woods themselves."

"What could have been in the river that's worse than the Cursed?" asked Aksel.

Jelena responded. "Things that hide from stars."

It was the first time I had heard her speak. Her voice was even but raspy, as if she had just been screaming, rather than entirely silent for many hours. I knew how that felt, after nights yelling in my rooms, hoping it would at least annoy the guards enough to come in to tell me off. Malina later told me that on those occasions, a group of guards would wait outside the tower door, afraid that I was turning Cursed, ready to kill me should I breach the door.

Jelena noticed me staring and sent a deep frown my way, which I returned.

"Those and more," a stranger's joyless voice added.

It belonged to an older man wearing the grey coat of a skinned wolf, its open maw a hood over the man's head. Straight, grey hair reached his chest over brown robes, while deep blue bags lay under cool, dark eyes. The wolfskin had to be old, since wolves had all been killed by the vukodlak over a decade ago, along with the rest of the northern forest's creatures.

"Ah. Protectors, please meet Elder Gorcha. The shaman of Midnight Gate."

"Caster, you are too generous." Gorcha's expression remained stony as he spoke, his voice flatter than the side of a knife. "I am merely another messenger of the wind between earth and stars."

Hartley introduced the Protectors one by one. When it was my turn, the elder's nose twitched. Smeared nectar had collected grit on my woollen garments over the course of the day. Twigs poked from my long, unravelled hair. Being naked would almost have felt better than standing here soiled. But Gorcha's attention was overtaken when Edric was introduced last.

"*Silvan?*" Gorcha's eyes widened. "I knew your brother. We must talk."

The man who hated me for that very brother's death visibly stiffened. Shoulders tensed like a dog raising its hackles. He pressed the little bird closer to his chest, his large hands a shield.

"I'm afraid," Edric gritted, "my Protector duties require my full attention."

"So," Gorcha spoke with the dry tartness of sour fruit. "You are not like your brother."

An awkward silence followed.

Take control, say something.

"Elder Gorcha," I said, stepping forward. "We are honoured to Protect Midnight Gate and its people. Please rest assured we will keep you safe with the magic granted to us."

It came out just as I had intended. Like someone who handled situations with control, like someone with power. I glanced at Hartley, hoping to see some appreciation for salvaging the good opinion of a clearly important leader.

But Gorcha's façade of strained courtesy swiftly tumbled away, along with a spark of my confidence.

"Keep *us* safe?" The sharpness in his tone matched his glare as he took in my state again. "The Midnight people live in a haven of safety. We *tolerate*," he spat, "the Council of Veligrad as far as it means we will be left in peace, but be this your notice that we do not take lightly any interference with our ways of life."

I shut my mouth with a snap.

Well.

If this was the town's elder, what did that say for how the rest of the town saw us? It could be anyone sabotaging the Protector's safe paths, then, even Gorcha himself. My plan for this season resurfaced with the ringing clarity of a bell. *Survive the season. Rank again for a better city. Take Malina with me to safety.*

"I will leave you to settle into your *duties*," Gorcha snarled towards Edric, before turning to the rest of us. "Never forget, *Protectors*. Do not disturb the teeth."

I had a feeling that the forest's beasts were not the only monsters at Midnight Gate.

CHAPTER NINE

"FROM TOMORROW WE'LL SPLIT the patrol shifts, three of us each for day and night. Tonight, everyone get some rest," said Hartley. "I'll stay up."

The spiralling walkway that wrapped the Night Tree led us high up to a flat landing where sets of doors were equally spaced around the entire width of the trunk.

"Those are your rooms. Pick any one, except that one's already mine." He pointed to the door closest to the walkway facing the town. He looked like he wanted to say something else but then wished us good night and ventured back down the tree.

Edric and Jelena shared a look, then split off to each claim a room either side of Hartley's.

So they're not a couple then.

I gained a twisted satisfaction from that realisation. Then quickly pushed it aside, not wanting to unpack wherever that thought had arisen from.

"Well, good night." Kavi smiled wearily to Aksel and I before they both chose their own rooms: Kavi next to Edric's, and Aksel next to Jelena's. I walked around the wide trunk to the last door, facing directly towards the silent river. Fewer zhivir trees appeared on the other side of the bank amongst the forest of oaks and beeches.

Inside was a spacious, wedge-shaped room. Thick, dark-grey quilts lay piled atop an enormous bed opposite a wardrobe and a tall, wood-framed mirror. A writing desk fitted in a perfect triangle into the nook of the room's wedge, holding a tray of bread and cheeses for a light dinner. Lit candles protruded from sconces all around the grooved walls. A door next to the wardrobe led to a bathing chamber, its fixtures all wood carved, too.

The rich wooden interior felt softer than the cold, heavy stone I had been surrounded by for thirteen years. I cricked some of the tension from my neck.

A small hollow window looked over the seemingly still river below. It was hard to tell how high up my room was. Not as high as Amber Gate tower. At least I could get out of this one. I slid dark velvet curtains to cover the view of black water, then finally pulled the crumpled "Do Tell" letters from my shirt, dropping them into the single desk drawer. They were safe. I had made it. The people who needed my advice would receive their replies.

I undressed and bathed in the adjoining chamber. The water quickly heated my muscles, but it did not reach deeper parts within me that remained cold.

"I've been meaning to thank you," said Kavi, her breath fogging the morning air. It was our third patrol as Protectors together. And my first with Edric. "For helping me at the Ranking. Ryker—" Kavi sighed. "He used to be an old friend."

Edric's broad back was far enough ahead not to overhear. The little bittern rode atop his shoulder, its long beak sweeping side to side, as if it was surveying the patrol, too. I tried to suppress the pocket of warmth in my chest at seeing the little thing happy.

We walked along the bank of the glossy Lutava River, careful not to step on any of the small white fangs that appeared every ten steps. Hartley had led my first few patrols, pointing out the main patrol routes, drilling our tasks into us: carefully watch and listen for signs of vukodlak, shoot dragul spheres if one appears, avoid giving the townspeople further reason to mistrust us.

I ignored Kavi's gratitude. It was hardly deserved. "Ryker seemed kind of . . . ruthless. Is that a Moon Gate thing, then?" I stifled a yawn. My first night shift wasn't until tomorrow, but already my eyes were fatigued with the hordes of new sights and sensations.

Kavi breathed a soft laugh, shaking her head. "Ruthlessness is not meant to be a Moon Gate thing. Competitiveness is, though." The laugh shifted to something more serious. "So is honouring debts."

"There's no debt. It wasn't even my plan to stop. It just happened."

"Okay," Kavi conceded with a soft smile. Perhaps the heat I felt across my cheeks had manifested into bright red. "So you were kept in a tower for most of your life. Never allowed to leave. Feared for your proximity to those bitten by the Cursed, and for the fear the Curse might spread after their death. You were quite intimidating at the Ranking."

"Intimidating?" It was almost laughable. "I looked like a lost sheep." Thankfully, Protectors were supplied with a closet of uniforms, pyjamas, and civilian clothing, and now I looked as sleek as a cat in my thick, fitted, indigo trousers and thigh-length, hooded jacket.

"If you were simply a sheep"—Kavi leaned her head closer to mine—"I wonder why Silvan's acting like you're his greatest threat."

Me a threat? That was not what it felt like. Edric stalked silently ahead, and the little bird gave an occasional honk.

"Who were you," asked Kavi softly, "before you became the Cursed Mortician?"

My stomach clenched. No one had asked me that question since those very first days of confusion and interrogations and stifling stone walls. Softly, I responded, "I don't remember."

Kavi reached out a hand to pat my shoulder, before pulling away. Maybe my stern thinking face was to blame. Or maybe a part of her didn't actually want to touch the Cursed Mortician. My shoulders curled forwards a touch.

"Someone else must have known who you were, though?" Kavi kept her focus on watching for wolf teeth ahead. Her questions didn't feel like probes or snipes, but rather like gently opening a flower bud's velvety petals.

I filled my lungs with the freshness of dew drops.

"They found me in the Smed near Amber Gate," I found myself saying. "It was after the Fall of the Fae, when mortals took the Seven Gates. I don't remember why I was in the forest. I don't remember anything before it. I just remember walking, like I was searching for someone, but I didn't know who." The memory was one I had revisited frequently as a child, but no other details ever revealed themselves. "Some guards found me. They could see I didn't look fae, but they thought something was wrong because I couldn't remember anything."

It was a story I never recounted aloud, apart from a single time with Malina. But now that I was free of Amber Gate, perhaps it would feel good for my story to be free, too. It was the kind of advice I would give to someone in "Do Tell."

"All that when you were only eleven years old," Kavi muttered.

"Well, they decided I *looked* eleven. But really, I don't even know. I could be twenty-four right now, or I could not."

Kavi lifted her gaze to the tall figure walking ahead. "Silvan is no better than Leden then, if he dislikes you for the things that were out of your control as a child. For who you were made to become." While Edric rarely spoke, it hadn't taken long for everyone to realise he had a particular aversion to me.

I scrunched my eyes, fighting against another memory. One that failed to leave me alone.

Let it out. It'll feel better. That was the advice I would give to someone else, right?

"Silvan hates me for something else."

The river's gurgle was the only sound beyond Kavi's steady breath, quietly waiting.

I rolled my shoulders back and gave in to the memory. Kavi had made space for me, had passed me a lit match, and now there was nothing to stop my words becoming an inferno. Even the ones I attempted to douse.

"Two years ago, I tried to escape my tower for the first time." I took a deep breath, focusing on the freshness of the forest, rather than the acrid smell of burnt hair that stuck to memories of the cremation chamber. "Some days I'd spend my time talking to whichever guard was on duty through the mortuary door. They were always bored, too, having to spend half a day by themselves. I would ask them about their lives, and they would tell me their problems. I liked helping them, actually." Between the guards and my advice column, I had plenty of practice. "But then a new guard started." *Toma.* "He was different from the others. He liked talking to me. He took more shifts guarding my door. He wanted to meet me."

"That guard who made you drink his nectar?"

I nodded. Since he had forced me to drink nectar against my will, any affection for Toma had decayed. I recalled the swelling of excitement on the night I finally let him open the door while I waited on the other side. He was taller than he had appeared when I had watched him in the courtyard below. He didn't come in right away. Didn't want to frighten me. Just wanted to help me. Then together, when we weren't spending time in my room, we weakened the bolt at the tower's only door, bit by bit, so it would look like I had done it myself.

"Toma caused a distraction. Said he saw some vukodlak. That gave him a reason to leave his post at my tower. It was the day some suspected witches had been found dead, so the guards were already on edge. I waited until I could hear everyone was gone, and then I finally broke open the door." I stopped walking, allowing green, mossy ground to fill my pupils. "Except when I tried to leave, somebody was already outside."

Ander Silvan. They told me his name after. Someone had clearly told his family mine.

"I had cremated dead fae before, so I knew the initial signs of the Curse. His eyes were bloodshot, the veins under them purple. I couldn't see the tips of his ears, but he looked . . . hungry. He came towards me, so I ran back to the kiln and found my hammer." The very hammer I still wore strapped to my waist. The one I used for smashing bones left over from cremation. "He must have thought I was hiding because he started looking around the preparation table where witches' bodies lay."

That was the moment I could have run for my freedom. The moment I had repeated in my mind, agonised over for many tortured days and nights. The moment Ander Silvan turned towards me with something more human in his expression than I had expected from a morphing Cursed. I had swung my hammer anyway, before I could slow to answer that question in my head. A question I had struggled to let go of since: *Was he really Cursed?*

"Who was he, Nevena?"

"Edric's brother."

Kavi's breathing paused while my chest heaved.

"You'd think when you see death every other week that another body wouldn't matter, that it would have no affect." My voice was hoarse, though surely I could not have been speaking for too long. "They never punished me for it. They never rewarded me for it, either. Just fixed another bolt to the door and locked me back inside. It had looked like Ander Silvan had broken in when everyone was away, and that I had defended myself. Toma wasn't found out. He was promoted away from tower duty not long after, and then that was it."

I tasted salt at the corner of my mouth.

A warm hand wrapped around mine, pulling me out of memory and back to the sight before me. Kavi's creased forehead. Columns of grey beech trees, brown oak trees, wide zhivir trees. Midnight Gate.

And then, stopped close enough to hear everything, a pair of dark-blue eyes.

Oh, Vuk.

I had been wrong. It did not feel good for my story to be free. It did not feel good to be a flower, opening myself for others to peer at the colour of my insides. I wanted to take it all back, keep it within me and never let anyone else in again. How could others do this in "Do Tell," venting out their secrets and awaiting the judgement of another, a judgement completely out of their own control? They had to have been really desperate.

"Nevena, I'm s—" Kavi began.

"Let's find another safe path to patrol." I pivoted away from Kavi's warm concern and Edric's hard intensity.

My eyeballs strained with more pressure, but I refused to give them the release they sought. No more giving away parts of myself. I needed no one's sympathy, nor advice. All I needed was to keep a hold of my control a little longer. Six months to the end of the season, and then I would Rank again. Somewhere far from Midnight Gate.

CHAPTER TEN

Dear Regretfully-Seeking-Closure,

My advice is this: First, write every word you wish to share to your unrequited love onto paper in great detail. Second, throw the pages into flames, and watch them burn until they become ash. Third, find your closest source of water. It can be a stream, a lake or the sea. Immerse yourself entirely below the water. Then scream. Reemerge for breath, and repeat this process. You should feel a sense of lightness achieved without the need to confront the source of your frustrations.

If a time arises that you feel the need to divulge your secrets and regrets—don't. Past hurts cannot be salvaged.

Yours Sincerely,

Do Tell

I sighed, folding my replies to "Do Tell," along with a letter to Malina, and shoved them into a large envelope. It had been two weeks since my arrival, and this was my first chance to write. Each patrol left me with barely enough energy to bathe before sleep dropped onto my head like a dull rock.

The Lutava River reflected Midnight Gate's canopy in twilight's slate shadows as I wound down the Night Tree's walkway, wincing with each stiff step of my aching legs. Day shifts and night shifts had been spent further familiarising ourselves with the woodland town's layout. Tooth-marked safe paths ran through clusters of zhivir trees to the north of the Night Tree, spilling across both banks of the Lutava. Paths also filed through the main thoroughfares of trade and food sellers to the east and south of the Night Tree. Hartley had directed us to look for any recent gouge marks in trees or footprints in the moss. We found nothing, and the safe paths remained safe. For now.

All of my activities and observations from the last two weeks were stuffed inside the sheets of rough paper squeezed between my fingers. I could already imagine Malina gripping my pages in her clay-caked hands, desperate to know every detail of my new world, of my freedom. Yet the first words that had spilled from my fountain pen had been something else.

I wish I could hug you again.

When the pen's nib paused above the page, waiting for permission to spill, I had reached for a fresh sheet instead. Last fortnight's incident with Kavi and Edric had been enough spilling. I hoped *Regretfully-Seeking-Closure* would learn from my mistakes and try a different method of emotional release.

I grasped the envelope tighter against another piece of information I could not compel myself to include. Like the guards at Amber Gate, all Protectors were encouraged to take microdoses of nectar on the transition shifts between day and night. A drop on the tongue *for the good of the town*, to make us well-rested and ready should there be an attack. I refused, unable to keep Malina's father Djordje's death from my mind. Nectar would have prevented it.

My choice was rewarded with fatigue.

Together with the constant exhaustion, I still couldn't quite comprehend the reality of my quasi-freedom as Protector. Every day I saw new shapes and colours, smelled different plants and food, felt the wind at its strengths and lulls. I was starting to think maybe this town wasn't as bad as it was feared. Perhaps the people didn't mind Protectors any more, either. Perhaps—

My dragul gave a sudden pulse, like the beat of a live heart.

I paused.

Over the side of the open walkway, a strange breeze stirred nearby branches. Slowly, I turned to face the river, gripping the smooth resin at my throat. Was it simply the wind that whispered closer, creating dark whisps of my hair? Or could I hear the syllables and consonants of words, like the voices that had spoken my name when I'd kissed the Midnight Gate? Lanterns peeked innocently through branches, while the town below twinkled with soft light, and glimmers of lively conversation twisted through the night.

My dragul pulsed again.

Go, it seemed to say. But where? Was it warning me, or encouraging me?

Air rushed against my ears as I hurried down the rest of the tree, ignoring the pain shooting through my legs as I tried to keep a hold of the whispers, searching for the lips from which they passed. I reached the mouth of the walkway and stilled my breath.

The whispers were gone.

"Nightfall." I heard the easy smile in Hartley's voice before I saw him. He pushed open the door of the common room, an oval door wedged between giant roots—taller than Hartley—at the Night Tree's base.

He nodded to my letters. "I'm taking Aksel to Step some post through the Gate tomorrow morning."

I gripped my dragul tighter, trying to feel its beat again. It remained silent, and the whispers were once again only wind. Perhaps it was simply part of the lingering fae magic at Midnight Gate, and nothing more. Hartley would have mentioned if it was something important. At the thought of asking him, embarrassment curled its hot tendrils around my neck. I didn't want Hartley thinking I was—I don't know—strange?

"Thanks." I released my dragul and handed him the letters, relieved Malina wouldn't have to wait too long.

"Got a second?"

A little thrill ran down my spine.

Hartley held the oval door open for me and I stepped past his thick, outstretched arm, into the dim warmth of the common room. Those giant roots made up its walls, gaps between roots serving as narrow windows. Fire crackled from a hearth surrounded by comfortable, crimson armchairs. I sat in one while Hartley dropped my letters into his outgoing mailbox on a bench next to a simple, wood-carved kitchenette.

He placed a bowl of walnuts on a side table between us, before sinking into the velvet armchair by my side. If I extended my hand, I could reach the fine hairs across his bare forearms where his navy shirtsleeves rolled up.

I clenched my fists in my lap.

"I never asked you something," said Hartley. "When you finished the Ranking, your bottle was broken. How much nectar did you collect before you fell?"

I popped a walnut into my mouth, grinding it between my teeth. I guess it was a natural assumption that I had simply fallen, judging by the amount of times Hartley had seen me trip in the Smed, but revealing exactly how the bottle had broken would lead to questions about why Edric hated me enough to sabotage me.

"Two bottles," I said, before swallowing the nut.

Hartley's dark-copper brows shot up. "Two *full* bottles? That's unheard of. Unless you're a—no." Hartley shook away a look that momentarily widened his eyes. "Witches' magic disappeared entirely. Huh. You must have just enough mortal blood to not be affected by the Curse, and enough magic blood to have more power."

I shrugged while Hartley considered me with fresh appraisal.

"I wonder who your family was."

"Guess we'll never know," I said casually, playing down the pain of a wound that I had picked at too many times.

Hartley settled back into the chair and gazed into the licking flames. "It's strange, isn't it, that our biggest strength—our magic—comes from the ones we hate the most?"

I blinked. Something jarred me about Hartley's words, like metal scraping metal. *Hate* seemed a heavy label, but perhaps Hartley carried an invisible wound, too.

I knew what brought me comfort when old hurts reopened. "*Spill away from the mountain, / away from my veins.*" My voice followed the lilt of the syllables. "*Though my blood will spill with you, / and I'll draw my own pain.*"

Hartley pulled his attention from the fire. "What?"

"Oh, it's a poem." My face felt hot, and it wasn't because of the fire. "About the irony of loving and hating something at the same time. You know, from the poetry book, *Water Music*? By the poet Rieka?"

Hartley considered me for a moment, then gave a slow head-shake. My stomach sank, as I tried to push away the irritating image of a face I knew would have understood the reference.

"Never mind."

Hartley's lips pulled into a smile. "Well," he said, voice smooth as mead. "Next time I get a cut, I'll ask you to bandage the blood."

His response wasn't quite the metaphor he thought it was. I forced myself from openly cringing. So he didn't quite understand metaphors. What of it? It didn't stop me from drinking in the sight of his face this close, the fullness of his rusty-golden stubble. It didn't stop my gaze from travelling down the column of his thick neck, snagging on the strong tendons that led to the swell of his pecs peeking out from the undone top buttons of his shirt. *Heightened strength.* I wondered how it would feel being picked up in those arms, with his hands closed tight around me. Or would I simply feel weightless? Held?

When I looked back to his warm eyes, Hartley was watching me as if he could read every thought. My cheeks warmed.

"You say *hate*," I said quickly, dropping my gaze to the bowl between us and seizing a handful of walnuts. *Vuk.* I already knew this was going to be a bad segue, but too late—I had to commit. "I don't see what's left for us to hate. The witches cursed the fae for their brute strength of magic against all others, and for laws that favoured only the fae. And now both witches and fae are either dead or turned into vukodlak."

Hartley inhaled slowly through his nose, then leant back into the chair, his gaze on the fire again.

I grimaced inwardly. I had certainly doused whatever embers had been stirring moments before.

"You have no memories before the Fall of the Fae, do you?"

I shook my head.

"When I was a boy, I couldn't wait to be a guard." He paused and half turned to look at me with a lopsided grin. "Promise you'll stop me if I bore you?"

I returned his smile with a slight crease of my eyes.

Hartley settled back into his chair, laying one hand over the armrest. "My parents and sister and I lived in a mortal settlement on the edge of the Suvan Desert near Tide Gate. Every day we had to fight, simply to live. It was a fight to find food. It was a fight to keep our shelter strong against the desert sands. Or against travelling fae who kicked our homes down when they passed—just because they could." Hartley ground a walnut in his hand, turning it to crumbs as if it were soft as bread. "The only people who fought for us were strong mortals who volunteered to guard our settlement. I wanted to be like that. Let people rest and live, instead of fight to barely survive."

He let fine grains of the once-solid walnut trickle from his fingers as I allowed the silence of his memories to settle over us like sand. Malina had once told me her father described the south-eastern desert as living in a kiln. Compared to the comfort of my tower bedroom—albeit mind-tearing—I could only imagine what it would have been like for Hartley's physical world to feel unsafe.

"Our life was about survival while the fae lived in an abundance that could never be my reality. Witches to a lesser extent, but still, they lived a better life than mortals. My father was even the son of a witch," Hartley scoffed, "but since he was mortal, his witch-mother abandoned him. Witches and fae, they never cared about how hard we fought to survive. And then," Hartley dropped his voice, "they lost every drop of power they once had over us." He huffed a dry laugh. "I always knew I'd fight to be free from them, but never did I imagine it could be like this. It's *their* magic that allows me to fulfil a life I only dreamed of in my childhood. Having power over *them*."

Hartley finished with his cheeks lifted in a sneer. There it was—hatred, jarring so oddly with the Hartley I knew so far. Hairs on the back of my scalp prickled. It must be because my bun was tied too tight at the base of my skull. In a small movement Hartley didn't notice, I undid the tie and loosened my hair to shake the feeling away. So he was driven to Protect against those who had kept his life insecure, unsafe. That was understandable, right? And plus, there was one thing he had done for me which I would forever be grateful. One thing that I never fully understood. I could ask about it now.

"Hartley," I raised my knees to my chest, my hair coating them like a blanket. "Why did you help me at the Ranking? You risked Leden's disapproval. What if it jeopardized your position?"

Slowly, he drew his gaze away from the depths of the hearth. "Leden holds power, Nightfall." Firelight and shadows flickered across the curves of his face, turning them harsh. "The more power you have, the more control you have of your own life. Of those who you care about."

Control over your own life.

The thought of it felt like the first taste of chocolate that Malina had left me one night for dinner—at once delightful and necessary.

Hartley watched me while his brown eyes gleamed with the reflection of golden flames. "You must hate Leden. What he did to you." He leaned closer to me, his breath smelling of peppermint. Clean. Composed. Yet there was something disconcerting I couldn't quite place. "Don't worry. I have a different vision for Veligrad."

I blinked. Did that mean Hartley was planning to take Leden's—

The door thudded open, revealing a large shadow against the backdrop of fallen night. I sprang back into my chair while heat dampened my underarms.

Of course, it was Edric.

He clutched a small envelope and strode unhurriedly into the common room. Each step felt like a stroke against the back of my neck. He dropped a letter into Hartley's mailbox, then unhurriedly filled a glass of water from a jug. Leaning back against the kitchen benchtop, Edric took a long drink, his wide throat bobbing with every swallow.

Hartley's eyebrows twitched, but his attention didn't leave me. "There's something special about you, Nevena. That's why I helped you. Someone who will take risks to fight back. Who will stop at nothing to reclaim their power. And I think you have far more of it than you know." Hartley stood abruptly. "Imagine what you could do with all that power." His eyes hardened, and then he strode past Edric to retrieve the letters.

Whether or not he noticed it, the Caster ignored the precision with which Edric watched him. An eagle tracking a mouse—or tracking a threat to its nest. Instead, Hartley acted as though Edric was nothing but an invisible phantom before leaving the room.

A tiny pyramid of fine, ground walnut dust remained beside his armchair. Something about it almost felt callous. I shifted uneasily in my seat.

Edric flicked his intelligent frown onto me. He was so tall the bench only reached his mid-thigh. I frowned back. His gaze travelled down the length of my unbound hair, flicked to my lips, then he abruptly turned to face the sink.

The sound of slopping water massaged the silence between us as Edric washed his glass.

I released my knees.

Time to go back now. Time to go to bed.

But my body felt warm right here. Why should I leave just because Edric had arrived?

Because you need to rest.

This was restful, too. Perhaps my thighs were slightly tensed, and my heart was beating faster than it had been moments ago, but that was only because I was waiting for Edric to leave, right?

"Do you remember the first poem of *Water Music*?" Edric's deep voice vibrated through my chest. How could it do that from all the way across the room? He was still facing the sink, neck slightly bent forward, emphasising the bulk of his broad shoulders straining against the fit of his shirt.

A river dammed is still water flowing. Battering rain makes a tranquil lake.

I didn't say it. I didn't say that now I heard that poem spoken in my head in a voice that sounded like Edric's, rather than my own.

Edric took my silence for acknowledgement.

"Then you know it means we each already hold the key to our own empowerment." His hands reached wide to grip the benchtop. A flat growl. "Obtaining power doesn't make you special."

My stomach contracted, joining my still-clenched thighs.

"Thanks," I snapped. "What a motivating interpretation. By your judgement, I had a well of power within me, and I simply chose to let Leden keep me locked up. It was my own fault that I wasted my potential burning corpses and shovelling ashes into urns."

Why was it that with Edric my words spilt from me like blood from sliced flesh?

"No," said Edric, his voice deeper than zhivir tree roots. "That's not what I meant. Being powerful is not what makes you special, Nevena. What makes you special is being able to discern right from wrong, and whether or not you act on your values—regardless of any power you possess."

Nevena. The timbre of his voice repeated in my head like a never-ending echo.

"Hartley wants to use you. He's just like Leden."

"Use me? He's the one who saved me from Leden."

Tendons strained against Edric's neck as he finally turned to me, clenching his perfect jaw. "*You* were the river that kept flowing when dammed. *You* were the lake that held itself while it was battered." His teeth were glaring metal as he parted his lips. "Hartley did not save you. You saved yourself."

Edric's heavy steps rang in my ears as he marched from the common room, leaving me alone.

I wanted to retrieve my letter to *Regretfully-Seeking-Closure*. Not even screaming into the depths of the Buran Sea would ease the burn of Edric Silvan's scorching words beneath my skin.

Chapter Eleven

I waited alongside a deep puddle at the base of the Night Tree. Not even the canopy's twinkling lanterns could penetrate the harsh chill of tonight's patrol. Hartley said a drop of nectar would warm my bones, and the rain would not bother me. That it would keep away illness.

I sniffled, not bothering to wipe my dripping nose. It mingled, anyway, with the water pattering down my face.

Two tall blurs appeared between droplets hanging heavy on my eyelashes.

"This way," Edric grunted from beneath his hood.

The temperature of my skin rose as he swept past. Those were the first words Edric had uttered to me in the five days since he had spoken my name with the intensity of the river roiling beside the Night Tree. Five days since his empowering words writhed like snakes within me while I tried to sleep.

Clearly, he regretted it. For whatever reason, Hartley simply got on his nerves, and Edric had wanted to contradict him. That was why he had given me five days of silence.

Fine. It was fine.

Besides, just because he decided to say one *vaguely nice* thing, it didn't undo how he had treated me before.

Jelena hardly offered me a glance as they continued towards the stone bridge over the Lutava River, her expression as sour as a pickled cabbage.

"Kavi's shift already did the eastern bank earlier today," I called, my voice creakier than unoiled door hinges. "We should patrol the western town border."

A snort ahead from Jelena was all I received in response, and my anger ignited like a ready, dry wick. Why was she always so unpleasant? She held more hatred against me towards Ander's death than even Edric did. When Aksel had once asked how they knew each other, Edric had said they were old friends. I suspected there was something deeper.

Aches in my joints were all I achieved as I tried to follow the pair, their nectar-fuelled paces already carrying them across the river's muddy, stone bridge. It was no use trying to catch up with them, and calling out again would be futile with my cracked voice. I halted in the centre of the bridge.

They couldn't simply order me around, picking random patrol routes as they pleased. If I hadn't made it clear to Edric before, I certainly would now. Like a rivulet, *no one* could control my flow. I defined my own—

Da-dum.

My dragul pulsed. Just like it had weeks before. The pendant at my neck felt like an extra heart, beating to its own rhythm.

It pulsed again.

No—it wasn't simply pulsing. It was *dragging* me, wanting to lead me towards the dark, whitecapped river surging beneath my feet, the water urgent, as though a storm was chasing it all the way from the Serpent Ranges.

Wet stomps splashed into the fringes of my hearing. "Come on," growled Edric. "There's something I want to show—"

"Do you feel that, too?" The question fell as if pushed from a high ledge. My voice barely sounded like my own.

For a long while, I heard no reply as I continued to gaze upstream at the heavy force of water.

"Feel what?" Edric finally asked. The reverberations of his voice bounced through my chest, hauling my attention back to Edric's proximity. Close enough to hear his steady breath.

"You can't feel that from your dragul? Like something's . . . pulling it."

Edric and Jelena shared a glance in the way siblings often did. Children would sometimes play in the courtyard beneath my window, and during my first months in the tower, I would watch them. Observing every interaction they made. Desperate to be one of them. I always wanted a sibling who knew my every thought simply from the twitch of an eyebrow. That was what Edric and Jelena seemed to share now.

"Maybe there's something over there. We should go and—*ahchoo!*" I bent over into my sleeve, holding my nose there until I could manage to sniff away the snot.

A deep, male sigh sounded, and then a square of navy fabric entered my vision. A handkerchief. "A lick of nectar would help, you know."

I ignored Edric's offer and wiped my nose on my sleeve instead. "Of course I know."

"Then why don't you take it?"

"Because I'm not a hypocrite, unlike *you*."

Edric was silent for a moment. He shoved his handkerchief back into a pocket. "*Turn, turn, tumble and jilt,*" he muttered. "*One sees the surface, while the other sees silt.*"

"Oh, really?" It was a poetic insult, implying I was unable to see complexity or underlying meanings. It was the wrong thing to say to someone exhausted and sick. The wick of my anger was aflame. "You know what I see? I see a hypocrite who vowed to Protect Veligrad from the Cursed but seems to have a problem with others doing just that." While Edric was already close, I stepped closer, nearly enough to touch. "All of the Cursed were once someone's family. You killed vukodlak at Amber Gate. They could've been mortals who were bitten and turned. Should their families hate you for killing their loved ones, then? Like you hate me?"

Edric's thick brows drew together, the muscles in his jaw popping. "You caved my brother's head in," he growled. "With a hammer."

"*That was all I had,*" I rasped. My damp skin itched with all the emotion I had suppressed. "I had nothing else, Silvan. Nothing. I never had a thing for myself, I never had a *life* for myself. And he looked Cursed—his eyes—he came after me. All I had to defend the life I had never had—that for the first time I *tried* to have—was that hammer." My throat was rough, grated shards. "So I'm sorry. I'm so sorry he died. And that it was my hand that did it. But your job"—I jabbed a finger at a hard sternum—"is to Protect Veligrad from the Cursed. So how can you hate me for doing just that? For doing what you voluntarily signed up to do right now. For what I had *not* asked to do back then."

I could no longer tell whether the wetness on my face was rain or my own tears.

"And you want to know why I don't take the nectar?" I heaved, unable to stop, more words pushing against each other to flee the cage of my heart. "Because people die when there's not enough to go around. The bottles you smashed during the Ranking could have helped dozens of people. Dozens of lives.

You know, I had one friend in Amber Gate. Her father became ill. She worked herself to sickness to try and afford nectar. But guess what? When she finally saved enough coin, there was no nectar in Amber Gate left." It was yet another memory I tried to wedge in a hidden corner and never look at. "He was the only person that had ever cared for me like a parent, and—" A sob welled in my chest, and I cut myself off. "With every drop of nectar you take to boost your own strength, people die."

Rain punctured through foliage, smacking against wet mud and increasing the roar of the rushing river. It matched how I felt—striking, then splattering, then roiling in emotions. But it did nothing to move Edric. Over a head taller than me, he peered down through long eyelashes with a familiar worried look that drew a line between his brows.

He dipped his chin. I lifted mine, anticipating the whip of his tongue to cast another lash.

"I'm sorry."

I released a sharp breath and stumbled back, surprise rendering me almost unstable. My mouth opened to say something—anything—at that damn genuine concern leaking from his eyes. The same look that had stopped me the moment we'd met. Before I could determine whether his apology was real or just another stroke of a lash, a different sound ripped through the darkening night.

A long, high howl.

The first I had heard in Midnight Gate.

"Nevena." Edric's breath shuddered over me as his gaze travelled the entire length of my body. "Your foot."

I lifted my boot with a squelch, and my heart thudded hard against my ribs. The tip of a small white tooth poked through soggy mud, disturbed from the line it usually lay in.

Don't disturb the teeth.

My vision swam.

I had just disturbed a safe path, and the vukodlak were ready to kill.

"No," I whispered.

With all my remaining energy, I twisted away from Edric and ran.

The path led all the way to the northern-most zhivir trees, but already a chorus of screams carried down the waves of the river.

"Vukodlak!" I shrieked to townspeople darting between zhivir trees in the rain, my voice so raw that my throat was surely bloody. "Get inside! *Vukodlak!*"

Edric and Jelena quickly outpaced me and were soon too far out of sight. My wet face was blasted to numbness as my exhausted, stiff legs pounded north along the riverbank. I felt unforgivably slow as more wails filtered between trees like phantoms.

Finally, I reached them. Edric and Jelena stood in the centre of a neighbourhood of zhivir trees, staring between tree trunks and drooping vines, under the light of their flaming indigo orbs. Only once the thuds of my feet softened did I hear it.

Nothing.

The screams had stopped abruptly. Not a single person was in sight. Lanterns twinkled knowingly in branches, illuminating paths that should be full of people at this time, even in the rain. The scent of food still wafted in the air, making my stomach churn against the guilt. If I hadn't been so sick, I would have focused more on where I had been stepping.

I conjured my dragul sphere to join Edric's and Jelena's, my lungs burning through whatever shreds of them were left.

"Where are those who were screaming?"

In answer, the sound of something heavy slapped to the ground in the trees beyond.

"Fuck," Edric breathed.

Jelena grunted as she threw a dragul sphere towards the direction of the sound, but it merely hit a skinny tree, engulfing it in blue flame before snuffing out. A charred husk.

The vukodlak were still nearby. And so was a drained, dead body.

This was all my fault. Panic clenched its icy fingers around my throat, tightening slowly. I couldn't breathe. My fingers gripped my necklace, wanting to rip it off. Maybe I should have never done any of this—left my tower, become a Protector—*any* of it.

Then a warm hand wrapped around mine.

"You're alright," Edric whispered. "Just focus."

Breath returned to my lungs.

I snatched my wrist from his gentle grasp.

"I *am* focused," I snapped. My palm tingled where his thumb had touched it.

"Good." Without making a sound, he stalked carefully forwards.

My attention shifted to the direction his thick, trunk-like legs moved, towards a cluster of young beech trees further away. Reedy and weak in comparison to the stoutness of zhivir trees. Had Edric seen something? I strained my exhausted eyes into the distance.

A second later, I heard it.

My skin crawled as the sound drew closer, becoming louder. Fast, panting breaths.

Vukodlak.

From between the young trees, the leaking, white eyes of a nightmarish creature rose. Its hairless muzzle was the colour of maggots, stretched taut over protruding bones, long fangs stained red from the blood of the victim it had just drained.

"There!" I called, and shot my dragul sphere towards it, at the same time Edric yelled "Wait!"

The vukodlak burst into an inferno of indigo and golden flames where my and Jelena's dragul hit, allowing it no time for a final cry of agony.

As I conjured another sphere of magic, several more vukodlak leapt over their packmate's dying body. The forest was cast in dark blue as I sent searing spheres of light against the incoming pack of vukodlak. Half a dozen wolf-like beasts charged in from all angles, clawed paws thundering against the ground. They moved fast, their stringy muscles popping from their skeletal frames and fangs exposed in anticipation of blood.

But my magic was faster. Each dragul sphere I conjured sent a stronger rush of magic racing through my limbs. I felt powerful.

I am powerful.

I matched every one of Jelena's dragul spheres with three of my own. Flames burst against vukodlak skin in a frenzy, releasing a putrid stench that churned my stomach.

And then there was silence.

Scorched limbs lay still and splayed across sombre soil. Maws were spread wide, displaying rotten fangs, capturing their final moments of agony. It was hard to believe these creatures had once been powerful fae.

"Edric," Jelena rasped. "Don't just stand there."

I turned to find one remaining vukodlak pinned to the ground on its belly and forearms, restrained by Edric's enchanted rope. The vukodlak's white eyes were wide, either with fear or hunger at warm blood so close. It snapped drooling jaws while its hairless back legs tried to kick out from its trap.

"They're sicker than they used to be," said Edric, a dagger poised in each hand. Pus streamed from the monster's eyes, polluting the forest air with the smell of rot.

"That's why we give them a quick death," Jelena snapped, striding with a frown to stand at the creature's feet.

I couldn't help but follow her. Close up, the vukodlak looked both terrifying and vulnerable. Its colourless eyes were wide, the dark veins around them twitching. Who had this vukodlak been before it had been Cursed?

"They're weaker, too," said Edric. "Slower. Look at its skin. It's covered in wounds. I think they're—"

With a strangled bark, the vukodlak burst free from Edric's rope and lunged—not at Edric, but at Jelena.

Time slowed and sped up simultaneously.

Jelena's eyes widened with the knowledge she had no time to conjure her magic. The creature's hind legs caught Edric in the stomach, kicking him to the ground.

Before the vukodlak's gaping maw could close onto Jelena's shoulder, I shoved into her middle, tackling her out of the vukodlak's path, and shot a dragul sphere into its face.

The tortured monster screamed in my ear as it landed heavily atop me, sounding more human than wolf, while my fire consumed its putrid eyes, its rotting mouth.

Breath squeezed from my lungs as clawed feet kicked me. I pushed against its burning flesh, the dragul sphere flames feeling as light as breath on my skin, but it was no use. The stench of foul body odour and decay filled my airways. I was either going to be squashed or choked to death by—

A whisper of slicing steel severed its howls, and then the heavy weight was lifted off me.

I lay still, my eyes closed. All that energy, magic, *power* that I had felt moments ago instantly vanished, and a wave of fatigue drained away any desire to move. Ever again, probably.

"Did it bite you?" My eyelids lifted a smidge at the edge of panic in Edric's voice. Warm hands lifted flaps of fabric off my skin where stinging lines had cut through. "Fuck. It's scratched you to shreds."

"Its face was on fire, cousin. Don't think biting was a priority." Despite her words, Jelena's tone didn't carry its usual punch.

"Nevena. I'm sorry, but you need to take this nectar. The vukodlak's claws are infected, and you're too sick to fight it."

Another apology from Edric? Maybe it was delirium. I could already feel the light stings sinking into something deeper, reaching into bones, leaving an agonising stabbing trail as if the vukodlak's claws were tunnelling into my marrow.

A small moan fell from my lips.

"Please, Nevena. Will you take it?"

"You keep saying my name," I mumbled.

It would only be moments before I blacked out, and then I could finally rest. It was just my sniffling sickness, probably, making me so tired.

"*Nevena.* I'll say it a thousand times more. Nevena, *please.*"

At the edge of my waning awareness, warmth flickered in my core. With a final mote of energy that flared at the tip of my tongue like a glowworm, I answered Edric. "Yes."

Something smooth pressed against my lips. The tang of bittersweet nectar trickled gently into my mouth. A firm hand held the back of my head.

My mind moved sluggishly between the sensations, as if observing from afar. As if it wasn't me who was fading away.

Suddenly, the trickle turned hot. Searing hot. I gasped weakly as every cut on my body stung with the unbearable strength of rubbed alcohol. My veins felt full of fire. I needed to kick. I needed water. I needed it to stop. I was going to *scream*—

Then all the pain disappeared.

Was I dead?

A warm thrumming under my skin mimicked the comfort of thick blankets, or the heartiness of hot broth. Even beneath the still-falling rain, I had never felt better since arriving at Midnight Gate.

Edric's deep voice mumbled over me to Jelena, "Your wife's going to find a way to strangle me for almost getting you killed."

"Sena has enough shit to deal with," said Jelena. "We're not telling her."

Rubbing my chest where my shirt was shredded, I slowly sat up to see Edric's dark brows pulled tighter together than I had ever seen. His arm immediately wrapped firmly around my back, supporting my weight in my sitting position. I didn't move away.

"What are you doing? There might be more."

"There aren't any more nearby," said Edric, with something like reassurance in his tone. "When they smell blood, they have no control, only bloodlust."

"I know that." It was almost instinctive to bite back—or at least to say *something* back. Perhaps snapping wasn't the right response, seeing as he still held me, and had just helped stop an agonising blood poisoning. Edric's lip twitched. Was that a smile?

Jelena looked between the two of us and rolled her eyes before striding away. "Don't get too comfortable," she called over her shoulder. "There are still bodies to count."

That washed away any heat. I leaned away from Edric and rose, avoiding those deep blue eyes that I knew were checking every scratch was healed, like his hands had moments before. Why was everything about Edric so deep? His voice, his eyes, his poetry?

The slow creaking of door hinges and the keening of low wails broke the stillness between us, just as Jelena came back from searching the bushes.

"Twenty-two dead."

It was the wrong timing.

A familiar voice rang out. "The puppets of Veligrad have failed us once again," Gorcha cried. "I *told* you. *Don't disturb the teeth.*" The grey man was seething. Froth speckled his lips, and the lantern lights reflected off his dead-brown eyes. Gorcha honed his attention onto Edric. "Your brother, he would have prevented this. He would never have allowed this to happen. Yet here you stand, one of *them.*"

Edric's eyes widened. It was the first time I had seen him look truly unnerved.

I shifted the weight in my feet. "Silvan didn't—"

Edric's wide back suddenly blocked my view of Gorcha, and Jelena tugged at my sleeve.

"Let's go," she muttered.

"But—"

"Let Edric deal with Gorcha."

Edric was already by the older man's side, murmuring con-
dolences and other words I couldn't catch against the wailing
of townspeople as they searched amongst trees, crying as they
carried stiff bodies out of bushes.

Gorcha barely seemed to notice Jelena and I were there at all.

Questions formed on the crest of my tongue, aching to
roll out. Who had Ander Silvan been to Gorcha, to instate
such admiration? Was he someone anti-Council, like Gorcha?
Wanting to live a traditional, though delusional, life?

The questions continued to bounce through my mind as I
reluctantly followed Jelena back to the Night Tree, no clear
answers in sight. And the only person who held their true
answers? I would rather take on another pack of vukodlak
than ask. Edric Silvan finally seemed not to hate me. For some
reason, I didn't want that to change.

CHAPTER TWELVE

I WASN'T ON PATROL when the first safe paths were deliberately disturbed.

My sleep was disrupted by a long howl near midnight. Then another. And then an agonising scream nearby.

Kavi's scream.

I tore down the Night Tree, following the direction of her voice, uncaring about my bare feet or my oversized nightshirt that only just covered to my mid-thigh. Light blazed through the trees ahead, a battle already in place. I begged the bright moon that I could reach Kavi in time. Footsteps raced behind me, and then a blur flew past.

Hartley. Thank Vuk for his Heightened Power.

I arrived at a thicket of zhivir trees a minute later.

Jelena's deadpanned face held a dragul sphere, casting indigo light as Aksel rubbed miran nectar into a tear along Kavi's neck. Hartley was wiping nectar from his lips too, three scratches down his face quickly disappearing. The carcasses of a pack of vukodlak lay strewn across the ground.

My heart clenched as I ran to Kavi's side. "Are you alright? What happened?"

"Someone must have accidentally stepped on a tooth." Hartley bared his teeth. "Didn't I tell you all? It's simple—*too* simple, in fact: You need to watch where you're walking to *not disturb the teeth.* My eye was nearly gouged out because of one of you, and I don't think that's something miran nectar can replace."

I winced at the unexpected harshness of his tone.

"We didn't!" Aksel exclaimed. "Don't blame us. It's probably the fucking Protector-haters."

"Look around, Ivkov. This is a cluster of homes. You think these people are reckless enough to draw the Cursed right before their doors?"

"Then why was this cluster completely empty of any people, *sir*?" Aksel spat, rising to his feet. "They did it. They knew about it."

"Enough." Kavi's voice cut through their argument. She shrugged her shoulders back and rose, her wound nearly healed. "Let's go back to the Night Tree. We'll wait until daylight in case any more Cursed come this way, and then we should speak to Gorcha."

So she thought Aksel was right. I did, too. While I wasn't as familiar with this part of the forest, the nocturnal habits of the townspeople meant there should be activity here. No fires were lit in the stone pits that usually roasted food at all hours of the night.

The walk back to the Night Tree was tense.

Instead of staying in the common room to discuss the attack like Kavi had suggested, Hartley shut himself in his own bedroom with a slammed door. Aksel exchanged glances with us before retiring himself. Of course, Jelena didn't hang around to wait, either.

"Kavi, can I tell you something?" I asked when it was just the two of us.

"Of course." She led me into her room, settling onto the bed and patting the spot beside her.

I sat stiffly. "I believe you and Aksel. I don't think the attack just now was a coincidence."

Kavi took a deep sigh. "At least that makes three of us." She gave a tight grin. "We'll be more careful now that we know someone is doing this. Better yet, hopefully it won't happen again. I'm sure Hartley will speak to Gorcha. He was just a bit . . . angry."

"Hopefully he will." It was twice now that I had seen a different version of the playful, confident Caster. Or maybe this version was always there, underneath a carefully controlled mask of ease.

"Thank you for coming to help." She smiled wearily, gesturing at my bare legs and dirty feet.

"It was nothing." Even after our last conversation that I had abruptly ended, Kavi had been gentle towards me. Friendly. Always ready to listen but never forcing conversation. "Also, I wanted to tell you . . . I'm sorry. About the other week. I was rude to you. After I told you about . . . about—"

A gentle hand clasped my shoulder. Just like I had once imagined happening. Warmth seeped from her touch. "It's fine. I can't imagine what you've been through."

"You've been so kind to me. I want you to know that I want to be there for you, too. If you ever need anything..." I couldn't imagine what she might need. She was strong, intelligent, secure in herself. But I let the offer hang anyway. I stood. "I hope you get some rest after all that."

"Nev?" My stomach squeezed at Malina's nickname for me. "You're a good friend." She smiled.

My heart swelled. I gave her a tiny smile back.

Suppressing the liquid that suddenly filled my eyesight, I quickly wished Kavi good night and left her room with a quiet snap of her door. Taking a deep inhale, I pressed the heels of my palms to my eyes.

Friendship was painfully beautiful. It was the reason for the courage I had gained to escape my tower and become a Protector—for Malina. And now, this growing friendship with Kavi was colouring in the grey stagnancy of my emotions.

"Nightfall?"

I jumped at the familiar voice. Edric was standing outside his room next to Kavi's, brow perplexed, flicking between my trouser-less legs and my watery eyes.

My heart thudded. We had been on opposite day and night shifts since the last time he had said my first name. *I'll say it a thousand times more.* I hadn't crossed paths with him since.

I sniffed. "Yes. I'm fine." *Ugh,* not that he'd asked. My cheeks flushed.

Edric frowned. Almost imperceptibly, he glanced at my legs once more, then to my lips, then he stiffly turned away.

"Wait. Edric, do you have time for . . . tea?" The hit of awkwardness I administered to myself was a blow to the gut. "I mean, I wanted to thank you for—"

"Don't." He cut me off sharply, keeping his attention averted.

"What?"

"Don't thank me."

A hitch in my chest. "Oh."

"I don't have time."

"Oh. Okay." I swallowed. "Good."

He turned to me then, one thick brow quirked.

"It's lucky you don't have time." I lifted my chin. "Because you clearly would have wasted mine."

I must have imagined the momentary widening of his eyes, his lips parting to say something else, because then his expression shuttered, and his jaw clenched tight.

I was already slamming the door to my room anyway.

Things only got worse.

It started with another attack a week later, when Hartley, Jelena, and Aksel were returning to the Night Tree. Townspeople had watched from a nearby safe path as a pack of twelve salivating vukodlak quickly overcame the patrol, nearly mauling Hartley to death. It took numerous vials to revive the Caster.

Then the attacks became more frequent. Every couple of days.

Exhaustion coated us all in sluggish, irritable muck. The allocated supply of nectar was dwindling. Hartley declared it only to be used for the growing number of serious injuries incurred against the Cursed. They kept appearing on our regular patrol paths when townspeople were nowhere in sight. It meant that the whole town was in on it. They wanted us gone.

"I swear I saw a walking vukodlak." Aksel's pale face was more concerned than usual when we started our night patrol.

"You mean a vampire? They're just a myth," I brushed off. "Believe me. I've heard plenty of rumours about myself, so I would know."

His light-blue eyes grew stormy. "Then how do you explain the fact that I saw a creepy shadow moving through the trees—upright on *two* feet?"

I sighed, too exhausted to respond. I probably wasn't far off hallucinating, too. Edric walked a little way ahead of Aksel and I as we patrolled through a busy thoroughfare. Where there were townspeople, those paths were definitely safe. Instead of patrolling for vukodlak, we were now essentially patrolling *them*.

"Silvan," Aksel called. "Why don't you speak to Gorcha? He knows you, right?"

"No." The answer came without a look back.

"Come on. Look, he's over there now with some of his followers. It's been over a month since Hartley *apparently* spoke to him. Nothing's changed. Why don't you try and get him to tell his minions to back the fuck off?"

A man pushing a cart of some kind of alcoholic drinks beside Aksel threw him a dirty glare.

"Why don't you tell him?" came Edric's tart response.

"Because—"

"*I'll* do it." I'd had enough. I wanted to survive this season, and at this point I would do anything in my means to achieve that. I brushed passed Edric and stormed towards the back of Gorcha's head where he and other diners sat cross-legged around a fire, roasting potatoes. The maw of his wolfskin hung backwards beneath his neck, limp and grotesque. A cloaked woman with deep-red hair broke her conversation with Gorcha to watch with curiosity as I approached. "Elder Gorcha. I—"

A scream tore through the crowd of diners somewhere beyond, and everything stilled.

"My child!" a man cried. "It was an accident. My child picked up a tooth!"

Silence.

And then chaos.

Townspeople scrambled to reach the nearest zhivir trees before the inevitable sound of pounding paws crashed between trunks.

Most had managed to find a tree to hide inside. Not everyone.

I willed my wooden legs to run towards the screams coming from further away, but Edric was already sprinting past.

It meant he was on his own when five vukodlak leapt at him at once.

A rotten maw closed around Edric's forearm. Even as he destroyed that one with a blast of indigo flame, another latched to his other arm. A third to his neck. It was only when a vukodlak lunged on Edric's back that he fell forwards, buried under frenzied fangs.

"*No!*"

My veins were on fire, burning me inside out as my power exploded into five flaming dragul spheres. I couldn't tell if the roaring I heard was the wind or my own screaming voice as I hurled magic at the pack of Cursed tearing Edric's skin apart.

They struck together in a blaze of indigo that flared nearly as tall as the canopy, charring the pack immediately. The sizzling sound of cooked flesh was all that was left stirring in the air.

I felt anything but relief.

"*Edric!*" What if I had killed him, too?

Aksel was beside me as we sprinted to the charred mess. No other vukodlak remained—the ones who had found victims had already dragged them deeper into the forest to gorge upon.

Aksel helped me as I pushed foul, steaming vukodlak corpses from Edric.

I suppressed a sob.

Edric's back was torn meat, his neck a bloody mess of gore.

"I brought four vials," said Aksel, promptly starting to pour one carefully into the side of Edric's mouth. "Come on, buddy. Swallow."

I didn't want to look at his lips to check whether Edric was conscious enough to listen. With a trembling hand, I spread the thick, silky fluid onto the gaping wounds at his neck where blood pooled freely, pinching his skin so the magic could knit it together more quickly. Then I moved to the deep gashes in his back. Then his scratched face. Then his arms.

I heard him swallow.

"There you go, buddy. Take some more."

I kept massaging the nectar into the wounds. His back rose, lungs lifted in a deep, clear breath.

There it was: *relief*. I let my head loll back as I took a shaky breath.

"The tooth is returned!" someone yelled from afar.

Good. I stood on wobbly legs.

"Nevena, here." Aksel tried to push a vial into my hand, a couple of drops left inside. "You used a lot of power."

"I'm fine."

I wasn't. Aksel was right: I *had* used a lot of power. More than I had ever felt, and now even standing on my feet was draining the remaining dregs.

That was enough for tonight.

I didn't wait for Edric to rise as I turned away, limping with fatigue. Faces watched me from zhivir tree hollows as I passed, but only one pair of eyes burned into my back like two dragul spheres. I knew whose they were without looking. I knew they were the shade of a deep, dark blue.

CHAPTER THIRTEEN

"T HERE CAN'T BE A fucking *ball* when these peasants keep moving the safe paths," said Aksel.

"Hey," Kavi admonished him with a frown.

Aksel, Kavi, and I strode back to the Night Tree at sunset, after a day full of glowering glares.

For not the first time, I silently agreed with Aksel.

The townspeople wanted us gone. And yet, after the latest attack, Gorcha had specifically invited all Protectors to attend the annual Blood Moon Ball in three weeks.

Just a little longer.

My chest always felt so tight these days. It was halfway into the season—three more months until I could Rank again and try to land a position at a safer Gate. My Protector wage was good, but not yet good enough to buy a home for Malina and I in one of the southern Gates. We could keep patrolling the townspeople's safe paths, but I could see the determination in their scowls. They didn't want us here. What would they do next?

Kavi fidgeted with the hilt of her Moon Gate short sword. "I've been thinking about something that could help."

My heart flipped. "What is it?"

Aksel and I watched Kavi expectantly while she twisted the end of her braid. Though Kavi was a student at Moon Gate, her knowledge of Veligrad's history was so deep she may as well have been an academic.

"You know how Midnight Gate was completed on the coldest night of shadow-light season, at midnight? Well, the coldest night is coming up, and it got me thinking." Her fingers relaxed. "There's a very old spell that bonds three people together to create a protective shield against malevolent forces. Kind of like what the zhivir trees do." Her voice rang clear in the quiet near the Night Tree, where townspeople loathed to pass. "The spell's meant to be undertaken by a fae, a witch, and a mortal, but since we're all part-magic and part-mortal, I think our blend of magic might make it work."

My heart rate picked up. "I'll do it."

If it could help prevent further deaths like those I had already caused—and protect *myself* in the process—then I was in.

"Me, too." Aksel gave a brisk nod. "The three of us will do it, then."

Kavi scrunched her face. "Well, there's a—"

"Do what?" Hartley stepped out of the common room between the Night Tree's giant roots, hands on his hips.

Kavi pressed her lips together. Fading light reflected off her high cheekbones, making her look taller. She took up space in the kind of way that made herself visible, but that still left room for others. "This is a conversation for everyone."

A beat of silence.

"Alright. I'll fetch Silvan and Altan. Meet me in the common room," Hartley instructed.

"No." The deep rumble of a familiar voice rolled down from above.

Tendrils of Edric's side-parted hair drooped over his fore-head as he peered down from the walkway above, clearly having overheard the conversation. "The day patrol will be hungry. Let's meet in the kitchen."

I met Kavi's glance with a side-eye. Was Edric . . . looking after us? The way her temples creased told me her thoughts. He wasn't looking after *us*, he was looking after—

"Thank Vuk," said Aksel, brushing past. "I've lost half my muscle mass since coming to this damn town. I miss chicken. I miss beef. I miss every animal that the Cursed have wiped out in the north. Speaking of," Aksel called up to Edric, "what happened to that bird of yours?"

Edric's firm jaw worked as he glared down at Aksel. "It healed. It's free."

Inside the kitchen, halfway up the Night Tree, Edric and Jelena sat beside each other at a round table next to the hearth. A pot of steaming bean soup stood in the table's centre, its comforting aroma making my stomach growl.

Umber pots hung from hooks over a low oven, while jars of grains, preserved vegetables, and spices lined full shelves hugging the walls. Although the townspeople hated us, kitchen staff still produced delicious meals with far more flavour than anything I had ever tasted while in the Amber Gate tower. The zhivir trees prevented anyone with malevolent intentions from entering, and that also meant preventing any interference with our food. I thanked Vuk for this small pleasure.

I was last in the door and took the only wooden seat remaining between Edric and Hartley.

Great.

I squashed into the small space between their big bodies. This close, it was difficult not to notice the sound of Edric's steady breath, or the gentle rise and fall of his chest beneath the fitted, woollen, thermal shirt. A single dagger remained missing from one side of his suspenders. The same dagger that was still wrapped in linen against the back of my wrist, covered by my sleeve. While I could conjure dragul spheres quicker than any other Protector, there was something oddly comforting about keeping the tiny blade near my skin.

To my other side, Hartley's attention was focused on Kavi.

She folded her hands on the table, her posture as strong and sure as the trunk of a zhivir tree. "There's something that can be done to Protect Midnight Gate from the Smed. But you're probably not going to like it."

Not going to like it? Some of my earlier enthusiasm flattened.

"The Gates of Veligrad," Kavi began, "possess magic that runs deep into the earth and spreads out like roots beneath each town. It's why our dragul are strongest at the Gate from which they come from."

I needed to crick my neck, to ease some of the strain that constantly lingered, but I was too squashed between the large bodies on either side.

"We all know that each Gate in Veligrad was built by a pair of fated mates. Their unbreakable bond is what made the Gates so powerful, the act symbolising unity."

Hartley leant his elbows on the table, his large bicep brushing against my arm. I squeezed my elbow closer into my ribs.

"Harmony only lasted a short time. Not long after the Gates were built, Veligrad became divided." Even the fire's crackling died down as it seemed to listen to Kavi's story. "The land wasn't divided between magic and non-magic peoples like it is now, but by cities. Each city had resources or skills that the other sought. People were killed or enslaved over them."

I could easily picture Kavi lecturing to a hall full of students, imparting her wisdom and knowledge. What was this intelligent woman doing here then, risking her life? My shoulders curled forwards at the realisation that I had never asked.

"That," continued Kavi, oblivious to the crumpling of my insides, "was when the Midnight Gate leaders—a fae, a witch, and a mortal—crafted a new spell. The Kora. The Kora bonded the three with the magic of Midnight Gate that runs underneath the whole town. The bond creates a protective shield as far as the roots of magic reach. When the Kora spell is activated, any intruding forces are repelled from entering and can be sensed by the bonded three."

"Wait, are you saying *we* can cast spells? I thought Protectors only had dragul spheres. And Heightened Powers," said Aksel, looking accusingly at Hartley, who was considering Kavi with an unreadable expression, deliberately blank.

"And Stepping," said Kavi. "But, yes. We can cast other spells. That's where Casters originally received their names. Only it can be dangerous. Spells can overcome those whose magic is not strong enough. That includes mortals like us who have small amounts of magic in our blood. That's why we're only taught to cast dragul spheres. Isn't that correct, Hartley?"

Hartley gave a stiff nod.

"So that's why we wouldn't like it? It can—what—kill us?" Aksel asked.

"Yes." A sombre nod. "The Kora is so powerful that even amongst the three intended—fae, witch, and mortal—the spell is only temporary, lasting a season at most."

Around the table, forearms folded across chests. Aksel leant back in his chair. "So you're saying the spell might be too strong for us to survive, and that we're probably not powerful enough to cast it in the first place. But you wouldn't be raising it unless you thought we could do it, right?"

Something shifted in my opinion of Aksel. The man had no filter between his mind and his mouth, but he clearly had enough common sense to trust Kavi's judgement.

"Right. Midnight Gate is most powerful in the middle of shadow-light season, on the anniversary it was built. It's our best shot. And I think there are three of us here who can take it." Kavi shifted to look directly at me, and I startled in my seat. "Nevena. Whoever your ancestors were, they must have been powerful. You only hold a fraction of the crystal that everyone else carries, yet you can cast more dragul spheres at once than us all. You have the most magic here, and I think you could undertake the spell."

Oh.

It was strange what happened when you truly felt someone believed in you. It was more than the words Kavi said, and more than how she said them—with her light brown eyes holding mine in a way that made me lift my chin. It was the bond of friendship that Kavi had extended to me the moment we met.

She squeezed her eyes in understanding.

"Hartley," Kavi continued. "Your Heightened Power developed earlier than anyone else I've heard of. That shows you possess a large amount of magic, too."

Of course. Hartley had told me his grandmother was a witch. Portions of magic were larger and stronger the closer the blood connection to a witch or fae.

"And the third person—"

"I'm wondering, Khalili," interrupted Hartley, "how can we rely on your word about this spell?" His shoulders appeared deceptively relaxed, but his arm stiffened against mine.

Aksel leant forwards so fast his chair scraped, speaking before Kavi could respond. "Her parents are academics specialising in fae history. They were some of the only mortals allowed to hold academic positions before the Curse, which shows just how smart they were. *And* she grew up at Moon Gate University and finished studying there before the Ranking. I don't think you'll find anyone more qualified."

If Hartley was as perplexed at Aksel's sudden defence of Kavi as I was, he didn't show it. Instead, a sly smile twitched at the corners of his mouth.

"Alright. Khalili, do *you* think you're qualified enough to risk mine and Nightfall's lives? And that of whoever the third person is?" While his expression remained the same, the back of Hartley's jaw twitched.

I didn't like the way he was speaking to Kavi. I shifted away from where his arm touched me. Space was so tight that my small movement meant I was now leaning into Edric. He moved to accommodate my space, bumping Jelena, who tutted and pushed him back into me. His bicep was huge and firm against my side, his warmth steady.

Just focus on the conversation. Be there for Kavi.

Kavi's braid hung heavily over the table as she leant forward, as if weighted with her knowledge. "Yes. Not only do I *think* I'm qualified enough, I *know* it."

Hartley opened his mouth to say something, but I beat him to it. "I trust you, Kavi. I'll do the Kora spell. You, Hartley?"

The Caster returned my question with a flicker of a bronze brow. "Who's the third?" he asked Kavi.

"Altan or Silvan. After Nev and Hartley, they're the next fastest at casting dragul spheres. Faster than any Protector I've seen at Moon Gate, too."

The pair didn't even look at each other, as if they had known this was coming.

"I'll do it," Jelena rasped at the same time Edric opened his mouth.

Brows raised at Jelena, he hooked his thumbs under his suspenders and muttered, "Sena won't be happy if you do it."

"Who's Sena?" asked Aksel.

Jelena narrowed her eyes at him. "My wife."

"She as pleasant as you are?"

Jelena slammed her palms on the table. "Don't talk about my wife. She shines brighter than the burning sun in the centre of the Suvan Desert. You would be lucky if she even glanced at a little shit like you."

"She must be real nice." Aksel grinned.

"I'll do it." Edric rose as he clamped a firm hand on Jelena's shoulder before she could lunge. He reached for the pot of bean soup and ladled some into a bowl. "I've journeyed a long time with seven wishes over seven moons. When none left me with what I sought, I returned."

My toes curled. It was the poem I had slung at him when we'd first argued in the Smed at the Ranking. Except he had changed some words, fitted them into his own story. Did he like to write, too? I had "Do Tell." I wondered what the sheets of paper in his bedroom desk would read, what lines they were filled with.

No. He was insulting me. Saying I was two-faced. Or was he? Poems had countless interpretations. What was he implying now?

"The fuck does that mean?" asked Aksel.

A realisation—then words hopped from my lips before I could catch them. "It means he's ready to try something new."

Edric's jaw twitched. My cheeks reddened. And everyone shot confused glances between us. The animosity between Edric and I was no secret. While patrol shifts were never easy, I especially knew no one looked forwards to being on patrol with Edric and I. We steadfastly ignored each other yet were all too aware of each other all the same. The way I had just—*I don't know, defended?*—Edric was enough to make heads spin. It was confusing to *me.*

"You're right." Edric broke the moment of silence, then, making my confusion whirl faster, he slid a bowl of steaming beans underneath my nose.

Eyes were definitely bulging now.

"*Fine*, you do it," Jelena spat from pursed lips. "This better be worth it."

"It is." Edric ladled a bowl for himself, then sat down and began to eat, carrying on as if nothing out of the ordinary had just happened. His shoulder lightly rubbing against mine with each spoonful. I was hyper-aware of the empty spaces before everyone else, and the carefully placed bowl before me. "You've got two of us, Khalili."

That flicked attention back to Hartley. Except from Edric, who continued eating his beans. Somehow, that was more inflammatory than if he were to have challenged Hartley openly. The Caster's confident grin was nowhere to be seen. The longer I knew Hartley, the more I realised that the polished statue I had first compared him to was perhaps only a veneer. One that cracked under a certain kind of pressure.

Finally, Hartley responded. "If we do this, no one can tell Leden. Agreed?"

Heads promptly nodded across the table.

Hartley crossed his arms, taking up more of my space. I didn't like it. "Then I'm your third."

Kavi sighed quietly. It wasn't a sigh of relief, and the sound dampened the racing of my heart. She looked solemn, a slight droop to her big eyes. I wasn't the only one who carried a burden. Even though she held her back straight, I sensed the pressure of responsibility beating down on her.

"Nev, Hartley, Silvan." Kavi spoke with gravity. "The spell needs to occur at Midnight Gate in two days' time. And then you will be bonded." My stomach flipped at the reminder. *Getting bonded to Edric?* This was probably why she hadn't raised her idea with me earlier. "Like I said, the spell is only temporary. Magic this large is too powerful to hold for long. Even so, if it lasts until the end of the season, I think it's worth it."

Yes. It had to be worth it. There was no other choice that would keep us all safe.

The others made to leave, but I remained. I'd take my choices where I could, no matter how small they were.

I picked up my spoon and took a swallow of soup.

Malina's most recent letter assured me everything was normal at Amber Gate, and her apprenticeship was moving along well. I completed my reply to her and hastily responded to the latest batch of "Do Tell" requests, leaving them in Hartley's tray of outgoing mail. If he did not make it through tonight, someone else would take his crystal and act in his place. If I did not make it—a thought that made my legs weak—at least *Forever-the-Third-Cart-Wheel* and *I'm-Everyone's-Type-Except-Hers* would have their replies, and all the coin I had earned so far was willed to Malina. All was neatly settled—unlike the swirling in my body that felt like my organs were flipping over each other.

It was close to midnight when Edric, Hartley and I crested the lip of the hilltop on the coldest night of the season. Harsh wind blew hard against us, a warning to say: *This is forbidden. Go back. Back to what you know.*

The sky was clear of clouds, and burning constellations hovered over the clearing where Midnight Gate stood. Unlike the first time I had seen it, the centre of the hilltop appeared a deeper black than the rest of the surrounding darkness. I felt as though I was seeing Midnight Gate in its true form. A reservoir of ancient power. A consciousness in and of itself.

We stood beneath the tall, reaching stone, just as Kavi had told us to.

"Bring your strength, Nightfall," Edric muttered to me. "This spell is not for the weak."

Despite the warning, I knew it was not an insult. I heard what was unspoken. *You are strong.*

An unbidden swell of emotion followed, whirring inside me along with a medley of nearly every single feeling I had ever experienced in my life. For a final time, I held the vision of Kavi's determined brow as she had wished me luck. The look that had told me she trusted me. If I allowed myself to do this, then countless people would be safe, and I could solve all of mine and Malina's problems.

I surrendered to my decision.

"Take a breath," said Edric. Hairs on my skin prickled in a wave like grass touched by a breeze.

Hartley glanced sideways, before growling, "Let's begin."

Udahnite svetlost zvezda
Uvuci mracnosti korena
Veza korena i krv
U polnoch, pochinje.

The spell was written in the Old Language, where words themselves were infused with a magic that mortals could not wield. The deep voices beside me mingled with mine to form a harmony that sounded like the wind itself.

Breathe in the light of stars, the spell sung. *Draw in darkness of roots. Bond of roots and blood. At midnight, it begins.*

As if we had called it, that strange whispering wind returned. The same one I had felt during my first moments at Midnight Gate. It tickled me now with familiarity, and with something else I couldn't quite place.

Then it was accompanied by something new.

A vibration of energy pricked my scalp before rolling into my body with a shuddering force. My limbs shook uncontrollably, jangling my head and chattering my teeth. It was so strong. Almost too strong, threatening to push its way out of my chest and tear me into shreds. All I could hear was the whooshing of blood in my ears, turning my body into a vessel for pain. Were Hartley and Edric experiencing the same fate? My body was not in my control any more, and I could not turn to see them. I was caught in a battle with a force of energy that could empower—or extinguish.

There was a good reason why Kavi had been hesitant. Why Edric had warned me to remain strong. This power could destroy us. Destroy me.

Only if I let it.

I will not let it.

A flood of another kind of power surged. Something ordinary but mighty that had been long repressed, waiting to be set free. Something that would devour me if I did not hold it back.

Suffering. Desperation. Yearning.

I tore away my mental restraints from these shackled emotions and unleashed them. My own power collided with the magic of Midnight Gate itself, intensifying both energies like oil poured over a bonfire.

The powers mingled.

A different sensation entered my veins. Like a stream of cold water through a hot bath. The dizzying intensified, and I dropped to my knees. Phantom spots dotted my vision, but I held on with a clenching force that would surely grind my teeth into sand.

All at once, the pain was gone.

Wholly and blissfully released.

The stars above distorted as if shining behind thrown silk, and then the spell was absorbed into the atmosphere around us. My hearing came back to me, and I realised I was panting. Heavily and ragged.

"Was-was that it?"

I turned to find Hartley in a crouch, coughing, gaze fixed on the earth between his knees. A puddle of vomit.

Edric remained standing, dark head raised to the stars with an emotion I could not read. "Yes." His voice was rough, the only indication he had gone through the same thing. "The Kora is complete."

Slowly and unsteadily, Edric dragged himself away from the arch.

I watched until he disappeared into the gnarled darkness. He didn't look back.

CHAPTER FOURTEEN

E VEN WHILE I SLEPT, I felt Edric's and Hartley's presences as if they lay in my very room. Edric was only a few rooms to my left, Hartley one room further. They felt closer.

Malina would look forward to hearing about this. From a forgotten, powerless woman, to suddenly being magically linked to the most powerful people in Veligrad.

I am one of them, too.

I needed a reminder. Would that ever feel true? It was either devastating or hilarious to think that I counted as powerful enough to survive a centuries-old spell that no one else in the last thirteen years since the Fall of the Fae had deigned to try. I—who had been unable to escape stone—was apparently more powerful than any other Protector before me.

It was enough to give me a headache.

On top of a new connection with Hartley and Edric was the bizarre connection to the Kora spell's shield. The reason we had done this.

During the walk back to the Night Tree, the sky felt as if it pressed down closer, within a tickle of the tallest tip of branch. The awareness continued like a dome encapsulating the whole of Midnight Gate, its zhivir trees and their very roots, its portion of the Lutava River.

An invisible shield now protected Midnight Gate, and it was a part of me.

While I sensed Edric and Hartley in my sleep, I briefly dreamt of Toma. At Amber Gate tower, it was he I would fantasise about before I fell asleep, pretending my hands were his. I hardly thought of him now at all.

Even in the dream, someone else held my attention, though I could not see his face. Someone who led me away as Toma already faded into the background. Then my knees were either side of a strong, thick torso. His broad hands swept up and down my bare thighs while my hair dangled over what I knew was a dangerously alluring smile. Hands brushed up my ribs, skipping over my aching breasts, then moved gently to hold my face. He knew I sought more, but he also knew how hungry he could make me by dragging out his touches, making me desperate. My tut of annoyance only broadened his smile, so I widened my knees until my hips dipped low enough to reach—

"Having a good sleep?" A gravelly voice woke me to soft light. I blinked my eyes open, mind still foggy from the sleep that had claimed me the moment we had arrived back. After a few seconds of squinting, I horrifyingly realised who it belonged to.

"*Edric.* What are you doing in my room?" Limbs flailed as I tried to rid myself of a tangle of blankets, adrenaline spiking and preparing me for a fight. It felt like only a moment ago that I had watched Edric's broad shoulders disappear into his bedroom when we had returned, while I wondered about the strange new sensations the spell had left in my body.

And now I was awake, and he was here.

The sconce closest to the door was lit, and Edric leant against a post at the end of my bed, watching me struggle, something glimmering in his eyes, though his face remained serious.

"You're late for patrol. Aksel already went off by himself."

It was full dark outside. Yep. I was definitely late for night patrol.

"So you didn't think to knock?" I spluttered while finally kicking my blankets to the foot of my bed. I sat up on my knees, fists bunching into my nightshirt, which was firmly pulled to my bare thighs, squinting through blurry eyes.

"I've knocked only about a thousand times. I thought something was wrong after the spell. But clearly, you're . . . fine."

Edric was annoyingly tall and ridiculously broad, with a perfectly straight nose, and a rude half-silver smile that I would do anything to turn upside down right now.

"Well maybe it was the spell that made me oversleep." I wasn't lying. Something in my core writhed and shifted. An energy that was both hot and cold, both harsh and tender.

"What does it feel like to you?"

I paused at his question and dragged the blanket up to my hips. Hartley and I hadn't spoken of it when we had trudged back from the Midnight Gate arch while the stars seemed to watch us in the sentient way that stars do. Talking about what was going on in my core would likely turn my face as red as the High Gate ruby dragul. Instead, I focused on the connection I felt with the magical roots of Midnight Gate, of the invisible wall I could feel at the town's perimeter.

"It's like . . . brushes of fog against a window. Something drawing close before dispersing." I left out the fact that Edric's presence triggered something else within the Kora magic running through my veins. A strong roiling, like simmering water trying to escape the heat of flame. "What does it feel like for you?"

For a split second, it seemed that Edric's eyes flicked to the curves of my thighs where the rumpled blanket didn't cover skin. Before I could be sure, he straightened and strode to my wardrobe, opening its doors and looking in drawers.

"Nothing much," he said with his back facing me.

"Nothing?" I repeated, distracted by Edric pulling out clothes and laying them over his arm.

"Some of what you said." Edric returned with my uniform while my mouth hung ajar. He threw my thermal undershirt, trousers, shirt, jacket—even a pair of socks and a hair tie—onto my lap.

He had not ventured into my underwear drawer.

This is... different. And infuriatingly, I was curious.

"I'll be outside." He closed the door behind him.

I watched the shadow of his boots as he took a stance directly before my door. I stared at the two smudges, my fingers absentmindedly stroking tangles from my long hair. Realising what I was doing, I quickly dropped them in my lap.

Someone needed to slap me.

Malina's shining face popped into my mind like a sunflower. The mirth of her giggles when I next wrote to her would rival the ringing of a bell.

The presence of Edric's shadow guarded my door while I pulled on the clothes he had—confusingly—provided for me. He had to be in a rush to get back on patrol; that must be it. And he surely had to feel more of the Kora than he had let on.

"Which path did Aksel go?"

Edric flashed me a glance as I emerged, and I momentarily thought his eyes widened. He whipped his head away and stepped out of my path, resolutely avoiding looking at me.

"West, towards the arch. But it doesn't matter. There's something I've been wanting to show you since the first attack."

I swallowed. "What is it?"

He was silent for a long while. I let him. It gave me a chance to study the back of his head. The waves of his dark hair stopped above the nape of his neck. Not long and not too short, just enough to grip if I were to run my hands through it and—

What in the Seven Gates of Veligrad am I thinking?

I dropped my gaze to my feet. Okay, so, he had nice hair, maybe. It was simply a fact. Nothing I needed to think anything further about. Nope. More important things. Like whatever mystery thing Edric wanted to show me.

Hartley's voice floated up from the base of the Night Tree, speaking to some townspeople.

"Follow me," Edric finally said. "I'll tell you when we're away from here."

Edric led me over the stone bridge. I tried not to be distracted by a light pull in my chest again towards the river. Its dark water flowed as inconspicuously as ever, making it seem even more guilty of holding a secret. Whatever it was, any investigating would have to wait.

When we were on the other side of the bridge, Edric breathed two words: "Miran flowers."

My heart skipped. "*Here?*" I wanted to seize the front of his jacket but opted for stopping before him instead. "They won't open for us until the end of shadow-light season. But that's . . .

that's *great*! If you've found miran flowers close by, then when they *do* open there'll be more nectar easily available! Where are they?" The warm mist of my excited breath met crisp night air in large, white puffs that reached Edric's face as he peered down at me. His eyes slightly widened, and my stomach leapt. An effect of the Kora spell, probably.

At the exact same time, we twisted away.

"I've heard they're at the peak of Ruined Hill," he responded as we strode side by side, slightly apart. "There's supposed to be a witches' curse on the hill that prevents anyone entering, but I haven't yet tested it. Maybe now with our connection to the Kora spell, we could access it."

"Didn't you say this is where you were going to take me the day the vukodlak first attacked?"

Edric nodded.

"But the Kora wasn't yet in place then."

He waited a beat before responding. "I thought it might be worth a try."

My lips parted but nothing came out.

Edric believes in me. In my strength.

Even before we had known about the Kora spell, he must have already thought I was powerful enough to overcome whatever obstacle Ruined Hill might have thrown at us. Was he trying to make amends for smashing my nectar at the Ranking? He couldn't be. He hated me. My eyes begged to look up at him, to study that sombre expression, but I willed my neck to remain bent over the overgrown gravel path barely visible under moss and dirt, where little wolf teeth peeked through.

All I could deduce was that this was a mutually beneficial exercise. Everyone always wanted more nectar. He probably did, too.

Edric led me south-east towards a heavily wooded rise devoid of zhivir trees. We cast our dragul spheres, no lanterns weaving in between branches past the town settlements.

Strange urges rose up from my gut as we walked in silence—urges to speak, ask him questions, ask him about that little bird he had rescued and set free. I pressed my lips tight to hold those question in.

Further up the inclining land, the oaks and beeches started to appear . . . *wrong.*

On days when I had been bored in Amber Gate, I would play spot-the-difference between each and every tree branch in sight of my tower. I loved their variations, their unique angles, their curves and whorls. But the trees that watched us on our way were shaped like some of the corpses I had received at my mortuary—arms and legs broken, jutting in unnatural directions.

Beneath indigo fire, the path abruptly stopped as the forest greedily reclaimed this land mortals had deemed undesirable. We continued on until Edric suddenly flung out his arm and gripped my forearm, his touch instantly doing something to the pressure of my blood, shifting something in my core. "The last wolf tooth was over ten paces away."

My chest tightened.

The Cursed could be waiting ahead. We held our breaths and listened carefully to the small sounds of the wilderness. A softly hooting owl. The creaks of branches in the night breeze.

Edric's hold did not loosen.

"It'll be fine." With reluctance, I pulled my arm away. "We have our dragul spheres."

He glared at me. Well—it didn't look much like a glare, but it couldn't be anything else. He wasn't blinking, those thick eyebrows drawn tensely together as he breathed heavily through his nose.

Heat crept up my neck under the burning intensity.

I lit four fiery orbs above our heads, ironically to diffuse the growing heat. "See? We'll be fine." I took a few sluggish steps up the hill. The Kora was still doing things inside my body. Maybe making space between Edric and I would help it settle.

A heavy sound hit hard ground.

Behind me, Edric had fallen on his ass.

My lips quirked. "I think that's the first clumsy thing I've ever seen you do."

"I wasn't clumsy," he deadpanned, raising to one knee. "There's something stopping me moving forward. It must be the witches' curse on this hill."

"How come I can still—*oh*. My legs. That's why they feel heavy."

Yet I was still standing, and Edric remained on the forest floor. I tested my next few steps towards the incline. My legs moved slower than usual, like walking through mud.

"Was your grandmother a witch by any chance?"

My blood froze. "You *know* that I don't know." As much as I wished my voice was steady, it trembled.

A low exhale. "I'm only trying to understand why you can carry on, and I can't."

Slowly, I turned to his piercing blue gaze. For once, I was taller than Edric, above him on the hill, a couple of paces away.

He exhaled roughly. "It doesn't matter. This was a bad idea. Let's leave."

"Edric, the miran flowers could be up there, and we need to know."

His nostrils flared. "You called me—" He pressed his lips together, then shook his head. "It's not safe. Come back."

"I have magic to defend myself. The people don't. And they need more nectar." I couldn't bring back Malina's father Djordje. Instead, I could help stop the grief of countless others who lost loved ones when there was no nectar to access, when its scarcity made it so dear. "I need to know if it's true. If there's nectar here."

I twisted to the hill. Edric couldn't stop me or slow me. Leaving the tower meant I was in control of what I did—mostly. Anyway, *this* was my choice.

"*Wait.*"

When I turned, Edric was on his knees with one hand outstretched, a pained stare on his face.

My feet stopped.

I forced them away from Edric, knowing if I halted too long, something would compel me to go to him.

"I'll be quick," I called over my shoulder, ignoring the skewer through my heart. Especially ignoring the man left begging on his knees. How could one simple word ring with so much torment? Why could I feel that torment like a hook to my gut, trying to reel me back?

My veins were rushing with too much—the Kora spell's magic, my emotions.

I extinguished my dragul spheres, bar one. Maybe even the vukodlak couldn't reach Ruined Hill. *Let's hope.*

The contorted trees stood out as eerily silent guardians amongst the thinning vegetation, overseeing an ever-changing yet ever-the-same landscape of stiff branches and spreading moss. Not even the protection of my dragul sphere could bring me comfort, its light making the forest look even colder than it actually was.

Soon, treetops began to level out. My eyes followed the curve of the hill, finding the shape of a wide pillar at the rounded top.

A zhivir tree.

That must be where the miran flowers grew. My chest tightened. Only a couple more minutes of this curse-slowed walk. I went to ignite another dragul sphere, just in case something sinister waited for me at its peak—and that was when I felt it.

Heaviness.

My knees crashed to the earth with the force of stone blocks. I barely managed to break my fall before my cheek fell flat onto hard mud, eyelids aching with fatigue as if I had not slept in a hundred years. Dirt stuck to my lolling tongue as I lay on the forest floor, but I was unwilling to use the little dregs of energy left in me to spit it out.

This must have been what had happened to Edric, why he couldn't carry on. Was it diluted witches' blood in my veins that had allowed me to progress further than Edric, but not all the way?

My dragul sphere shrank, still remaining lit above me, a reluctant observer to my powerless, helpless state. My lack of control.

Panic started to build in whirls in my stomach, threatening to rise in my throat and suffocate me.

You're a Protector, Nev. You're free.

The voice in my head sounded a higher pitch than my own.

You better be here next season, Nevena Nightfall.

Malina's voice.

By the Seven Gates of Veligrad, did I miss her. I didn't miss my tower, nor Caster Leden's casual cruelty, but I missed Malina's freckled smile. She was the only person who had fully cared for me in the thirteen years of my life that I carried memories of. I needed to finish this season at Midnight Gate for her. And I wanted to find more nectar to help people just like her. It wasn't the magic of my dragul nor the spell of the Kora that rushed beneath my skin now. It was the magic of friendship.

My head faced the hilltop. Where I had fallen was about twenty paces from the crest.

The zhivir tree was so close.

I flexed my toes so that the balls of my feet dug into soil, then pushed. Next, my fingers crept forwards like two injured spiders until they gripped a protruding tree root above my head, then pulled. I repeated the movement. Push. Pull. Pause for breath.

Inch by inch, I crawled along. Branches, roots, and bushes took turns scratching me, never leaving me in peace. I was soon coated in dirt and blood. Maybe that was why the broken trees were here, to oversee fools who decided to continue up Ruined Hill, their twiggen fingers aimed to tease and taunt without mercy.

I wondered if Edric still waited for me. Or maybe he had simply left me here. Panic constricted my chest.

Breathe. That was something I could control. The forest air was colder along the ground, biting my lungs with sharp teeth. It was better than choking on fear.

Push. Pull. Breath.

The hill stopped slanting, and I pulled the rest of my body onto the level top.

Broken, charred tree limbs littered the base of what looked like the hollow remains of a burnt zhivir tree. Wrapped around the tree's roots were the stems of miran flowers, buds tightly closed. A slight moan escaped my lips as I reached one. The stem was supple and strong, but it loosened at my tug as I plucked the flower away and tucked it into my shirt.

And then my awareness fell away to nothing.

The shuffle of leaves nearby woke me.

The forest was pitch black. I let my senses check in with my body. It felt no different to before I lost consciousness. Which meant that I could move. Stifling a cry, I tipped myself towards the hill's descent.

Leaves rustled again, and another sound.

A grunt.

Was it a vukodlak? My heart beat harder, threatening to drain the little energy I had left, but I managed enough strength to dip my chin towards its origin.

The first thing I saw was the clench of silver teeth, bared in fury and pain, lit from a hovering dragul sphere the size of a small fist.

Edric.

Harsh lines of pain twisted deep into his stubbled, dirt-streaked face. Edric crawled, agonisingly slowly, towards me. He was smeared with mud, dragging his body over the night-dampened forest floor, punctuating the still air with a painful grunt every time he gained ground.

My head pounded as hard as my heart as a conflicting mess of emotions swarmed through me. Relief. Confusion. Wonder. No label settled as Edric hauled himself towards me.

The nearer he drew, the faster he could move. Life began to throb in my body again, too, as if Edric's presence was the warmth that thawed my ice. I painfully pushed myself onto all fours, and our gazes locked. I couldn't look away, and I couldn't move. A part of me wanted to relish in his suffering for all the ways he had hurt me, yet I suffered to watch him, too, feeling every throb of his agony as if it was my own.

He made it within reaching distance, and his heaving breath cast heat across my frozen cheeks.

I was panting, too.

Edric reached trembling fingers towards my crystal, and my skin pebbled in anticipation of his touch. The ghost of his fingers reached my throat before he suddenly dropped his hand to clasp around my wrist.

I saw the change in him as I felt it in myself.

Lightness. Strength.

He drew a shuddering breath and dipped his head into the curve of my neck, soft lips brushing my cold skin. I shivered. My hand found his giant bicep and I gripped the arc of its bulge, energy filling me further, like hot tea pouring into a mug.

Together we staggered to our feet.

"Nevena," he whispered hoarsely.

I could only stare back at him, my heart beating harder and faster. In my delirium I feared he could hear it sounding his name with each double beat.

Before I could break his stare, he slipped from my grip to his knees, his dragul extinguishing on the impact.

Edric was too weak. It was up to me to get us out of here.

On his knees, he still nearly reached my eye level. I hauled a heavy arm over my shoulder, letting his weight settle on me as he unsteadily rose again. With his arm secured with my hand, we stepped forwards.

There was no light to guide us, only the tipping of the earth downwards as we followed its descent.

Every so often, we stumbled and fell. Then we made it to our feet again, or sometimes our knees, drawing on each other for strength.

Step by shaky step, Edric and I staggered down the hill, clutching each other. I had no idea how far we had progressed, only that it was past the point where the magic had hit me on the ascent, the bubble of energy-draining power seeming to expand and follow after us, a punishment for daring enter its forbidden ground.

Despair seemed almost too exhausting of an emotion to host in my current state, but it seeped into me anyway.

Only a little further, I told both myself and Edric, hoping he could feel my thoughts in his head.

A moment later, Edric's balance faltered once more. He fell on his side with a heavy thud.

This time, he stayed down.

Oh, Vuk. I dropped to his feet, gripped his ankles and tugged. He barely moved a fraction, his mass of muscles as heavy as the earth itself.

I stopped and put my dizzy head in my arms while Edric lay quiet and still. I knew I would not make it back on my own without whatever connection of energy moved between us. Any thoughts of resting here were quickly driven out by how cold and weak I was, let alone Edric. It was the middle of shadow-light season. If we stayed the night, what little of us would remain in the morning?

I pulled at his feet again, a whimper escaping my lips.

"Edric," I rasped.

The desire to rest numbed away the very real knowledge that we should keep moving. I walked my trembling hands against the length of his body. Curling up next to him, my back moulded to his front, a shelter from the freezing, draining air, if only for a moment. His body twitched in response.

I stared blankly ahead at the frigid darkness. The jacket I wore was a hard, cold shell encasing my body, impenetrable even to Edric's warmth behind me. Wasn't that what I wanted? To be unbreakable from the outside. Let nothing else inside. Do everything on my own.

If being numb and unbreakable was this uncomfortable physically, why would I do this to my heart, too?

You don't know what could get inside.

I did not. Allowing room for friendship was one thing, but the muddle of feelings I felt for Edric? It was too draining to consider at this moment.

Especially as another noise penetrated the silent forest.

My body froze even more than it already was. Something large and heavy broke through the trees below. Before I could decide whether to spend my remaining strength trying to fight it, I noticed a glow.

An indigo light.

Hartley.

The Caster's face was a mask of furious determination. One that I regretted being at the receiving end of. He lurched his body onto a tree trunk, then stopped, breathing heavily. Spotting us, he lunged again and gripped a low branch.

The Kora: That's how he must know we're here. And it must have been his Heightened Power lending Hartley enough strength to reach us against the curse of Ruined Hill.

Just like with Edric, a wave of strength seeped into my limbs when Hartley neared. Edric stirred, feeling the Kora's bond melding and settling around us, too.

I had enough strength to shift to my knees, though my movements were still restricted. As though hands were pushing me into the earth.

Edric rose alongside me. Grasping each other, we unsteadily heaved to our feet, my face bumping clumsily into his chest. Edric's grip tightened on my arms. He did not let go.

Hartley lurched himself away from the nearest tree. His usual pleasant expression was livid with an anger that I never could have imagined on his face. Hartley snatched Edric's hand away from me and centred himself between us, an arm around my ribs. I could not tell if he did the same to Edric.

None of us had the energy to speak. I could hardly see the shape of land before our feet as we staggered across roots and rough earth, picking up pace as we moved further away. It was lucky Hartley held me up as my feet slipped and caught. The curse wasn't the only culprit. It was more to do with the fact that a different set of visions filled my mind. Gritted silver teeth. An outreached hand. A dark-haired man crawling. I was too tired to push them away. It was only that fatigue which kept me from staring at the object of my visions on Hartley's other side.

Finally, we were spat from Ruined Hill's curse and onto the meagre path where starlight twinkled like secrets through the canopy. The three of us collapsed on top of each other in a heap as power came flooding back. I lay still, simply breathing into the feeling of wholeness again, allowing arms and legs to remain intermingled amongst the others. I could hardly distinguish whose body part was whose. Somebody's legs were intertwined with mine, while my head lay on a squishy limb I gathered to be an arm. Another heavy arm lay across my ribs.

Both Edric and Hartley groaned deeply at the same time. The exhaustion had clearly affected me, because I wanted to laugh when I realised I could tell their groans apart. Hartley's sounded aggravated. Edric's was more like a warning.

Two more breaths passed, then limbs disentangled, the three of us crawling apart.

"What the *fuck*," rasped Hartley as he rose, "were you two thinking?"

The change in Hartley's demeanour was that of day to night, his usual calm confidence replaced with a look so violent it could rival the Cursed.

Edric stared ahead, resolutely avoiding Hartley's gaze, his chest heaving.

"I said, *what the fuck?*"

"Don't speak to her like that," Edric snapped.

Hartley's eyes widened, and then his brows contracted so fiercely they could have burst into flame. "I am your superior, Silvan. I can speak in whatever manner I choose. If I wanted you to, I could make you lick the filth from my shoes right now. You know why I won't? Because I use my fucking *head* when I make decisions. Not whatever reckless, unthinking reasons allowed you to even consider going up Ruined Hill."

"But there are—"

"I know there are miran flowers up there, Nightfall. Blocked by *another fucking witches' curse*. If it wasn't for the Kora bond, no one would have been able to retrieve the two of you.

That's another two Protectors down in Midnight Gate, and this power-sucking bond done for no fucking reason."

He kicked the trunk of a young nearby tree. It snapped like a broken neck, supple bark still attached on one side, but irreparably damaged forever.

Hartley stopped to stare at the pitiful mess he had made, then abruptly left, taking with him the light of his dragul sphere.

Neither Edric nor I lit another one.

"Why did you come for me?" I whispered. I knew the Kora had something to do with the pull we felt, but he could have sought help from others, knowing what would happen to him once he entered Ruined Hill.

Edric ignited an indigo orb. Slowly, he turned towards me with an unreadable expression. His jaw clenched hard, as though words were trying to burst through his lips, and he was holding them back. I knew how that felt.

Instead, he swallowed.

Wide shoulders hiked to his neck, he trudged in the direction of the Night Tree, glancing back to make sure I was coming, too.

The crimson flower was still tucked into my chest. It didn't matter if it was dry of nectar at this time of the season. I placed a tingling palm over the fabric where it rested. Now I knew I could reach Ruined Hill's peak, and Edric would follow me.

CHAPTER FIFTEEN

"**E**DRIC SILVAN *CRAWLED* TO you? Edric *Silvan?*" My gentle, steady friend was the closest I had seen to shocked. "I mean, I know the Kora creates a bond, but I didn't know it would be this . . . intense."

I had finished recounting the events of seven days prior, as Kavi and I patrolled a slate-grey afternoon through a neighbourhood of zhivir trees, their hollows spilling soft glowing light into the cold, dense air.

It was just her and I while Jelena took her rest shift between switching from day patrol to night patrol. I must have debriefed my thoughts to Malina more than I had realised, because without her communication, my need to share what had happened to me felt like it would burst through my eyeballs if not through my lips. Maybe—just maybe—it felt a tiny bit better to share my load with Kavi, even if it stung. Or maybe it was the way I knew Kavi listened with no judgement, leaving space for thoughts and feelings to take up as much time as they needed.

Maybe I needed to write a follow-up letter to *Regretfully-Seeking-Closure*, retracting some of my recommendations.

What I didn't tell Kavi was that I had chosen this particular route on our northern town patrol hoping to feel that strange tug towards the water that I had experienced before. That was something that could stay inside a little longer.

"It was lucky, really, that Hartley felt us through the bond. We would've been compost by now if no one had been able to help us. Even if Hartley was a prick." I frowned.

"Well, Nev," I squirmed through the ache at the nickname Kavi had adopted, unbeknownst to her that it was Malina's name for me, too. "You've just discovered that you *can* make it up Ruined Hill and back. Maybe that means when the miran flower blooms in between seasons, you'll be able to extract more nectar. It was worth it."

She was right. The miran flower had been empty of liquid when I had opened it, the inner buds a deep purple that had signified its immaturity. But I *could* access it again. A small smile twitched at the edges of my lips. As fast as it arrived, it was wiped away by something else that pressed against the insides of my skin, begging me to release it.

It probably wasn't important

It's important. Fatally important.

The voice in my head sounded like the one I used to respond to "Do Tell" letters.

Fine.

"Kavi, recently I've felt things . . . touch the Kora's shield," I admitted. "The day the spell was first cast, it felt like a light brush. But now"—I swept fingers along the cool curves of my hammer—"it feels more like something trying to poke through."

Kavi stopped walking. "Have Hartley and Edric felt the same?"

"I haven't spoken to them."

"It must be the Kora activating, telling you there's something at the border. You should speak to the others. The spell's only temporary, so any sudden uses of magic might destabilise it." Kavi's brow was scrunched in and up. "It's best to check."

She was clever and wise, and she was right. I had been thoroughly avoiding the two men all week, even on patrol. Meeting Edric's eyes would undeniably release a burn of embarrassment at all the ways we had held and helped each other. And Hartley? Thinking about him brought a sour tang to my mouth. That sourness felt more bearable than the flush I experienced in Edric's proximity.

"Alright." I sighed. "I'll find Hartley after our shift." Facing Hartley after last week would undeniably make my stomach curdle, but if there was a horde of vukodlak waiting at the border, Hartley needed to know.

The river remained silent for the rest of our patrol, electing to deny me the secret she had desperately wanted to share before. Begrudgingly, I let Lutava keep her silence.

At the end of our shift, Kavi stayed out in the town, having actually managed to befriend a townsperson or two. If anyone could do it, it was her.

As promised to my friend, I headed to the Night Tree to find Hartley. Edric's and Hartley's presences guided my way like following a rope.

But which one was which?

One presence felt like the heady sweetness of lemon rakija. The other held more tartness, like apple cider. The latter sounded like Edric.

Ignoring the taste of cider, I focused on the pull I knew would take me to Hartley, allowing my feet to lead as if following a route they had taken a thousand times before. Like running Amber Gate tower's spiralling stone steps, just like I was now spiralling around the walkway of the Night Tree—

Stop. I'm free from that place. Let it go.

Well, I wasn't really free. Not yet. Not until I could retire by the ocean with Malina.

I blew another breath out. I knew escaping Amber Gate's tower wouldn't solve all my problems right away, though I hadn't realised how many more problems could pile up. At least at Amber Gate I had been safe and close to Malina. But neither of us had been truly living. This was the price.

Not needing to think where I was going, I continued around the Night Tree's wide trunk, over a section of the walkway where branches twined above the path in dozens of miniature arches.

It led to the library.

I had never been here before—exhaustion, lack of time, and everything in between—and I hadn't expected this was where I would find Hartley.

That's because it wasn't.

Sitting beside a low desk in the dim, multi-levelled room, Edric stared at me with a slack jaw, silver lower teeth gleaming between shocked lips.

I stared back—frozen.

Images flashed before me of the pain on his face at Ruined Hill, of curling up next to his large body, of gripping each other as we fell and rose over and over again.

At the same time, we said, "What are you doing here?"

"Nothing," I said, as Edric said, "Reading."

Of course he was.

Mezzanine levels filled with shelves layered the space overhead, with winding stairs crossing the air to reach them. Edric sat in a red, oversized armchair, with *The Northern Serpent* spread open on the low desk before him, beside a stack of books. One dangled from his hand.

As if in a daze, Edric slowly rose and approached me with careful steps. "I, uh, was going to show you—"

Five paces away from me, Edric stopped, his jaw tense and eyes wide, as if I had just thrown him a blow. At the same time, something in my core throbbed in response to his nearness.

And then I was engulfed in an all-consuming agony—of desire.

Oh, Vuk.

I clenched every muscle and sinew and joint in my body to remain exactly where I stood while struggling against an overwhelming need to leap at the tall figure only steps away from me.

My skin felt too sensitive, my clothes too scratchy. They needed to come off so I could experience a grip I knew would be the perfect pressure of firm. This was stronger than any other lust I had felt, even in my wildest moments with Toma.

Why was this happening? Could Edric sense this, too? He had not moved closer, and while all this had occurred in the space of a blink, I prayed that Edric had not noticed.

Run. No, stay. Wrap your arms around his neck. NO, go back. Even my "Do Tell" voice was confused.

"W-what did you want to show me?"

Stay *it is, then.*

I trembled. Enough for him to notice. A bead of sweat rolled down my temple. My face had to be redder than a ruby with the effort of self-restraint, though my core urged me to give in with the ferocity of a thirsty gambler watching a fight where their favourite was winning against all odds.

Edric faltered, and the longer I stood there, the stronger the impulse became.

By the Seven Gates of Veligrad, resist, I told myself. *Stay.*

My feet took a step forward.

Oh, Vuk. It was the spell. This was all the Kora's fault.

"I found another volume of Rieka's poetry." Edric's deep voice was strained. His expression held the shocked look of someone caught doing something they shouldn't.

"Oh?" It was almost enough to intrigue me.

Almost.

On any other day, I would yearn for another volume of the words that had soothed and kept me sane the last thirteen years. There had been rumours of another piece of work, though Malina could never find a copy in Amber Gate. The reason for my visit faded to near insignificance, though I attempted to raise it back up, trying to ignore the thought that all I wanted was to cover myself in the sound of his voice. He could say anything into the shell of my ear, or whisper it over my skin, or trace it over my lips.

"It's called"—he took a dry swallow, making me aware of the corded thickness of his neck—"it's called *Sighing Winds.*" This time Edric took a step towards me, carefully, controlled, the book by his side. "I think you'd like it," he whispered.

My stomach fluttered like a flock of birds weaving and diving inside.

"Oh. Is-is there a theme?"

Edric did not move as I took another step towards him, leaving only a handbreadth of space between us. Only to see the book better, I told myself, but my limbs trembled with the effort of resisting touching him. I wanted to cry out his name.

Wanted to latch my fingers into the thick waves of his hair and not let go until all this tension was wrung from me.

His throat bobbed. "Acceptance."

Edric's blue eyes rivalled the illustrations I had seen of the ocean. The one place I longed to escape to. Those eyes bore into me with an intensity so deep that if I didn't drop my gaze, I would dive right in.

Where my gaze landed did not help. The thin, fitted shirt Edric wore was now damp with perspiration against his broad chest and beneath his arms. Higher up, the neckline was low enough to reveal prominent collarbones and a hint of his pecs beaded with moisture. Edric watched me with lips slightly parted, as if it was my hands travelling over him rather than my gaze.

Then he cleared his throat and snapped his gaze away.

We both spoke at the same time.

"I'll leave the book for you—"

"My patrol is finished so—"

We both made to move into the narrow gap between chairs—Edric's giant step two of mine—and collided directly into each other.

He caught me by the shoulders and attempted to quickly pull me away from him while I made to push against his chest, but it was too late.

The Kora had already won.

My fists clenched the fabric of his shirt as he held my arms. Neither of us could move. I felt his warm breath on my mouth as we stood frozen. The tang of citrus was on my tongue as if I had just drunk a bottle of lemon rakija.

He was probably hating this. Hating that the Kora was making us do this. *I still hated him, didn't I?* He was callous and careless and—

He took me to find nectar to atone. He crawled to me when I was stuck.

Even if I moved, I was afraid I would somehow fall closer. Was he thinking the same?

Edric finally managed to speak first, his words whispered rough and urgent. "Are you alright?"

"Yes," I breathed, and his grip on my shoulders tightened in the exact way my core ached for his touch, making me stomach leap.

"You should go," Edric said, but he only slid his hands slowly down my arms, like he was memorising their shape. Then he slipped them under my ribs, his fingers spread broad, pressing into me.

A tiny arch in my back pushed my chest forward.

"I should go," I repeated, my voice hardly better than a murmur. It was a lie, anyway. I did not want to go. My hands flattened onto his firm chest, with nowhere near enough pressure to move him away. Instead, I was introduced to the feel of his solid warmth, and his heart beating under my hand. I wondered if the look in Edric's expression reflected my own—a deep intensity, a hint of panic, and an undercurrent of need, heating my tingling skin. That heat spread across me like warm nectar, and I knew I was not made of paper any more, my chest no longer brittle wood, my heart no longer a fist.

Now, I was hot wax. Melting, malleable, willing to mould into any shape this man could bend me in.

His first name slipped from my tongue, like honey dripping into steaming water. "Edric." I pulled his chest closer, holding his gaze.

Edric's lips parted, and a short exhale escaped while his eyes flicked desperately between longing and wariness.

"This isn't what you want. You're not in your right mind," he breathed against my mouth.

But he was completely wrong. Between entering the library and landing in Edric's arms, I had come to accept that my desire was clear, and my mind was certain.

I pressed my lips to his.

Hard.

Edric groaned. His mouth opened together with mine. And everything exploded from our kiss.

A thrill raced through my centre, and my skin felt like it was on fire. He smelled of citrus and of the extinguished wick of candleflame, and I drowned in his scent, his breath, his tongue. *Him.*

With Toma, things had always been frenzied as we'd raced the clock, fearful of anyone discovering us. This kind of urgency with Edric was different.

There was a desperation in him to taste me, to know the feel of my entire mouth, to never leave it alone. Every stroke was deliberate—impatient from lack, not from external influence.

"Say it again. Say my name again."

My breathing turned ragged. "*Edric,*" I said into his mouth.

He exhaled sharply as his name released from my lips again, at the same time wrapping one arm around my waist and the other behind my neck. Holding me in a hard, warm trap.

Everything vanished while he held me and kissed me—any care of where we stood, any consideration of what might follow. Only the feeling of his hold on my body and his mouth meeting mine. The Kora bond seemed to sigh in release, almost satisfied with us. But not quite.

Edric's kisses deepened, his tongue moving further into my throat. Willingly, I let him, melting into his touch. At the periphery of my mind, a tinkle of wonder sparked a thought. Was it really the Kora's influence doing this? Kavi had said the bond it created was of protection, never a mention of . . . this. What if it meant I actually—

A throat cleared behind us, and Edric and I sprang apart like burnt hands.

It was Hartley, looking as sour as over-fermented apple cider, glaring at us with arms folded.

"What do you want, Hartley?" Edric's hard voice rasped, at the same time I shouted, "It's the spell!"

"Is it, now?" Hartley addressed Edric coolly. "That's funny. I haven't felt an urge to shove my tongue down *your* throat, Silvan."

My ears pounded. "We didn't even—"

"You know Casters can expel Protectors for improper conduct."

"There's no such rule." I clenched my fists.

"There is," said Hartley simply.

"She didn't do anything," Edric's deep voice grated. "It was me."

Hartley's lips twisted into a strange smile, as if that's what he had been waiting to hear. He ignored my weak protest of, "No, it wasn't." I didn't like the way the lines around his mouth twisted.

"Alright. Nightfall, what would you like Silvan's punishment to be?"

Edric was stone beside me, hardly breathing. He didn't object.

"Nothing. I don't want you to do anything." I resisted the urge to clutch my torso where embarrassment bloomed like a miran flower at the Ranking.

"I thought the two of you didn't get along. I thought you would want this, no? A chance to finally get back at the man who looks at you like you're half-Cursed, if he looks at you at all?"

"I said, I don't want you to do anything."

Hartley let out a soft exhale. "Well. As the Caster here, *I* could do something. But you know what I'm going to do? I'll grant you your request. And you know why that is? It's because I know when to make the right decision. I'm good at *using my head*." The false benevolence slipped off his face. "The two of you should try it."

It was then I realised Hartley could very well exert his power over us. All those weeks ago by the fireplace in the common room, he had told me he had a different vision for Veligrad—different to Leden's. Edric had doubted it then. I was certainly doubting it now, too.

Hartley composed himself to that calm, entitled expression I was familiar with. "Right then. Off you go to night patrol, Silvan."

Edric opened his mouth to speak, then closed it. Abruptly he strode away, leaving his notes behind on the table. I itched to swipe the pages filled with words written by his own hand. What did they say?

At the entrance hollow, Edric threw me a final glance. One that was as confused as I felt. I surely imagined the way it looked as though his hunger was not sated.

Then he was gone.

Hartley stood there for a moment longer, his cool glare sending a thousand warnings, before he left the library, too.

I let out a shaky breath. My skin felt cold without Edric's touch. Why had the Kora pushed me to want him, but not Hartley? When I chose to kiss Edric, I could accept it was because there was *something* like an underlying lust towards him. Whatever. His stubbled jawline was nice. So were his eyes. The sheer size of his body. How firm it was, and how comforting it felt to be enclosed in it. These were simply objective facts. Nothing more.

Once, there might have been some of that towards Hartley, too, but certainly no longer.

A familiar tinkling thought floated closer to the front of my mind. Surely everything that had happened tonight wasn't because I actually *liked* Edric?

Nope.

Not possible.

Something—the Kora bond or Ruined Hill or both—had simply triggered that small strain of lust. There was no *actual* want for him. No thoughts like that existed.

Except for the way he was curious to know me after he helped me escape the Amber Gate tower. And the way his lips are always begging to be bitten when he throws poetry at me with a scowl. Or the thought of him crawling, *literally* crawling *towards me. And the way that I knew it was his arm that I rested against when we finally made it out of Ruined Hill. The care in his actions when he saved that little, trapped bird. And—*

As these realisations whirled through my head, my body was not torn paper, nor was it melting wax.

It was all-consuming fire itself.

Oh, Vuk.

CHAPTER SIXTEEN

FOR THE FIRST TIME since arriving at Midnight Gate, a strain of something akin to excitement permeated the air. The Blood Moon Ball was soon to occur. There had been no further attacks thanks to the Kora spell. And amongst the Protectors, there was a certain momentum about the fact that it was over halfway through the season.

I could focus on being excited, too, when I blocked Edric and Hartley from my sight. Patrols had been reduced, deemed unnecessary, and most were conducted in pairs. The lax schedule had allowed me to avoid patrols with Hartley and Edric since the library incident.

"I just don't understand," said Aksel from under a thick scarf. "If doing this spell was all it took to Protect everyone from the vukodlak here, why didn't they do it before?"

Aksel and I were returning from patrol. I had made him walk along the river with me, secretly hoping to feel that tug again, but there was no repeat. Maybe whatever it had been was gone. Who knew what ancient magic still floated amongst this forgotten Gate.

"Ask Kavi." I yawned as the soft evening breeze caressed my cheek. "She said me, Hartley, and Edric had a lot of power, so I guess the others before us didn't."

"*Edric?* Not Silvan? He finally warming up to you then, Nev?" Aksel smirked. My cheeks prickled with heat. If there was one thing I could never hope to have total control over, it was that.

Aksel was not finished. "But surely the Casters could have been actively searching for the right three Protectors, and we should have all known about it. What's so special about *you?*"

Though I did not appreciate Aksel's unfiltered thoughts, his words mirrored my own doubts. "To be honest, Aksel, I've wondered that, too." But he was already focusing on something else. Two figures in the distance.

"Hey, is that Kavi? And why's she with fucking Dejan again?"

Dejan was a flutist who was to play at the ball, and one of the townspeople whom Kavi had befriended. He was also one of the few townspeople in Midnight Gate who appeared to have no issue with the Protectors. That was probably thanks to Kavi's nature. With a grunt, Aksel rushed off to confront the pair amicably strolling down a walkway of a nearby zhivir tree. Words of reproach towards Aksel died on my tongue as I felt something prick against the Kora's shield and winced. I was all but accustomed to the presence now, but instead of brushes and the occasional poke, they had turned into sharp prods. Every few days, I felt a twang at my awareness at the outer edges of the town, as if a needle was stabbing the invisible boundary, but it would always clear away after a few moments.

Edric and Hartley need to know. Speak to them.

Facing a pack of vukodlak would induce a lower heart rate than speaking to the two men who drew heat to my neck—both of a different variety.

Towards one: the simmering heat of anger. The other: a squirming heat that curled my toes, the memory of a certain act. An act that kept replaying in my head, over and over again. I couldn't stop it. The intensity with which Edric had kissed me. The taste of his tongue. Heat of his breath, his skin. Most nights were spent writhing in my bedsheets, torturously alone. It was fine. It was simply the after-effects of the Kora spell. That was all.

I yawned again.

Despite my feelings, I would have tried to find Hartley to tell him about the strange intrusions against the shield, but in the two weeks since the library incident, he had been distracted with other business. In celebration of the Kora spell's safety—which I suspected Hartley had communicated to the Council with credit on his behalf—delegates from all other six Gates in Veligrad would attend the Blood Moon Ball. It was common for congregations to be held at a different city each year, but Midnight Gate was never included in the rotation, except for now. The deaths of those killed by the first attack made me uncomfortable with the fanfare.

Kavi and Dejan recommenced their walk towards us while Aksel stomped his way around the Night Tree walkway and to his room. Snippets of their conversation reached me.

". . . I'm so sorry again."

"Don't." Dejan smiled reassuringly. "You have nothing to apologise for. I'm sure he's just tired after patrol."

Kavi returned a strained smile while I regarded Dejan's kindness. It was strange that in such a confined settlement, I still knew hardly any of the people who lived here. There was the town's general suspicion against Protectors and then there was my resting face. A repellent, for sure. Kavi certainly did not have that problem.

She sighed in greeting as she approached me. "Ball update. Needleworker will be here tomorrow at dawn."

"They're still insisting we wear civilian clothes then?" I had become quite comfortable in my midnight-coloured uniform.

"Not just clothes, Nev. *Gowns*."

"Let me guess." Dejan smiled at Kavi. "Yours will be a raucous yellow."

"Why do you say that?"

"It's the colour of miran nectar. Of something precious. It would suit you."

Kavi accepted the compliment with a bright laugh. "And what about for Nev, then? What would suit her?"

"Ah, for your friend, I would say . . . the colour of night. Of midnight."

Friend. My chest warmed.

"That's too easy," Kavi teased. "You're only saying that because we're at Midnight Gate. Or because of Nev's surname. Come on, we're making you in charge of picking the *perfect* colour for my friend."

Friend, again. One side of my lip quirked in the beginnings of a smile.

"No, really." Chestnut ringlets framed Dejan's honest face. "Without sun, the night both covers everything and contains everything within it. It's a powerful colour. The perfect colour for Nevena Nightfall."

The earnestness in his voice had me drawing back. "Do they teach poetry to flutists in this town?" I asked.

"They do at Moon Gate University."

Kavi's mouth fell open. "You studied at Moon Gate University? So did I."

Kavi and Dejan carried on chatting while the flutist's strange words clanged through my mind. I reached the bedroom floor up the walkway when Aksel quickly slammed his door from where he had clearly still been watching Kavi and Dejan, partially concealed from sight by the Night Tree's branches. At least I was not the only one having their emotions battered.

The next morning, it turned out Dejan had been right about our dresses.

And wrong.

As soon as the needleworker had placed a deep indigo fabric against my skin, I hurriedly suggested another. The colour of midnight made me look too different, somehow. Like I . . . belonged here at Midnight Gate. Something that was not in my plans. No, I would leave any plans—including the colour of my dress—to my own choice. My own control.

Snow only fell in the far northern Serpent Ranges. Its sweet, cold scent blew into Midnight Gate on the evening of the Ball, as I mistrustfully eyed my gown in the wardrobe mirror. It was the blue of glaciers that now sliced through the northern peaks of the mountains, leaving chunks of pale ice floating down the Lutava River. And although it was floor length, one entire leg was on display, thanks to a wide slit in my gown that parted all the way to my hip bone.

"It'll be fine, Nev. It's what everyone else will be wearing," said Kavi, while inserting small gold hoop earrings that matched the richness of her velvet, daffodil-yellow, halter dress, reaching all the way to her heeled, golden shoes. Kavi's usual braid had been unravelled and piled into an intricate bun, her face framed by two strands of loose curls. My hair had been styled by a member of the kitchen staff that Kavi had, of course, also befriended. It now flowed in uniform, dark waves to my waist. It was the only part of my ensemble I was pleased with.

"I can't walk in this thing—it's going to show my ass." I swung my hips from side to side, testing where the silky material swayed when momentum was applied. The only underwear suitable with this outfit was little more than strings, which I had to hike higher than my hips to hide.

"It won't," Kavi soothed. "Look, the skirt panel crosses over itself at your hip. That stops it from widening any further, see?"

From my mirror swishing test, that appeared to be true. For now. I sighed and re-examined the clingy bodice, which was hardly any better. Seemingly innocent at first, it sported long sleeves that flared wide at the wrists, and a neckline that flirted just beneath my collarbones. But anyone standing close to me would be able to notice how the fabric clinging to every curve and point was slightly transparent. The needleworker forbade me from wearing anything else underneath, should it lessen the effect of her design.

I wanted to like it. Worn on anyone else, I *would* like it. "If another attack happens, the Cursed are going to get a good look before they combust."

I stopped swishing and faced her reflection in the mirror. A thin, horizontal line creased her forehead as she fiddled with her earrings. Something heavy pressed onto my chest at seeing her . . . not herself.

"Are you alright?"

"Hm? Oh, sorry. Yes, I'm fine."

I let the silence remain for a few beats, something I had learnt from my friend. "Are you sure you're alright?"

She sighed and dropped her arms. "Actually, there is something." Another pause. "Remember Ryker Rada? At the Ranking?" I nodded. There was no way I would forget that hulking ball of anger. "Hartley said some Casters are sending Protectors as delegates for tonight, and I'm worried he might be here."

Kavi's brow was usually only furrowed when she was worrying about someone else. Whatever Kavi's history with Ryker, it had to be bad. I recalled at the Ranking he had made some sort of threat to Kavi's parents.

"There's nothing he can do to harm you here." I lifted my chest. "I'll stay by your side. What else can he do but act like the whiny brat he is?"

Kavi looked straight into her reflection, as if she wished she was someone different.

"Ask me to marry him."

My mouth fell open. "*What?*"

Kavi turned away from the mirror and sat on the edge of my bed, her shoulders slumped. I settled next to her, not quite touching, but close.

"Caster Rada of Moon Gate is his mother, and she's been trying to arrange this for years. At one point we nearly did, but then—" Kavi gave her head a slight shake. "I left Moon Gate because people are constantly trying to use me. My parents want me to live out a life they chose for me. Caster Rada wants me to marry his son. And Ryker . . ." Kavi's shoulders sagged. "This was the one way I could definitely leave Moon Gate without being summoned back. I think I was the only one glad to be posted at Midnight Gate." She gave a humourless laugh before her brow scrunched once more. "I can't stand Ryker or his mother. They're selfish. And they're . . . cruel."

Hug her. My arms twitched. I clasped my hands tightly in my lap. "That's why Ryker was trying to sabotage you in the Ranking—so that you wouldn't become a Protector. To keep you close." And marriage was the tool of choice. Not that Ryker had looked keen at the prospect. Perhaps his mother had him well under her control. "But why you? I didn't get a sense he . . . loved you, exactly."

Kavi fiddled with her glittering dragul pendant. "My mother is the Chancellor of Moon Gate University. My father's a history professor. The university still has some old fae magic around in certain rooms or objects. Many of the rooms are sealed. Caster Rada thinks the academics can access them." Kavi opened her mouth and snapped it shut. I knew what it was like to not want to divulge one's inner workings all at once.

"She wants something from the university?" I ventured.

"She wants power." Kavi exhaled harshly. "She always wants more power. When the fae fell, she went for political control of Veligrad with Caster Leden. She didn't think about the value of the university, so the academics quietly took it over. They avoid her as much as they can, so she doesn't read their minds, and my parents don't tell me what they do in case she reads *my* mind. There are mental practices that can shield one from her Heightened Power, but it's hard to know how effective they are."

"Shit."

"Exactly." The word was a weary sigh.

"So she wants to get close to your family and access the university. But you can refuse Ryker's proposal, right? Just like you've been refusing an arrangement over the years. And Protectors hardly ever marry anyway."

Kavi lifted her head to meet my gaze in the mirror. "So far, Rada hasn't used force against the university. But if I keep denying her what she wants, it'll keep adding marks against my family's name. I'm getting worried she's going to try and do something to them."

I didn't know what to say. So I didn't say anything. We sat beside each other, blinking at our reflections. While I had lived a life physically trapped, Kavi had been running from a different kind of enclosure. Perhaps we were more alike than I had thought. Maybe that was what Kavi saw in me, why she had sought our friendship from the start. That ache in my chest that I maintained only for Malina had long changed. My care for Kavi lay firmly there, too. I took a quiet inhale, and my heart sped faster as I reached a hand towards Kavi's where it lay in her lap.

A knock sounded at the door.

I let my hand fall back.

It was Aksel. He wore a dark jacket with a black shirt underneath, appearing almost too harsh in contrast with his pale hair and light eyes.

"Well, you look beautiful." His eyes were only on Kavi.

Kavi was back to her composed self again. "Are you here for a reason?"

He shrugged. "Just checking to see when we're all heading there."

Kavi eyed him suspiciously before asking me, "Are you ready, Nev?"

I stood and glanced in the mirror once more, cringing again at my dress. But there were some things to be happy for. After over three months spending time amongst trees, fresh air, *life*—my hair was no longer limp, my skin no longer ashen. Midnight Gate had plumped both, and I looked healthy. Living in Amber Gate tower, I had never really been ill, but the absence of life lived to its full potential was a different kind of illness.

I turned away from my reflection and joined Kavi and Aksel at the door.

"I'm ready. Let's go."

CHAPTER SEVENTEEN

C LOSE TO THE RIVERBANK, a little way from the Night Tree, hundreds of tealight lanterns strung along ropes entwined through branches. A ceiling of soft, twinkling stars spread above a dance floor of moss, while a red-tinged moon watched from high above. Gentle light refracted off sparkling gowns and suits of every colour, like dragul crystals. Pretty, but not pretty enough to make me forget I felt almost naked. A dressed-up icicle.

My heart beat faster as we strode beneath the first row of lanterns where magic kept the cold air out. Thank Vuk for that mercy.

"Will you stay beside me?" Kavi said in my ear, glancing around for any sign of Ryker's brunet head across dozens of round tables, and the open dance floor where couples and groups already danced and mingled. Next to the Ranking, this was the most people I had ever seen in one place.

I nodded—more times than usual—as much to reassure Kavi as to reassure myself.

Aksel overheard. "Aren't I good enough to escort you?"

"I don't need an—" Kavi paused, attention narrowing onto Aksel. "Actually, you might be perfect. There's someone who . . . I'm trying to avoid." Aksel quirked a brow, interested. "He's a Protector. From Amber Gate." Her cheeks flushed, before she added, "He wants to propose to me."

Aksel stiffened, then ran a hand through his blond hair. "You want us to fake date?"

Pulling back slightly, Kavi nodded, hands clasped beneath her chin.

"Aren't you dating Dejan?"

"We're just friends."

Aksel glanced between Dejan on the podium and Kavi, who was slightly taller than him in her heels. His brow smoothed a touch. "Okay, then."

Kavi threw him a grateful smile and slipped a hand around his forearm. Slowly and languidly, like warm honey, contentment oozed from their linked arms. The warmth was contagious, and my shoulders dropped a touch away from my ears. I realised I was grateful for both of their company, too. On my own, I might have felt as lost as a dropped leaf amongst litter.

A dropped, *naked* leaf.

I folded my arms across my thin, ice-blue gown, as Aksel led us to an unoccupied table. Kavi's cheeks flushed again as Aksel pulled her chair out for her. I suppressed a grin when he proved too distracted to do the same for me.

"Protector Nightfall." A sleek, rich voice interrupted me before I could take a seat.

Turning, I found plump, red lips stretched into a smile. They belonged to the woman who had been with Gorcha during the last vukodlak attack. She ignored Kavi and Aksel while taking in every detail of my attire beneath my crossed arms. Eyes darted over my hair, my face.

"How good to see you celebrating the Blood Moon in the spirit of the occasion. We are gathered here to surrender to the darkness tonight, after all. To chaos." She tossed thick, red hair over a backless, black gown and laughed. Not unpleasantly, yet somehow I felt the joke was at my expense. Dirt-stained fingers motioned over a staff member carrying a tray of wine. The dirt was a strange contrast to the impeccable wave of her hair, the dark gloss of her gown. She plucked two glasses, only for us.

Kavi's stiff posture told me she was listening. Closely. Aksel settled back into his seat, one arm draped across the back of Kavi's chair, position deceptively relaxed, but his movements were too still to be natural.

My friends.

"You are Gorcha's . . . associate?" I asked carefully as I politely accepted the glass filled with blood-like liquid.

Another rich laugh chortled in her throat where a bone-white crystal sat. Smooth as a pearl, though marred by a dozen hairline fissures. A patter of creeping spider legs ran down my spine as I realised they were real bones. Tiny joints of some kind.

"Not quite, dear. *I* extended the invitation to Protectors this evening." She dropped her smooth voice, her brown eyes glimmering. "I am Mother Noche. Of the Coven Noche. But that's between us." She winked.

Coven. The wineglass paused halfway to my mouth, its fumes already filling my nostrils with tangy strength. A warning.

"Were the covens not . . ." *Hunted. Murdered. Obliterated.* When the witches' magic faded away at the same time as the fae became Cursed, Caster Leden ordered witches to be killed, afraid that their loss of magic meant that they, too, were corrupt. They were not. I had seen enough of their bodies in my mortuary to know. In front of this woman who looked like the personification of lifeblood, it did not feel right to say it. "Diminished?"

Mother Noche laughed through her nose into her glass, then took a deep sip. She ignored my comment. "Are you aware, Protector Nightfall, of the extent of the Kora spell which you control?"

Control. Now I felt like I should laugh. That would mean I possessed power over it, which was far from the case. I was not sure if I liked this woman. Her eyes laughed at me, yet behind them was something hungry looking. Too intense. "Not entirely," I admitted.

Kavi shifted in her seat. *Be careful*; I could almost hear her words in my mind.

Mother Noche scrutinised me. "You are aware that the spell amplifies your strengths, your emotions?"

It certainly heightened a particular emotion.

I unclenched my thighs from where they had involuntarily tensed.

"I have awareness of the Kora's field of protection. And a kind of awareness towards Caster Hartley and Protector Silvan," I said delicately. "But nothing else."

"Nothing else? Not the knowledge of how to control it? How to wield it?" The woman's smile fell with the grace of a diving bird. "So much wisdom has been lost amongst the Casters and their little underlings." Elegant, dirty fingers curled around the stem of her glass. "Now, I wonder. Whether you are the same as them. Or whether you are curious to know more."

Her challenge rang clear. Part of it rang true. There was so much I did not know about Midnight Gate, about the Kora, about my own power. Here was someone offering more. But what reason did she have to share this with me?

Dejan's band of flutes and fiddles and drums abruptly ceased.

A smooth, amplified voice interrupted from the podium. "Welcome, people of Midnight Gate. Casters and delegates of Veligrad," said Hartley.

I kept my gaze on the deep-red liquid in my wineglass, avoiding looking up at his entitled face. Hartley was different to Leden in the casual cruelty and manipulations Leden wove. But Hartley had proven he was just another man trying to exert power and control over others. Despite all that, the prodding against my Kora shield was still there, and Hartley still needed to know. Maybe more wine would ease my reluctance.

I held my glass tighter and did not raise it to my lips.

"Tonight, we celebrate the alignment of the sun, the earth, and the moon. We celebrate the offerings of darkness. We celebrate the Blood Moon Ball."

Mother Noche kept her back to the podium as Hartley continued with introductions to the ball and the delegates, watching me with the intensity of a hungry hawk, waiting for my answer.

Could I trust whatever knowledge she claimed to offer?

I revisited my memories of Midnight Gate's people. The suspicion towards Protectors. The dedication to old fae ways. Their wariness collided with my own misgivings—my unpleasant impressions of Leden, of Hartley—cracking open a window of doubt.

I wondered if my assumptions of Midnight Gate's people were all wrong. Did they have a good reason to be wary? I thought Gorcha despised the Veligrad Protectors out of threat to his old ways, or even of threat to his swollen ego, perhaps. And maybe that was not entirely wrong. But the Council was led by Leden, and Hartley had turned out to be more power-hungry than I had once thought. Were they right to be mistrustful?

Meeting this woman—a witch—was like looking at light through different facets of a crystal, different angles revealing new shapes and shades.

What did I have to base my trust on Mother Noche, though? Her and Gorcha's disdain for the Protectors was evident. They could've been the ones risking our lives by moving the wolves' teeth. What motive could she have to speak to me now?

"I am pledged to the Protector's Vow," I finally said. The words were thick on my tongue.

"So you choose ignorance." Mother Noche's fierce gaze shifted into something pained, something urgent. "Reconsider, Nevena, dear. The Coven and our people will meet at midnight by the Gate. Our ritual. You can join us there if you seek more . . ." She paused, lids half lowered. "*Control.*"

Hartley finished his speech, and music recommenced, a faster pace than before, matching the speed of my racing heart. Mother Noche made to move away, then stopped. "And, daughter? Know that the Kora spell will only heighten what is already there. Enjoy the Blood Moon Ball." With a knowing look, she disappeared into the throng of dancing bodies.

Daughter.

How could one simple word be both disquieting and comforting at the same time? It was simply a term of endearment, wasn't it? Her name was *Mother* Noche. Maybe she called everyone *daughter*.

Or maybe she knows something about me.

"You're not really going to meet with someone who thinks she's a witch?" Kavi asked. Pushing away the strange urge to follow her, I reluctantly lowered into my seat.

"I don't know."

I twisted my neck, trying to catch a glimpse of Mother Noche through the crowd again, but someone else stood directly in my line of sight as the crowd parted almost deliberately.

Under lantern light, Edric's hair gleamed dark like nighttime water, his head topping the dancers as he shifted his weight slowly, comfortably, from foot to foot. Was he . . . *dancing*? A glass in one hand, the other hooked at the base of his dagger-lined suspenders over a clean, white shirt, fitted perfectly to the swell of his torso. Tight enough to encapsulate the bulk of his arms. Not so tight that he looked like those men who thought smaller-fitting clothing would make their muscles appear larger. No, Edric needed no help from his attire to look thigh-clenchingly *huge*.

I swallowed, trying to hydrate my suddenly dry mouth. My stomach flipped, and a small voice asked if I was certain if this was even the Kora's effects any more when Edric wasn't physically near enough for anything like *that* to happen again.

He made no move closer to me, didn't look my way, yet I knew he was aware I was sitting here, watching him.

Though Edric was clearly a Protector, townspeople's eyes tracked him with desire. Dancing bodies neared him, moving with suppleness and invitation. Edric paid them no attention. He pulled a small leather book from his pocket, and started reading it, as if it was the most normal thing in the world to dance alone and read. I knew what silver letters embossed the title: *Sighing Winds*.

I uncrossed my arms, chest suddenly feeling hotter and tighter.

"I don't think Ryker is here. Neither is Rada. Or Leden," I observed aloud, trying to distract myself from the fact that the bristles of Edric's stubble looked just soft enough to run my hands over. I dragged my foolishly reluctant eyes away from him. Our kiss was a mistake. It would never happen again. He wouldn't want that again, anyway. Of course he wouldn't. Edric hated me. The kiss was entirely the fault of the Kora bond.

"Thank the Gates of Veligrad." Kavi took an audible swallow of wine that Aksel had procured while I had been . . . distracted.

Aksel leaned his forearms on the table. "Let's go dance, then."

Kavi blinked. "We don't have to fake date any more."

"Maybe we still should. In case he comes late." Aksel wore his usual tetchy frown, but for the first time I noticed a steadiness behind it. Something sturdy, something honest.

A slow smile parted Kavi's lips. "You like to dance?"

Aksel shrugged. "I'm good at it. There are dances at Tide Gate all the time."

"I know, I've been to some."

"I know. I've seen you there."

Kavi's jaw dropped, and I didn't miss the quirk of Aksel's lips at her reaction. She quickly closed it and swallowed before turning to me, a slight breathiness to her voice. "Okay. Let's go. Nev?"

"You go. I'm fine here." Dancing meant exposing the thinness of my dress. People weren't drunk enough yet for that.

Before Kavi's sympathy could stop her, I added, "Really, I am. Go and enjoy yourself."

The lines above her cheeks crinkled slightly. "I will." With a squeeze of my hand, she swept away with Aksel, her long, velvet gown standing out with the brightness of the sun over Midnight Gate's cold landscape.

Good for her.

I pushed my drink away from me. Speaking to Hartley could wait until *he* had drunk a few glasses of wine. I didn't want to know what would happen if I let myself go with Edric only about eleven people's widths away. Not that I had counted.

If I sat right here, nothing unexpected would happen. I was in full control. I could relax. Or try to.

"Nevvy."

Oh, Vuk.

Not relaxing.

"Toma." I stood. "What are you doing here?"

His brown hair was shorter than before, closer to his scalp. Something else was different about him, too. Deep lines in his forehead. Brackets around his mouth.

"Caster Leden sent me and a couple others as delegates. He didn't want to leave Amber Gate unprotected." Toma's eyes roamed over the top of my dress and down to my bare leg. I pressed my arms tighter around myself. "But really, Nevvy. I've missed you."

Before I could react, Toma lifted me into an embrace, my feet rising off the ground, the scene drawing laughs from tables nearby. Of course it would bring them mirth, witnessing a loathed Protector finally looking less powerful than what my dragul pendant granted.

I pushed at his chest, but his hold was tight.

"Miss me, too?" He spoke into the crook of my neck, the sharp blades of his freshly shaved skin pricking uncomfortably. I was wholly aware of every inch of unwanted contact. The thinness of my gown pressed into the bulk of his frame. The fact that this was all in public where it had once been private left my cheeks warm and my forehead beading with sweat.

"Put me down," I hissed, smacking against his shoulders. I could do *so* much more than a hard smack, but we'd drawn enough attention already.

"Wait, I wanted to talk to you. It's important." He placed me back on my feet but held on to a wrist. "It's about something happening at Amber Gate."

I snatched my hand away and glared up at his height. "What about Amber Gate?"

Toma sat down heavily next to my seat.

Great.

What gentle light reached his face highlighted shadows beneath his eyes, which were obvious now that no smile creased his cheeks. "More townspeople have been going missing."

My chest exploded. "Malina?"

"Who? Oh, your ceramicist. No, no. But over three dozen people have. I've spoken with Caster Hartley already, but I wanted to tell you myself."

The sharpness of my fear transmuted into a deep tension in my neck. I slid into the chair beside Toma. *Three dozen people.* That was even more than all the deaths at Midnight Gate combined.

"How are the Cursed doing this? And since when?"

Toma looked directly at me with a hollowness in his eyes that had never been present in all our time at Amber Gate. The magical warmth in the air seemed to dissipate, the twinkling lights no longer so pretty.

"We haven't been able to figure out a pattern, but it happens often enough. Sometimes we find them in the Smed. Drained and dried out. Telling their families is . . ." He left the sentence unfinished, his voice raw. "When we don't find them at all, I worry even more. That they've become Cursed, too. That there'll be even more of them out there."

A memory I struggled to suppress resurfaced. Ander Silvan's hollow face. His widened eyes before my hammer hit his skull. Clenching my fists, I willed the memory away, focusing all of my attention on the too-close proximity of Toma's knee to mine.

"Shit."

Toma's attention suddenly narrowed to my lips at that word, and his eyelids half closed. I felt his full awareness on me like it had never been before. His voice came out rough. "In all our time at Amber Gate, I don't think I've ever heard you swear before."

A hand snaked onto my knee.

I smacked it. Hard. "Don't touch me, Toma."

He pouted like a scolded child. "What do you mean? I thought you wanted this?"

I spluttered with indignance. I had told him time and time again what I didn't want. Why couldn't he *listen*? Why did I need to keep repeating myself, only for my actual wants to be ignored?

Before a coherent response could form on my lips, a deep, curt voice rumbled, "She *said* she doesn't want you to touch her."

Edric was behind me, one hand resting on the back of my chair while his gaze locked onto Toma.

"Edric," I bit out and slammed my hands to the table edge, gripping hard to prevent my body jumping out of my control. "Get away from me." I did not know how he had managed to draw so close to me without the Kora's awareness activating, but now his presence consumed me as if I was wood in the middle of a hearth, engulfing me, burning me.

Toma's chair scraped loudly back, and he took a threatening step towards Edric. "What have you done that she doesn't want you around?"

The revelry in our vicinity dipped, as people took notice of the unfolding spectacle. Edric returned Toma's move and stepped closer to him, so that I was almost sandwiched in between them where I sat.

"The thing is, *guard*, I think it's *you* she doesn't want around."

Toma growled, then shoved Edric with all his strength.

Except Edric didn't budge. He glanced down to where Toma's hands had touched him, as if they were coated in grime. Then he skewered Toma with a look that threatened violence.

"Touch her again," Edric purred, "and I'll break off your hands. I'll string your knuckles on a pretty necklace, then I'll offer it to her as a gift. That is the only way your rancid fingers will ever meet her skin again." Silver teeth bared in a growl, white canines on display like a wolf.

I clamped my thighs together. Then suddenly Toma was flying. He landed three tables away with a crash.

Good.

The space created a moment for me to jolt out of my seat. To run before the yearning inside me made me do something

I would regret in front of every person already watching me with far too much attention.

I sped as swiftly as I could through the dancing crowd. There was no time to notice whether the part in my dress slit revealed anything more than my leg. Behind me, glass shattered and raised voices intervened.

Frozen air assailed my skin as soon as I left the ball, imparting blessed clarity to mind as I sped towards the Night Tree walkway.

These *men*.

Clearly, big egos needed little fuel to explode. Neither of them owned me, had ever attempted to make any claim for a title as partner, for neither of them truly cared about me. Who would want to lay claim over a Mortician or a murderer? If it wasn't for the Kora, I would enjoy seeing the damage they caused each other over *nothing*.

A quiet voice in the back of my head reminded me there might have been something potentially *thrilling* about seeing Edric defend me.

Had it felt good?

Okay, yes.

Was it necessary?

Absolutely not.

Did it maybe feel a little bit more than just *good*?

I shut a heavy door on that thought, my chest heaving. Sparkling lanterns watched me through branches like little giggling guardians as I hurried around the Night Tree's wide trunk.

My room passed as I sped on, needing more space, more air. When the library door came into sight, I ground to a halt, panting. Though I was used to the incline, it was not the run that made me breathless.

My pulse refused to slow as hard footsteps sounded, nearer and nearer. I knew whose they belonged to before he appeared around the curve of the thick tree.

Edric stopped when he found me, his lips slightly parted and eyes wide. One cheek had a purple tinge, and his hair looked tousled. I tried to ignore the hitch in my breath at the sight of him and took a step backwards.

"Why did you follow me? You know what will happen."

He remained where he was, deliberately still. "We can control it."

This was the second time this evening I had heard that. But now was not the time for tests. The effects of the Kora began to burn my centre again, and I spun away from Edric, focusing on leaping the few more steps to the library door. Clutching the doorknob felt like hanging on to a rope on the edge of a tower and—*Nope. Not a helpful analogy.*

"Been there before, Silvan," I said without looking back. "And I could not control it."

"Nevena, listen." *Nevena*. "There's a gemstone that suppresses the effects of the spell."

"How do you know?" I peered over my shoulder to find he hadn't moved. Had Mother Noche spoken to him, too?

"I've used it. You can use it, too." His whole body was still, steady, as if worried of frightening a small creature.

"Why are you even doing this? I would've thought you'd be glad. This is your reason to stay as far away from me as possible. Isn't that what you've always wanted?" I thought of every time Edric had clearly stated his displeasure towards me. I remembered every clenched jaw and narrowed gaze. "You told me to run, Edric, and I did. Why are you here now?"

Edric said nothing, muscles in his jaw standing out, while my chest rose and fell.

Through his deep-blue eyes, he saw a murderer. Through my brown eyes, I saw a stubborn, unforgiving man. Why, then, was he holding my gaze with the intensity of smouldering wood? The beginnings of wonder trickled through my mind like leaks through a cracked jug. Perhaps Edric also saw . . . something more. Together, in my glacier dress and his white shirt, I was starlight and he was moon. Did they ever touch, the stars and moon?

"I'm here now." His gravelly whisper sounded pained. "Because I was wrong." *Oh.* My heart raced as Edric reached into his pocket without breaking our gaze. "Catch."

Something small shimmered in the air. I caught it, a soft coolness landing in my hand. Inside my unfurled fingers was a bracelet. Its chain looked to be made of the same fine silver as the dragul necklace at my throat. Small gems dangled from tiny links, the colour of midnight.

"What is this?"

"A family heirloom. It lifts enchantments for the wearer." His voice was the low rumble of distant thunder. "Put it on."

Curiosity burned hotter than confusion.

A soft gasp escaped my lips once the bracelet slid onto my wrist. The sensation of the Kora spell disappeared. No more stabs at the edges of my awareness. No more shield.

"Can I come closer?" The thunder in his voice grew heavier, a storm on the verge of breaking.

I nodded, facing him fully.

He took a step towards me, then waited. Completely still. Attention fixed wholly on my reaction. Eyes flicking between mine, over my loosening arms as they moved to my sides.

"Closer?" Edric asked, explicitly waiting on my consent.

I nodded.

He took another step. The same question appeared in the slight dip of his chin, thick brows raised. Waiting again for my nod.

And again.

Tingling in my palms spread up my pebbled skin with each step Edric took. My heart pounded so heavily inside my chest he could surely hear it. I knew the Kora was no longer working its bond between us. That meant it was my own body's fault my breathing was ragged as the distance closed between us, and that it was my own eyes' fault for drinking in every curve of muscle bulging from his arms and shoulders.

Edric stopped when the gap between his chest and mine was as small as the bud of a flower—tight yet delicate. So close that I could see the wetness on the inside of his full lower lip, touching his silver teeth.

"Is it working?" His murmur was as soft as rainfall kissing stone.

It will only strengthen what is already there.

"Yes," I whispered.

And then I fully relinquished control.

CHAPTER EIGHTEEN

M Y LIPS CRASHED INTO Edric's with the ferocity of a hailstorm as I pulled his thick leather suspenders into my chest, not caring about the discomfort of cold metal hilts digging through my fine dress.

My control was not relinquished, I realised. Rather, I held it in full. Taking it back from the Kora's influence and wielding it to my own will.

Edric stumbled backwards a half step, our lips connected.

Vuk. Maybe he doesn't want thi—

Strong hands seized my waist and pulled me against him even more firmly.

The moon and a star colliding.

Edric kissed me back, mouth covering mine in a hunger that outmatched anything I had ever experienced—could ever imagine experiencing. Was this truly what Edric wanted? To be kissing me?

It only strengthens what is already there.

The bracelets gave us our own control back, and still Edric chose this, just as I did. A thrill reverberated through me so strong it would either burst into a sob or laughter. It culminated in a desperate moan that reached the back of my throat, stifled from escaping any further by the pressure of our mouths.

I suppressed a whimper when he suddenly broke away from our kiss.

Hoarsely, between heavy breaths, Edric said, "The Slom bracelet—I don't know how, but it isn't working. We should—"

"It works," I breathed back. "This is all me."

Our chests heaved against each other in tandem. Edric searched my face. His brows furrowed, a slight gap between his lips. An unspoken question.

This is all me. My stomach knotted at the truth of my words spoken aloud while my frantic mind darted to answer the question, *Why?* Maybe it was the ropes of tension we had tied between us, fibres too taut and ready to snap. Maybe it was the curiosity from our very first meeting, desperate to be satisfied. Was that all it took to ignite a spark?

Something deeper stirred in my gut, gurgling with words like *compassionate* and *intelligent* and *empowering*, then the words of his admission, *I was wrong.* I pushed them away in favour of the licks of desire that clambered higher in my core. Thoughts like that could cut deep if they were wrong. No reason mattered. It just felt right. Necessary, even.

A curved lock of Edric's hair touched the tip of his long, dark lashes, quivering as he blinked, eyes flicking while his hold on me remained firm. "This is all me, too."

It was a murmur, soft as a feather that knocked the breath from my lungs. Then Edric's mouth covered back over mine, desperate for us to only breathe the same air. Each stroke of his tongue tasted as sweet as sugar thrills riding through my veins, and my chest rocked against him in time with his mouth. Another roll of excitement roamed over my skin when my tongue swiped the smoothness of his silver teeth, the part of him that all others saw, but that only I touched. He groaned into my mouth, the reverberations drilling into my core.

From below, deep drums and fast fiddles whirled their music into the evening air that coated us like a secret veil. Edric's hasty breaths and deep grunts were the only thing I truly heard.

I swept my tongue against his smooth, silver teeth again, slipping my arms around his strong neck, eliciting another deep groan. Edric rewarded my daring tongue by winding long strands of my hair around his fingers until his fists were wrapped, drawing a hint of tension at my scalp.

Nothing in my life had ever made me feel so *alive.*

I shuddered, pressing my breasts into his torso, sweeping side to side against the stiffness of leather suspenders. The friction against my nipples was too good.

Something about that action did it for Edric. Through the thinness of my gown, I felt the hard bulge of his length.

He growled into my mouth. One fist of hair released, then his hand was immediately on my hip, as if he couldn't bear to not touch me. Rough bark hit my back as Edric pressed me into the trunk. I didn't care. I wanted to feel more. To make up for every stolen moment from life that had been taken from me. I wanted Edric to be the one to make it up.

He pulled back. Only a little, so our noses nearly touched, while his eyes flicked between mine, curious and searching. They were a perfect shade of ink blue, so deep my mouth dried with thirst.

"This is familiar," Edric rasped low. Head bowed over mine, dark locks dangling over his forehead. "You and I, alone next to a tower, while the whole town is distracted." Reverberations rumbled through my chest, drawing a shudder. "Or maybe you liked it more when I had you at the miran flower. You never returned that dagger, by the way."

Memories of the Ranking flashed through my mind. I narrowed my eyes.

"That's because you were a prick," I said, but the lack of air from our previous exchange made it sound softer than I had intended.

Warm breath skated over my mouth. "Hm, was I?" His lips skimmed mine as he spoke, the barest hint of contact somehow throwing me to a ledge where everything coiled tighter with anticipation.

"Yes," I breathed, pressing my hips into his hard cock. He held unnaturally still. "Edric, the prick." I immediately cringed. *Vuk.* Why did words always fail me with this man?

Head tilted, Edric tutted. "When I have you, I'll make you regret calling me that."

"Oh."

He nipped my bottom lip, the gesture of familiarity sending a tingle of pleasant surprise down my spine. "Besides, I have a much better name for you, Nevena Nightfall. I think"—another nip—"you just might be my *nightmare.*"

Oh. It was a reminder of our first meetings together. His hatred towards me. My anger towards him. Perhaps I truly was his nightmare. Behind the newness of this banter, I felt as if we held each other not against the solid trunk of this tree, but at the opposite edge of the walkway, one wrong move from hurtling a long way to the forest floor.

"How is that much better?"

His voice rumbled low, like boulders rolling against each other. "It's a compliment." Strands of hair touched my forehead as he bent over me. "It means you're in my dreams."

Edric skimmed his lips past my mouth, my cheek, landing on my neck, while I let his words sink to a place deep within me that I hardly knew existed. I responded with a violent shudder as he kissed a sensitive spot below my jaw. Then his hot tongue slid across my flushed skin. I bit my lip at the sensation and rolled my hips against him, the ridge of his cock pressing against me in return.

By the Seven Gates of Veligrad did I want this.

I lifted my bare leg around his hip, the slit in my dress now fulfilling a purpose. Edric finished what I started and hoisted my ass up so both my legs wrapped around him. I gasped at the sensation of my clit perfectly positioned against him, the tiny material of my underwear hardly providing a barrier to the intensity of sensation. Edric would surely feel my slickness seep through his trousers, too.

Somewhere far below the walkway, the thud of a door slammed shut. Without breaking our contact, Edric lifted me properly into his arms, and carried me with his lips still on mine, uncaring for anyone that might be looking up. I didn't care either. Possessing his whole attention made me giddy and light-headed. My lips were swollen and stinging by the time he stopped outside his bedroom door.

Edric pulled away, the motion appearing controlled, but his gaze was feral. "Is this what you want?"

"Yes." I arched my chest against him, urging him with my body to hurry into his room. He remained still.

"I need you to be sure." His whisper was a muzzle over the desperation that strained his neck tendons. "Are you sure this is what you want?"

"*Yes*, Edric," I rasped. "*Yes*," I urged again as another slamming door sounded. My chest felt lighter at that one word.

Edric's expression shifted into determination. Mouth closing over mine once more with a groan, he hauled me into his room.

The door remained open when he dropped to the edge of his bed with me still wrapped in his arms. My knees slid to either side of his hips in a straddle, the angle giving me a foretaste of what was to come without the barriers of clothes.

"Fuck," he breathed, then pulled back. Edric's eyes roamed the view before him while his thumbs swept back and forth across my ribs, tipping the underside of my breasts, reminding me of a dream I recently had.

I felt him harden even more—*was that possible?*—as his gaze fell over my peaked nipples, their darker colour fully visible now through the thinness of my dress. His lips parted, and he ran his tongue over his silver teeth.

"Why did you choose this dress, my nightmare?" His calloused palms roamed the curve of my hips, fingers spread wide as they swept over my thighs, then squeezed my calves.

I tipped my head back at the tingling sensation that trailed from his touch. I needed him all over me. Whatever the Kora had made me feel before was nothing compared to the need I felt now.

"Did you do it to torture me? To make me watch you be yearned for by others—*touched* by others?" His voice broke. "Knowing it could never be me?"

Vuk help me, Edric's words mingled with his presence and overwhelmed my senses. The strength of his intoxicating, saline skin. The hold of his large hands gripping me. I imagined this was what it would feel like to dunk myself whole into the Lutava River at once—no air, all panic and thrill, covering me, holding me and pressing into me all at once. Whatever I had expected Edric's thoughts about me to be—I had not expected this. How long had he been watching me? My mind tinkered with a realisation that made my mouth dry. Longer than just tonight.

"Edric—the door," I urged, now needy to have him all to myself.

He breathed one short, harsh laugh, then slid me off his lap to sit on the bed. Heat roiled in my core as he dropped to his knees before me, ignoring the open frame of night.

Large, gentle hands unbuckled each of my heels, pulling them from my feet and dropping them on the floor with a loud thud.

"Did you enjoy thinking to yourself how I would lose my damn mind," he said, his voice rougher now, "when I could finally see every curve? Every single detail?" He swept his hands over me again, and this time he did not hesitate to travel higher, his thumbs swiping my nipples.

I gasped, the sensation heightened by the friction of the fabric, sending pleasure directly to my core as if he was touching me there.

"You could have worn anything," he continued, kneeling before me, "and I still would have torn apart anyone who tried to claim your attention."

Oh, Vuk. "What did you do to Toma?"

Edric stilled. From his position, his gaze was a level height with mine, carrying a deepening ferocity that should have been terrifying.

It was exhilarating.

My veins rushed with energy while my heart pounded with a greater intensity than I could ever recall having experienced.

"I'd prefer if you don't speak about others when you're with me, *my* nightmare." Edric swiftly rose to shut the door. When he turned back, his muscled forearms were tense at either side of his body, bulging through the sleeves of his shirt.

His voice as soft as rustling leaves. "Only mine."

The words themselves felt like they formed fingers and stroked my core, clamping my slick thighs together.

Edric stalked towards me. I leant on my forearms, but he pulled me backwards onto his lap and sat on the edge of the bed again, facing our reflections in his full-length mirror.

My eyes latched onto Edric as he trailed his lips down the curve of my neck while one strong hand squeezed my ribs, pressing me back into him. The other hand moved to the slit in my dress, peeling it away from the bareness beneath. Languidly, reverently, he parted my legs until they were wide.

"Mine," he whispered. And then he slid black lace to one side, exposing me to the mirror's reflection.

There was no space to feel shy when Edric released a ragged breath at the sight of my slickness. He pulled my underwear further aside to make room for his fingers, then circled my clit in firm, tight motions. Another ragged breath reverberated against my back, blowing warm air into my ear.

"What's your favourite poem?"

There was no way that question could be so erotic. Slowly, he pushed a finger into my centre, allowing me to adjust before he repeated the motion.

"The one"—I gasped, eyes fluttering closed—"you told me."

"The one I told you?" The curve of a smile pressed against my temple. "Which one, my terrible nightmare?" he rumbled. "You'll need to use more words."

Coherent words proved to be difficult as he moved in and out. Faster. A furious bliss bloomed and ran through my entire body, tingling in my palms. I was alight. Not like a flame, but like a burning star in the midnight sky. My body welcomed him when he slid in a second finger, soaking his knuckles instantly.

"River. Rivulet."

"Hmm."

I relished in the strength of the vibration from his chest.

His arm wrapped around me, reaching to circle my clit while his other hand kept pumping. "'*Rivulets may disappear while / Rivers spill into seas high.*'" His voice was a deep purr. "'*One defines existence while / Another defines itself.*' That the one?"

I nodded, my cheek rubbing against his jaw. I had been right: His stubble *was* soft. But also rough. Perfectly in-between.

"Open your eyes," he commanded. I was surprised at how quickly my eyelids obeyed. "Tell me why it's your favourite."

My throat was tight with the effort of suppressing a moan. "I don't want . . . to be pushed down a current," I managed. "I want to be free to choose my own course."

His teeth flashed silver, mouth pulled to halfway between a grimace and a smile. "You are free, Nevena. You are free."

A hoarse moan escaped my throat, and Edric answered by pumping into me faster. I hardly recognised the woman looking back at me in the mirror. Splayed and slick and panting. But that wasn't all. Held against Edric, I looked comfortable. Safe.

My cheeks strained with building pressure while his reflection absentmindedly swept his tongue across his teeth, attention solely on watching me rise closer to my peak. Even now, there was that genuine curiosity, a desire to *know* me, rather than place a cage around me. I wanted to ask him his favourite poem in return, but it was difficult, as my moans were starting to make me light-headed.

Everything was so tight.

I needed it to be tighter. Or looser. To *break*.

Edric glanced up in the mirror, catching me watching him. Those silver teeth found my earlobe and bit down.

Finally, there was nowhere higher left for me to climb.

All tension exploded.

I screamed, in freefall, as ecstasy burst from that one spot and everywhere simultaneously, shuddering through every nerve in my body.

Over and over again.

I reached the other side of the climax, but still Edric did not slow, drawing the same motions with his hands, low voice murmuring against my cheek saying, "Look at you," and, "That's it," and, "Only mine."

Almost immediately, a second wave of pleasure built upon the first. I let my head loll backwards over his shoulder as all that I held tight was released.

"You define yourself, Nevena." Lips whispered against my temple. "Remember that."

How could I ever forget those words now?

It took time for the violent shudders to ease. Only when my chest slowed its rocking did Edric withdraw, his hand entirely soaked.

He rested it on top of my wet centre. The gesture was sooth-ing, almost more intimate than anything else he had just done.

Edric pressed a gentle kiss below my jaw. Carefully, he shift-ed me off his lap and laid me back on the bed. His body followed over mine, knees shifting outside my hips and hands on either side of my neck. I stared up at him as he watched my face relax and my breath return to some semblance of normal. Beads of sweat rolled down the waves of his hair that drooped over his brow. Dripped onto his straight nose. Onto mine. What was he thinking now? What did he see? His face was flushed along his prominent cheekbones, flickering eyes wide, dark brows slightly drawn. Was he regretting this already? Before I could analyse his expression further, he dipped down to kiss me. Another wave of arousal reared itself.

"I'm going to keep you here all night," he mumbled against my lips, lowering his hips.

"Oh." It was all I could say as I felt his long, thick column meet my swollen centre through his trousers.

Definitely not regretting anything, then.

I briefly thought to our absence from the Blood Moon Ball, reassuring myself that everyone would be distracted, and anyone noticing our absence would likely not think to look for us here. Definitely not together.

I curled my legs around him and pressed him into me harder, but he made no rush to finish himself how he had finished me.

He wasn't exaggerating. He is going to keep me here all night.

Edric kissed me harder, fuelling my reignited arousal further as his tongue stroked mine in building intensity. A warm hand moved to my breast. Through the spiderweb-thin material, the tip of one finger flicked my nipple, shooting pleasure like lightning directly back to my core.

I exhaled sharply and rolled into the fabric of his trousers, grinding with as much force as I could from where he kept me trapped beneath him, making his trousers damp with my own come. He smiled against my lips and tightened the gap between us so I could hardly move my hips. Keeping me from sating myself too soon. Working to build my desire so it would burn even brighter if he held me off.

He knew exactly what he was doing.

"Edric, I *need*—"

Bang.

From outside the window, the loud sound of a collision carried to our room.

Hands gripped tightly on each other, we both froze, ears straining to identify its cause. And that's when I heard something else.

Shouted orders. Cries of pain.

Scrambling apart, Edric darted to the window. Shock plunged into me like a knife as I joined him. All lanterns were extinguished, and bursts of magic lit the darkened forest floor in bright flashes beneath the Night Tree.

The Cursed.

CHAPTER NINETEEN

I HURTLED DOWN THE trunk's walkway, dread twisting my gut, Edric pulling my hand.

This was my fault.

I should have said something. All the prods and pokes and stabs. I never told Edric and Hartley what I felt against the shield, and then I went and gave up my control of the Kora.

No, you took back your control. Is that what my "Do Tell" voice would say to someone else? It didn't matter. It was definitely my fault.

"The bracelet broke the Kora shield," I cried. "Why did it break the spell?"

Each round of the wide trunk revealed clearer flashes of the scene below. Casters and Protectors blasted orbs of multi-coloured fire, and delegates hacked with swords while packs of vukodlak surrounded the helpless townspeople in a writhing circle of snatching claws and teeth—preventing escape into the protection of nearby zhivir trees.

"I don't understand." Edric's voice was edged with pain. "I thought Hartley's portion of the Kora would still hold, even with the Slom gems."

I thought back to the sound I'd heard before entering Edric's room, and my throat burned. While we were so consumed by each other, Midnight Gate had been under attack. Why was it that the first time I felt fully alive, it was immediately followed by death?

A crushing fear that my legacy as the Cursed Mortician would never truly leave me squeezed my heart. Maybe, after what I had done to Ander Silvan, I didn't deserve anything better. The darkly twinkling bracelet at my wrist now felt like a shackle. I pulled it off as we reached the base of the tree.

A split second later, Edric collapsed onto one knee, framing it with his fists. "*Fuuuuck.*"

"What is—"

The returned presence of the Kora's power hit me like shards of exploding glass. My veins were fissures from which magic burst and agonisingly cracked apart. My lungs emptied, and I dropped to the earth, clawing against the hem of my neckline as spots sparkled in my vision and everything else turned black. All I could hear was the rushing of my own desperate blood in my ears. All I could see were black spots and stars. I couldn't breathe and I was going to lose consciousness and—

The explosion of magic disappeared. My senses settled back, and I knew the Kora spell was completely shattered.

Gone.

I heaved with relief that my lungs were my own again, but it was short-lived. Tearing screams sliced my insides into ribbons, throwing my attention to the vivid horror before the river-bank. Vukodlak held back by the line of dragul orbs, snatching in between the gaps to steal limbs. The panting, snarling creatures fell as magic blasted into them, yet the sheer number of Cursed meant there was always more behind them.

All my fault.

"I've got you." Firm hands raised me to trembling feet.

His breath was unsteady as he held me for a beat longer than we had time for, dark hair falling across his brow. And then he let go.

My heart hammered. Something more was left unfinished between us, but now was not the time to dwell. Our dragul spheres burned like two indigo suns, ready to fulfill their purpose, and together we ran into chaos.

The ball had turned into a slaughter pen.

Mossy ground squelched with blood though it was empty of bodies. My stomach churned with nausea, and I clenched my abdomen to keep down the contents that threatened to spill. This needed to end before any more mortals fell to the painful, undeserved deaths of their neighbours and friends.

All my fault.

Guilt was a whip that lashed my back, as I fired orbs of killing magic at the grey, ridged spines of the closest vukodlak about to break through a line of delegates' slashing swords. Yellow pus and fractured bones burst where my magic hit its target. I was already moving before their corpses fell.

The after-effects of the broken Kora were gone, and it felt almost effortless to draw my power. Four orbs of indigo fire ignited at my will, their flames hungry. Expelling the dragul spheres felt like ridding my body of excess heat, but it never cooled down.

I deserved the corrosive burn in my stomach that fuelled my need to kill. If it wasn't for my cowardice in simply *speaking* to Hartley or Edric of what I had felt against the shield, this might never have happened.

Edric remained beside me wherever I moved, the shadow to my flame. He threw magic after mine, helping carve out gaps in the circle of vukodlak.

"Make their deaths fast," Edric rasped in my ear, almost pleading.

"I'm trying." Of course I was. This needed to be over before anyone else could die because of me.

The Cursed salivated at wriggling flesh entrapped before them, so focused on the mass of blood that their slimy backs were exposed. Vulnerable.

I made it fast, decimating a quarter of the vukodlak's circle into steaming piles of stringy flesh and sticky pus.

"Go! Get to the Night Tree!" I bellowed at the frightened townspeople. The ball of light I now conjured was a beacon illuminating a pathway of safety. Edric joined my shouts, his booming voice reverberating through my bones.

At first, only a few frightened faces broke out of their huddle and sprinted towards us. Others noticed the fierce magic propelling from Edric in steady throws, and the safety of my indigo light, ready to be hurled should any monsters venture towards us.

Soon, a trail connected the former dance floor to the Night Tree while Casters and Protectors continued to thin the number of Cursed with their own magic.

Pus-filled eyes noticed their prey escaping, but Edric and I remained in their way, side by side while townspeople scurried behind us.

The vukodlak's awareness shifted. Assessed. Were we an easy target, or were we a threat?

"Vukodlak are retreating!" someone called.

The first trickles of relief felt like cool water on my neck as I watched the backs of their rotten skin canter away, parallel to the safe path that led east.

Then that cool water turned frozen.

The Coven and our people will meet at midnight by the Gate.

Sudden tightness gripped my chest as Mother Noche's voice resounded in my head. If all the Protectors and Casters were here, there was no one to protect Mother Noche's coven.

"There's people at the Gate," I screamed to Edric.

Not stopping to check if he followed, I drove my feet as fast as I could into frost-hardened ground towards the arch's safe path. Dark columns of trees blurred past. It felt like running on the spot, never progressing. I cursed the distance to the Gate. The trek on foot took nearly an hour, and even if I ran at this pace the entire way, the vukodlak were still undeniably faster. Were they already there?

I couldn't stop. All of this was my fault.

Crunches and snaps sounded behind me, not dissimilar to the sound of hundreds of tiny bones cracking. Even in the darkness, I knew who the footsteps belonged to.

"Here." Edric's deep voice rumbled as he joined my side, pulling something out of his pocket. I briefly felt the heat of his skin before my fingers clasped the smooth vial in my hand.

Miran nectar.

It was as though two beasts reared their heads within me. One uncurled from deep within my gut with flames snorting from its nose, threatening to tear at any notion of defiling the values I held close. The other beast dropped from the depths of my mind with graceful agility, analysing the most practical course.

At least both beasts were my own. The choice lay solely with me.

I threw the bitter, floral liquid down my throat.

The first beast roared with rage, adding to the corrosive guilt and shame in my stomach. It was a consequence I would have to deal with, damaging my own values to prevent more damage to others.

Edric ran silently by my side, nectar propelling our speed up the gradual incline towards the Midnight Gate. Darkness seeped through the forest, leaving our path devoid of any sign of assault, the crunching and slipping of our feet over mud and twigs the only unwelcome disturbance. Even with the nectar, the run was agonisingly slow.

Finally, the lip of the hill came into view, tossing the sound of cries and howls towards us while flashes of bright light illuminated the final steps of our path.

On the hilltop, two small groups of townspeople huddled against each of the arch's columns, facing a barrage of vukodlak. Fangs snapped and snarled, but the Cursed remained a distance from the arch, as if it repelled them like the zhivir trees. A blast of red light exploded a handful of vukodlak backwards, and under the clear, midnight sky, the magic wielder of the light was revealed.

Mother Noche.

How was a witch in possession of magic? If the witches were this powerful, they would never have allowed mortals to drive them out of Veligrad's cities.

There was no time to ponder.

Edric and I ignited the hilltop in the blue light of our flames and cast burning magic at the wriggling mass of large bodies.

The dragul spheres struck and blasted. Large white eyeballs and clacking jaws shifted their attention to the source preventing them from hoarding their prey. Before their pounding paws could reach us, something in my dragul pendant twitched.

Do it.

Those two words wafted into my head like smoke. Potent smoke. Like the product of cremated bodies.

Do what?

Make them do it. Make them stop.

A rush of energy surged through my limbs like too much sugar.

Sickly sweet. Nausea-inducing.

And then pain like I had never felt before exploded from my head, so strong I didn't even have the energy to scream.

The skin of my forehead split, blood spurting out as two horns suddenly erupted from my skull.

My stomach heaved with bile.

What in the Seven Gates of Veligrad is happening?

My hand flew up to feel thick bones protruding from my skull before curving in to face each other, their points sharp. They weren't horns, I realised.

Pincers.

Not made of bone, but shell.

What the fuck?

Blood poured down my face from the split skin, but I didn't need to see as the pincers instinctively sensed the strands of consciousness of every living being in my vicinity, touching and tasting until they found the invisible threads that reeked of decay.

The pincers twanged the strands. Collectively, the vukodlak hesitated their assault, as if struck. Because of . . . me?

In the flashing darkness, Edric still hadn't noticed the disgusting protuberances from my head. He mistook my pause for fatigue and clamped me to his side, enveloping me in his hot, salty scent, while he continued to blast spheres of his magic at vukodlak that peeled away from the arch.

Realisation crept over my scalp like spider's legs.

This was my Heightened Power. To *control*.

Those two beasts within me roared again. One with exhilaration, the other with horror. I reached a trembling thought to this new magic that felt different to the energy I used for conjuring spheres of destruction. This magic was heavier, sharper. Perfect for slicing against the resistance of willpower and implanting mine.

My stomach heaved again. I tasted vomit.

Mother Noche's magic had slowed, and only Edric remained in his assault. Vukodlak bounded closer and closer. Edric couldn't hold them back on his own.

My pincers clicked together.

I felt along those sharp points of magic. And then I released them. Invisible hooks latched into the spinal cords of the nearest pack of vukodlak, and my head exploded with pure agony. The vukodlak minds were fractured spikes that I was impaling myself upon, as I wormed further inside like a parasite. I was going to die trapped in their heads, in the excruciating thirst that propelled their need to drink blood.

But it was working.

The vukodlak slowed, then stilled, howling at my invasion, but unable to resist it.

"Nevena!" Edric held me against his front as my body slumped with the effort of making the vukodlak *stop running*. His voice pulled me from the torture chamber of tormented vukodlak minds. I twitched in Edric's arms, mimicking the movement of vukodlak yanking away from the coven, from us. Edric held me as I convulsed. "Your . . . your head," he rasped, hot breath against my face. "Are you doing this?"

One inner beast feasted on the elation of finally being in true control, while the other from my belly roared at me to stop. This was a vile act. Controlling them felt like *being* them. Being worse than them. I knew what it was like to have my life controlled, and the feeling of compelling another being to do *my* bidding—was sickening. But it was better than anyone else dying. I took a shaky breath and reached for those rotten strands.

Then I told the vukodlak to tear each other apart.

Under Edric's sphere of indigo fire, long claws scratched and tore, jaws snapped, limbs ripped. Their brutal frenzy was over in minutes, until only one remained. Edric ended it with a sphere of magic before the nausea overtook me completely, swilling my stomach. The solid warmth of Edric's chest was the only thing not spinning, keeping me from falling as Edric held me close.

Darkness followed the final blaze of light.

His voice reached me as a deep rumble that could have been an ancient language of trees. "I think you've just discovered your Heightened Power."

He was disgusted; I knew it. I felt it in his searing attention, his tightened grip.

I willed myself to release the hold on my pincers. Slowly, reluctantly, they retracted back into my skull, the sliding sensation making me want to vomit again.

"Don't tell anyone." A trembling whisper. I blinked stinging blood out of my eyes. "S-say it was the Kora breaking . . . that made the vukodlak turn on each other. Please."

My Heightened Power was something I could never use again. It made me a monster. A parasite. And if anyone else found out, how could they ever feel safe in my presence? They wouldn't. They would surely take away my dragul or trap me again, rendering me powerless.

This ability was worse than Caster Rada's. Worse than the Curse of the fae.

I was a curse.

Edric nodded into my hair. Was he afraid I would use my Heightened Power on him if he disagreed? The only reason Edric was still holding me to his body was likely shock.

Deep, red light illuminated the hilltop as Mother Noche conjured a sphere of her magic. Beneath the sinister, bloodred fire, the coven picked through the remains of the vukodlak. Not picking, I realised, but pulling away those lost under the weight of fallen monsters. My heart seized at the sight of bodies being retrieved. I focused my attention on the two figures approaching us. Mother Noche's footsteps were deliberate, and by her side strode Gorcha, like her second-in-command.

"Keep away from her," Edric snarled. It made my heart sink. He didn't care about me any more. He was only doing this so I wouldn't hurt them like I had the vukodlak.

"Are you truly this pressed under the Council's thumb?" barked Gorcha. His wolfskin was despoiled with black blood.

"Your brother sought peace with witches, while *you* perpetuate the Council's hatred like this?"

Ander sought peace with the witches? I thought back to the unshakeable memory of Ander Silvan following me into the mortuary. He had approached the witches on my worktable. What if he had not been seeking to harm me at all? I pressed harder into Edric, guilt threatening to burst against the brittle, useless twigs of my rib cage.

Edric said nothing in reply, but his grip tightened. I let myself seek comfort, even though I knew it wasn't real.

Mother Noche ignored both Edric and Gorcha, speaking to me in a steady, flat tone. "You broke the Kora spell." I could not tell if she spoke in fury or fact. At least she attributed the vukodlak's deaths to the spell. "Do you remember who you are now, Nightfall?"

Blood was still streaking down my face from the wounds in my forehead, slippery and hot. "What are you saying?"

Edric's arm stiffened around me.

"You can find out—" Mother Noche began, and then came to a choking halt.

The air thickened. Beyond the cast of Mother Noche's light, a shadow dragged itself forwards like a solitary pillar, obscured by roiling shadows darker than the deepest thicket of the Smed. The shape of a man stood in the centre of the darkness, and the breath in my lungs was reluctant to pump any more.

A vampir. A Cursed fae able to shift between wolf and human form. It was supposed to be a myth.

My limbs were long roots, tangled under solid earth, unable to withdraw themselves from where they were weighted. Even the pincers of my Heightened Power didn't rear, remaining firmly beneath my split skin.

Mother Noche tossed a red dragul sphere with dwindled strength. It fizzled into nothing against a dark sphere that appeared in return, furious black fire.

Edric pushed me behind him before rushing at the shadow as it released magic of its own.

There was no time to move as a black orb zoomed directly at Mother Noche—and collided with another body that jumped in front of her.

Gorcha.

The elder crumpled to the ground, a crater of destruction concaving his chest.

The vampir disappeared back into the darkness with a hiss of wind against branches, just shy of Edric's reaching silver blades.

A firm grip pushed me towards Gorcha's fallen body. "I am too weak. Heal him," Mother Noche rasped. Her hair was matted in places, reminding me of the corpses that ended up in my mortuary.

I cried out as her nails broke my skin, and Edric was back at my side wrenching me away from her claw-like fingers.

"You can heal," she stressed. "It's in your blood."

"What? I'm not a—"

My shoulders felt suddenly cold as Edric's hands lifted away. "*Heal him.*"

Gorcha's open eyes were unnaturally still. Empty. Unblinking.

Mother Noche released a growl. "You're too late."

No. I might be responsible for breaking the Kora. But I was not responsible for this. Healing magic didn't exist any more—apart from the miran nectar—and more importantly, I was not a witch.

"If I could heal," I said, with as much bite as my exhaustion would allow, "I would've saved someone dear to me long ago." *Malina's father, Djordje.*

Mother Noche placed her hand over the charred hole in Gorcha's chest, her dark-red hair splayed against her back like spilt blood. The coven's quiet keening prickled tiny hairs on my neck and arms. In between their wails, I felt the empty space of the Kora spell. No more awareness of Edric or Hartley. Instead, all that remained was the presence of my filthy Heightened Power.

"Gorcha advocated for witches and mortals to live in peace." Mother Noche's tone was accusatory, as she stood to face me. "For witches to have a place of safety after our power died."

"Your power isn't dead." I had seen the evidence of that tonight.

"Just like mortals, there are ways for us to channel dormant magic." Mother Noche's hand twitched towards the strange pendant at her neck—a hemisphere of fractured, polished bone.

"You," Edric hissed, baring his silver teeth. His hair was mussed, and perspiration dripped down his temples. "*Witch.*" Slowly, he turned to me, eyes wide as if looking at me properly for the first time.

"No. I'm not a—"

At that moment, a person with blood-soaked hands streaked towards us, while others grappled at their vest. Their arms flailed as they were pulled back.

"You did this! You did this!" They screamed, over and over again. Every cry sent a blow straight to my heart, their voice as bludgeoning as a hammer. "If it wasn't for the promise of your spell," they spat, "we would have prepared safety routes into the zhivir trees. We trusted you, and now my wife is dead. You did this! Get out!"

The Kora spell did not fail—I did.

Edric rubbed his sternum with his knuckles, expression unreadable as he glanced between Mother Noche and me.

You did this. You did this.

"Edric, I'm not—"

He stormed away, disappearing into the forest without a second glance. My heart splintered into shards.

You did this. You did this.

The retracted pincers in my head quivered, as if trying to console my misery. As I strained against building pressure behind my eyes, the ghost of a pincer reaching to brush against the side of the screaming witch's mind and—

Bile burned at the back of my throat, and my pincer recoiled. The drop of the person's essence tasted like an anguished tear, bitter and caustic and leaking with raw wounds unhealed. Those wounds threatened to live in me, too.

No. I'll never use it again. Control it.

If only those pincers within me would turn on myself.

I cast a burning, indigo dragul sphere. The least I could do was protect the coven from the vampir if it returned.

"Go. Find me tomorrow. Sunset." Mother Noche's blunt instructions interrupted my thoughts. "Don't stray from the toothed paths."

"But the vampir. It might come back for you." Even if they screamed at me, I wanted to stay. At least it was something I could do to atone.

Mother Noche's bloodred lips were a sickly contrast to the dullness in her dark eyes. "It was not aiming for me, dear." Her voice hung with the melancholy cadence of a flute played in minor scale. "It was aiming for you."

My mouth felt dry, and I shuddered beneath my spider-web-thin gown.

Was this the truth? I had been beside Mother Noche when the spectre struck. If she was right, I wondered if Gorcha knew, too. Had he sacrificed himself to save Mother Noche? Or had he known the shadow's aim was me?

Cold dread filled me like a well as I stepped into the forest's darkness, which now seemed fuller than before. Like every living particle was a knowing eye. Every rough scrape of branch against branch someone listening in. Every sparkling piece of frost an informer, threatening to whisper to the vampir that roamed somewhere between the trees.

Cries carried across gusts of wind that pebbled the skin under my gown, the forest conspiring to torment me deliberately for everything I had done or had been helpless to do.

My head throbbed and stung from the open wounds in my forehead, evidence of something so repulsive living within me, that was somehow *part* of me. How could I ever accept this parasitic power of a monster?

For the first time since my arrival at Midnight Gate, I allowed a tear to slip through the defence of my lashes. It silently slid down my cheek, mingling with my blood. When the bloodied tear reached the edge of my jaw, I brushed it out of existence.

Tomorrow at sunset, I was going to find out the secrets hidden from me for far too long.

CHAPTER TWENTY

E DRIC SILVAN KNEW ABOUT my vile, corrupt Heightened Power. Whatever desires had burned for me last
night were surely now ashes blowing from the acrid smoke that
filled the inside of my nose. Too similar to the stench of my old
cremation chamber.

No one rested for the remainder of the night, searching for
bodies, piling them onto a sombre bonfire that burned in place
of the Ball's dance floor, throwing glares my way that the Kora
had only lasted three weeks while guilt consumed me like a
dragul sphere burning me inside out.

Kavi had rubbed miran nectar onto my head, concerned
when I didn't offer an explanation as to the twin wounds
open to my skull or the crimson streaks down my face. Nausea
threatened to upturn my stomach at the disgusting reminder
that parasitic pincers lived in my head. Caster Rada's power
allowed her to violate the minds of others as a voyeur to one's
deepest thoughts. But I could control bodies, force them to do
things outside their control.

That was unforgivably worse.

Mother Noche's suggestion of healing was a twisted joke,
too. What I could do was more sickening than any Heightened
Power I had ever heard of. More intrusive than sucking blood
from veins.

The visitors soberly Stepped through Midnight Gate shortly before dawn. I almost managed to avoid a black-eyed Toma
until the last moment before he left, during which he hauled
me into a hug. I didn't even have the energy to punch him, like
I knew I should. Instead, I felt nothing.

Numbness was good. Numbness encased guilt.

Sleeping all the next day, I rose only to eat in the late afternoon. I splashed cold water over my face as I prepared for night
patrol, not allowing myself the comfort of warmth.

All my life I had wanted control. Of myself. Of others
around me. Of complete strangers who wrote to me in "Do
Tell." But this kind of control—it felt as destructive as a
vukodlak's bite, and I wanted to cleanse myself of it.

There was still an hour until my patrol at sunset. The forest
offered silence, and I craved its space, away from cloying walls
and the all too familiar stench of melting corpses.

Westward, I passed through the town. Past burnt batches of
forest floor. Past muted sobs that thumped against the insides
of their wooden homes, then inside of my skull. A headache I
deserved.

Da-dum.

The pounding in my head felt strange.

Da-dum.

It moved into my chest.

Da-dum.

This was not a headache. This was something different.
Something . . . familiar.

Pivoting on the packed earth, I quickened my pace back east.
The beating was a tug, pulling to the river that rushed below
the stone bridge, a mirror to the churning in my stomach.

I took a breath of the Lutava, the scent of damp rock and earth battling to cleanse away the traces of pus I still imagined blotched my skin.

And then I ran.

Uncaring of who saw, I followed the river upstream, along its muddy bank, the sticky earth pulling at my feet like congealing blood.

Da-dum.

I ran towards what had been calling me since the first moment I had arrived at Midnight Gate. Something was waiting for me—whether to harm or help me, I no longer cared. Either way I knew it would bring me release. Even the threat of the vampir did not slow my pumping arms.

Away from mortal settlements, the woods were a different kind of wild. Gnarly tree roots twisted from the riverbanks all the way into the water, as if the earth's moisture was not enough, as if they thirsted for nourishment directly from its pure source. I slowed as roots created hurdles of the riverbank, desperate limbs reaching and crossing one other.

This was further than any point I had been on during my patrols, definitely well past the range of safe paths. The air was thick with moisture and cold, the river's song loud against the forest's stillness. The pull of whatever called to me was stronger now. My jaw chattered with the fear I would arrive face-to-face with last night's threat—the vampir. But I couldn't stop.

Another pulse at my chest nearly rocked me off my feet. And then I knew where I was being led.

I leapt from the riverbank and crashed into the vicious torrent of freezing darkness. Cold punctured through layers of all my senses—a beast that tore away comfort, leaving my skin and organs exposed.

It did not matter I couldn't swim. I needed to sink. The weight of my clothes pulled me down, only willing to assist.

Da-dum.

I startled as the whole body of water around me pulsed.

Da-dum.

My hair swirled back and forth with the force, and I whirled, trying to locate the source. The water was murky tea, and I could not sense which way was up or down. I followed the pull. My blurry, ghost-pale hands reached out, hoping to break the surface. Instead, they grasped into the riverbed, swirling silt into whip-like whisps.

And then my fingernails skimmed something hard. A glint like starlight, and my hands closed over an object as if on their own.

Da-dum.

The next beat no longer moved the water, beating only within my hand as if I held a live heart. I kicked off the bed with nowhere near enough force to reach the surface. It didn't matter. Another power surged through my weightless body until my head was above water. The current pushed me onto the river's slanting bank.

Under the cover of branches that stretched and criss-crossed over the river, I opened my pulsing fingers. A teardrop-shaped garnet crystal lay in my palm. Deep and endless and raw. It reflected glints of light across its many facets, ominous like stars on a moonless night when there is no guardian orb to watch them.

Was this an old crystal of the fae? During times of deadening boredom in my tower, I'd re-read every worn book Malina had ever delivered to me about Veligrad's fae and mortal histories. I couldn't recall a mention of anything like this.

Numb, sopping feet carried me over crooked roots and ruts without so much as a stumble as I gazed into the stone's earthy, wine-coloured depths. My magic shifted in my veins, as if adapting to the new addition. Why had this crystal called to me? There was a neediness to it, like it wanted to bond with me. Or to claim me.

A tinkling laugh broke into my thoughts.

I shot my head towards branches above to follow the sound. That was when I noticed I was no longer walking alongside the river. The Lutava rushed somewhere in the distance, but my vision was entirely dominated by a large zhivir tree.

Its moss-coated bark was covered in lolling vines that draped across branches and crossed around its trunk like a living net. Blue flowers the colour of a pale dawn blossomed along the vines, from which glowing fireflies dipped in and out. Circular windows showed soft candlelight emanating from the rooms within, casting a warmth to the deep emerald forest whose branches crowded out the day's ending light.

"Look who decided to come to us." A light, feminine voice glimmered from above me again, like rain whose drops catch sparkles of sun. "Wise."

I finally spotted her. Along a branch next to a hollow leading into the central trunk, a young woman with tightly curled dark hair lay on her side. Her fair face rested on an outstretched arm. Her eyes gleamed with alertness, unnervingly reminding me of a sour domestic cat.

"I didn't come to you, I-I don't know where I am," I said, my jaw chattering against the river's cold sinking into my skin.

It was the truth, and it was also a lie. There was no other place I could be—this was the home of the Coven Noche.

The witch smiled, sensing my thoughts—or perhaps she sneered. "Well, then. Why don't I introduce you to your host?" She leapt up onto the branch with feline gracefulness. "Come inside."

There was no opening into the tree from the ground. The witch pointed to a low branch hanging over my head, as thin as my forearm.

At my touch, the wood lost its stiffness. Twigs wrapped around my arm with the suppleness of strong vines, and yanked me off the ground, depositing me before a hollow doorway with a *slop* of saturated clothing.

Inside, curved shelves with rounded edges had been carved into the trunk's interior, supporting thousands of books. No shelf was linear, curling down to accommodate taller volumes and sliding closer to contain slight novels. The shelves were the tree's own arms, holding the books dearly. Armchairs and large, stuffed cushions were piled in perfect tiny alcoves and nooks, and sconces had been lit against the dimness of the canopy outside. In the centre of the room, a low wooden table held a jumble of twigs, dried herbs, candles, and cards facing down.

My shivering limbs staggered closer to the room that felt like some semblance of home. A flash of fear stiffened my legs. *I am not a witch.* After Noche's absurd remark last night, I felt the need to affirm it. Anyone would surely be entranced by the comfort this room offered. Not that I deserved comfort any more.

"Oh, *Mother*," the young witch called. She landed into the room from a separate window, then leant against a bookshelf with the confidence of a cat cornering its mouse. Her eyes flicked to the crystal in my hand, almost imperceptibly, and then away. I clenched my fist tighter to cover the hard, silken edges from sight, and slipped my hand into my pocket.

Mother Noche stepped down from a spiralled staircase at the back of the wide, circular room. She wore a white shirt tucked into a skirt of deep red wool, matching her full red lips. A black vest cinched her waist with green embroidery that mimicked vines climbing the tree outside. She looked clean from the previous night's events, but the weight of mourning darkened her eyes. Four others—*witches*—stepped down after her.

"Daughter of night. Have you decided you wish to learn?"

Daughter of night. She had called me *daughter* before, but this title struck me as strange. True, it could be a monicker of my surname, but I did not think that was what Mother Noche referred to.

Enough riddles and half-truths.

The cold tightened my muscles and hardened my resolve.

"Am I a daughter of night, or a daughter of one of you?"

Mother Noche gave a rich hum. "So she *does* want to learn."

Her smile twisted into something more sly. And then kept twisting.

The witch suddenly bent in half and retched. Over and over again—violent and wild. I moved forward, unsure what to do, but the catlike witch held me back. No humour remained in her face as she and her coven watched as one while Mother Noche coughed and heaved on all fours with struggling breaths. Just as I was about to demand an explanation, Mother Noche shoved her fingers to the back of her throat and pulled something out, long and thin. She pulled and pulled until it was all finally drawn into a wet puddle into her palm.

A tangle of dark hair.

"The mothers send a vision," whispered the curly-haired witch, her fingers digging into my biceps.

The coven leader righted herself to stand, not bothering to wipe away strands of saliva that streamed down her chin. She dropped the wet slosh of hair onto the low table. The witches leaned forwards like reeds in water.

"Show me what is in your pocket."

I startled at the clarity in Mother Noche's voice after the violence of her fit. Something had shifted in the room, something I did not understand. Mother Noche held answers to questions I had not asked, avoiding the ones that I had. I knew the witches always sought an exchange for their spells or their wisdom. This was no different.

Reluctantly, I pulled out the burgundy gem.

"Ah." Her fingers twitched over the low table, and I snatched the crystal to my heart possessively. Mother Noche smiled and made no move to take it from me. There was no reason to feel attached to the stone, but I did. The other witches stared at it with hunger. Sweat beaded my upper lip under their scrutiny. "So you really are *hers*."

My breath hitched. *She knows something.*

"If you know who I am, tell me." My voice quivered, a failure at hiding my desperation. I was close—*so* close to learning about my past. *They all know.* It was obvious in the sets of narrowed gazes, homed in on every flinch and quirk of my shivering body. They knew who I was, and it was something not good. "Please. I have no memories since I was found in the Smed and—"

In a whirl of her skirts, Mother Noche was suddenly before me. She shoved me hard, so that my shoulders hit bumpy spines of books. Shelf-branches shifted away, and I fell back onto flat wood. Books dropped in heavy thuds, and before I could understand what was happening, the knots of the trunk spilled over my shoulders and around my legs, as if the wood fibres had turned into honey. Then they hardened once more.

I was effectively encased.

"How did you attain the Traitor Stone?" Mother Noche said calmly, as if we were lounging on cushions over rosehip tea.

Traitor Stone? *For Vuk's sake.* Squirming under the prison of the tree, I gave a swift rendition of how I had found the earth-coloured teardrop.

"Do you remember what I told you last night?" Mother Noche did not seem to mind that I was almost squeezing one shoulder out of the tree's grip, ready to escape. Why wasn't she noticing that I could—*oh.* This was not a trap. It was a test.

"You told me that I can heal. Do you think I'm a witch?"

It was almost laughable. Not only because witches had lost the magic to heal, but that if I *could* I wouldn't have allowed Malina's father to suffer.

"What else did I tell you?" Mother Noche's intelligent gaze tracked my every expression as if she could read my thoughts.

I reeled my memory back to earlier that evening, before the Kora broke. Before the gut-clenching guilt I would likely never shake had settled into my stomach.

"You told me the Kora only strengthens what already exists. But the Kora is broken now. I don't understand why—"

She knows about my Heightened Power.

The realisation cut me off. The Kora had not only strengthened whatever irrational bursts of desire I'd had for Edric, but maybe it had triggered the emergence of my Heightened Power. My desire for control. Was this vile power my own doing? Those uninvited pincers perked at my thoughts, pressing lightly against the inside of my skin. I shoved them back down, sucking in air against a rising panic. I would rather remain trapped in this tree than induce the nausea and disgust of those pincers protruding through my forehead again.

"Well." Those full lips stretched into a cold smile. "This may be mutually beneficial. There's something you can do for us, dear. But the mothers' vision tells me we don't know if we can trust you."

The feeling was mutual. How could I trust someone who traded secrets and knowledge for favours? This was what mortals had suffered from witches before the Curse.

Were they going to try taking my dragul? They couldn't. I could cast a dragul sphere right now if I wanted to.

"Nevena Nightfall, do you know what happened to witches' magic?"

Wet fabric scrubbed harshly against my skin, chafing against the tree prison. I allowed the pain as I recalled what brief information I knew. "The witches tried to Curse the fae to strip them of their magic and power, because of the fae's harsh rule. But the witches lost their magic, too. I thought you were essentially mortals now." Hissed murmurs passed between the women like angry snakes. "How were you able to use so much power last night?"

"It's as I told you. There are other ways of channelling magic. Just as mortals found their way to magic through stealing the dragul from the Fae Gates, we found our own ways."

I glanced at the round bone pendant at her neck whose origin was probably another question she would refuse to answer. Then I noticed small pieces of bone jewellery on other women. Little teeth around a bracelet. Pointed fangs dangling from long necklaces. What bones did Mother Noche wear fused into her pendant that were a conduit to her power? A vukodlak's? A—*oh.*

"The wolf teeth. It's *you* who spelled them to protect against the vukodlak. It's *you* who have been moving them to kill us. Yet you protect the mortals here. They don't worship the old fae, do they? They worship witches."

It all made sense.

Mother Noche prowled closer to me, and I pressed my trouser pocket tighter against the tree, the Traitor Stone's hard edges digging into my leg.

"Tell me." Mother Noche stood close enough to touch. "Why did the mortal Council of Veligrad take the dragul magic upon themselves?"

I frowned. "They wanted to protect Veligrad against the vukodlak."

Slowly, the witch wiped thick saliva from her chin. "Why were the dragul not handed to the witches, then, who can wield greater magic than mortals and provide better protection against the vukodlak?"

"Well, the witches mistreated mortals. The Council of Veligrad, they . . . wanted to maintain safety for mortals, and peace."

The room seemed to dip in temperature. I looked around at the witches and now noticed the hunger I had seen in their eyes was more akin to pain. Torn from their magic, their essence, their identity. My words had been thoughtless, inflammatory as hard shoes to a heel blister.

"Is that right?" Mother Noche's voice was almost a whisper. "Peace for whom?"

"The people of . . ."

I faltered. The people of Amber Gate, like Malina and her father Djordje, were always struggling, suffering. As were countless others who desperately sought work so they could feed their families or scrape enough coin together for drops of miran nectar. They placed trust in Leden to Protect them. Yet week after week, I had cremated the bodies of those drained by vukodlak. Those the Casters and Protectors of Veligrad had failed.

"Hm." Mother Noche lifted her chin. "Beware those who demand you devote your entirety to a cause. Assuredness is often arrogance disguised as knowledge."

I couldn't deny the truth in her words. It applied to the Council of Veligrad. To this whole Protector system. Yet I had had no choice but to participate in it. I needed to keep my position, to keep my dragul, or else I would lose any control I had gained over my life.

As if proving her message applied even to herself, Mother Noche drew back. "Well, we shan't keep you any longer, daughter."

The zhivir tree reeled itself away and merged its shelves into place once more, dropping me onto the floor amongst piles of fallen books.

"Wait, you still haven't answered my questions. Am I one of your daughters?" I struggled to keep trembling frustration from my tone. Had I failed whatever test she had set for me here?

"Take that book with you and come back in three days. Then tell me your learnings. If you do that, we shall move on from there." Mother Noche indicated a book that my palm had fallen flat against. Its back cover was plain mauve cloth, giving no indication as to what lay within, or how Mother Noche knew what it was. "And, daughter? I would suggest you keep the Traitor Stone with you. Many seek its power, but the stone chooses its own carrier."

The witches parted, forming a path to an open hollow. My welcome had been withdrawn, and my questions would need to wait until three days' time.

Glints of that predatory hunger met me from the silent, staring women, but they remained where they were as I scrambled to my feet, book in hand.

I clambered down the coven's zhivir tree, branch by branch, the weight of my cold, wet clothes heavier than ever.

CHAPTER TWENTY-ONE

Dear Regretfully-Seeking-Closure,
Your last letter indicated no closure was received from
screaming into your local river. I apologise for my hasty
advice.
You also informed me that you are unable to speak to your
unrequited love about your feelings. For a long time, I was
in a similar situation, with limited ability to interact with
those around me. To assuage myself, the following line of
poetry brought me comfort:
Strong currents carry gentle ripples.
Formed of salt, heed them both.
It reminds us not to underestimate our own actions, no
matter our path, no matter how few or many choices lie
before us. Both currents and ripples can sting with the bite
of salt. Or they can soothe and heal.
If you still seek closure, I suggest the following: Write the
words you wish to speak onto paper, then release them to a
sighing wind. Your love will hear the wind, and you will
know your words have reached them.
I trust this will bring you comfort, like it did to me.
Yours Sincerely,
Do Tell

I should have been reading the damn witches' book or sleeping before my patrol commenced at sunset, but the book told me nothing of my past, and I was too jittery to rest.

The witches did not trust me. Why? To get my answers, I *needed* their trust.

I spent most of the morning skimming through the old book that smelt as fresh as cut wood, scrabbling for answers as if they would slip through my grasp forever if I did not find them soon. The book was as the title suggested—*A Botanist's Most Faithful Companion*. Dry and obscure, the author prattled on in extreme detail about the anatomy of plants. Did they expect me to memorise them? As much as I tried to concentrate, the *anthodium* and *involucre* of chamomile were labels that blurred into a meaningless jumble.

Descending the tall trunk's walkway, I promised myself I would read it again tomorrow, before my two remaining days came to a close.

I sighed a misty breath into the late afternoon air. My purpose had been so clear—undertake the Ranking, live out a season here, then find a better a post where Malina and I could live in peace, ideally by the sea. Now the rope of control that I had tightly wound around myself was loosening. So much change had happened in such a short space of time, so many things I couldn't control: I had a Heightened Power—one that could be summarised as *fucked up* at best, I might be a witch—and witches apparently still possessed some magic—and I was beginning to question the whole dragul-and-Council-of-Veligrad system.

And, of course, there was Edric. There had been barely any time to process what had happened between us. Yet even with everything going on, why was it that the only thing bringing me comfort was recalling the sensation of his warm breath against my ear? The firmness of his large, steady arms holding me securely in his lap? Air blew out hard from my puffed cheeks. After seeing my power, those were things Edric would never want to experience with me again. Not even reading *Water Music* poetry could loosen the knots of my worries.

"You're still here." Jelena's hard, husky voice broke into my thoughts from the common room entrance. Any gratitude for saving her after the vukodlak's first attack had been short-lived. Maybe Edric had in fact told her about my Heightened Power. She smiled unpleasantly at the confusion written on my brow. "Hasn't Hartley spoken to you yet?"

I dropped my letters into Hartley's outbox—the one addressed to Malina was a highly abridged version of recent events including nothing about my power or the witches—then I folded one arm across my chest, the other stroking my pale resin pendant. "Spoken to me about what?"

"He's sending you away."

"What are you talking about?"

"Caster Leden's daughter is to be married at Amber Gate, and after the bloodbath here, they're worried the Cursed might attack there next. They want extra Protectors in case anything happens."

It was only the tinge of resentment underlying Jelena's words that made me think she was telling the truth.

This was unprecedented. A Protector's dragul was most powerful at their own Gate. That notwithstanding, one privileged woman with her father's connections should not receive more protection than any other citizen of Veligrad. Just like guards and Protectors should not be plied with nectar unless they were gravely ill. It was the same corruption.

Indignation sharpened my words. "I am no one's personal guard to be used at the Council's whim."

"Maybe that's just how they see you." Jelena was enjoying this conversation far too much. If this was all she had to force her sour face into a smile, I almost pitied her. Almost. The only reason I could think of Jelena becoming a Protector was for the enjoyment of kills. Kavi had told me she had been seen screaming right back at a howling group of vukodlak at the Blood Moon Ball—now known throughout Midnight Gate as the *Blood Bath Ball*—before massacring them with her sword, not her dragul spheres. "He's in the library."

Resisting shoving my shoulder into Jelena as I passed, I left her smirking face to find Hartley.

The sweet smell of book pages did nothing to soften the stomps of my feet as I stormed towards the same red armchair Edric had once sat in. Pushing aside the pang of that memory, I inhaled the bitterness of anger at all that had happened, at everything I had lost control over.

"You're not seriously sending me to another Gate for a *wedding*, are you?"

Hartley did not raise his gaze from a stack of papers before him, his pen furiously scribbling. "Nightfall."

"And why did I learn this from Jelena, and not you?"

He lifted his gaze from beneath bronze brows. "I've been busy responding to correspondence about exactly why the Kora coincidentally broke on the same evening Midnight Gate received visitors for the first time. Leden is questioning my Castership and implying I step down from my role."

Oh. My ears felt hot. It was lucky Kavi had given early warning of the Kora's temporality, otherwise Hartley would probably have been much more suspicious of the spell's sudden collapse.

"He's using the excuse of this wedding to publicly humiliate me. Strip me from my dragul, probably."

"But no one can force our dragul from us once we're bonded to it, right?"

"Right." He set his pen down. "Do you remember how easily Leden made your confinement sound like a mercy? Exactly. He'll do something similar to me. Make me look unreasonable. Dangerous, even. He'll craft a story that leaves me with no choice but to resign, unless I want the rest of the Council against me. Veligrad needs Leden gone, Nightfall, and I'm not going to give up my position. At least if someone else takes my place for the wedding, it won't look like dissent. I need more time for Veligrad to build trust in me and to doubt Leden."

The flame-licked spectacles of my vision bled away, while the harsh contours of Hartley's bracketed mouth ignited his face with determination, hatred. How different he appeared compared to the jovial Caster who had first introduced me to Midnight Gate. His peppermint scent no longer felt soothing. Now, I detected a cloying hint, like rotting leaves.

I said nothing as Hartley shared his instructions of when and where to meet—Midnight Gate, tomorrow at midday. I still said nothing as he retreated back into his armchair and letters without waiting for a response from me.

The day quickly faded into dark cobalt while I prepared for patrol, mulling over Hartley's words, his demands. He was right. Veligrad needed to be rid of Leden, and Hartley clearly considered himself the best candidate to take Leden's place.

Did Veligrad really need another leader who clung to power with a tight fist? I doubted it. But Hartley had momentum. He already had a plan. And still, he *had* advocated to free me from my tower. Despite peeking at what really lay under Hartley's mask, it was still better than Leden. For now, I needed to attend Amber Gate's wedding.

Vuk—the witches' book.

There would be no time to finish it. Returning it late and without explanation would easily lose the witches' trust in me and lose any hope of finding out what they knew. To the east, twilight already sprinkled the sky. I could speak to the witches and be back before dark. Hopefully. The vampir was still a concern, but it had disappeared after Edric had rushed it. And it appeared that the safe paths worked against it, too. Wherever in the Smed that shadow now pooled, my dragul could surely handle it.

I slipped a note under Kavi's bedroom door, letting her know where I would be tomorrow. We had hardly spent any time together since the Blood Moon Ball, and I itched to debrief with my friend. It would need to wait until I returned.

Tonight was colder, even more so along the riverbank, the Lutava deflecting the icy breeze and throwing it back even harder, as I searched for the path to the witches' coven. A shiver passed over me as I imagined that water submerging me again, turning my skin to thousands of tiny pebbles. After reaching the part along the riverbank where trees grew wilder and the safe path was long behind me, I turned into the forest, hoping to find the coven's zhivir tree close by.

In mere minutes, my surroundings were familiar—but not in the way I had been expecting. Lantern lights swung indifferently ahead of me, already lit in the ever-growing gloom. Somehow, I had circled back towards the town.

That couldn't be right. Yet here I was before the paths that led to the now-subdued town centre.

Shaking off a creeping strangeness, I made my way to the riverbank and tried again. The route I had taken last time must have been deeper. I continued further north along the river, a dragul sphere hovering above each palm, before turning into the forest again.

This time, it took less than a minute to see familiar lights before me.

What is going on?

My fists trembled with nail-digging frustration. I gripped my backpack straps and sprinted the short distance back to the riverbank. The waterside earth was sticky, but I didn't care as I slammed my book-shaped bag into the ground before shooting my dragul spheres high into the sky where they burst like fireworks. Panting, I bent over my knees and squeezed my eyes shut. I didn't need to look to know those same lanterns floated innocently behind me, the town's borders within easy reach. It smelled dank here, as if even the land was trying to deter my search. I needed to get to the witches. I needed to ensure their trust. Then find out what they knew about me.

Unless they don't want me to find them tonight?

When my breaths slowed, I retrieved my pack again, ready to make my way through the twilight, but upon my first step, a protruding root caught my foot, sending me sprawling. My palms slammed into hard, sticky earth.

Great. Did I need to be either drenched or mud-soiled to find the witches?

As I swiped cold earth from my palms and knees, the sound of my palms against skin, against trousers, was . . . loud. Usually, the settling of birds signalled the coming of night's vast veil. But not here, even with the town so close. I cursed myself inwardly for not paying closer attention. The river's bubbling descent over rocks and logs was the only noise that broke the stillness around me.

Apart from that, it was unnaturally quiet.

Slowly, I dropped into a crouch, aware that the absence of sound meant the presence of something *other*.

Vuk.

A movement in the corner of my vision nearly had me hurtling dragul spheres on reflex, but I forced myself to turn ever so slowly to search for the source. It was across the other side of the river—a shade of indigo slightly different to the night-shadowed trees through which it passed.

Shivers brushed across my skin.

The shadow moved closer to the riverbank, unconcerned with the loud rustles it now made. I shuffled carefully towards an abandoned zhivir tree nearby. If I could remain unseen, then I could strike it with a dragul sphere when it least expected it. I used the cover of its noise to creep backwards towards the open hollow while hair prickled across my arms and the back of my neck.

It finally appeared, standing at the bank opposite me. What light remained highlighted the different depths of shadow, distinguishing a stomach-dropping familiar shape.

"*Edric?*" Rather than relief, my heart rate picked up at the sight of his solid frame, his wind-mussed hair. "What are you doing? I thought you were the vampir."

"I could ask you the same thing." Edric's reply was measured. The stillness of the silent air carried his words across the ten paces of river between us. "Looking for anything in particular?"

His words held a cold hardness. Of course they did. I was no better than a vukodlak to him now. A parasite. His touches would only ever be phantom memories against my skin.

"Just..." I glanced up at the darkened canopy. "On patrol."

Edric's hands shifted to his suspenders, feeling the edges of his daggers. "I would advise you against being friendly with the witches."

"Why do you think that's where I'm going?"

Edric deadpanned me.

Right, so I was way off any patrol route, and he had somehow mapped the coven's tree already.

"Okay, fine. Edric, I don't think they're our enemies here."

His teeth glinted as if with silver flame. "They are not your friends."

"I don't understand. You helped fight with them at the Gate's hilltop. You saved them. Why are you acting like this now?"

"I didn't do that for them." Edric's eyebrows knitted together, something between worry and anger etched into the lines of his angular face. His eye sockets were soaked in shadow, but I could still feel the intensity of his stare shooting into me with the force of dragul spheres.

He hadn't done that for *them*.

My heart beat so hard it was surely rocking my whole chest.

Edric stepped to the edge of the riverbank. "I've travelled Veligrad a long time, Nevena. Some of those years were spent avoiding witches with long grudges against my family." I wanted to ask what had happened, but his next, low words held the warning of wind gusts preceding a storm. "Beware the wrath of a witch—they do not forgive." More softly, he added, "They only seek to use you, my nightmare."

The instant he said my monicker, I was in his bedroom with his lips against my skin.

Control. I needed to be better at it. I needed to not want it. Both of those wishes seemed out of reach right now. What irony. I could control anyone around me, except myself. Not that I ever, *ever* would again.

I stepped closer to the riverbank, too, mud softly sucking my feet. "What if you're just like those witches you spoke about, then? Holding a grudge against someone you don't know. Do you know how awful it is to be on the other end of that?"

Edric's broad shoulders softened, before stiffening once more, solid and unyielding. "It's not like that. It's different with the witches. I . . ." Edric fluttered his eyes closed before taking a breath. "Please. Don't look for them. Come back with me."

Come back with him? It must have been the strength of my heart pounding inside my ribs that knocked the air from my lungs. After everything that had happened, Edric didn't hate me? The river rushing between us now felt thunderous.

"Why?" I breathed. "After you know that I can . . . What my power . . ." I couldn't even bring myself to speak aloud the corruption that lived within me.

"Nevena, you won't even take nectar that's allocated to you. The only time you did was when others were at risk, but you never did it for yourself. Your willpower is stronger than any Heightened Power. I've never seen you make a decision that isn't formed after evaluating the impact on others. There's nothing the witches can offer you that you don't already possess within yourself."

How could words punch like fists? And why did it feel good?

I wet my dry mouth. "They know things about me. I think they know who I am. Who my mother was. I want to finally understand what happened to me. Why I was left alone in the Smed when I was a child. It might not change anything, but . . ." It could change everything. For one, it could explain why leaving me to be trapped in a tower had been better than allowing me to grow up living a full life. Unless I had been the only survivor of a vukodlak attack. Then at least I would know their decision hadn't been intentional. "I need to understand."

Edric's eyes flicked like fingers leafing through pages of a book. "You think the witches know who you are?" He inhaled sharply through his straight nose.

"'Rivulets may disappear while
Rivers spill into seas high.
One defines existence while
Another defines itself.'

"You know which you are. I know which you are," he said in his deep, rumbling voice. "Do they?"

The river rushing through the divide between us was the only sound. The wind was as still as my breath.

"I don't know. They know *something*." Before Edric could argue, I dropped my voice to a whisper, almost afraid to admit my next words, but I knew this was needed. To let words leave the confinement of my straining heart. Something I should have advised *Regretfully-Seeking-Closure* in their first letter. "It was our fault, Edric. Everything that happened. All the deaths. It was because of us."

"No." Edric closed his fists. "It's my fault alone. I should have known how powerful the Slom bracelet is." He opened his palm and, even from the other side of the bank, I caught the familiar glint of dark jewels. "You sought freedom, and instead you were offered another cage."

More punches to my heart. This ache was a different kind of pain.

"It was my choice. It was my choice to become a Protector. My choice to undertake the Kora spell. *My choice* for what we did."

Edric shook his head slowly while his eyes remained fastened on me, as if it wasn't good enough, as if *he* wasn't good enough. My toes curled at the intensity of his gaze.

"How is it a true choice when you never had the freedom to pursue any other options?"

A deep pang struck the centre of my being. I shut my gaping mouth, unable to comprehend the genuine concern—the genuine *care* this man had for me.

"Come back with me." The words were a brush of soft wind, caressing the air with promises unspoken. He moved down the embankment and placed a foot onto a mossy stone. My heart thudded at the realisation of what he was about to do. He stepped further down the bank, bending his knees where it became steeper.

"Careful," I whispered.

Edric's mouth curved upwards slightly. "Worried?"

My cheeks heated. *Yes.* I was worried about more than just him slipping on a rock. A bloom of paranoia wound vines around my chest. How could he truly want to be near me after what he knew?

Edric reached the waterline, and unhesitatingly plunged his boots into its body, forcing water to part as he made his way to me. The river would be as freezing as it had been yesterday, yet Edric moved with ease, as if nothing could hinder his path. The bottom dipped rapidly, and he was soon at his neck. Long dimples appeared around his mouth as he gave me a smile as rare as mine, then dipped himself wholly in the river before bursting his head back out to swim.

My chest rose and fell sharply. I was just another twisted root implanted in the soil, unable to pick myself up and away. If the Kora spell was a being, it would have laughed at me, as if daring me try and blame it for how I felt. But I knew it was all me. Again.

Edric stood when the water reached his hips. The river foamed around him, as if he were a rock hewn into the waterbed, and not a man of flesh. His clothes clung to his massive form. The river should have reduced him to shivers, but he gave no indication of cold as he calmly waded towards me.

"I want you to take this." Water sloshed sullenly as if reluctant to release his legs as Edric dragged himself to the river's edge, stopping before stepping onto the sloping bank. His dark shirt was plastered against the ridges of his body, dripping loudly against the dark metal of water glinting like his silver-lined teeth. "You should never feel trapped again."

My breath felt stuck in my throat as Edric held out the Slom bracelet. "But the Kora is broken now."

"We don't know what's coming next. It's better if you know you can keep yourself safe."

The vampir. It clearly had enough magic to produce some form of dragul sphere, but what else could it do?

I swallowed. Reduced my voice to a whisper. "And what about keeping people safe from me?"

Pincers clicked within my head in reminder of the sickening power I held, a parasite living under my skin. But it was me—*I* was the parasite, capable of burrowing beneath the safety of others' skin and playing with their bones like dolls.

"Like I said," his voice rough, "you know what it's like to feel trapped under another's control. There's no doubt in my mind that you would know when to use your power. Or when to not." He exhaled, his words more breath than voice. "I trust you."

"You trust me?" The sudden lightness I felt must have been the sensation of a breeze around my knees.

"Mm-hm. I trust you. I *know* you." The night had well and truly fallen. I shivered, though it was nothing to do with the river's seeping cold. "I want you to be completely in control of your own choices. Always." He gently tossed the Slom bracelet from where he stood beneath the small slope of riverbank, chest heaving. "Put it on for me," he whispered.

I released a shuddering breath. Then I did.

CHAPTER
TWENTY-TWO

THE BRACELET WAS WARM against my skin, as if it had been heated by a fire instead of crossed through a freezing river. My heart sped as Edric pulled himself up the bank with ease, then stopped when he stood close enough to touch.

"Don't take it off. Ever again."

"Why?" I breathed, my thoughts as tangled as the river weeds peeking from the shallows.

"Because if I do something like this..." He traced the curve of my jaw with a burning knuckle that drew tingles across my skin. "I need you to tell me if you don't like it. I need to be sure it's you." The timbre of his voice was surely deeper than the foundations of the Gates buried deep within the earth.

I tilted my chin higher to allow Edric's fingers to spill down the column of my neck. "The Kora's fully broken, Edric. This is me. It's always been me."

"Yes," he whispered, so close I felt the hiss of his breath against my lips. His warm fingers spread to grasp my whole neck. "It's always been you."

Oh, Vuk. My inner walls crumpled like steel in a furnace. But some smouldering part of me still held.

I watched beads of water drip from his hair, his nose, twinkling like stars as they fell. "We should go. You're going to freeze."

"I'm not." His soft smile was a hook, lifting my stomach, my core.

I shivered as he gripped my wrist, then placed my hand in between the swells of his pecs. Edric was hot. Burning beneath the thin material of his clothes. *How?* Was it the mass of his muscles that kept his body warm?

Edric sucked a breath between his teeth, then shuddered, raising his wide, bulging shoulder muscles.

"See? You are cold. We should go."

"It's not that," he grunted. "It's your touch."

Oh. I blinked.

My other hand found his chest as well, and he exhaled hoarsely through his open mouth. Dear Vuk, I wanted to lick those silver teeth.

So I stood on my tip-toes, pulled his neck towards me, and did.

Edric groaned, deep and gravelly, as the tip of my tongue slid over his lower teeth.

Then he captured my lips with his own. Hungrily. Sloppily. As if all he wanted to do was to consume me as thoroughly as possible.

"Do you like my touch?" I managed to say. The thought of this hulking man being reduced to shudders by *my touch* was extraordinary. Intoxicating. Unbelievable.

He exhaled a harsh breath into my mouth, a half laugh. "Want to find out how much I like it?"

"Yes."

He backed me into the abandoned zhivir tree behind me. Vines hung over its opening like parting curtains. I let him lead me inside the surprisingly warm, dark hollow.

It was clear I would not be finding the coven tonight. Either I had somehow mislocated the tree, or the coven did not want me to reach it. I would have to take the book with me on my journey and hope for their forgiveness at the delay. Even if I could have found them tonight, I wondered if I would have exchanged this moment with Edric. I decided I didn't really want to answer that.

Edric gently gripped my wrist at his chest, then slid it all the way down the ridges of his muscled torso, down to his waistband, then to the thick outline tenting his trousers. My stomach tightened and squirmed.

"Oh." My palm tingled as I closed over his shape. "You do like it."

He growled in confirmation. Then he dropped heavily to his knees and began unlacing my boots. I gripped his shoulders, watching every deliberate movement. Even lowered at this height, he was massive, the top of his head reaching my eyes.

After discarding my second boot, he held my foot and tickled the underside. I shrieked and tried to jerk it away. Those long dimples appeared at the sides of his mouth.

"So that's your only weakness. A tickly foot." His teeth showed when he grinned. "Noted."

I laughed again. Short and bright. By the Seven Gates of Veligrad, it felt good to do that. He must've liked it, too, because suddenly he was back on his feet. Kissing me hard. Large fingers unfastened the buckle at my collarbones and slid my coat from my shoulders.

"Are you going to undress me in the middle of the forest? What if someone walks past?"

Edric stiffened momentarily. "Good point," he mumbled. "The problem is I don't think I can walk back to the tree like this." His length was well and truly *hard*.

A whispered laugh against his lips. "Guess we'd better stay here, then."

Edric's eyes darkened, his mouth curving. "Guess you're right." With one hand, he slowly unbuttoned the front of my trousers. His eyes locked onto mine, then he slid his warm hand over my centre.

I gasped. Everything tingled in anticipation of what I knew those fingers could do.

"I'm going to tell you about my favourite poem now." He whispered into my ear while a finger circled at the exact spot I needed. "It's from *Sighing Winds*. I wanted to show you that day you found me in the library. But then someone gave me the best kiss of my life."

"Oh." I gasped against the already building pleasure. "That's fair."

"Mm-hm." One hand gripped my hip firmly—the side where I usually kept my hammer. I realised I hadn't worn it since . . . since the day Edric kissed me in the library. I couldn't help but moan, as his fingers slid smoothly between my folds, my centre already soaking wet. "It goes like this, Nevena. Are you listening?" His breath tickled my ear.

All I could do was nod against his cheek.

"Good." I felt the curve of his lips smiling. The heel of his hand joined in to rub against my clit.

"'*Louder than the rattling pane*
That shudders in the storm,
I bate my breath, force lungs to wait,
To only hear your own.'

"That's it, Nevena. What do you think of my favourite poem?"

His length pressed against my stomach through his trousers. I closed around it once again, and Edric groaned, pushing into the pressure of my hand.

"I think . . . it's great."

"Hmm." The hum of approval shot another thrill up my centre. "Is-is that all?" Now we both were struggling for words.

"No." My voice sounded different—high and pitchy. The strength of heat in my core was coiled so tight. I was close. How was I this close so quickly? I clenched my thighs around Edric's slick hand. "Edric. I want it to be you inside me."

"*Fuck.*"

"Edric," I breathed his name again.

"Yes?" He drove his finger into me faster.

"*Edric.*"

"Fuck." He groaned the word directly into my ear, warm and raspy.

My control snapped, and everything exploded in pleasure. Lights burst behind my squeezed eyes, as I moaned and shrieked and cried, while Edric kept driving, my body shuddering onto him.

"That's it. Keep going."

At his roughly spoken words, another wave crashed ferociously from my centre atop the first. I ground against his hand, letting any restraint free, allowing myself to feel every mote of pleasure Edric wrung from me.

"You're so beautiful," he whispered against my temple as the tremors in my core slowly eased. It still felt incredible, every pulse a jolt of pleasure. "You're so pretty when you come, too. Do you know that?" I could only gaze up at him through half-lidded eyes. Gently, Edric laid me on the ground, atop my spread coat, then he lay alongside me. One arm curled protectively around the back of my neck, the other around my waist. "I love seeing you like this. Relaxed. Taken care of."

I exhaled. Fully. All tension loosened from my limbs. When some energy returned, I planned to return the favour to Edric. For now, he seemed just as content holding me in his arms.

I shuffled closer into his firm, steady warmth.

The movement shifted something in my pocket, poking it painfully into my hip. *Ugh.* The Traitor Stone. Moving felt like the last thing I wanted do right now. But my skin was sensitive to touch after the intensity of my orgasm, and the teardrop shape dug its pointed end into me hard.

Reluctantly, I started to pull the stone from my side pocket, when something sharp stabbed into my finger. I retracted my hand with a hiss. A drop of blood already beaded on my skin.

"Ow."

"Are you al—"

"*Ah!*" Sharp pain suddenly speared through my hip where the crystal sat, as though a dagger had been pushed through skin, muscle and my very bone. My body convulsed beyond my control. I couldn't move. I couldn't focus on anything except the pain.

"*Nevena.* What is it? Did I do something?" He frantically searched my body for a wound. I grasped weakly at my pocket, the pain barring me from forming coherent speech.

His hand was immediately at my side, skimming my hip. Then he stilled.

He plucked the garnet crystal from my pocket and dropped it on the ground, as if it stung to touch.

My body collapsed into relief, and I groaned, sweat coating my forehead. I opened my mouth to thank him, then stopped. Edric gaped at the garnet stone. My blood was smeared onto its multi-faceted surface, more blood than what I thought could have come from the small cut.

"You carry the Traitor Stone." Edric's words were dangerously soft.

"What?" How did Edric know about this stone, too?

He shifted upright onto his knees, the space leaving me feeling as cold as if I was naked in the river. I longed to grab his wrist and pull it back towards me.

"That," he swallowed, "is the stone responsible for cursing the fae."

"What do you mean?" I gasped. "The witches Cursed the fae. Are you saying they used a stone?" That was never in the renditions I had heard from guards passing rumours, or even from *The Northern Serpent.*

"You don't know the full story, do you?"

At my confusion, Edric fluttered his eyes closed, as if pained. I wanted to reach out and stroke the stubble on his cheek, but Edric was too distant.

"The fae king, Hvalimir, was a jealous, possessive man." He ground the words like stones. "He was jealous of the witches' earth magic, so he forced his indentured witch to create a spell to access her power. Hvalimir was a cruel, hated ruler." An emotion I couldn't place passed over his face. Something like fury, maybe. "The witch used the opportunity to imbue a gem with all of her hatred towards her master."

Edric leant further away from me as I tried to lean closer. I suppressed a trembling sob.

"When Hvalimir placed the jewelled ring on his finger, the corrupting magic was ready to claim more than just the king. It was intended for all fae." His voice was so hoarse. "You now carry the origin of the Cursed. The Traitor Stone. A witch's stone. And it responds to your touch." Edric looked at me with a hollowness that ripped my paper chest. I was his brother's murderer all over again. I was a repulsive parasite that could control bodies like puppets. I was everything ruinous in his life. "Who are you, Nevena Nightfall?"

CHAPTER
TWENTY-THREE

"TELL ME. TELL ME who you are." Desperation etched lines in Edric's brow.

My lips parted, but I had no reply to offer him. I shook my head.

I had been the Cursed Mortician. A forgotten girl, kept away from any and all. Now a Protector. But those were not the words which finally made their way to Edric. Three quiet syllables fell from my lips, as staccato as a knock on a door.

"I don't know."

It was the truth. He knew it, gazing down at me with a mixture of pity and fear and devastation. Something about his expression reminded me of the families who came to collect urns of ashes from my tower. Like nothing beautiful could ever bloom in their world again.

Edric closed his eyes and dipped his head, nodding as if coming to a decision. "Until you do . . ." His voice cracked. "Keep away from me."

No. Surely, no. Not after the depth of his words. Why was he sliding away from me, when his fingers still lingered in protest at being parted from my skin?

Boots scuffed earth as Edric twisted and stood. His hands raked through mussed hair. Across his shoulder, he shot me a once-over.

Then he was striding through the vine curtain, leaving me utterly alone in the abandoned zhivir tree.

The whirring sound of blood filled my ears. Spikes of twigs beneath my coat sent pinpricks of pain through my knees and palms, urging me to move. It was nothing to the tearing pain of my heart shredding itself apart, oozing with cold blood.

Edric hated witches. And now he hated me. Again.

He had put Ander's death behind him; he had overlooked the parasitic monster that lived inside me, my Heightened Power, but suspecting I was a witch—why was that the only part of me he could not forgive?

I brushed prickly burrs off my night-dark cloak, but what made me curse was not their nips, but the bracelet still sparkling contentedly on my wrist. My eyelids burned with the pressure of tears. Yanking it off my hand, I stashed the damn bracelet in a trouser pocket. What I was going to do with it, I didn't know. Why did everything good in my life turn out to be cursed?

I pressed a cool palm to each eye before crouching towards the small object responsible for dismantling the foundations of trust Edric and I had only just started to build. Carefully, I prodded the Traitor Stone, testing whether I could touch it again.

Its facet looked richer, like fresh earth. The smear of my blood was gone, as if the stone had drunk it and was now satiated.

Strange.

Nothing triggered any pain as I tested it. With a trembling hand, I dropped it back in my pocket, opposite to the bracelet, before trudging down the river towards the Night Tree, struggling to keep tears behind my waterline.

Half the night was wasted. The moments spent with Edric in the zhivir tree had been for nothing, robbing me of opportunities of my original plans, and pushing me under the weight of Edric's rejection. Fine. That was fine. I knew I was strong enough to lift it.

Strong currents carry gentle ripples.

Formed of salt, heed them both.

Vuk. Even my favourite poem struggled to lend me strength. Why was it still Edric's voice which spoke Rieka's words in my thoughts?

At midday, I waited atop Midnight Gate's hill as the cold sun hung precisely above the arch's pointed peak. Wind tugged at my unbound hair, and I gripped my woollen coat tighter, trying to forget what it had been used for mere hours ago, hoping the crisp air would blow away Edric's salty scent from its fibres. Maybe at Amber Gate I would find a new coat.

The frigid sky was open and clear, unlike my murky thoughts. What had occurred on this hilltop was also too fresh. The attack. Gorcha's death. The vampir. Nothing made sense. Apart from the fact that the witches knew something, and I needed to prove myself to them.

"Nightfall." Hartley's steady voice rang loudly against the flat expanse as he crested the hill's lip.

"Hartley." My hands twitched at my sides under Hartley's gaze, wanting to clutch my pockets hiding the two pieces of jewellery. I had thought about leaving behind the disturbing stone. And the bracelet that only reminded me of broken hopes. They ended up accompanying me just the same. As did that little dagger Edric had given me all those months ago, which sat at the bottom of my pack beneath the witches' book. The dagger was at least practical, never mind the hurt it carried.

Without preamble, Hartley placed a hand on a flat piece of stone, avoiding the Stepping symbols so he didn't Step alongside me. "Right. Be careful of Leden."

Like I needed reminding. Though the dragul at my neck meant Leden and the guards couldn't recapture me if they wanted to, my shoulders still pressed into my spine. I ignored the clicking of pincers inside my head, trying to comfort me in reminder of what they could do. The only thought bringing me true comfort was the knowledge that I would try and see Malina.

"You should take this with you. Now's not the time for upholding your own values, but for doing the right thing by others."

I narrowed my eyes at the glass vial Hartley shook in front of my face. For someone who had experienced a childhood of bare survival, he seemed to have difficulty grasping what the *right thing by others* meant to those struggling to survive.

At my silence, he sighed, as if giving in to a child's tantrum. "Alright. Ready?"

Well, there wasn't much choice. Offering Hartley a tight nod, I touched the symbol of Amber Gate, an etching of a leaf.

As soon as the rough carving met my fingers, that familiar sugar-like rush tore through my limbs. Fierce energy twisted around me like a possessive lover, ready to carry me away.

My feet were about to leave the ground when Hartley's face suddenly contorted. I startled as a strong hand gripped my wrist from behind. Hartley began to yell something as I faced the intruder, but it was too late. The Stepping spell plucked me from the hilltop, and I was deposited moments later at Amber Gate.

With Edric by my side.

CHAPTER
TWENTY-FOUR

"WHAT IN THE SEVEN Gates of Veligrad are you *doing*, Silvan?" I yelled as soon as my feet hit the cracked paving of Amber Gate. His surname came easier to my lips. "Don't you think this will make *keeping away from you* a bit hard?"

Edric's final words from last night still bit at the encasing of my chest like frost, his touch a mocking reminder of where his hands had been last night. I yanked my arm out of his grip—and was hit with the reality that I stood back in my old prison. Amber Gate. The scent of beech trees and chimney smoke. The lingering memory of ashes that made me feel trapped and alone and—*Stop.*

Edric peered down at me, dark brows bunched in ever-present curiosity. Why did he still look at me like that, after making it as clear as the Lutava's water that all he wanted was distance?

"It's not because I—" He broke off and exhaled. "There's something I need to tell you." No sun hung over the quiet emptiness of the Amber Gate arch, only clouds loaded with looming tension, mirroring the deep, storm blue of Edric's eyes. "What if there was a way to break the Curse?"

Something in my stomach fluttered and rose before I smacked it back down. How could he possibly think he could break a witches' curse? A curse the witches themselves had not been able to break to reclaim their lost power? It was almost a pity to crush the earnestness in his expression. Almost. "I see you've skipped through the parts about abandoning me, telling me to keep away from you, then apparently stalking me through the Smed so you could escape Midnight Gate."

His gaze flicked to my bare wrist, and his jaw stiffened. "I see you've skipped the part about never taking off the Slom bracelet. You need to keep safe," he growled.

I folded my arms, long hair running in tendrils past my elbows like snakes ready to rear. Edric had made it clear from the moment we'd met that we should remain far apart from each other. Last night was the freshest reminder yet. Why would he not take his own advice and let me be? *More importantly, why could I not, either?* I shook away the thought.

"You don't want to answer questions? Fine." I squeezed my arms into a tighter knot. "I'm staying here for two nights, and you can't get back without a Caster dragul. Good luck asking Leden to Step you back to Midnight Gate, because you're not sharing a bed with me."

Edric's gaze dipped to my lips before flicking away in a frown, one hand gripping the base of his suspenders like a crutch. *Vuk.* Bad choice of words. Why did that always happen with him? Now thoughts of last night were at the front of both our minds, when I had been determined to push them way back. Spinning on my heels to hide my cherry-red cheeks, I strode to the wild grass field, trying not to shiver at how his absence left a creeping draft or at the way curiosity pulled at my sleeve.

Edric's suggestion was ridiculous. If it could have been done by now, either the witches or the Casters would have figured it out. I tightened my jacket buckle above my collarbones, trying to ignore the bulk of presence that had absconded his post and followed me to another Gate. Nothing good would come of it. Even if his company somehow made my legs less shaky in the wake of a tall, grey shadow in the distance—Amber Gate tower.

"Wait." Edric was suddenly close, blocking my path. "I'm sorry. I just—" He opened his mouth then shut it, knuckles twitching towards me. He lifted them to his sternum instead and slowly rubbed between the two rows of daggers on his suspenders, taking a deep breath. "I think we can do it. You and I. Break the Curse. People would never have to fear the vukodlak again, or the Smed. Anyone could freely access miran nectar."

That fluttering rose up again, higher this time. Edric knew how much it meant to me for miran nectar to be accessed fairly—and apparently, he still cared? It didn't matter. The Curse couldn't really be broken by *us*, could it? When it came to Edric, hope was like a thin ceramic urn—once dropped, it smashed apart, and it was painful to put the pieces back together.

"This is . . . sudden of you."

"It isn't sudden, Nevena," he whispered, neck bending like a heavy bough. "I've been searching for a long, long time."

As the shapes of his words brushed my face, threads of memories wove themselves onto the blank fabric of a tapestry, constructing a picture I had not stepped back to observe as a whole. There was Edric, prowling around Amber Gate buildings in the dark. Ander Silvan standing before my mortuary table. Elder Gorcha, and his connection to the two brothers.

My stomach dropped. Edric followed as I abruptly strode through the barren field, towards buildings that would shelter me from my tower's lone window.

"That's what your brother was searching for, wasn't he?" I breathed, fixing my head to the weed-ridden ground. "A way to break the Curse."

His dark head slowly nodded. "We both had different ideas on how to achieve it, but yes. He was working with Gorcha and the witches. Ander wanted peace for Veligrad."

An invisible rope tightened around my chest, throttling my windpipe. My vision turned into dark blotches of clotting blood against a dented head. It was those wide eyes I saw now—*Cursed* eyes, I had thought. I must have imagined it out of fear. Imagined it and murdered an innocent person.

I stumbled to a stop. "Ander . . ." It came out thick, my tongue bloated, reluctant to admit the horror of what I had done. "Was Ander looking for my . . . for the *Traitor* Stone? Is that why you want it?" It had to be why Ander had entered the mortuary. Not to chase me, but to search the deceased witches that lay on my worktable. I reached in my pocket for the teardrop of garnet crystal that had nicked me and swallowed some of my blood. Could it break the Curse?

Edric was suddenly close before me, halting my arm before I could lift it out of my pocket. "I don't want that stone. Just put the Slom bracelet on for me. Please." Concern lined his brow beneath hanging locks of dark hair. Salt and citrus sailed into my lungs, his scent inflating my chest again, releasing the hold of that rope. Was I imagining it, or was his hand heating my skin even through my jacket?

I swallowed. "The witches are keeping something from me. You are, too. I'm sick of it, Edric. Tell me. *Trust* me." It came out hoarse. That was the thing, wasn't it? Nobody, except Malina, had ever trusted me, or my word that I wasn't Cursed. Readers of "Do Tell" only trusted the ebony, printed ink that offered them advice for their deepest worries. The witches didn't trust me, though it was becoming increasingly clear that I had to be one of them. And Edric. That genuine concern, ever-present from the moment we had first met. He *cared*. He had *said* he trusted me. But did he truly?

Edric exhaled with a deep hum through his nose. "Nevena, I don't believe Leden's claim he has no Heightened Power."

"Oh." *Oh, Vuk.* "Then you think . . ."

Edric's voice was as subtle and deep as burrowing roots. "He has a Heightened Power. One he doesn't want anyone else to know about."

I knew how that felt.

It could only mean one thing. Leden's power was something as terrible as mine.

We were alone in the barren field, bar the busy sounds of the town floating over the low stone border wall. Edric dipped his head closer to mine, as if to share a secret. "Have you ever wondered why Leden has never tried to find a way to break the Curse?"

It had always been assumed there was no way. *The Northern Serpent* had included articles on how to protect against the Curse but never any insights on ending it. Instead, harsh punishments were doled onto Amber Gate's witches, their deaths justified by the Curse's permanence.

"I never lied when I said I was a traveller," Edric continued. "It took many years to find lost books, lost people who knew about curses and how to break them. But someone else was searching for this information, too. People disappeared before

I could find them. Books went missing. But there were enough pieces left for me to figure it out." Wind shook reedy grass, creating a rustling cover for what Edric was about to say. "The Curse can be broken with the strongest dragul. That's why the witches couldn't break their own spell. Jelena and I became Protectors so we could try it with our own dragul, but they're not strong enough. It needs to be a Caster dragul. At least one."

My heart punched the inside of my chest in rhythmic thuds. This whole season at Midnight Gate, Edric and Jelena had been trying to break the Curse. In secret, so that word wouldn't spread to Leden. Their reluctance to engage with others made sense now, and warmth cracked through the shell of my frostbitten heart with the strength of the hammer I had left behind at Midnight Gate. Edric's hardness all season had been borne from a burden: trying to end the suffering of every citizen of Veligrad who lived beneath the threat of the vukodlak, the Cursed fae.

Edric's brows quivered, curving into a shape he was trying to suppress. A question he didn't want to ask. Understanding dawned on me.

"You want me to use my Heightened Power on Leden," I said, my voice flat. That's why he had followed me here.

His brow cleared, and the deep blue in Edric's eyes gleamed. "You could—"

"No." I swallowed the trickle of vomit that had already burned its way to my tonsils. It wasn't only the pain and revulsion accompanying the memory of pincers erupting from my head, or the dizzying nausea of controlling another that made my skin crawl with rotten maggots. It was the fear of becoming as vile as the act itself. Of being a violator, an intruder, and never feeling clean of the filthy grit that accompanied that act. I remembered the part of me that felt exhilaration at the power of control. What if I released those pincers again, and they didn't want to retract? What if I lost myself, trapped as a monster forever? "Using my power . . . It could change me."

Half a beat of silence passed, then, "I understand."

He said it without further question, without expectation of anything other than my decision as it had been made. Edric gazed up at the tall, narrow tower somewhere behind me, then offered one of his rare smiles that made those long dimples appear at either side of his mouth.

"There's only one current left for me to follow then," he said softly. "Find a way to kill Leden and take his Caster stone."

The quiet words made me shiver.

What Edric was saying about Leden had to be true. Leden was cruel, an orchestrator of murders against anyone threatening his reign, to the extent of destroying any chances of anyone else breaking the Curse. He needed to be stopped, and this was the cleanest path forward. I would not sully my own life to spare Leden's. If that made me callous, it was an easier burden to bear than the consequences of losing myself to my power. I straightened my back and lifted my chin. "Fine. I'll help you. But you need to do one thing for me first."

Before Edric could ask what it was, a familiar whining voice called from over the low stone wall separating the abandoned field from the town's buildings. "Mortician? What are you doing here? Where's Hartley? Why are there two of you?" Jakov Prosek marched towards us, his moustache as pronounced as his displeasure.

Edric held my gaze, unmoving. Making space for me to decide our next move.

Reluctantly, I stepped out of the protective curve of his body. "Caster Hartley said Protectors were needed for the wedding. Here we are," I said simply, hoping it sounded innocuous.

"*No*, Caster Leden needed *Hartley. Specifically.*" Jakov's moustache was angry with me.

Edric hooked his thumbs into his waistband, unperturbed. His biceps strained firmly through his coat while his forefingers stroked the hilts of his daggers. "We volunteer to patrol the wedding, to ensure the safety of Amber Gate's citizens."

"No, no, *no*. I do *not* want you. Go back from wherever you came."

"We need a Caster to do that, Jakov," said Edric. I swallowed a chuckle at his use of Leden's assistant's first name, though it didn't help our cause.

"That's a problem you *Protectors* will need to resolve yourselves. And don't expect any free lodgings here, either."

"But you will tell Caster Leden, won't you?" I asked. "That we've arrived?" The whole point of coming here was to not throw suspicion onto Hartley's absence. Hartley had a strategy to be rid of Leden, too. If whatever Edric wanted to try didn't work out, at least I had done what I could for Hartley to continue his own plan.

With a mutter of, "Wasting my Gates-given time," Jakov marched away, shaking his greasy head.

"So, Protector." Edric's lips spread into sharp smile. "Looks like we have some spare time to put our plan forward."

My back straightened as I came to a decision and slipped the protective bracelet back on. Edric watched as I did, and his smile grew.

Chapter
Twenty-five

"First, I want to find the nectar," I muttered to Edric, as we strode down a lane in Amber Gate's outer circle of streets, squeezed with crumbly, unkept stone townhouses. He nodded, strong chin dipping close to my head to hear my words. Passersby flashed confused glances at our indigo Protector uniforms before averting their eyes. I tucked my dragul necklace inside my top. Not that it would help much. "If we try to take Leden's stone and we fail, I want the nectar out of Leden's hands. Even if it's only for the rest of this season. I have a friend we can give the nectar to. She has a . . . distribution network."

If Edric could harbor secret plans, then so could I. Malina's freckled face would smile so wide when I met her with a crateload of nectar. She could spread the word through "Do Tell," figure out some method of alerting people in the town. Some code, maybe? I smiled at the thought. We could work on the details together.

Edric gave me a sideways look. "Only you could still make friends while trapped in a tower."

I blinked. "Well, there was only the one."

"You sure?" Edric muttered. "Because my fist seems to remember punching some guy who claimed to know you pretty well."

My stomach flipped. "He wasn't really—okay, fine. Two then."

"And then on Ranking Eve, there were a pair of guards I overheard whining about their in-laws, and that they were going to talk about it with you when they returned from the ceremony."

"Well, we only spoke through the *door*. They were hardly friends."

He hummed darkly, his mouth close to my ear, the deep vibration somehow penetrating to my core. "I think you underestimate the impact you have on others, Nevena Nightfall."

Well. I looked directly ahead as my cheeks heated. If I turned to him now, I knew I'd find that smile again. "Malina is a ceramicist," I blurted out, trying to deflect his... compliment? Surely not. Not after the way he'd expressed his hatred for witches last night. "She should be at her master's workshop."

A nod, and Edric followed dutifully like the once-worshipped, protective wolf-god Vuk, as I searched the narrow lanes of the smoke-stained artisan district. Edric's shoulders hunched almost imperceptibly, but I noticed. They were raised hackles, defensive, alert. It made something within me lighten.

A wooden sign swung from an iron rod, bearing an image of a vase.

"There it is." I hurried to the latticed shopfront window of Master Patrizia's workshop, searching for Malina's frizzy silver-blonde hair bent over a pottery wheel.

Except that it was empty. Both the workshop and living quarters were entirely closed.

Of course. They had to be preparing for the wedding. Malina's last letter had been over a fortnight ago, and she had spoken about her increasing work.

Edric's shoulder brushed mine as I stood with my arms slack by my sides. "Let's find an inn, then we can come back and leave a message letting her know where you're staying."

I cricked my neck from side to side, trying to ease some creeping tension. "Yes. Okay. She can find us later. Gives us time to locate the nectar first."

"That's right," he soothed, our arms still touching.

We were potentially about to steal Amber Gate's nectar, possibly kill Leden, and maybe break the Curse. If I could see Malina before we changed the course of life for Veligrad, it would ease at least a little strain.

Closer to the inner circles of town, the air sparked with a different energy. The clean, whitewashed houses were larger, the streets wider and filled with people. In the outer districts from which we'd come, heads scurried like cockroaches revealed under a rock. But here, orange-clad townspeople moved with happy purpose, wearing the Gate's colour, which was worn for special occasions. Something about the bright eyes and nods between neighbours passing by felt . . . contagious. Lightening the load of the nearness of my old prison, somehow.

"Over there." Edric pointed to a tiny, whitewashed shopfront with swathes of cloth almost bursting from its windows. "We won't get far if we don't blend in."

Two young men, a couple, worked in smooth synchronisation to pull ready-made garments for our stipulations. We walked out of the store wearing matching formal clothing—Edric, a shirt, coat, and trousers, while under my coat I wore a thick, fitted, button-down dress, cut to accentuate every curve as if it was made of silk instead of cotton and wool—all in the colour of bright turmeric. Only my thigh-high stockings were a sheer black.

"Go on," said Edric, narrowing his eyes at me, but the corners of his lips tugged upwards, and I realised I'd been staring at him with a hand covering my mouth.

I dropped it, barking out a laugh. "It's just that—"

"I know."

"No, no—I mean, you're always so serious, and the colour doesn't quite—"

"Yep. Let it all out, Nev. Tell me just how inadequate I look beside you."

The laughter gently drained away, leaving something warm in my belly. "You called me 'Nev.'"

"Is that allowed? Or should I call you . . ." He looked me up and down. "*Breskvica?* You've had breskvica, right? Those little peach cookies?"

Joy bubbled inside me again. "It's just that only people who *know* me call me *Nev*." Only Malina. Then Kavi. Now . . . Edric, too?

"I feel like I know you." Those lips still tugged upwards, but something more serious lay behind the playfulness. Something warm and firm and safe. "You're a rivulet. While a river rages on without control, you disappear onto your own course. You define yourself."

Blood rushed through my veins and my spine arched towards Edric.

I snapped it upright. "I'm not sure I can say the same about you."

"You don't feel like you know me?"

I shook my head, smile sliding away.

He slipped his fingers under the shoulders of his dagger-studded suspenders, coat parting to reveal the tight fit of his orange shirt over his broad chest.

"You sure you want to?"

"Yes."

He took an inhale through his nose, and his eyes fluttered closed momentarily before looking over my head. "Further up this street there's an inn named after High Gate. The walls hold paintings of the sea. The furniture is crafted in High Gate fashion. It reminds me of my old home. One day, all I'd like my life to involve is simply sitting by the ocean, reading a good book." His face relaxed as he dipped his head towards me again. "That's the most important thing you need to know about me."

I shut my open mouth. It was almost a mirror to the dream I had spoken to Malina about. Swallowing, I said, "Let's stay at that inn. And before you ask—yes, I'm sure."

Edric's shoulder brushed against mine as we strolled towards a sign that read The Bellowing Cliff, never losing contact. "I can call you Nev, then?"

I smiled, and pushed open the wooden door of the wide, double-storied building set between an apothecary and blacksmith. It seemed to be happening more frequently lately—smiling.

Inside the inn's dining hall, walls had been painted beige to mimic the sandstone buildings of High Gate. Cluttered tables and chairs of a pale, white wood filled the quiet room, empty of lunchtime patrons. Large oil paintings stood above booths and tables, parting my lips. I spied the canvas sails of boats docked in a wide bay of turquoise water, the sun setting over deep violet and rose and ochre waves. Could the ocean be so many colours? I always pictured it a simple blue. Now, I envisioned a tall, wide man with dark hair, book in hand, passing sandstone buildings to land on white sand by water of every possible hue.

"We're after lodgings for two nights. Two beds." Edric's voice spoke from a distance.

"The two of you together?" asked a young woman's voice.

"Yes."

That one word jolted me back into the room. It shouldn't have. Sure, Edric was being kind of pleasant to me, but it didn't rub out his reaction to realising I was likely a witch. Maybe it was easier for him to be civil when we both wanted Leden gone.

The innkeeper rolled her eyes, retrieving an iron key, then pushed it into Edric's hand before returning to the kitchen behind the bar. "Upstairs. Last chamber on the right."

"You've only given us one key. Isn't there a second room?"

Over her shoulder, the innkeeper said, "You should thank the Gates I'm giving you one. Tonight is the mirror ceremony. Other chambers are reserved by the hour at twice the rate."

Edric's expression tightened. We avoided looking at each other as Edric's rigid shoulders led us up narrow, ruby-carpeted stairs to our chamber. The room was small but clean, with a wide painting over a hearth depicting another ocean scene. But that wasn't what caused us to both pause in front of the open door. Pressed white sheets covered a curtainless four-post bed.

The only bed.

"I'll sleep on the floor." The bronze skin of his neck flushed. Gruff and stiff, Edric looked even less comfortable under the garments far too sunny for his disposition.

"It's fine," I said. "We'll hardly be sleeping anyway—I mean—we'll be retrieving nectar." Now my cheeks matched the colour of his neck and of the deep red rug that was a nod to High Gate's ruby dragul.

"Are you hungry?" Edric asked as I dropped my pack beside the bed. He shut the door behind him but didn't move further inside. Was Edric thinking about the last time we had been alone together?

"I had lunch before Stepping through," I said, unclenching my thighs. *Focus.* "About the nectar. It'll either be in the armoury or near the old stables. I know they used to change its location from time to time." Was it only because I had been confined in my tower so long that the urge to lunge at Edric—alone in a room together—felt this strong? I didn't want to visit those thoughts anyway. Every time I got close to Edric, something pulled him away. There was a very important task ahead, and I needed my mind focused on that, and not floating amongst the tingling sensations that started in my palms, swimming to other body parts.

"I'll go find out." His sharp jaw was clenched. "Most other Gates have their nectar held in a chamber near headquarters, so I'll search near the manor to start. We can break in tonight while the guards are focused on the ceremony. If your friend has come back to by you then, do you think we can leave the nectar in a safe location with her?"

"Yes." Now my whole body tingled with a different feeling. Our plan was real and approaching swiftly. Veligrad's freedom was close. My *true* freedom was close. A blue ocean unfurled in my future. "Okay. Let's go."

Edric fluttered his eyes closed before speaking to the ceiling. "I think you should stay. You might be recognised by guards. It'll be suspicious if you're seen asking around." My mouth opened in protest, but Edric continued, "They won't recognise me. Better you stay out of sight until evening, and then we can take the nectar together."

Tension rose to my shoulders, and I folded my arms. Before I could argue, Edric took out a pocket notebook and leant against his large, muscled thigh to write a message. "I'll leave a note at the potter's workshop for your friend."

Reluctantly, I agreed. Edric left without glancing back, the room feeling larger without him as soon as his solid footsteps faded away on the other side of the closed door. Maybe it was a good thing. Maybe we both needed some space. If Malina found my note, at least I would be here for her, waiting.

Without removing my boots, I flopped back on the smooth quilt sheet, then rubbed my face. The blank, beige ceiling stretched above me, and I avoided glancing to the painting opposite me, a dream I couldn't bear to allow inside while I lay here alone. Who knew what tonight would bring? Where would Edric and I be tomorrow? Where would Veligrad be? I blew a loud breath through puffed cheeks, needing to do something to distract the restless energy that prickled my veins.

The witches' book.

The chamber's silence amplified the gentle hiss of lamps as I ignited two wall sconces framing the bed. Grey afternoon light filtered through gauze curtains over a small window. Cautiously, I collected *A Botanist's Most Faithful Companion* and settled against the pale wooden headboard.

The moment I opened the book's cover, a thick draft of wind blew against my neck, the flavour of Midnight Gate. A sweet scent of zhivir trees and river water. Shivers skittered over my skin, but I kept my eyes on the page, knowing the bedroom door and window were both shut. A childish fear told me that if I did not look, then nothing sinister would see me, either. I flipped to the middle of the book's thick, cream pages, where I had last left off. When I raised it higher onto my thighs, a small square of paper slipped onto my stomach in a whisper. It was blank.

Weird.

I flipped both sides and carefully held it up to the soft wall light, but no writing shone through. Still bare.

And then the note burst into a ball of ruby-red flame.

Startled, my back hit the headboard as I cast a dragul sphere. The two energies collided in a blaze of coloured light, sending me tumbling off the side of the bed. Light twisted and flared as I scrambled backwards, elbows burning from the friction of the rug, ready to send forth another sphere. But the blaze stumbled, as if doused with water, and then it shrunk. Finally, it flickered into a single flame above my bed.

Rising slowly to the red flame, I blew it out.

My chest heaved, and ghosts of orbs flashed in my vision with every blink. The slip of paper lay innocently blank once more, as unscathed as the quilt on which it rested.

It was hot to the touch. Was the paper some sort of key? A clue?

My attention flicked back to the witches' book. Carefully, I clambered onto the bed once more, sliding the book into my lap. This time, I held my palms flat beneath the front and back cover and imagined initiating a dragul sphere without bringing forth its flame.

My hands grew warm.

Words on the page began melting, separating apart and then melding back together again. My jaw slackened as pages and pages of new text revealed themselves. These words were not printed by a press but written by a bold hand. One that seemed narrow and hasty in some stanzas, and lazily cursive in others, but still the same hand.

A different title now spread over the mauve, cloth cover in silver foiling. *The Coven Nightfall.*

The thudding of my heart could have broken steel. My name. A witches' book. I was part of some coven belonging to my own family.

I was a witch.

My breaths came quick and shallow as a small, missing piece was restored to the tapestry of my history. So this was the test from Mother Noche. I could hardly wait to speak with her as I scanned through the pages of new text, searching for other secrets to reveal themselves. But there was no coven history, no family tree. Instead, I faced scribbled paragraphs describing healing plants and recipes and various remedies for illness. Not all required magic.

My eyes caught on a particular heading that sent a pang through my bones: Remedies for Respiratory Sickness. It detailed healing plants, and their locations in the Smed, that could ease and cure the illness that had caused Malina's father's death. If Leden had not ordered the deaths of witches, perhaps Djordje could have been saved with medicine that required no magic at all, only knowledge. Instead, Leden chose to exterminate these women who could have helped so many, and hoarded nectar that was out of reach for most. Dryness itched my eyes as I refused to blink, refused to allow a single tear to fall. Leden's cruel reign was going to end soon.

I cleared my throat and allowed intrigue to pull my eyes onwards. There were other forms of magic I had never heard of. The more languid handwriting occurred when the author described complex spells, such as ones that created illusions of past memories to help work through old wounds of the spirit. Hours passed as I pored over the forest-scented pages, corners of the room darkening with the day's ending. Every entry in the book had a common purpose: healing and nurturing for both witches and those they helped. What would it be like to weave these spells? To not only exert brute force of destructive dragul spheres, but to do more? I recalled what Mother Noche had said to me on the night of the Midnight Gate attack.

You can heal.

Had she thought to unlock a magical healing gift within me by handing me this book? As I absorbed the ink's secrets like a sponge, a different kind of heading caught my eye.

Cunnilingus and Its Significance in Healing.

The next few paragraphs described techniques in detail on pleasuring a partner, then instructing a partner on delivering pleasure. As I read through this section with more attention than the others, my skin tightened and my body squirmed, each word drawing a picture of Edric's mouth, silver-lined teeth glinting, lowering over my stomach, then further down. Heat pulsed in my core.

The "Significance in Healing" portion of this section shared a belief that regular climaxes cleared the mind and built connection to one's uninhibited self. A factor, the author claimed, that was vital for healing magic to flourish.

Well, this version of the book was certainly interesting. I nestled further into the soft pillow behind me, the tasks ahead easing to the back of my mind as I eagerly consumed the words that stoked a growing, liquid heat that spread from my centre and outwards, making my warm skin sensitive.

Until the door flung open without warning.

I slammed the book shut and shoved it behind me as Edric's bulking frame filled the entranceway, a plate of hot burek in his hand.

"You shouldn't leave the door unlocked."

His furrowed brow separated as soon as his gaze landed on my knees pressed close to my chest and hands behind my back. Not a natural pose.

"Who doesn't knock before opening a bedroom door?" I snapped, pressing harder into the headboard, though the book's hard edges dug into my spine. It was best Edric didn't know about me possessing a witches' book.

Edric's lips parted, and his widened eyes flicked over my suspicious position. "Sorry for . . . interrupting." The corner of his mouth curved slightly upwards as my cheeks heated further. "I can come back if you need to finish something."

"No. *No.* I don't need to—I've just got to . . . put my shoes on."

Edric flicked his gaze to my boots still on my feet. *Vuk.*

"Okay." He smiled a ridiculously attractive smile with his straight, white and silver teeth. "I've found out how we can get the nectar. Make sure you put your shoes on."

CHAPTER TWENTY-SIX

T HE MIRROR CEREMONY OCCURRED the night before a marriage ceremony, where anyone the couple knew would brandish mirrors and strike instruments to ward off evil spirits. It was one of the only other occasions apart from Ranking Eve when Amber Gate townspeople came out at night, when Protectors and guards were on full duty.

Essentially, the mirror ceremony was a party.

Leden's daughter Marta and her wife-to-be were clearly known by most of Amber Gate. All streets leading up to the Amber Gate manor were alive with clashes of cymbals and drums, the trilling of frula and strings of tambura. Light reflected in flashes from small mirrors worn around necks or waved in the air as people danced, while the scent of roasting nuts and pastries wafted over the streets of Amber Gate like a delicious blanket.

"This is for you," said Edric, as we crammed up a crowded, inclined street that led to the Amber Gate manor. Small, rounded pieces of mirrored glass dangled from a silver bracelet. "To blend in with everyone. Keeps away bad luck. Apparently."

I took a final swallow of the burek, the cheese pastry sliding slowly down my throat. He kept his eyes averted as I accepted the gift. Was Edric being . . . *shy*? The mirrored bracelet glimmered in opposition to the Slom bracelet, its dark gems absorbing the surrounding darkness.

"You know," I said, "if you really want to blend in, I think you could look a little more . . . relaxed." Edric raised a suspicious brow. "Everyone else is drinking or dancing," I suggested innocently, adjusting the two canvas satchels Edric had procured, invisible beneath my coat. Two hid inside Edric's coat, too.

"You want me to dance?"

"Well—"

A heavy body shouldered into me, driving me into Edric's chest.

A young man with hazed eyes raised his hands in apology, offering a sloppy smile. Before he could utter the words, Edric gripped the man's throat and shoved him roughly onto cobblestones.

Around us, sounds of joviality turned to surprise.

"S-sorry, sir." His hands were splayed in front of his face as he shakily gasped on his back, the mirror necklace around his neck askew, but Edric's worried gaze flittered over me.

"It shouldn't be me you apologise to."

"Of course, lady, I'm sorry," he choked. "Please, please . . ."

I deadpanned Edric. This was not helping our plan to *blend in*.

"Right," Edric muttered, flicking his gaze to the surrounding stares homing in on us. Reluctantly, he lifted the male onto his feet as easily as if he was a doll, then gave him a single pat on the shoulder. The young man staggered and stared up at Edric, no less fearful. The nearby crowd looked equally unconvinced at Edric's supposed civility.

Releasing an exasperated growl, Edric pulled me away from the pocket of suspicion.

"What?" he asked at my narrowed gaze as we blended into the crowd halfway up the street. "They don't know our plan. They're not about to follow us to the armoury."

"You look too angry. Relax your shoulders. And your face."

"You're right, I am angry." Edric gazed straight ahead, shoulders tense. "You were hurt."

My stomach fluttered. "Alright, just . . . put your—put your arm around me. At least pretend to be drunk, or something."

The gentle weight of Edric's arm immediately settled across my shoulders. His salt and citrus scent did something to my legs. How could I feel heavy and weightless at the same time? A different kind of tension thrummed from Edric's body now, the anger transmuted into something else.

"Like this?" That rumbling voice was deeper than sleep.

I nodded from somewhere beneath his armpit, avoiding glancing up, unwilling to vocalise how . . . *right* this felt. Only last night, we had been more intimate than this, yet the simplicity of Edric's arm around me now made me feel closer. A statement to all around us that we belonged exclusively to each other. Even if it was only a performance.

Vuk, I was overthinking this.

"Fuck." Edric suddenly stiffened and gripped me tighter to his side.

I made to pull away. "If you don't like this, we can—"

"No, over there." I followed his gaze up the rising incline of the street to see the jaunty crowd splitting around a group of four guards. One of the guards was Toma—and speaking with them was Hartley.

"Oh, Vuk." If Hartley was risking attending Amber Gate and running into Leden after everything he had told me, he had to be really angry about Edric sneaking through the Stepping. "He's probably here to take you back to Midnight Gate."

"Let's go down that laneway." Edric nodded immediately to his left. "We'll take some other streets."

Before we could rush away, Hartley and Toma shook hands with the guards, then headed up the incline of the street in the same direction we needed to go.

"If we take a different way, we might run into them front on." I grimaced. "Let's keep going. At least we can see them ahead of us."

Edric kept me pressed firmly into his side, arm still around my shoulders, as we followed Hartley and Toma from a distance, Hartley's bronze head reflecting under lamps along the street. The pair stopped at a small inn and ducked inside, expressions grim.

"Quick." I tucked my head into Edric's warm chest, and he bent into my hair. With our faces hidden into each other like infatuated lovers, the crowd melded us into its revelry, carrying us past the inn whose doors remained shut with Hartley and Toma on the other side. Amongst the jostles of our uneven steps, Edric took a deep inhale. His hand crept up the side of my neck, entwining his fingers gently through strands of my hair.

"How's this?" he whispered, nose still buried in my hair even after the inn faded behind us.

My hand snaked its way to grip his forearm. "It's—yes," I stammered back.

A warm huff of air prickled my scalp. "*It's yes?*" Edric repeated, a smile in his voice. "That's not an answer."

I gripped his forearm tighter with a tingling palm. Did he want me to admit how good this felt? Maybe Edric really was drunk. I was spared stumbling over another response when we reached the top of the sloped street.

Before us, the tiered, formal gardens of Amber Gate manor sprawled from its small hill, guarded by my old tower at its peak beside the grand, pillared manor. The armoury was a short, square building standing to one side of Leden's residence—nice and close should anything befall its privileged residents.

"I only see two guards by the manor entrance," I said. The stars had sprinkled their luck on us tonight. From this distance, the pair of guards seemed pleasantly occupied in conversation, sharing covert swigs from a flask, clearly at ease that the mirror ceremony was no threat to the manor. Neither of them had been guards at my tower—even better. Other couples also seemed to have found their way from the street parties to the privacy provided by tall hedges and weeping tree branches. Breathy sounds and quiet giggles carried down from the tiered gardens.

"Mm?" Edric didn't move from his position draped over me, as I stopped before a hedge at the lowest tier. My heart thudded hard.

"The armoury," I breathed. "It's just up there. But we should . . . keep doing this. In case the guards look at us."

Edric finally lifted his head, his eyes blurry as if waking from a dream. "Okay." A rustle of fabric, and he shifted me in front of him, so our bodies pressed flush against each other, all without removing his hand from my hair. "Still fine?" That deep voice rumbled through my core from the contact with his chest.

I nodded up at his half-lidded gaze. Edric inhaled deeply again, then slowly walked me backwards through a parting in the hedges, and into the garden. He stopped every few paces to brush his lips past my ear or swipe a thumb over my jaw. I clenched the bulking muscles between his neck and shoulders as we wound our way closer, my head tilted back. It was all I could do to keep myself from whimpering as each touch made my skin tighter, more sensitive.

"Nearly there," he grunted. I could see nothing of where we walked. Only Edric. The intensity of his deep blue eyes travelling over me, his lips parted to reveal those darkly glinting lower teeth.

"Like the ocean," I whispered.

"Mm?"

"Your eyes. They look the same as the painting of the ocean in our room."

"Our room," Edric whispered back. "Yes." A lazy smile spread across his face. I returned it, only for Edric's expression to tighten, replaced by drawn brows and a clenched jaw. His lips barely moved when he said, "Someone's coming."

A pair of crunching boots neared. Edric tightened his arms around me, protective and strong. I gasped when my back touched cold stone. The armoury.

"They're going to make us leave," Edric murmured. "What do you want to do?"

The footsteps grew louder. Amber Gate's supply of nectar appeared in easy reach, but it was only an illusion. When Djordje was sick, of course we had considered if Malina could find a way to steal some, just a single vial. Desperation had been deflated by the risk of punishment—hanging for theft. Then there was the fact the armoury was always locked and within sight of guards. Apparently, tonight was no different.

"Just come here and—" I shoved my lips to Edric's, wrapping my arms around his neck. There was a short pause, an inhale through his nose, then Edric kissed me back. Slowly. His lips moving softly against mine, as if this was our first time. Shivers passed over my skin at his gentleness. But it wasn't enough for our act. We needed to look more convincing, fully distracted. I slipped my tongue through Edric's teeth, pushing deeper into his throat, pressing my breasts into his chest.

It was like igniting straw coated in oil.

Edric released a long groan and pushed his heaviness onto me, squeezing me between his large body and hard stone. His lips moved faster. Hungrier. Making my kisses sloppier and harder. I could hardly breathe.

"Is this okay?" I panted into his mouth.

"Of course," Edric mumbled without lifting his lips, filling spaces between words with more kisses. "Why wouldn't it be?"

"Because. Of last time." When he had ripped himself away from me after discovering the Traitor Stone.

"Hey," a high, male voice called. "You're not supposed to be up here."

Vuk. If we didn't listen, it would only draw more attention. Casting my dragul sphere could derail everything if we were discovered causing a scene, and I wanted to keep Leden's secret Heightened Power away from us, whatever it was.

Take the nectar tonight, then face Leden tomorrow night. That was the plan. To make it through this first part, we needed to pretend we were really, *really* drunk.

I moaned against Edric's mouth, loud, knowing the sound would carry down the path to the approaching guard. Edric gripped my hair tighter, his other hand grasping my waist in an almost painful hold, and then something hard and thick pressed perfectly against my throbbing centre. My legs went weak.

"Don't make me get closer. You can be in the gardens, but you know you're not permitted up here."

Edric hiked my thighs on either side of him, and my hips offered an involuntary roll onto his stomach. Edric groaned in return, deep and heavy, like tumbling rocks. The sound alone was incredible, enough to send pleasure flooding to my core in a hot ache.

A perfect performance.

It's not a performance, fool.

I whimpered. The evidence of his arousal was a strong shaft that I made tiny circles against. My skin was too hot. My core was liquid, dripping.

"Fuck's sake," muttered the nearing guard, and I gripped Edric tighter, grinding against him faster, all the way up and down his thickness, uncaring of the scraping against my back. My mouth found his neck, and I rolled my tongue from the base of his column, licking the salt from his skin.

Go away. Just go. Away. I prayed to the stars, the earth, the wolf-god Vuk.

"Noric, over here!" a female voice called. "Someone's tried to get into the tower."

If my lips were in my own control, I would have released a thanks to any and all of the gods listening to my prayers. But my lower lip was currently pinched between Edric's teeth as he pulled and sucked, helping lift my hips steadily up and down with his sturdy grip.

Gravel crunched again, but this time it was the sound of a pivot. The first guard grumbled something about the mirror ceremony being "an excuse for everyone to get off in public," before his footsteps sounded moving away, leaving us against the armoury wall.

When the sound of shifting gravel was no longer audible, I reluctantly extracted my lips from Edric's with a wet, sucking sound. His forehead dripped with perspiration as we both heaved hot air against each other's mouths.

"Are you alright?" Edric asked.

Yes. No. That wasn't enough. Instead, I nodded, not trusting myself to speak.

"Good," he breathed against my lips. My bare legs were still hooked against his hips, and Edric appeared entirely unbothered by it as he held me with one arm, the other slipping a thin dagger from his suspenders. He blinked at me while my heart raced erratically like the drumbeats from the mirror ceremony down the hill.

He shifted his gaze away to the door of the armoury. I swallowed the irrational disappointment. This was why we were here.

With a few jiggles of his strong forearm, Edric picked the lock of the armoury door, and we were inside. Reluctantly, I unhooked my legs, sliding down Edric's hips while still pressed tight. The sensation was stimulating, making my thighs clench, and I was somewhat aware Edric's shirt was now damp where I had been pressed against him. He had felt so hard. I refrained from brushing my hand against his front, aching to feel that length again.

"Best we do this quick, before that guard returns," said Edric against my forehead. He was still so close. I didn't ever want to part from his feel, his scent again. But we needed to do this for the people of Amber Gate, people like Malina's father, whose lives could be saved by a small vial of nectar. Lamplights from outside illuminated enough for us to see inside the dark room, and with a disappointed inhale, I turned away from Edric.

The room was stocked with shelves of weapons and shields and leathers, and in one corner—a glass-front cabinet of nectar. Small, wooden racks held tiny vials, the size of a thumb, but the majority of the racks were empty. There was a month until the next Ranking, and supply was clearly low. Still, there were at least four dozen remaining. With my trembling fingers, and Edric's steady hands, we plucked the vials, quickly adding them to our satchels between layers of towels from the inn.

It was done in mere moments.

"There's no one outside—let's go," said Edric. He took my hand and swiftly pulled me after him through the entrance.

It felt like we floated all the way back to the inn, all the way to *our* room. Edric held my hand the entire time or wrapped his arm across my chest where the crowds were too thick to stand side by side.

The door closed with a snap as we finally landed back inside the quiet, undisturbed bedroom bearing the painting coloured with Edric's eyes. Ocean blue. For a moment, all we could do was stare at each other's swollen lips.

"We did it," I breathed.

Edric nodded, his mouth ajar, pupils dilating, staring at me like he'd never seen me before. The curiosity he'd always had for me intensified to a blaze. He wasn't just curious, he looked . . . captivated. *Obsessed.*

My hands tingled and ached.

Trembling, I took off my coat, then my satchels, and placed them next to a bedside table. Through the thin walls of the inn, passionate moans filtered in, making my already sensitive skin hotter. Rooms rented by the hour, as the innkeeper had advised us.

I took a shaky breath. "Help me with my boots?"

Edric was on his knees before me faster than I had ever seen him move. Gently, attentively, he unlaced one boot.

"Every day," Edric's voice was rough, "when you take off your shoes"—he dropped the boot to the ground—"you need to let me do it for you."

His words hit deep in my core. "Why?"

"Because"—he moved to the other one—"you should be treated like a queen"—the boot slid from my stockinged foot—"and queens aren't allowed to take off their own shoes."

"I didn't know that was a rule." My tingling hands moved to Edric's hair of their own accord, as if they couldn't bear not to touch him. His dark locks were silky between my fingers. He fluttered his eyes closed.

"It's my rule."

Large, warm hands moved up the back of my calves, inside my dress, all the way up the curves of my ass. Edric walked forwards on his knees, pushing me gently until I sat on the bed. I lay back, pulling Edric's collar until he sat above me in a straddle, two fists beside my head, every muscle under his shirt taut. Enclosed by the cage of his body, I knew this was the only trap I would ever willingly choose.

My dress swept against skin as I lifted my hips, pulling the fabric to bunch at my waist.

"What other rules are there?" I said, unbuttoning my front.

Edric's gaze followed my fingers as they revealed my bare breasts. "If you want to stop, we stop."

"I don't want this to stop. Trust me on this." *Trust me on everything,* I wanted to say, but I didn't need to. I knew we were so close, and only getting closer.

"I don't deserve you." Edric's throat bobbed, gaze roaming from my thigh-high stockings, over my breasts exposed between my unbuttoned dress, and up to my lips. "I haven't been truthful to you."

"Edric." I reached a palm to his stubbled cheek. "Every time I think you've run away from me, I find that you're always following. That's all I want. I can let go of my control when I'm with you, because I know you're there to catch me. To support me. This is only our start. You'll tell me your truths, and I'll tell you mine." I caught the quiver in my throat as my own truth poured out. "I just want you."

"You just want me?" He breathed, eyes half-lidded. "Always?"

"Always." It was simple. Edric was curious, intelligent, genuine. *Kind.* He had saved me from the vukodlak after the Ranking. He had released that trapped bittern when it had been suffering, despite its rumoured bad luck. He'd followed me up Ruined Hill, not for the miran flower, but for me. He'd followed me to Amber Gate, wanting Leden's death, but prioritising my wish to retrieve the miran nectar first. *Poetry. Justice. The ocean. Empowerment.* He shared my values, my dreams. It was time to put aside the things that had divided us and be together.

"Always," Edric repeated. "I promise you'll be safe and free. You'll be with me. Always."

"Good," I said, my chest rising and falling. "Now," I said, my voice unrecognisably husky, "I want you to fuck me."

Edric's eyes darkened, emanating liquid heat. The ocean on fire. "I will."

Edric hooked his thumbs underneath his suspenders and let them drop to his sides before swiftly unbuttoning the top of his shirt, roughly pulling it over his head. Buttons pinged and seams ripped in his haste.

I will never unsee this.

No matter what happened after this moment, it would not be possible to look at Edric again without picturing his bare torso and suspenders hanging loosely off his trousers. His muscles were gigantic, bulking swells of power and strength. An old scar of shiny skin ran vertically between his packed pecs. My limbs tingled—lack of oxygen, anticipation, excitement, awe—I couldn't keep up with the rushing beneath my skin.

Edric pushed my dress over my head and threw it carelessly to the ground. "These stay on," he said, fingering the top of my thigh-high stockings. "These come off." He tugged off my plain, black underwear, scrunched them in a fist, then shoved them in his pocket.

That act alone was enough to make me dripping wet.

He exhaled roughly, eyes on the slickness between my thighs. "You're so ready for me, aren't you?"

"Yes." I gripped my own breasts, pinching my nipples to satiate some of the fiery energy yearning to be set further alight. "Fuck me."

"I said I will." He smiled dangerously, eyes narrowed, voice hardly a rasp. The rest of his clothes were off in a blink, and Edric bracketed my body again, his indigo dragul crystal dangling over my breasts. My mouth dried at the sight of his huge, erect cock above my entrance.

"It's going to be perfect for you," he rasped, pumping with one hand.

It looked perfect. Everything about this moment was perfect. I wet my lips and replaced his hand with mine, guiding his cock to my entrance, my palm full with his thickness. Edric shuddered at my touch, then slowly, he pushed it through.

"Oh," I breathed. "*Edric.*"

A few more slow thrusts, and then he was in. Deep. All the way to the hilt. "That's it. So perfect."

It was. I gaped at him as unimaginable pleasure hit every single mote of my body with each thrust of his cock. A shriek escaped my lips as his hilt ground against my clit.

"That's right. You're so good at this. Did you know how good you'd make me feel?"

Someone else's breathy moans carried through the wall beside our room. The heat in my lower belly twisted. I raised my own cries.

"You love this, don't you?" He knew it from the way I rocked up and down with what limited range of motion I had from lying on my back. "You're my queen. You're my nightmare. You're my everything."

Edric interlaced his fingers through mine, our hands gripping each other so tightly that the two bracelets' dangling charms pricked into my wrist. The tinge of pain was perfect. I wanted to sit up, to switch positions and ride him instead. To taste his cock. I wanted everything, but I was already coiling too tight, threatening to come loose. I squeezed my fingers into Edric's, something like panic burning through me.

"*Edric*, I'm going to—"

Edric groaned at the same time I shrieked as I exploded, coming right on his cock. Pleasure burst from my core to my heart, radiating through my limbs, tingling and burning everywhere. It was like nothing I had ever experienced in my life. More intense than the times before. I felt at once whole and splintered into thousands of pieces. Edric moaned my name as he came, too, warmth spilling from where we joined, as he continued to thrust in and out.

"*Nevena.*" It sounded like he was begging. His hair was drenched, sweat dropping onto my face. "I'm yours, Nevena."

A sob hiccupped my chest.

I ran my fingers through the wet hair across his forehead as we both slowed, our panting still heavy. Twin tears fell from the creases of my eyes and into the hair at my temples. Edric kissed them at either side.

"So beautiful," he breathed. "I've never felt—"

Suddenly, Edric's eyes widened as his attention caught on something beside me.

Warmth trickled down my right wrist where my hand was still intertwined with Edric's. His face was aghast, petrified. Afraid he had hurt me.

"It's okay. My bracelet, it dug into—"

The two bracelets dangled halfway down my forearm, nowhere near my palm. I extracted my hand from Edric's stiff fingers. A curved, red line cut deep into my skin from the base of my little finger to the base of my thumb, as if sliced with a knife.

"How did . . ."

My stomach dropped. Something Kavi had said. And a memory from a book Malina had found about the Fae Gates of Veligrad. Each Gate had been built so strong because of the magic imbued with the bond of those fated to live their lives as one, signalled by the bond mark. A red crescent.

Edric's mouth opened and closed; colour drained from his lips. "You're my . . ."

Mate.

"How?" I whimpered. "That can only occur if one of us is—"

An urgent knock on the door sounded.

"Fae," I said, my voice little more than a whisper.

Edric lifted himself off me in a blur. My heart thrashed in my throat and my stomach all at once, hard enough to pierce through skin. He was bigger, faster, and stronger than anyone I had seen. He was intent on breaking the Curse. He was constantly drawn to me. But it wasn't possible. Couldn't be possible.

"Edric?"

He held his cut hand before him, slick chest heaving. "I—"

The knock banged louder. "Nightfall. Silvan." Hartley's voice rang clearly from the other side, and I jolted from the bed. "I know you're in here. Something has happened. I need you both."

CHAPTER
TWENTY-SEVEN

E DRIC RIPPED FABRIC OFF one of the canvas satchels and tied it around my hand while I sat naked and numb. My bones felt hollow, but my blood rushed wildly, desperate for an explanation. It couldn't be real. If Edric was fae, he would be a vukodlak.

Say something, I willed him, unable to lift the words off my tongue.

He said nothing as he pulled on his trousers and shirt, his thick brows bent into two hands praying. Maybe he was just as confused as I was?

Hartley knocked again, harder, and Edric flashed me a glance. *Oh*, he knew something. That expression wasn't praying, it was begging.

"I'll explain everything," he finally uttered, tying fabric around the red crescent across his left palm. "I swear to you, I didn't know—"

"Don't make me smash this door open," Hartley threatened from the other side. Still in shock, I slipped on my dress and unlaced shoes, just as Hartley broke off the door handle and strode inside.

"What are you—" Hartley looked between our dishevelled states. Behind him stood Toma, eyes bulging. "I don't even want to—it doesn't matter. Nevena, there's something you need to see in the tower. It's to do with Leden."

That was the last thing I had expected. I resisted exchanging a glance with Edric.

"What is it?" Edric demanded roughly. His legs stood apart in a protective stance in front of me.

"We can't discuss it here."

The journey back towards Amber Gate manor was tense; Edric and I unable to speak about the red crescents that marked our palms, and Hartley unable to tell us what was so serious he hadn't even berated Edric for Stepping through to Amber Gate with me. Toma flicked pinched glances my way, fearful glances at Edric. Why was Toma even here?

The drunken mirror ceremony crowd was thinner, those who lingered moving slower. Only a few hours remained of this cold night.

Each footstep closer to my tower made my ribs echo with hollowness. All the while, my bleeding palm tingled and itched with an urge to grip Edric's skin, to feel the warmth of his blood and the beat of his heart. Walking beside him wasn't close enough. The gap of space between our stiff arms felt like the vast distance between stars.

It was a gap I maintained.

Avoiding guards, Hartley eventually led us around the back of the manor, stopping before the courtyard that I had looked down upon every day for thirteen years. An instinct to press into Edric intensified. Hartley nodded to Toma in some unspoken signal, and my previous lover left to approach the two guards stationed before my old tower.

Waiting in the deep shadows of the manor's side, Hartley turned to Edric and I. "Toma has been suspicious of Leden's intentions for a while. He started corresponding with me after the Ranking about Leden's movements. Every few weeks, Leden releases the guards from duty near the manor for a night. Did that ever happen while you were here?"

I shook my head, frowning. Gravel shifted under boots as Edric moved a fraction closer towards me, still not touching.

Hartley grimaced and continued. "No guards have been allowed to enter the tower. Some have been dismissed, neither they nor their families seen again. Only Leden has a key."

In the distance, Toma was having a hurried conversation with the guards. I heard the word "vukodlak." My insides twisted at the memory of him doing something similar the first night I tried to escape. The night Edric's innocent brother died by my hand.

"Earlier tonight, I broke the lock and tried to open the door when guards were distracted. I only had time to look quickly, but—" Toma signalled to Hartley with a wave. "I want you to look inside," Hartley continued. "Tell me if what you see was normal while you worked as Mortician. Quickly, before the guards return."

He wanted me to go back inside the tower that had held me trapped while I'd yearned for freedom, life, self-control. Nearing it was one thing, but the thought of going inside made my skin crawl and my lungs compress with heaviness. What if I went in and I couldn't ever get out again?

"I'll be right beside you," said Edric, voice low and gravelly. Could he feel the sensations running through my body? Or was I visibly trembling?

"It'll be too obvious if there's too many of us near the tower and someone sees. You keep a lookout here, Silvan."

"I'm going. To be. Right. Beside. Her," Edric said to Hartley, slowly, dangerously.

My knees trembled harder. *Who are you, Edric Silvan?* I wanted to ask. *What are you keeping from me?* My palm tingled with dull pain at the deep cut between my thumb and little finger. *Who am I?* All those times I'd felt the tingling sensation when Edric and I had been close, I'd never thought it had been anything more than—I don't know, excitement? Could we really be . . .

Hartley was waiting for me to move. This could be the moment I find something on Leden that could bring about his downfall. Regardless with what was going on between Edric and I, our plan was to end Leden. Before I could mull over it any longer, I strode towards the arched wooden door. Two pairs of footsteps followed. Toma was there waiting, the lock's hasp and staple already wrenched off.

Sweat broke out above my upper lip, under my arms. The heat of Edric's presence was the only thing reassuring me against the fear I was being trapped again. Alone. Forgotten. Powerless.

No. I was none of those things any more.

I straightened my spine and pushed against heavy wood.

A putrid stench wafted from inside the mortuary chamber. Worse than any of the deaths I'd ever had to clean up.

"*What the fuck,*" I choked.

The room was full of corpses.

Piled atop each other across every surface—preparation tables, the floor, propped up against the kiln door, blocking the winding stairway. Stiff limbs and matted hair. Not cleaned, nor prepared, nor incinerated. Simply dumped.

All had one element in common: Their throats were ripped open, and their shrivelled bodies lay devoid of fluid. Drained of blood.

Edric dragged me back into his chest, arm across my front, the contact doing little to assuage the sight of tortured corpses.

"Did you ever see anything like this?" asked Hartley, sleeve across his mouth.

"Never," I uttered. I had always prepared the dead immediately, wasting no time before placing them in the kiln.

"We didn't think so." He exchanged a concerned glance with Toma. "We suspect Leden is Cursed. He's always said he never had a Heightened Power, but what if his power is a glamour? What if Leden is a vampir?"

It all aligned with Edric's theory, too, and his grip across my chest tightened. Leden was known for a severity borne from a vukodlak that had killed his eldest child, and nearly bitten him. But what if it really had? And now, Leden didn't want the Curse to break because it could break him, too—break his *power*, at the very least. The night of the Blood Moon Ball, it must have been Leden who had killed Gorcha, aiming for me.

What did that make Edric? Was he a vampir as well, wearing a glamour?

Edric stiffened, as if sensing the thought cross my mind. "Nev, I *promise* I'm not like him." Lightning fast, he spun me to face him, grabbing my marked palm and pressing my fingers to his sternum, over the scar I had seen.

"Do you feel that?" Distinct bumps ran down the centre of the flat bone. "They're Slom gems. Inside of me."

I wanted to thrash out of his grip, but there was no denying it. Another piece of the tapestry revealed itself, threads unknotting and smoothing themselves into a picture. *It lifts enchantments*, Edric had told me.

"You're fae," I uttered.

His neck was corded, his stare pained. "The Slom gems protected me from the Curse, Nev. I'm not Cursed. Not a vampir. I'm simply fae."

A dragul sphere lit the room in indigo. Toma stood behind Hartley, whose jaw was slack, but gaze determined, ready to strike. "Let her go, and step away."

"You have no idea what's going on here, Tavion."

Hartley's dragul sphere grew larger at the use of his first name.

I needed space. Not a fight. Disentangling myself from Edric's grip, I turned away, ready to run from this cursed tower that had never nourished me with anything of my choosing. That was when my eyes caught a tangle of frizzy blonde hair poking out from the base of a pile of bodies.

No.

My legs moved of their own volition. Hands vaguely aware of pressing against cold, stiff skin, pushing against mounds of stacked heaviness. Bodies hit the floor in sickening smacks and cracks before the others could comprehend what I was doing.

And then I brushed hair aside, revealing her face.

"No!" My scream was a tearing, grating beast.

Someone's hand clapped over my mouth, but I didn't care. I screamed the muffled word over and over again, and then her name.

Malina's skin was so withered it could have blown away in flakes, wrinkles aging her by decades. The one person who had brought life into my world of death. The only one who had cared, who had risked herself to give me comfort. How was it fair for her life to end like this?

Someone large and strong hoisted me against his chest, as I grappled to clasp her cold hand. There was no purchase, and I was carried out, screams still tearing from my throat into torn fabric wrapped around a palm.

He was running. Tears streamed from my eyes, pulled by the cold speed of wind as Edric ran faster than I had ever thought he could.

Somewhere in the Smed, we stopped in complete darkness. Edric cast a dragul sphere, not releasing me from his arms, as Hartley deposited Toma from his back.

"So Leden's got to be a vampir under glamour. What the fuck are *you*, Silvan?" Hartley demanded, casting a dragul sphere of his own.

"I'm the result of Leden's hatred against anyone trying to break the Curse." Edric's anger rumbled from his chest through to mine, where I still clung, my heart torn, slashed, ruptured. *Empty*. Edric could be a vampir, and I would still hang here, picturing Malina's death. It had not been gentle, unlike her spirit. It had been hard, like her life. Nothing was so undeserved as this.

"What the fuck is that supposed to mean?" Toma unsheathed a short sword.

"Put that away before you hurt yourself."

"*Silvan*," Hartley admonished, "I am your superior, and you *will* tell me exactly who you are."

Edric ignored Hartley, peering down at my frozen form, my expressionless gaze. Some of his hardness fell away like water splashed over ice. "There are protective gems which defend its holder from any spell. You know they work," he said only to me, disregarding the others. "When the Curse fell, my mother embedded the Slom stones into me." He gently placed my fingers on his sternum again. "Others who possessed the gems did the same to their loved ones." There were ridges. Five bumps. The size of the gems that dangled from my wrist.

"Why didn't you tell me?" I croaked.

"What would you have thought? Would you have believed me? You would have thought it impossible." That was exactly what I *had* thought. "Leden declared all fae Cursed, all witches a threat. Anyone remotely suspected of having power to break the Curse, Leden deterred by manipulating others' beliefs, convincing them the individual was a danger. Even you were locked in the Amber Gate tower in case you possessed a hint of magic, and no one thought to help you. If I told you any of this, you would have run from me, and I would have followed. And kept following. And *kept* following. I didn't want to frighten you. I wanted to tell you when the time was right." Edric encircled my bandaged hand with his. "But this? It happens so rarely. I *never* suspected. I never even considered I was deserving of . . . keeping you."

Some feeling returned to my skin as Edric held me. His breath on my face. The warmth of his fingers. A dull splash of a tear on my cheek—Edric's tear—its salt leaking into the crevice of my lips. His eyes were an ocean of anguish.

I squirmed in his grip, and he placed me lightly on the quiet forest floor.

"What will happen to the fae if the Curse is broken? Or to those bitten and turned?" I asked, standing close enough to feel heat emanating from his chest.

"The only certain thing is that the vukodlak will be no more. Whether they perish or return to their original form . . . that I don't know. Either way, it will be a better fate than the tortured forms they dwell in now. They're suffering."

That's why Edric had given them quick, efficient deaths. He had asked me to do the same at the Blood Moon Ball.

Hartley stepped forward, his dragul sphere slightly shrunken. "You know how to break the Curse?"

Edric considered Hartley before responding. "Yes. It's going to take a huge wave of power. A Caster dragul." His eyes lowered to Hartley's collarbones. "At least one."

Hartley closed a fist around his indigo crystal. "Leden's dragul. Right?"

After a long pause, Edric inclined his chin a fraction.

"You want to kill Leden," Hartley observed, his eyes flicking between Edric and I, understanding of our planning fitting into the slots of his own. Leden's demise, with Hartley to take his place as Head of the Council. "This is delicate," said Hartley. Those three words were a deluge of cold water penetrating through my numbness. "I was planning on speaking with the other Casters first. Now I have evidence that Leden is doing something untoward, I can raise it with them. Unseat Leden publicly through the Council."

My insides stirred again. An unpleasant swill. "Things might be *delicate* for you." My fists clenched, drawing the pain of the red crescent's cut. "But for the townspeople here, they're as solid and real as those"—I choked—"*bodies* in the tower. These people aren't safe." Not even the stolen nectar hidden in the inn would help Amber Gate if Leden was stealing people, draining them of life. "What's the point of being a Protector if we don't *Protect*? We need to act for them. Now."

It didn't matter if Hartley didn't want to participate in this. My mind was set, my choices made, and I didn't need the rotten pincers of my Heightened Power in order to feel a sense of control. Edric's warm presence—no matter how twisted and confusing—was at my back to support and empower my decision. My free choice.

"Fine." Hartley lifted his chin. "But we can't rush this. We need to wait until he's vulnerable. Our power isn't as strong this far away from Midnight Gate, and Leden's Protectors surround him at all times. I don't know if he's manipulated them, too." Hartley extinguished his dragul sphere, so only Edric's remained, casting dark light on our circle. "We'll wait until the end of the wedding. He'll least expect it after everyone's drunk, when he makes his way from the ceremony back to the manor."

The agreement was stiff and suspicious. But the details were confirmed. Tomorrow night. After the wedding. Leden would be dead, and the Curse broken.

Hartley left hurriedly, carrying Toma on his back to speed away from the forest. They needn't have run. The Smed no longer felt so sinister compared to the Amber Gate tower.

The night was lifting, filtering to grey, when we returned to the quiet inn subdued with the after-effects of rakija. Edric pulled off my boots as soon as I sat on the bed, delivering on a promise made before my heart had been uprooted. He didn't join me when I crept into the jaws of the covers, standing in the middle of the still-dark room.

"Edric?"

"Yes?" He was by my bedside before I even finished saying his name. Attentive, alert. His fae speed was going to take some time getting used to. Especially if we were *fated mates*. It was an ache in my palm, a wriggling energy in my veins, but there was too much grief tonight to contemplate it further. He was still so tentative about it. So was I.

"The bracelet you gave me. Whose was it?" I asked, though I knew the answer already.

"My brother's." I squeezed my eyes shut. "It was in his pocket when I collected his body. When the Curse descended, there was no time to safely embed them under his skin, like mine." Softer, Edric said, "I buried Ander next to the Lutava River. It leads to the ocean where we're from."

The guards had taken Ander's body away after his death, saying they would dispose of it themselves, seeing as I had been too traumatised.

"Why wasn't he wearing it?" I whispered. "He looked Cursed when I—" A thick lump lodged in my throat.

Edric sat cautiously on the bed. My body shuddered at his proximity. I could touch him if I wanted to. If he wanted to. My shredded heart panged with whatever was left of it as I recalled these were the same thoughts I'd had towards Malina. I had held her in my arms once, and now I never could again.

I grasped Edric's marked hand and pulled him under the covers. The length of his frame curled around mine, large and steady and soft.

"Sometimes he took off the gems to try and test a way to break the Curse." Edric spoke against the top of my head. "The Curse starts at the eyes and takes some time to fully transform."

Oh. That was why Ander had looked Cursed. I scrunched my face, squeezed my arms, my legs, holding inside all the parts of me that felt too unstable to release.

"Let it go," Edric whispered. "Let the salt flow. Let it cleanse."

I sniffed, eyes still bunched. "Is that another Rieka poem?" I hadn't heard of it.

"No," he breathed, deep and soothing. "That's just me."

Shifting to face into his chest, I did what Edric said, and I let go. My sobs wracked my body, as everything, *everything* pushed to the surface. Salt stung. It stung at the memories of a smaller Nevena, waiting for a parent that had left her all alone, no one to care for her, to come back and save her. It stung at the grief that weighted my limbs with the knowledge that Malina's kind smile was forever gone. It stung at the fears I held with clenched hands of losing control, then at the irony of my vile Heightened Power.

Salt pricked and prodded and pushed, until the rivulets spilling down my raw cheeks emptied their source. Everything still hurt, but that was what happened when salt cleansed wounds.

Edric held me until I felt weightless. He entwined his left hand into my right, our fae marks kissing as my lungs softened and slowed.

Eventually, I took a breath where my grief didn't feel so spiky any more.

"That's it," he soothed as I drifted towards the comfort of dark sleep. "I'm here for you, Nev. I'll follow you, always." Before heaviness sealed my senses, I thought he whispered something against my temple, but I couldn't be sure. *"And I'll impale silver into the eyes of anyone who tries to ever hurt you again."*

As my breath deepened, my lips slipped into a smile.

CHAPTER
TWENTY-EIGHT

T HE DRUMBEATS OF THE wedding reception were meant to be joyful. The two brides certainly danced like the happiest women in Veligrad, linking hands in a circle with townspeople to dance the traditional *kolo*, a chain of laughter and kicking feet. The Amber Gate arch reflected light from the relit bonfire, making dancing shadows flicker. Long feasting tables to one side had been abandoned in favour of the twining dance. To me, the drums sounded like a warning. An all-knowing, menacing threat that beat within my skull.

Go back in your cage, they seemed to drum. *It's safer in there.*

No. My own voice was stronger. I rubbed the bandage over the red crescent on my right palm. Whatever happened next, I *chose* to embrace it.

"I don't like this," muttered Hartley from beside me. "You should have listened to me. We should have waited."

Leden had spied the three of us earlier with suspicion but had been too preoccupied with the ceremony to approach. His daughter Marta appeared completely ignorant of anything but her wife's smile, thin gold circlets around their heads as bright as their joy. The only time I saw the harsh rigidity of Leden's frame soften was when he looked at his daughter. It did nothing, however, to soften my own resolve.

"Not a single other life deserves to be wasted for Leden's greed and cruelty, and—" I stopped. The tears had dried before the ceremony commenced, but a pressure still built in my throat when I thought of Malina.

"I get it. But it's not the most convincing plan. Leden could suspect us."

"We have three dragul against his one," I said, cricking my tense neck to each shoulder. Those rotten pincers perked up beneath my skin like they wanted to be counted, too, and I wrenched them back down. *I won't need it. I won't defile myself—especially not for Leden.*

On my other side, Edric's little finger brushed against mine. It was agony to do nothing, picturing the corpses of those Leden had destroyed in the tower, while his amber dragul sparkled humbly at his neck. Leden's assistant had begrudgingly accepted our story about Hartley deciding to come last minute to express his congratulations, and we were stationed where the clearing met the forest line, as far from the celebrations as possible, as if he worried we would spoil the festivity.

Which we would.

All the formalities of the evening had long passed, and the revellers were as drunk as the night before. I didn't blame them, when there were little occasions to celebrate and feel safe in their own town. Thanks to Leden.

"Where's he going?" Hartley growled as the Caster promptly rose from his seat near the head of a feasting table, moving towards the direction of the town. Two Amber Gate Protectors followed, one of them Kavi's nemesis, Ryker. I narrowed my eyes at the back of his shorn head. Surely, Ryker and his companions weren't oblivious to Leden's actions. "Toma said Leden planned to stay until the very end."

Toma's chestnut head gave a shake in our direction, from where he stood amongst guards. Absconding our post to follow Leden now would be obvious. Not the inconspicuous ambush we had planned.

Edric looked only to me, gaze unwavering, voice low and soothing, even against the urgency of decision before us. "What would you like to do?"

The question made my heart squeeze. While I wanted Leden's downfall for what he had done to my life, to Malina, to the people of Amber Gate, Edric surely wanted it just as much, or more. For him, this would end the Curse that had destroyed his entire people, derailed his life, separated him from his family. What had Edric's life been before the Curse? There was so much I wanted to know. If we did this, we could have space, safety, *time* to speak openly. To learn. I would find Mother Noche, too, and finally discover who I truly was.

"We do it now."

Hartley frowned. "But the people—"

"They can see him for what he is," I snapped. These people had lost their loved ones to Leden, and they deserved the truth, too.

Edric spread his shoulder blades back. "Then we do it now."

The certainty in his tone made my chest expand. He held my gaze until I gave him a nod. Then together we cut through the centre of the dance floor, Hartley begrudgingly following. There was no point in hiding our intentions any more. Drums followed the beat of our footsteps through the middle of the dancers who faltered their steps, sensing something amiss. Music faded into mutters.

"Leden," I called between the parting crowd. He stopped at the clearing's edge where pavement met wild grass, offering me the back of his stiff, narrow shoulders.

"Caster Hartley," Leden responded over his shoulder, ignoring me entirely. "You and your Protectors seem to be inept at following orders lately. Surely on the wedding of my only surviving child, it is not too much to ask?"

Ryker and his companion tensed beside Leden. Ryker looked different. Haggard. That fiery spirit beaten into grey ashes.

I was done wasting time. I pulled the thin dagger Edric had given me in the first ever moments of freedom from my confinement and cut a stinging gash on my forearm. Blood spilt down my arm all the way to my palm, just as a gust of wind blew from the forest behind me, carrying the metallic scent and whirling it across the clearing to where Leden stood.

"Ah," he said calmly and finally turned to face three indigo dragul spheres.

Townspeople scurried away, leaving a crater of space. My stomach tensed at the moments before the final proof of Leden's depravity. Vampir couldn't resist blood. In moments, we would have what we need to end Leden and end the Curse.

Seconds passed. Sweat trickled down my forehead.

"Caster Hartley, care to explain what it is you think you and your Protectors are doing?" Leden's stiff, mortal form remained.

Vuk. Did we get it wrong? Was it all conjecture? All the signs pointed at Leden being a vukodlak. If he wasn't, then—

"Fuck it," Edric growled, drawing his arm back. "I know it's you."

Blazing indigo flames shot towards Leden across the clearing, enough to incinerate him whole—and ricocheted against a white dragul sphere cast by Leden. Edric gripped the collar of my neck, and we dove hard to the ground, droplets splattering from my cut arm. Hartley dropped beside us, too, as Edric's magic burst against the side of the Amber Gate arch in a shower of sparks. Screams raked the air as townspeople scrambled away like scurrying ants.

Leden took a deep breath. His form quivered around the edges—and then he morphed. Fangs extended from his jaw like stalactites. His chest and limbs expanded, ripping through the orange ceremonial jacket to reveal slimy, grey skin over stringy muscles, wiry grey hair running down his back. His irises disappeared, eyeballs globes of maggot-white, and his ears grew long and pointed. A dozen flaming white dragul spheres hovered above his palms, the colour of a vukodlak's pus-coated eye.

Shouting guards and Protectors gathered into confused formation, swords and bows directed at their leader, where Leden now stood in his vampir form.

"Witch blood has always been my favourite," he hissed between fangs. Teeth first, his clawed legs pounded towards me.

Edric was a spring of muscles, already on his feet and hurtling another dragul sphere at Leden's approach. The vampir paused his charge to block Edric's magic with his own, a collision of combusting flame. Hartley and I rose to add our own flames against Leden—which he blocked again. And again. Neither my power nor Hartley's or Edric's speeds could do anything to penetrate through the near-constant blazing power surrounding Leden. A shield of spheres. Without Midnight Gate's magic, the three of us were slow, and Leden was so powerful. As we threw sphere after sphere, Leden pushed closer, driving us back towards the arch.

"The witch," he hissed. "Give me the witch." Then he blasted his burning, white orbs in a chaotic parry.

Searing heat hit my shoulder as the edge of Leden's power sheared past. I cried out as my skin blistered and blood poured out.

"Nev!" Edric hauled me behind the arch's column, away from Leden. "I have a vial of nectar." He fumbled in his pocket while his eyes remained locked on me, but I lay a trembling hand on his forearm to stop him.

"Edric." My voice shook. The pincers of my power nipped me hard. *We can fix this*, they promised. *This is what we're for.* It was true. What was it for, if not to protect the innocent from monsters like this? "My power. I could—"

"*No.*" Edric gripped the sides of my face, his jaw set. "I don't want you to change yourself. Not for *him*. We can do this." He was fierce and strong and beautiful. Whether it was what I had told him, or some awareness through our new bond, he understood what I feared using my power would do to me.

Hartley lugged himself around the column, panting. "I said we should've *waited*," he hissed. "Right now he's licking the ground where Nightfall's blood spilt, but those fucking spheres are still around him."

"Don't blame Nev," Edric growled. "We all decided we'd do this together."

Together.

A flame ignited in my mind.

"The Kora," I said, drawing Hartley's puzzled brows. "I know it's broken, but what if we join our power together?

There's a reason we were able to connect in the first place. We can't do this alone."

That was it, wasn't it? I had thought I was alone for so long in my tower, even when Malina had urged me it didn't need to be that way. I wanted to hold on to control myself. I wasn't sure if I could accept my Heightened Power, but I *could* accept the help of others. It didn't mean I was losing control over myself.

"Nev's right," said Edric. "We have to try."

Leden's sickly grunts sounded from nearby, slurping and grazing the stone paving.

I cast a sphere of indigo flame and placed a hand on the arch. Hartley watched doubtfully as Edric lightly placed his hand over mine. A shudder ran through my body at his warm touch, and then again when he cast his own sphere.

With a reluctant growl, Hartley pressed his hand over Edric's, too.

There was no need for a spell as my magic neared Edric's and Hartley's of its own accord, led by an instinct. Gargoyle faces and carved vines were illuminated under the cool light of our growing dragul spheres.

Our hands pressed tight against the Gate, against each other, as three orbs merged into one.

Power soared through my veins. Rushing sugar, strength, thrills, *love*. The single dragul sphere grew wider, spitting flames of indigo and gold that licked at the air, tasting the corruption it sought to destroy.

My hand pushed off the Gate. Hartley moved his hand to my shoulder, while Edric wound his fingers through mine. Magic surged like a current of the Lutava River through the places our touch connected to each other.

Together, we stepped out from the arch's protection.

"There she is." Leden raised himself from the cracked ground, his voice rasping like steel against stone. A chuckle rasped from between cracked lips. "You know, it was only after your departure that I found I never needed you to clean up my messes. Mortals are so gullible when they're afraid. What a pity I hadn't known you were a witch." He licked a swollen, purple tongue over his fangs, and then he leapt.

Magic surged through me with blazing heat, and the giant dragul sphere collided with Leden's magic.

Everything exploded in brilliant light, as if the sun crashed into the earth.

The impact flung me backwards, Edric and Hartley skidding across the clearing alongside me, tearing skin and cracking ribs. At the same time, Leden was thrown into the Gate's stone column with a sickening crack.

Air sizzled as magic dissolved. Heat warped the air. Silence.

A hot hand clamped around my bleeding forearm. "Nev."

Blood trickled from Edric's temple; his brow furrowed into desperate grooves.

"Yes," I gasped, and Edric's face softened. "Did we do it?"

Hartley raised onto an elbow behind Edric, panting. "He's not moving."

Warm blood dribbled rivulets down my skin as we limped carefully towards Leden's still body, but the pain hardly registered, screaming somewhere distant.

Leden lay crumpled on his side at the base of one column in tattered shreds of clothing, returned to his mortal form except for his eery white eyes still open. No breath lifted his chest.

Footsteps pounded as Toma and the guards ran forwards. The explosion had blasted tables apart, and pained cries rang out across its path of destruction. Guards administered what remaining nectar they possessed, and guilt tugged at my sleeve for the nectar that still hid in the inn room. At the clearing's furthest edge, Leden's daughter clutched her wife in the distance, crying while her wife stroked her head and wailing, "I don't understand. I just don't understand."

"Is he dead?" Toma reached us, leaning over Leden's corpse. Hartley nodded. "He's dead."

"I don't only want him dead. I want him eradicated." The daggers along Edric's suspenders unsheathed themselves in a whisper, as if seven invisible hands pulled them free, then merged to form one spike. Too many events had occurred for this to even shock me any more. Edric had a Heightened Power. Or was it a fae power? "This ends now." He handed the spike to me. It was cool and warm at the same time. "Finish Leden first, then we break the Curse."

I nodded at my . . . *mate*. His eyes glimmered, light over an ocean that we would one day visit together. This was about to end, and we were going to have our new beginning.

"Straight through his heart." Edric positioned me in front of him, his breath tickling the hairs behind my ear.

My stomach fluttered. Ribs aching, I raised my arms. No pain could hinder me. For my life. For Malina's life.

"*Ah!*" The cry was Toma's, as Leden's hand suddenly shot out and gripped his leg. Before we could react, Leden clambered up Toma's back and latched his teeth into his neck.

"NO!" Hartley cried, but it was Edric who reached Leden first, ripping him from Toma and smashing his back into the Gate's column.

Edric pinned Leden's arms against stone, but it couldn't stop Leden's long neck from stretching and sinking his teeth into Edric's shoulder, nor could it stop the dragul spheres Leden ignited to surround them.

"Edric!" I scrambled forwards but was helpless to do anything as Edric thrashed, punching and elbowing, trying to remove Leden draped across his back. Leden's white orbs circled the two of them to form a barrier. The silver spear was useless, and I couldn't throw a dragul sphere at Leden without risking it hitting Edric, too. The vampir was hooked on to Edric like a leech.

There was only one thing left to do.

With deliberate intention, I called forth my Heightened Power.

Blood spattered down my face as my skin split painfully. Those pincers rose at once on a giddy wave of power. They clacked in anticipation as I released them towards Leden, seeking for the invisible threads of his consciousness, the strings that would make him my sick puppet. I reached for the column of Leden's spine, accepting the rotten burden that would inevitably follow—

Only there was nothing to grasp.

Leden's consciousness was a solid wall of stone that my power could not penetrate.

No.

My head spun, and I dropped to all fours, my entire body shuddering as Leden sucked Edric's blood, pale eyes bulging over Edric's shoulder as he drank. Leden's wiry forearm was fastened across Edric's chest, unable to be shifted, even as Edric choked Leden's neck from behind and bashed himself against the Gate to try and loosen Leden's hold.

Again, I drove those pincers towards Leden. They clicked in agitation, searching for something that wasn't there.

I know it is there.

Kavi had said there were ways of building mental shields around the mind when she had been speaking about Caster Rada. That must be what Leden had done. My power was untrained, but I had to try. Reaching a trembling arm in Leden's direction, I pushed the invisible magic of my pincers again. This time they scraped away some stone, trickling like sand.

I can do this.

Hartley was trying to staunch the blood flowing from Toma's neck. The other guards and Protectors merely watched on as horror slackened their jaws, too shocked or frightened to act. Not that they could penetrate the dragul spheres surrounding Leden anyway.

"*Edric.* Hold on. I'm nearly there!" I cried, picking away at invisible stone that crumbled easier now.

Tendons in Edric's bloody neck strained as his ocean-blue eyes found mine, then flicked to the pincers protruding from my head. Emotion flitted over his grimaced face. With all his weight, he lunged against the column a final time, then released the hand around Leden's neck to drop it lower. The vukodlak continued to suck as Edric's grip landed on Leden's amber pendant.

"What are you—?"

Edric breathed two words—"My mate"—and then smashed his palm onto the Stepping symbols.

In a blaze of vivid orange light, Edric and Leden disappeared.

CHAPTER TWENTY-NINE

"WHICH GATE DID HE go to? *Which Gate did he go to?*" Frantically, I rubbed my hands over rough carvings on the arch, feeling where Edric had placed his hands only moments ago, as if his warmth might still linger on the stone. "Hartley!"

Hartley massaged miran nectar onto Toma's gaping wound.

"Please." My voice was hoarse, splintered like my ribs. My heart was shards like the pendant at my neck that had been no use in saving Edric.

The Caster's gaze remained transfixed on the red and pink fibres of Toma's flesh knitting themselves back together. His neck sealed. Only then did Hartley twist towards me, deliberate and slow.

"You didn't listen to me," he snarled. "We should have waited." He noticed my pincers, disgust crossing his face.

My stomach dropped at the same time my knees thudded to the ground. Hartley wasn't distracted but was choosing not to help me.

"I'm sorry. I'm sorry." My knees grazed rough pavement as I shuffled into the warm puddle of blood surrounding Toma. The red crescent on my palm burned in agony, and my pincers clicked. I hadn't been able to control Leden, but Hartley . . . the threads of Hartley's mind were so close.

I couldn't lose Edric. My *mate*. I didn't know what it meant to have a mate, only that a deep part of my soul promised my existence would be agony without him. A cage worse than my tower. One with no light, no feeling, no taste. Only endless pain. Alone.

"Tavion," Toma murmured, eyes fluttering open. His chest gently rose and fell. "I'm here."

Hartley collapsed over his chest, hands twining behind Toma's neck.

Dirt and stones caught in the skin of my torn knees as I continued closer to the pair, mumbles of "please, please, please," tumbling from my lips in a desperate, monotonous prayer.

Please help me. Please don't make me make you. Please forgive me when I do.

"Tavion," Toma blinked, threading a hand into Hartley's bronze hair. "I've tried to help Nevvy, but I couldn't. I didn't do it right. You can help her now."

Carefully, Hartley lifted his head. "Is this what you want me to do?" When Toma nodded, Hartley carefully stood, looming over me still on my knees.

"What's that coming out of your head?"

"I-I don't know," I stammered. "It just happened now."

Hartley glared at me a beat longer.

"If anything happens to him while I'm gone," he said, peering down. "You're finished."

With trembling effort, I retracted the pincers that were about to latch on to Hartley's spinal cord. They slid back beneath my split skin. If only Hartley had offered up his dragul to begin with, maybe none of this would have happened. Maybe he deserved to be—*stop.* I touched the arch, blood still falling like tears as it dripped down my eyes.

With his broad stance unapologetic, Hartley pressed a hand to the arch, then Stepped through.

Toma sat beside me as we waited and waited and waited. Guards and Protectors attended to the injured, clearing wreckage from the blast, warily eyeing the forest line should any vukodlak be attracted to the spilt blood. I felt glances thrown my way. Uneasy looks at my blood-streaked face, at the wounds from which they had seen my pincers protruding. All I could do now was keep my eyes peeled, even if they stung from the trickling blood. I wouldn't miss the moment Edric returned.

Light burst from the arch and Hartley strode back through. Alone.

Three days passed with no news from any of Veligrad's Gates about Edric and Leden. They had Stepped during the darkest part of night before bakers rose to make bread, when no one was awake. No one had seen them. No untoward attacks had occurred since. No bodies had been found. There was nothing.

When I had begged Hartley to Step between the Gates again to help me search for Edric and Leden, he only pointed to the fact that the rest of Veligrad needed a leader that would protect them right now, and the other Gates were on alert anyway. When I had pleaded for him to gather the other Casters' draguls—or at least his own—to try to break the Curse, he had spoken to me as if I was an irritating child, explaining the Council was investigating how to break the Curse, but that it was too risky to try it without full research and guidance. I hated that it made sense, that it would leave Veligrad unprotected if we tried and it failed, but it didn't stop me from screaming at him until Kavi dragged me away.

I had cried so hard I vomited more than once, while Kavi and Aksel took turns sitting in my room at Midnight Gate, making sure I kept down the food they put before me, making sure I was safe from my own harm. Grief for Malina, despair for Edric, guilt for those hurt on the wedding night. Helplessness for myself. The only mote of reassurance was knowing the Slom gems in Edric's chest would prevent him from turning into a vukodlak himself, and I knew he had a vial of nectar, but it did nothing to staunch the flow of grating pain that he was gone, nor the weeping wound of the red crescent on my right palm.

As soon as Hartley had recounted the events upon returning to Midnight Gate, Jelena had disappeared. The only person that might have helped me find Edric. She was probably fae, too, and didn't trust Hartley with this new knowledge. Hartley was mostly absent, Kavi told me, in frequent meetings with the Council whom he had convinced to name him their Head. It seemed the new leader of Veligrad had got all that he'd wanted.

It was that burst of bitterness on my tongue that propelled me to finally rise on the third evening since Edric had disappeared. Aksel's soft snores rose in gentle sweeps from a corner of my room as I swapped my sweat-stained nightshirt for my Protector uniform, fitting looser against my grief-withered frame.

This time when I strolled under Midnight Gate's moonlit canopies, I located the witches' zhivir tree with ease, as if it wanted to be found.

A giant limb lowered itself, shaking the ground as it dropped at my feet. It was large enough for me to walk on without slipping off its rounded edge. In my current state, I was not sure if I could care anyway.

"You return to us late," said Mother Noche, as the branch deposited me in the library. "You return to Midnight Gate without your lover." I flinched. "What else is emptied upon your return?"

Myself. My insides were hollow, a void only visited by grief and fear.

Atop the low table, Mother Noche stirred a pot heated by a woodless fire, flames hugging the pewter's curves. The bone pendant necklace hung dully from her neck.

"Help me find him. Please."

Or I'll make you, said the pincers.

I was weaker at swatting them away now when their points pricked the inside of my skin.

"You'll have to ask the Earth Mother, not I."

I squeezed my fists and shoved those pincers down harder. Mother Noche's next words were not spoken aloud—they were in my head.

Sit beside me, daughter. Lean forward. Look. The voice was hers, but it was also mine, and it was also a thousand others'. *Our mothers tell us stories. Will you listen?*

Stiffly, I knelt on the hard wood next to the pot. Hunter-green tea water swirled and swirled. Then stopped.

It was now a glass the colour of a forest river's reflection, even as Mother Noche continued to stir. The witch dropped a strand of dark hair into the pot, before snatching one of mine, the pain twanging at my temple.

Look.

A familiar woman with waist-length hair the colour of night held a cupped hand filled with her own blood. In the centre sat a garnet crystal cut into a teardrop. *The Traitor Stone.* The very same stone that still sat in my pocket. She muttered words that made her body shudder while tears fell over rage-pinked cheeks.

The surface rippled into swirling water, dissipating the images, and bringing new ones forth. The dark-haired witch, this time her face composed and head bowed in subservience, offering a tiny box to the fae king as he sat imperiously on his dais.

"It is imbued with witches' power, my lord. Our might is now yours."

Hvalimir was a large man with wavy dark hair past his shoulders, blue eyes permanently narrowed in greed. He plucked the Traitor Stone from its box, inspecting the crystal now imbedded onto a silver ring, then slipped the ring on his finger.

My mouth fell open as I realised what I was watching. The inception of the Curse.

"Very well, Nightfall, you shall be rewarded with—" The king flinched. "It pricked me." Wiping at a bead of blood that sank into the stone, he frowned at the witch. "What is—"

The king's head dropped back as his chest thrust forwards, a guttural scream tearing from his throat, then morphing into a strangled howl.

"*May the fae deserve their Curse.*"

The water rippled again. Strain pulled the tendons in my neck as I leaned in further.

The Nightfall witch stood in a sandstone building overlooking a dusk-reddened ocean, panting with rage.

"My power is *failing*," she screamed through the glassless window. Howls rose in the distance, the only response. She turned and stormed through large, lavish rooms, looking for something. Portraits lining the walls marked this as the king's residence.

When she reached the kitchen, she stopped. A teenage boy stood in front of a smaller blond boy, butter knives hovering in the air around him. My heart panged at the terror and determination in his ocean eyes.

"Leave my brother alone," Edric yelled. His bloody shirt was torn in two, fresh stitches running down his sternum.

"Verily, child." The witch stretched her mouth into a strained smile. "Let us make a bargain. Your teeth for your brother's life."

Water swirled faster as the echoes of a boy's scream faded, and what I knew would be the final image appeared.

The crest of a hill atop a thick forest. The dark-haired witch, gaunt and thin, clutching the shoulders of a girl. Loose hair to her waist. Determination in her expression.

Me.

"Remember your name, my daughter, and run far away from here. Do not stop until you are safe. Do not look back at me."

Young me began to protest, but the witch—*my mother*—gripped my head, muttering words until I stilled, my eyes out of focus. "Go," she commanded before kissing my forehead, and under her compulsion, I turned.

A pendant of small, fused bones sat at her neck now. She stood before a tall zhivir tree, watching until I disappeared, but I never glanced back, running down a hill coated in tall miran flowers. Ruined Hill.

Simmering water tore the images apart, until the pot was only roiling tea water once more. Cold sweat soaked my back.

"What did you see?"

"The Fall of the Fae." A tear prickled my cheek as it lamented down my face. "Edric in his king father's castle." Edric had to be Hvalimir's son. He was not only fae, but a fae prince. "My mother."

"Yes." It was a hiss. "The Destroyer. Nada Nightfall." *My mother's name.* "When she cursed the stone with the magic of her mothers and sisters, she knew what she was risking."

"Where is she now?"

"With the Earth Mother," Mother Noche said simply.

I raised my eyes from the pot. They landed at the witch's neck, and pieces of understanding clicked together. Corrosive rage rose up my stomach, up the backs of my eyes.

"Hand. Me. My mate's. *Teeth*," I demanded.

This was why Edric's lower teeth were silver. He must have moulded them himself into his empty tooth sockets using his power, after my *mother* took them to wield what magic she could from his fae bones.

"Hand me the midnight dragul," Mother Noche parried.

"I need to find Edric, and I need my magic."

"You do not need the crystal to access your magic, daughter. Your blood is in the Traitor Stone. That is why you possess power when other witches do not. You will still have your magic when we make this trade, just like you always have."

"If I always had magic, I would not have let myself stay trapped in a tower for thirteen years."

"Are you quite certain? Your dragul may have unlocked some additional magic that had been repressed." She looked up, red lips plump with blood. "Think about your Heightened Power. How did you spend your days while you were *trapped*?"

My vision trembled, and my pincers twitched again. Out of all the ignorant—

Oh.

A key turned in my mind, unlocking a realisation. I had spent my life in the tower giving advice to guards, in my articles in "Do Tell," to Malina . . . In a way, perhaps I had always been compelling people to do as I told them. As for remaining trapped, maybe I had accepted it after a while. As a child, I had cried and begged to be released. But maybe my power hadn't been developed then. After my first few years, had I ever *told* the guards to let me out? I could not recall.

I pulled the Traitor Stone from my pocket and placed it with a dull thud onto the floor. The zhivir tree quivered, as if burned by its touch.

"I want to end the Curse."

Mother Noche stopped stirring. "Daughter of the Destroyer. Blood of the Traitor Stone." She lifted the pendant of Edric's teeth from her neck and placed it next to the Traitor Stone. An offer. "You are the only one who can."

Another memory pulled to me. The night of the Blood Moon Ball. Gorcha sparing me from the deadly magic of the vampir. That was why. He had sacrificed himself for the chance that I could destroy the Curse.

I swallowed. "Tell me how."

"You will need the Traitor Stone, and you will need a source of the strongest magic. To access this, there are different streams from which you may choose. Collecting each of the seven seed crystals of the Fae Gates would be one way." Hartley had made it clear the Council wouldn't relinquish their Caster draguls, and the seventh had been lost with Leden anyway. "Another stream is to channel the magic of two fated mates." My stomach flipped. "When you have your source, you must cast a spell from your heart to end the Curse. Your intention must be pure and clear: to end the Curse's suffering."

The void within me shrank a little, as the beginnings of a path laid itself before me.

"Fated mates . . . would feel it if the other died, wouldn't they?"

The witch poured the pot's contents into two ceramic cups. My heart panged for Malina at the reminder. "You would feel the agony of their death in each waking moment of your life and even in sleep."

I dropped the resin-coated shards of the Midnight Gate dragul and scooped up the Traitor Stone and the pendant of Edric's teeth. My right palm burned as I pressed the bone pendant to my lips, taking any essence of Edric I could.

"Then I need to find my mate and end this Curse."

Mother Noche blew cool air over the wafting steam of her tea, as if my response meant nothing, but her eyes shone.

"*Zhiveli*." She raised her mug, the toast an old word meaning "to life."

"*Zhiveli*." I swallowed a sip of the boiling tea, even as it scorched my mouth.

I welcomed the burn.

CHAPTER THIRTY

"**W**HAT ARE YOU DOING?"

I jumped at Hartley's voice, hand flying to the hilt of my hammer strapped into my belt. Without the midnight dragul, I felt defenceless, despite confirming that I surprisingly could, in fact, still conjure spheres without my crystal shards. After collecting supplies and leaving a note for Kavi, I had practiced all the way to the Midnight Gate arch in the pre-dawn gloom.

"I'm trying to figure out the Gate symbol that Edric touched." It was the truth. Reconstructing Edric's touch would help me choose where to begin my travels.

"Why are you packed like you're going away then?"

I shrugged. "In case I can figure it out and find him."

Hartley's shoulders sagged. He thought I was desperate, pitiful. There was no point asking Hartley to help me any more. I would journey by foot.

"I've been meaning to speak to you, but . . . Well. This was found at Amber Gate. I think it fell from Edric's pocket."

At the mention of Edric's name, I moved almost as fast as Hartley's Heightened Power to reach for the item in his hand. A small, dark, leather book with a silver-embossed title.

Sighing Winds.

The red crescent on my right palm throbbed. It was the same poetry from which he had recited to me, what felt like years ago, rather than days. I flicked through, inhaling the smell of worn pages, seeking Edric's scent amongst them. Lines of handwritten annotations filled the margins. I flipped to the end, where a half-finished letter lay folded for safekeeping against the back page. Then I noticed something that made my heart halt.

"You seem . . . better," Hartley tested. "Find out anything further about those horns from your head?"

I swallowed, trying to keep my breathing steady and my hands from trembling, then gave a tight shake of my head.

He took my silence for sorrow. "Alright. Well, I might as well Step through since you're here. I'm expected in Amber Gate this afternoon to decide what we do about their Protectors. Apparently, Leden threatened them to keep quiet about his Curse, but after Leden's reveal, we can't take any chances." He patted a silver dagger at his waist. "Another thing. More nectar was recovered from Leden's personal quarters. Thought you'd be happy to know."

It was Hartley's way of extending an apology.

I nodded in response. From the beginning, we'd both had different priorities. Sometimes they aligned, and other times they didn't. Hartley's mask of joviality had slipped off in the process of attaining his goals. What lay underneath wasn't *bad*, but I wasn't sure if it was the markings of the leader Veligrad needed. Sure, some bond lay between us—the Ranking, the Kora, the dragul sphere connection at Amber Gate—but it was one of necessity rather than sincerity. I wasn't sure if I forgave him for his hesitations to find Edric. It didn't matter anyway. Something more urgent was suspended between my fingers.

Hartley placed a hand on the leaf engraving along the row of Stepping symbols. A hand on my own dragul, I placed a palm on an unengraved portion of stone, and in a flash of light, Hartley Stepped through.

My heart pounded in my ears as I held a breath as still and silent as the white-capped Serpent Ranges on the grey northern horizon. I opened to the back page of Edric's book.

Outlined in dark ink was a small gargoyle with a lolling tongue. Releasing a shuddering breath, I lifted my gaze to a carving on the Gate that lay slightly beneath the seven Stepping symbols.

There it was. Smaller than my palm, the engraving of a gargoyle head, just like the one drawn in Edric's book. It was similar to the gargoyle faces covering fae architecture—the Gates, my old tower—except for one difference. A triangular protuberance sat on the end of its unfurled tongue. A crystal?

The Traitor Stone throbbed in my pocket, resonating in my bones. Shaking, I withdrew the stone and compared the same teardrop shape as the miniature version on the gargoyle's tongue. How were the Traitor Stone and this gargoyle carving connected? And why did Edric have it drawn in his book? The gargoyle seemed a different tinge to the other engravings, slightly lighter, and I pressed my hand to its shape to feel—

Rushing sugar in my veins. A hook in my stomach as my feet lifted beneath me. Bright light obscuring my vision. Then—

Flat, red sandstone painfully met my grazed forearms and knees.

The air was warm and thick with salt, coating the inside of my nose, the back of my mouth. Blood roared in my ears as my heart thudded against the tender bones of my rib cage.

I was no longer in Midnight Gate.

The roaring wasn't only my blood—it was the sound of giant waves. Raising myself on shaking legs, a crinkled ocean stretched languidly before me from the edge of a tall cliff. Surging water crashed against the red cliff face far below, spraying foam that speckled my cheeks.

Above, carmine-red stone spread in a giant arch, deep fissures running through its columns.

An eighth Gate.

How is this possible?

There was only one place in Veligrad known for its impenetrable red cliffs, impossible to reach. South-west off the coast of High Gate, the islands of the Glancing Isles.

My legs threatened to give way as I stumbled away from the cliff, pulling the arch into full view. A large garnet crystal lay embedded at its pinnacle, sparkling contentedly in the dawn sun. A twin to the burgundy stone clutched in my hand.

The Traitor Stone was a dragul, too, its power so great it didn't even need a second dragul to Step.

Edric's book shook in my trembling hand. Was this where he had Stepped? Warm wind turned the strands of my hair into whips, lashing at my face, into my mouth. The loose slip of paper fluttered where it poked out. Maybe it was a message? Ears still roaring, I unfolded its page, and my heart dropped further and faster than falling from a red cliff.

> *Dear Do Tell,*
>
> *The lines of poetry you shared are, in fact, the same as those I read to myself each evening, trying to seek comfort in their strength.*
>
> *They are, unfortunately, unable to give me comfort any longer. When I see their words, my mind only speaks in her voice, as if she is reading them to me.*
>
> *I have dived into the river and screamed her name, but the water is not large enough to contain my yearning. Perhaps the ocean would cleanse me, but it is far from my reach.*
>
> *I am longing to tell her—*

Edric's hand ended there. Salt from my tears mingled with the salt spray on my face.

"Hey!" A firm female voice called from behind me, followed by several sets of pounding feet.

My muscles stiffened. The three islands of the Glancing Isles were meant to be empty, barren, unreachable, yet when I turned, a red stone palace rose from the end of a long path leading from the Gate. Intricately carved pillars connected to form a row of pointed arched frames, guarding a long, covered terrace. The design was repeated on two levels above, each set further backwards. Beyond the palace, a fruit orchard bloomed over undulating land.

How?

A more pressing issue approached. Tall strangers in light linen shirts and trousers sprinted at me on bare feet, drawing curved cutlasses. Ten of them at least. They halted with a dozen feet to spare.

I exhaled a slow, shaky breath, restraining an impulse to conjure a dragul sphere until I understood how in Veligrad's *Seven* Gates this was possible.

The strangers' expressions ranged from suspicion to fear to something else that glinted a little more softly.

"Sena, she's not one of us," snarled a shorter pale-skinned woman with cropped, chestnut hair that revealed her ears. Elongated. Pointed.

Fae.

That was when I noticed their necks or wrists adorned with familiar ebony stones. Slom gems.

"Who are you?" Sena, the woman who had first called to me spoke, deep red hair in one plait reaching her elbows. Why did her name seem familiar? Her sleeveless tunic revealed bronze shoulders so toned they could knock someone unconscious. "The Gate is broken. How have you arrived? Why are you here?"

Salty wind blew hard, carrying with it another layer of something sweet. Orange blossoms. A knee-buckling realisation. *Salt and citrus. Edric's scent.*

A searing sensation ran through the cut of my red crescent mark. The rushing of sugar racing through my veins now wasn't magic.

"I'm looking for my mate."

If you loved Midnight Gate, please support the author by leaving a review.
www.skstapar.com/books

Desperate to find out what happens next? Connect with S. K. Stapar to hear all the updates first.
@skstapar.author

Have you read the **free prequel e-novella** to Midnight Gate yet? Sign up to the S. K. Stapar newsletter to get your copy!
www.skstapar.com/newsletter

GLOSSARY OF POEMS

Water Music

I

A river dammed is still water flowing. Battering rain makes a tranquil lake.

II

Strong currents carry gentle ripples.
Formed of salt, heed them both.

III

Rivulets may disappear while
Rivers spill into seas high.
One defines existence while
Another defines itself.

IV

Seven wishes over seven moons,
None of them left me with what you returned.

V
Spill away from the mountain,
Away from my veins,
Though my blood will spill with you,
And I'll draw my own pain.

VI
Turn, turn, tumble and jilt
One sees the surface, while the other sees silt.

Sighing Winds

I
Louder than the rattling pane
That shudders in the storm,
I bate my breath, force lungs to wait,
To only hear your own.

Acknowledgements

This is the part I can't write without tears spilling down my face.

Thank you to James, my best friend, for your complete, unwavering belief in me. The way Edric's character empowers Nevena was wholly based on one thing you said to me on our very first date: that your role in a relationship is to empower your partner. I'm incredibly lucky to call you my hubby.

Thank you to my Mama and Tata, for the years of stories and poems that you lovingly told Sara and I. Your lives were uprooted when we came to Australia, yet you poured endless love and magic into our home, and plied me with as many books as our library could offer. It's because of you that magic has always been such a big part of my life.

Thank you to my sister Sara, for being there for every mote of emotion I experienced in writing this book, and always knowing the exact right thing to say to fix any problem. I don't know how you do it (sister magic, probably), and I don't know where you find the energy to be always there, but I do know that you are the goodness and hilarity that brings light to any darkness.

To Erica Parkes, my incredible friend of over two decades involving many sleepovers reading ghost stories into the night—and then being too afraid to sleep. Thank you for your wonderful creativity in drawing the most gorgeous map of my dreams. I appreciate your kindness, your intelligence, your creativity, and I am so grateful for your friendship.

Thank you to the Saturday Writing Crew, for the support I would have sorely missed had it not been for our coffee chats and writing sessions. To Steph Huddleston, for being such a helpful and conscientious critique partner—Midnight Gate was shaped by your thoughtful feedback. To Bridie Blake, for being a ready, listening ear to all the unexpected ups and downs that publishing brings. To Lisa M. Matlin, Emily Nixon, Katrina Toone and Bridie again, for undertaking the shortest beta read ever asked of you, yet still sharing incredibly detailed and considerate feedback that changed trajectories, added chapters and made Midnight Gate a better story—I appreciate you. To Nicko Place for your specialist First Chapter advice and thoughtful brainstorming. To Holly Brunnbauer, who somehow was able to pluck my imagination directly from my brain, and create the most beautiful website that represented me perfectly—you definitely possess some sort of magic. And to Kat Turner, for inviting me into this group of kind and talented writers. I am genuinely thankful to each of you.

Thank you to the editors who polished Midnight Gate to perfection. To Kaitlin Slowik, for your beta feedback and brilliant copyediting, and to Rebecca at Scrollwork Edits for your wonderful line editing. You are both the best humans, and I appreciate your warmth, professionalism and humour—I cackled at your respective comments many times.

To every single person who has ever asked me how my book writing is going, or who has shared a word to others about Midnight Gate. You probably never know how excited it makes me feel to know that others remember, are interested, *care*. It means so much.

And to you, reader, thank you for opening the pages of this book and taking a dive inside. I hope its magic found you.

About the Author

Born in Former Yugoslavia, I came to Australia as a refugee at four years old with my family. I always loved the folk and fairy tales my parents used to tell of the magical woods of our homeland. They made magic feel real, totally and undeniably tangible.

That feeling stayed with me as I pored over every fantasy book our local library could provide, and then into my adulthood where I discovered the BEST genre I had ever read: romantasy.

Today, my own stories have little nods to Slavic tales and culture, while stepping up the values I hold close: equality, inclusiveness and empowerment for all.

Those values led me to a (very) short career as a high school English teacher. (Shoutout to those who do it – I could not!) I went on to study a Master of Public Policy, and put my social justice and environmental values to use.

There is no other life I would live than this, pouring magic out of my heart and into pages that I hope others feel too. Romantasy is empowering, healing, mysterious and suspenseful. It's an escape, and it's immersive.

Outside of my books, I'm married to a legit dream of a man, and our daughter is a little pup called Ivy. We love going to pet-friendly cafes and restaurants around the beautiful Yarra Valley winery region in Victoria near where we live.

While I competed internationally in Taekwon-do as a young adult, today I enjoy the gentleness of yoga, gardening in our little yard, and reading all the delicious romantasy books that bookshops and the online book community recommend.

Community

Want to be part of my community? Make sure you're signed up to the **S. K. Stapar newsletter**, and we can stay in touch! I love hearing any book recommendations, and I'd love you to be the first to know about exciting book release updates, Advance Review Copy (ARC) call-outs, events news, and more! Head to skstapar.com/newsletter to sign up.

Made in United States
Troutdale, OR
02/02/2026

46549225R00215